British Weird

Also published by Handheld Press

British Weird

Selected Short Fiction,

1893–1937

edited by James Machin

Handheld Classic 17

This edition published in 2020 by Handheld Press
72 Warminster Road, Bath BA2 6RU, United Kingdom.
www.handheldpress.co.uk

ISBN 978-1-912766-21-5

1 2 3 4 5 6 7 8 9 0

Series design by Nadja Guggi and typeset in Adobe Caslon Pro
and Open Sans.

Printed and bound in Great Britain by Short Run Press, Exeter.

MIX
Paper from
responsible sources
FSC
www.fsc.org   FSC® C014540

Contents

Acknowledgements

Kate Macdonald would like to thank Greg MacThomais of the University of the Highlands and Islands, and Anne O'Brien, for Gaelic advice; and Ursula Buchan for information about her grandfather's knowledge of Gaelic.

James Machin would like to thank the owners of the estate of L A Lewis for permission to republish 'Lost Keep', and United Agents for their permission on behalf of Susan Reeve-Jones to republish Algernon Blackwood's story 'The Willows'.

Handheld Press would welcome information on how to contact the estates of Alexander Leydenfrost, John Metcalfe and Eleanor Scott.

James Machin teaches at the Royal College of Art, London. He published *Weird Fiction in Britain, 1880–1939* (2018), and he co-edits *Faunus*, the Journal of the Friends of Arthur Machen. He has had short fiction published in various places including *The Shadow Booth*, *Supernatural Tales* and *Weirdbook*.

Introduction

BY JAMES MACHIN

The 'thing you can't quite see is more weird than the thing exposed' wrote Arthur Conan Doyle in 1912. This selection of stories for the most part bears out his observation (Fallon 2020, 180). If there is one aspect of British weird writing in the period covered by this volume that distinguishes it from the stories being published in North America in the pulp magazine *Weird Tales* in the 1920s and 1930s, it may be this tendency to keep things 'off screen'. Most of the stories selected here are effective because of their refusal to fully reveal their horrors, relying on ominous hints, telling detail and atmosphere, instead of the full reveal. Arthur Machen (1863–1947) was a pioneer of this technique. His novella *The Great God Pan* (1894) was so oblique that reviewers complained of feeling cheated by the lack of any clear resolution or explanation of what exactly was being suggested darkly by the narrative. However, that story has only grown in reputation because of the queasy uncertainty it evokes rather than despite it. This is writing that relies on the peripheral for its power – foregrounding the nebulous shadows flitting about at the edge of the page. M R James used the term 'reticence', arguing in 1929 that 'reticence conduces to effect, blatancy ruins it', also noting with disapproval that to be 'merely nauseating' is easy (James 1929, 171). This demarcation is echoed in H P Lovecraft's claim that the 'true' weird tale had to consist of 'something more than secret murder, bloody bones, or a sheeted form clanking chains according to rule' (Lovecraft 1985, 426). The emphasis is firmly on the creation of atmosphere and what Edgar Allan Poe called the unity of effect, rather than the multi-character drama, plotting and intrigue of the Gothic novel (Poe 1984, 15).

Uncertainty always lurks somewhere at the heart of weird fiction, in terms of both content *and* form. China Miéville calls it 'a rather breathless and generically slippery macabre fiction, a dark fantastic' (Miéville 2009, 510). It is most famously associated with Lovecraft, Clark Ashton Smith, and Robert E Howard, whose delirious mixtures of Gothic horror, science fiction and fantasy were all to be found within *Weird Tales*. This gave the designation 'weird' traction as a catch-all for writing that belonged to any of those genres, slipped between them, or bodged together into strange new combinations (Luckhurst 2015, 195). This version of weird fiction – as a marker for genre hybridity or impurity – was subsequently redeployed at the turn of the millennium as 'New Weird' and applied to the restless genre-bending experimentalism of writers like M John Harrison (who suggested the label) and Miéville. However, Miéville, taking his lead from Lovecraft's biographer S T Joshi, has also suggested using the term 'Haute Weird' as a way of grouping together those British writers of the period covered by this book, some of whom Lovecraft considered to be the 'Masters' of the weird tale (Miéville 2009, 511). A key commonality of these writers, which drew Lovecraft's attention and praise, was their refusal to rely on traditional Gothic tropes for their literary engagement with the supernatural.

Although the supernatural fiction of the nineteenth century – from Mary Shelley's *Frankenstein* (1819) to Bram Stoker's *Dracula* (1898) – enthusiastically incorporated contemporaneous scientific and technological advancements and discourses, the 'Haute Weird' looked backward as much as forward. Lovecraft was explicitly concerned with the fragility of civilisation, and with what he saw as the futile insignificance of human endeavour from the cosmic perspective; much has been made of his atheism in underpinning this worldview. However, metaphysical beliefs or (in Machen's and Buchan's case) religious certainties, didn't offer much protection from similar anxieties about the fragility of modernity. Disturbing atavistic forces from the past were ever-present, and the flipside of Victorian Imperial self-confidence was a terrible fear that it was all paper-thin and liable to come crashing down around our ears at any moment. Religious, evolutionary and cultural decadence was immanent in modernity. In literary terms, this decadence flowered as a controversial movement (controversial not least in whether or not it actually *was* a movement) in what became known as the 'Yellow Nineties', which aestheticised and celebrated the alleged social rot that vexed the bourgeoisie. Several of the writers in this volume emerged from this hothouse atmosphere, associated with the trial of Oscar Wilde, the *Yellow Book*, and the publisher John Lane's 'Keynotes' series of risqué literature, all sharing the visual branding and sinister androgynous *diablerie* of Aubrey Beardsley's illustrations and design work.

Edith Nesbit (1858–1924, writing usually as 'E Nesbit') is best remembered today for her children's fiction, especially *The Story of the Treasure Seekers* (1899), *Five Children and It* (1902, which continues to be adapted regularly for film and television), and *The Railway Children* (1906). However, like Machen and M P Shiel, she published a volume in the 'Keynotes' series (*In Homespun*, 1896) and had found initial publication success contributing to the then booming periodical market, writing for *Longman's Magazine*, *Temple Bar*, the *Argosy*, *Home Chimes*, and the *Illustrated London News*. She was part of the generation of writers who took full advantage of what M R James referred to as 'the deluge' of the early 1890s: 'the deluge of the illustrated monthly magazines' that made it 'no longer possible to keep pace with the output either of single stories or of volumes of collected ones' (James 1929, 171). This remarkable expansion in the sheer quantity of print media resulted from several coinciding factors, including the growth of literacy resulting from the 1870 Education Act, and the repeal of various printing and publishing taxes. There was also a loosening of the vice-like grip that the lending libraries had on dictating what sort of material was fit to be put before the newly-expanded reading public. Subscription libraries like Mudie's, which – thanks to their library network and purchasing power – once had a powerful influence on publishers, could no longer impose the unofficial censorship that had until then ensured that literature should be morally improving, preferably with an explicitly Christian message. Rid of their control of the market, writers at the end of the nineteenth century were newly able to test the boundaries of what was possible, without the obligation to provide reassuring resolution and conventional endings in which good prevailed over evil. This combination of circumstances contributed to what James described in 1929 as an 'astonishingly fertile' period for what he called 'ghost stories' (James 1929, 169).

Nesbit's own collection of such stories was *Grim Tales*, published in 1893 – the same year in which a reviewer (also in the *Bookman*) commented that Nesbit was a writer 'with a strong leaning towards the weird' (Anon 1893, 184). The tale presented here, **'Man-Size in Marble'**, was described by Nesbit's biographer, Julia Briggs, as 'the most disturbing ghost story she ever wrote' (Briggs 2000, 265). The tale is not without its flaws, and a reviewer for the *Athenaeum* was certainly justified in the complaint, 'Why is it almost always considered necessary in ghost stories to make the characters irredeemably middle-class and uninteresting?' (Anon 1893, 535). However, 'Man-Size in Marble' distinguishes itself through the power of its central conceit. As the narrator observes, there is 'a certain weird force and uncanniness about the phrase "drawed out man-size in marble"' in itself, and although the notion of ambulant statuary was likely inspired by Prosper Mérimée's 1837 story 'La Vénus d'Ille', the very mundanity of its cosy Kentish village setting contrasts jarringly with the suggestion of the nocturnal shambling of masonry, the exact nature of which remains unaccounted for. The reader remains *uncertain*.

From his comparatively modest beginnings John Buchan (1875–1940) had an extraordinary career encompassing colonial work, publishing, law, politics, and spending the Great War directing the British propaganda effort. While still a student at Brasenose College, he was already a published author and earned additional income by being a publisher's 'reader', evaluating submissions and advising on their suitability for acceptance. For someone so closely associated with ruddy-complexioned *Boys' Own* yarns such as *Prester John* (1910) and *The Thirty-Nine Steps* (1915), the fact that he spent some of the 1890s working for John Lane, the publisher of the notorious 'Keynotes' series, as well as contributing to the *Yellow Book*, might be surprising. However, one of the reasons why weird fiction enjoyed such a boom period from the 1880s onwards was precisely because of the confluence and interchanges of literary styles and markets. As detailed by Peter McDonald, behind the scenes influential editors and taste-makers such as W E Henley were busy establishing the notion of 'literary' fiction as a more robust concept, but in the meantime, writers like Buchan could experiment (McDonald 2002). And experiment he did: **'No-Man's Land'** was serialised in *Blackwood's Edinburgh Magazine* in 1899, following its first publication of Joseph Conrad's 'The [sic] Heart of Darkness'. The latter is now considered to be a literary classic, while Buchan's weird fiction is largely forgotten. Though Buchan's spy thrillers endure, they are treated usually as middlebrow entertainments. 'No-Man's Land' and Conrad's novella do bear comparison in terms of their subject matter. Both draw their horror from a threatened shattering of the line between civilisation and barbarity, and their protagonists are confronted with the perilous fragility of a complacent sense of superior, secure modernity.

Buchan's tale owes much to Machen's better-known stories of isolated pre-human populations lurking within the obscure corners of the British Isles, most fully drawn in 'The Novel of the Black Seal', an episode in his 1895 novel *The Three Impostors*. Drawing upon the 'euhemerist' theory of Scottish folklorist and antiquarian David Macritchie (1851–1925), Machen postulated that a hidden pre-human race endured in the fastnesses of the Welsh mountains, and that the glimpses and signs of their existence are responsible for the stories of the 'little people' or fairy folk (Fergus 2015). However, whereas Machen was an expert in keeping his sinister race of troglodytes at the periphery of his readers' consciousness, thereby intensifying their weird mystery and ambiguity, Buchan is less hesitant. His cave-dwelling, Highland 'Folk' are flesh and blood, and bullets have the same effect on them as they would on any man. 'No-Man's Land' ably demonstrates Buchan's supreme talent for both evoking a sense of place and keeping the reader gripped, though the clarity with which he delineates the 'Folk' means it lacks the power of Machen's original. Buchan ultimately demonstrates both Conan Doyle's observation above and Lovecraft's dictum that 'atmosphere, not action, is the great desideratum of weird fiction' (Lovecraft 2004, 177). Nevertheless, and despite the protagonist's muscular efforts at escaping his captors, the encounter with this atavistic relict people ruins his reputation and shatters his sanity, as it does the lowly shepherd couple with whom he shares the encounter. There is no reassertion of order or offer of resolution at the end of the narrative: our understanding of man's place in the universe has been destabilised and damaged, and with it all sorts of certainties about 'progress' and 'civilisation'. The fundamental tension dramatised here – the 'conflict between his mystical, pagan empathies and his Calvinist conscience' (Bell 2019, 186) – can be identified to greater or lesser extents in much of Buchan's weird fiction, and resonates with the weird fiction of the period more generally.

Also concerned with these porous borderlands – literal, spiritual, psychological – was Algernon Blackwood, whose 1910 story 'The Willows' is similarly engaged with the civilised, modern – and in this case, sceptical – protagonist being stripped of the comforting trappings of progress, psychological as well as material. Born into a comfortably wealthy – though austerely religious – family in Shooters Hill in what was then Kent, Blackwood led an adventurous and peripatetic life, which included time spent as a hotelier in Canada, a Pinkerton detective in New York, an artists' model, and ultimately a BBC television personality. One line of continuity through all these endeavours was his love of the wilderness, and of being in nature, a predisposition he developed into a pantheistic or animistic worldview explored in his fiction. 'The Willows' is perhaps his most successful effort at capturing the essential contradiction at the heart of the desire to escape oneself in the natural world, with its corollary dread of becoming engulfed or absorbed. The story has its origins in some travel writing by Blackwood based on a canoe trip along the Danube. The eerie atmosphere of the delta's reed-beds and shifting sands evidently seeded his imagination, and the hook for the story is the concept of the *temenos* or sacred grove. As Mary Butts writes:

> In the past certain holy spots, caves and 'temenoi' were, at one and the same time, a place on this earth; a place where once a supernatural event had happened; and a place where, by luck of devotion or the *quality* of the initiate, it might happen again. (252)

The narrator of 'The Willows' observes of the particularly isolated stretch of the Danube that he finds himself in: 'The Romans must have haunted all this region more or less with their shrines and sacred groves and elemental deities.' James C G Greig also identifies 'temenoi' as a recurring theme in Buchan's work, and Peter Bell has argued that it is one Buchan shares with Arthur Machen (Greig 1997, xii–xx; Bell 2019). Its vogue at the fin de siècle and in the early twentieth century no doubt owes a debt to the classical scholarship and neo-Paganism of influential figures like James George Frazer, Gilbert Murray, and Walter Pater. However, John Clute also connects the 'Pan-worship engaged upon by the many Edwardian fantasists' to a deep anxiety over the expanding suburbs and the loss of greenbelt land, citing writers including J M Barrie, E M Forster, Kenneth Grahame, Machen, Barry Pain and 'Saki', 'who bemoaned the loss of childhood and the rise of suburbia' (Clute 1997). At root of course was a sense of loss of a connection to nature associated with modernity. However, as Butts observes, *temenoi* are 'not always places you would expect', and not always tied to nature, and Butts' own story in the present volume, as well as Machen's, demonstrates that point ably.

A prolific novelist, E F Benson (1867–1940) found enduring literary success relatively late in his career as an author with the celebrated 'Mapp and Lucia' series. These were set in a fictionalised version of Rye, in East Sussex, where he lived and even served as mayor. Like Nesbit, Buchan, and Machen, he was very much a product of the 1890s, and he too produced a *succès de scandale* indicative of that period in the form of his first novel *Dodo: A Detail of the Day* (1893). He was from a prodigiously talented family, and his siblings R H, A C, and Margaret Benson (one of the first female students admitted to Oxford) all had multifaceted and successful careers in various fields, including literary. S T Joshi notes that E F Benson was an attendee at 'a celebrated meeting of the Chitchat Society in 1893 at which M R James read some of his earliest ghost stories' (Joshi 2012, II). While Benson only occasionally dedicated his energies to the form, his efforts resulted in several stories that have entered the supernatural canon. Perhaps most notable of these in terms of its influence has been 'The Bus-Conductor' from the 1912 collection *The Room in the Tower*, adapted for the 1945 portmanteau horror film *Dead of Night* and for a 1961 episode of *The Twilight Zone*. One contemporaneous reviewer summed up Benson's talent for the short weird tale as follows:

> One great rule in the art of the ghost-storyteller the author has borne in mind – he has kept his ghosts at a distance. The apparition which can be reduced to cubic inches of fog, or expressed in candle-power of phosphorescent luminosity, is incapable of evoking one solitary shudder from the average reader. Mr Benson has left his readers to guess at causes for the effects which he describes. (Anon 1912, 527)

'**Caterpillars**' is an especially potent demonstration of this point, which once again echoes Conan Doyle's observation. While Benson was quite capable of using more traditional hauntings as the central conceit of a story ('How Fear Departed from the

Long Gallery' being a good example), he also experimented with more ambiguous entities – including strange slug-like elemental monsters in '*Negotium Perambulans* ...' (1923) and 'And No Birds Sing' (1928). He also contributed to the weird hominin survivals trope (represented by Buchan's story) with 'The Horror Horn' (1923). 'Caterpillars' (1912) is particularly effective as a story, due to the alien quality of the eponymous infestation, and the sinister link made between them and the very real fear of cancer and its inexorable spread. Although the protagonist experiences a nightmare vision of giant caterpillars haunting a particular room and moving with strange agency, Benson makes sure to give the 'real' normal-sized caterpillar found on the grounds of the villa the peculiar feature of crab-like pincers instead of legs. The reader cannot take comfort in a straightforward interpretation of the story as a projection of a subconscious perception of someone's disease.

John Metcalfe (1891–1965) remains an obscure and slightly mysterious figure, whose itinerant career included service in both the Royal Navy and Royal Air Force during both wars, and teaching positions in Paris and London (at Highgate Junior School). He also spent time in the United States where he found employment as a barge captain on New York City's East River and married the Modernist author Evelyn Scott. Although he went on to write several novels, Metcalfe's first book was *The Smoking Leg and Other Stories* (1925), a collection of memorable weird tales, including **'The Bad Lands'**, effective due to what L P Hartley identified as a 'whole armoury of suggestions and apprehensions' (Hartley 1925, 123). Also praising Metcalfe's writing for its occasional attainment of 'a rare pitch of potency', Lovecraft singled out 'The Bad Lands' for approval, describing it as 'containing graduations of horror that strongly savour of genius' (Lovecraft 1985, 488). Machen's friend and biographer, the poet John Gawsworth (pen-name of Terence Ian Fytton Armstrong, 1912–1970), was a drinking companion of Metcalfe and regarded him as the 'third great Musketeer of the modern macabre *conte*, following his friend Arthur Machen, and

Redondan King M P Shiel, whose Lord High Admiral he proudly and frequently signed himself' (Gawsworth 1970; the Caribbean 'Kingdom' of Redonda being a ludic conceit established by Shiel, a Montserratian, and continued to this day by the present 'King', Spanish novelist Javier Marías).

As with Blackwood and Buchan, Metcalfe's story is centred on the notion of a *temenos*, or *genius loci*, this time an area of countryside in coastal Norfolk, the reality of which is somehow unstable, with unpleasant consequences for some visitors. Mary Butts identified this trope in British supernatural fiction and associated it with fairy lore and related legends of the Celtic Fringe, and those areas where a 'transition took place, which has been observed before and after, when a place becomes another place; and you know what you have suspected before – that all the time it has been two places at once' (245). This connection neatly dovetails several recurring themes of the stories in this book: fairies as folk memories of pre-human survivals and atavistic threat; the sacred grove; and unstable geographies, or the landscape as a palimpsest or psychic reliquary of history. All these concerns persist into the contemporary moment, and recent years have again seen an upsurge in interest in what Robert Macfarlane has called the 'English Eerie' and – less subtly – the radical and transgressive potential of the 'hidden' pagan underpinnings of modernity explored in the 'folk horror' movement (Macfarlane 2015).

The contemporary critical application of the term 'folk horror' was almost single-handedly formulated by writer and actor Mark Gatiss in his 2010 BBC documentary series *A History of Horror*. Gatiss coined the term to label a cycle of British films from the late 1960s and early 1970s: *Witchfinder General* (1968), *The Blood on Satan's Claw* (1971), and most famously *The Wicker Man* (1973). However, the anxieties exploited by these films had been engaged with decades earlier in the weird fiction of the period covered by this book. One of the hallmarks of the classic Gothic novel was an associated concern with the recrudescence of the superstitious pre-Reformation past, often represented by crudely caricatured 'backward' Catholic societies. This awareness of the precariousness of modernity and civilisation was exacerbated by a new understanding of mankind's place in the universe, its status acutely diminished in the context of geological and evolutionary 'deep time', astronomical space, and the associated loss of Biblical authority (Worth 2018, xxiii). Towards the end of the nineteenth century, Machen especially seized upon these anxieties with his fiction, but the concern with evolutionary and cultural recidivism as the threat to civilisation and modernity remained a preoccupation of weird fiction into the twentieth century. John Buchan's 1927 novel *Witch Wood* certainly contains all the central ingredients of the *Wicker Man*-brand of folk horror: villagers seduced by nebulous pagan forces, indicated by the persistence of superficially innocuous folk customs; a lone, uprightly Christian protagonist acting as a bulwark against the atavistic threat; and a final revelation of terrible existential peril. One year earlier, Sylvia Townsend Warner's *Lolly Willowes* (1926) had neatly subverted these elements in feminist folk horror, in which women evade male attempts to control them. While Buchan gives his story a distinctly Scottish slant, with its Calvinist preoccupation with 'backsliding', in Eleanor Scott's 1929 short story **'Randalls Round'**, we get a far more economical and English iteration of this prototypical folk horror narrative.

Eleanor Scott was the penname of Helen M Leys (1892–1965). Melissa Edmundson notes that she had a 'lifelong interest in history [...] eventually becoming Principal of an Oxfordshire teacher training college' (Edmundson 2019, xxix). Her single collection of supernatural fiction (also titled *Randalls Round*, 1929) contains tales that Scott claimed were all based on 'dream experiences', to which she added some narrative shape but endeavoured to keep the overall atmosphere intact (Anon 1929, 93). 'Randalls Round' is striking not only in how specifically it anticipates the folk horror archetype of the educated interloper stumbling across terrifying primordial rites darkly hinted at in quaint village traditions, but also in how its structure maps on to the quintessential Lovecraft plot, complete with the protagonist's initial perusal of antiquarian texts, gleaning sinister details foreshadowing the final sanity-threatening denouement.

As well as an uneasy relationship with the natural world, some – for example Michel Houellebecq in his 1991 study of Lovecraft – have identified markedly unnatural architecture as a key aesthetic aspect of weird fiction. This has links with the Gothic tradition of the sublime; of bewildering castles and endless dungeons, and of Piranesi-like built environments which dwarf the human drama being enacted within. Lovecraft's sensitivity to architecture and the emotional response he had to his native skylines of Providence and Boston found their inversion in the horrific and sanity-threatening angles of the impossible architecture of R'lyeh and his other alien topologies.

However, similar experiments were also being undertaken by British writers, an example being **'Lost Keep'** (1934) by L A Lewis (1899–1961). In this tale, Lewis evokes a sense of weird horror through – and here one of Lovecraft's favourite adjectives seems appropriate – cyclopean architecture. Lewis exacerbates the queasy dread of the protagonist, who is wandering in a strange twilit landscape under the shadow of ominous masonry. Abrupt changes in focus switch the reader between the keep as a scale model and the subjective nightmare of those trapped in it. As with another remarkable story by Lewis ('The Tower of Moab', 1934), the keep is a supernatural structure, the actuality of which is uncertain, and exerts a baleful influence over the protagonists. Although 'Lost Keep' is weakened by a slightly trite ending involving the rightful punishment of moral transgression, the reader might be reminded again of the oppressive, alien edifices that dominate the landscapes of Lovecraft's tales, and how the human figure seems diminished. 'Lovecraft needs the human world,' wrote Mark Fisher, 'for much the same reason that a painter of a vast edifice might insert a standard human figure standing before it: to provide a sense of scale' (Fisher 2016, 20–21). Lewis's story is of course also beholden to the Gothic trope of the imposing castle, and associated notions of the sublime. However, Lewis (who, like Metcalfe, served in both world wars) also loads his writing with a psychological acuity. The hallucinatory visions experienced by his characters, and their associated compulsions, were likely informed by his own struggles with mental illness. According to his widow (when interviewed by editor Richard Dalby) he destroyed some of his papers towards the end of his life, when suffering from one of his regular bouts of depression (Dalby 2014, 4). His literary output is sadly limited to a single collection, *Tales of the Grotesque*, published in 1934.

Arthur Machen's (1863–1947) work could book-end the period of British weird fiction encompassed in this collection. Perhaps his most well-known story remains the novella *The Great God Pan* (1894), which is both a definitive product of the fervid 'Yellow Nineties' and became a springboard for much weird fiction that followed, concerned as it is with neo-Pagan revivals and mystic evil lurking within the wildernesses of the Celtic fringe. However, 'N' (1934), the story included here, was written towards the end of Machen's creative life, when he was in his mid-seventies. Much of Machen's later writing is overlooked or even disparaged, yet 'N' emerges as even now almost *sui generis*. As a sometime publisher's reader, Machen kept up to speed with literary developments and – with the stream-of-consciousness story 'The White People' (1906) – even anticipated some of them. 'N', with its lack of narrative, and its fractal, kaleidoscopic superimpositions of the real and the visionary, is certainly Modernist. It is also a good demonstration of how a text can remain distinctly 'weird' without any corollary horrific element; in other words, that a weird tale can be something different than a horror story. Miéville identifies this potential of weird fiction to resist any generic dependency on horror as its 'focus [...] on awe, and its undermining of the quotidian', adding that this 'obsession with numinosity under the everyday is at the heart of Weird Fiction' (Miéville 2009, 510).

Machen once complained that he considered his literary failures to be the translation of 'awe, or awfulness, into evil', but in this respect at very least 'N' is an unarguable success (Machen 1923, 127). In his attempt to penetrate this 'numinosity' – or what Machen might call 'quiddity' – of London, Machen is also very much under the spell of Dickens. One is reminded by 'N' of Mr Micawber's caution to David Copperfield that when attempting to penetrate 'the arcana of the Modern Babylon' one may very well end up lost.

In **'Mappa Mundi'** (1937), Mary Butts issues a comparable warning, though this time the metropolis is Paris, and the loss is a more literal one, though just as compelling and replete with mystery. Butts (1890–1937) was involved in several different yet overlapping circles of creative and intellectual life in the early twentieth century, including an acquaintanceship with literary Modernists such as Ezra Pound and Wyndham Lewis, artists such as Jean Cocteau, and having had a sojourn at Aleister Crowley's notorious 'Abbey of Thelema' at Cefalù in Sicily. Typically, in his 'autohagiography', Crowley is breathtakingly obnoxious about Butts before going on to acknowledge casually her intellectual gifts and insight that led to their association and her co-authorship of at least one of his occult works. Butts was interested in supernatural fiction in theory and in practice, and her essay 'Ghosts and Ghoulies', published in the *Bookman* in 1933, remains a tour de force in its examination of the subject. It also makes clear her belief in the reality of the supernatural and contains several allusions to personal insight into such encounters: 'To quote again one's own experience: there is a part of Lincoln's Inn which does not always 'stay put'.' (254) Like Blackwood's Danube delta, Metcalfe's Norfolk, and Machen's Stoke Newington, Butts' Paris in 'Mappa Mundi' refuses to 'stay put', and a young American tourist slips between the ever-shifting city's cracks. This quality of Paris – both wonderful and perilous – is explained by Butts through a meta-textual reference to another of Buchan's weird tales, 'Space' (1911): 'Now we began to walk again, and into my mind flashed images of men who had been too far [...] the man in Buchan's story who discovered the corridors and that space, like murder, "is full of holes".' (228) Once again, although there is a more overtly-sinister tragedy lurking somewhere at the centre of its labyrinth, like Machen's 'N', 'Mappa Mundi' is most powerful as an evocation of the numinous rather than horror.

Butts was a perspicacious critic of Weird fiction, and we have reprinted here her essay 'Ghosties and Ghoulies' in full. Despite its glib title, this essay gives full expression to the depth and range of her insights into the supernatural tradition in Britain. It should be read alongside Lovecraft's celebrated study 'Supernatural Horror in Literature' (1927), especially since Butts discusses her subject with an unapologetic sincerity in her belief in the reality of supernatural or 'psychic' phenomena, simultaneously adopting a stance of vigilant scepticism towards any claims she regards as credulous or opportunistic. This of course contrasts with Lovecraft's own avowedly scientific disbelief in the occult. Interestingly, Butts argues that the authors of 1920s and 1930s supernatural fiction have in common 'an absence of the facetiousness or stressed scepticism which the Victorians thought essential' (262). Butts makes several allusive references to her own supernatural experiences in the essay, and at least one such *vignette* reads as a perfectly-formed weird tale in miniature. It is a brief anecdote about an 'abnormal sleep' and a vision of Stonehenge:

> Hanging above the grove that crowns the earthworks was a face. Fifteen years later I met the owner of the face; or rather the translation of its unthinkable loveliness into flesh and blood. We stared and immediately recognised each other. And with that began another sequence. (254)

In her various classifications of supernatural fiction, Butts rates most highly those authors 'who seek only to produce horror and wonder; or at best, and without explanation, the consciousness of a universe enlarged.' I hope that the present volume demonstrates the soundness of her judgement.

Works Cited

Anon, 'Something Wrong', *The Bookman*, 4.24 (1893), 184.

— 'Book Review', *The Athenaeum; London*, 3418 (1893), 535.

— 'Randalls Round', *The Bookman*, 77.457 (1929), 93–94.

— 'The Room in the Tower', *The Academy and Literature*, 2086 (1912), 526–257.

Peter Bell, 'Of Sacred Groves and Ancient Mysteries: Parallel Themes in the Writings of Arthur Machen and John Buchan', in *The Secret Ceremonies: Critical Essays on Arthur Machen*, (ed.) Mark Valentine and Timothy J Jarvis (New York 2019), 181–197.

Julia Briggs, *A Woman of Passion: The Life of E Nesbit* (New York 2000).

John Clute, 'Thinning', in *Encyclopedia of Fantasy* (1997). http://sf-encyclopedia.uk/fe.php?nm=thinning [accessed 18 May 2015].

Richard Dalby, 'The Quest for Lewis', in *Tales of the Grotesque*, by L A Lewis (Birmingham 2014), 1–5.

Melissa Edmundson, 'Biographical Notes', in *Women's Weird. Strange Stories by Women, 1890–1940*, (ed.) Melissa Edmundson (Bath 2020), xxv–xxxii.

Richard Fallon, 'Arthur Conan Doyle's The Lost World: Illustrating the Romance of Science', *English Literature in Transition, 1880–1920*, 63.2 (2020), 162–192.

Emily Fergus, "A Wilder Reality': Euhemerism and Arthur Machen's 'Little People", *Faunus: The Journal of the Friends of Arthur Machen*, Autumn 2015, 3–17.

Mark Fisher, *The Weird and The Eerie* (London 2016).

John Gawsworth, 'In Memoriam: John Metcalfe', *The Antigonish Review*, 1.2 (1970), 73–5.

The Rev James C G Greig, 'Introduction', in *Supernatural Tales*, by John Buchan (Edinburgh 1997), vii–xxiv.

L P Hartley, 'Imagination and Reality', *The Bookman,* 69.410 (1925), 123–124.

M R James, 'Some Remarks on Ghost Stories', *The Bookman*, 77.459 (1929), 169–172.

S T Joshi, *Unutterable Horror: A History of Supernatural Fiction*, 2 vols (Hornsea 2012).

H P Lovecraft, 'Notes on Writing Weird Fiction', in *Collected Essays Volume 2: Literary Criticism*, (ed.) S T Joshi (New York 2004), 175–178.

H P Lovecraft, 'Supernatural Horror in Literature', in *Dagon and Other Macabre Tales* (London 1985), 421–512.

Roger Luckhurst, 'American Weird', in *The Cambridge Companion to American Science Fiction*, (ed.) Eric Carl Link and Gerry Canavan (New York 2015), 194–204.

Arthur Machen, *Far Off Things* (London 1923).

Peter D McDonald, *British Literary Culture and Publishing Practice, 1880–1914* (Cambridge 2002).

Robert Macfarlane, 'The eeriness of the English countryside', in *The Guardian*, 10 April 2015.

China Miéville, 'Weird Fiction', in *The Routledge Companion to Science Fiction* (ed.) Mark Bould and others (London 2009), 510–515.

Aaron Worth, 'Introduction', in *The Great God Pan and Other Horror Stories*, by Arthur Machen, Oxford World Classics (New York 2018), ix–xxxvi.

1 Man-size in Marble

BY EDITH NESBIT (1893)

Although every word of this story is as true as despair, I do not expect people to believe it. Nowadays a 'rational explanation' is required before belief is possible. Let me then, at once, offer the 'rational explanation' which finds most favour among those who have heard the tale of my life's tragedy. It is held that we were 'under a delusion', Laura and I, on that 31st of October; and that this supposition places the whole matter on a satisfactory and believable basis. The reader can judge, when he, too, has heard my story, how far this is an 'explanation', and in what sense it is 'rational'. There were three who took part in this: Laura and I and another man. The other man still lives, and can speak to the truth of the least credible part of my story.

I never in my life knew what it was to have as much money as I required to supply the most ordinary needs – good colours, books, and cab-fares – and when we were married we knew quite well that we should only be able to live at all by 'strict punctuality and attention to business'. I used to paint in those days, and Laura used to write, and we felt sure we could keep the pot at least simmering. Living in town was out of the question, so we went to look for a cottage in the country, which should be at once sanitary and picturesque. So rarely do these two qualities meet in one cottage that our search was for some time quite fruitless. We tried advertisements, but most of the desirable rural residences which we did look at proved to be lacking in both essentials, and when a cottage chanced to have drains it always had stucco as well and was shaped like a tea-caddy. And if we found a vine or rose-covered porch, corruption invariably lurked within. Our minds got so befogged by the eloquence of house-agents and the rival disadvantages of the fever-traps and outrages to beauty which we had seen and scorned, that I very much doubt whether either of us, on our wedding morning, knew the difference between a house and a haystack. But when we got away from friends and house-agents, on our honeymoon, our wits grew clear again, and we knew a pretty cottage when at last we saw one. It was at Brenzett – a little village set on a hill over against the southern marshes. We had gone there, from the seaside village where we were staying, to see the church, and two fields from the church we found this cottage. It stood quite by itself, about two miles from the village. It was a long, low building, with rooms sticking out in unexpected places. There was a bit of stone-work – ivy-covered and moss-grown, just two old rooms, all that was left of a big house that had once stood there – and round this stone-work the house had grown up. Stripped of its roses and jasmine it would have been hideous. As it stood it was charming, and after a brief examination we took it. It was absurdly cheap. The rest of our honeymoon we spent in grubbing about in second-hand shops in the county town, picking up bits of old oak and Chippendale chairs for our furnishing. We wound up with a run up to town and a visit to Liberty's, and soon the low oak-beamed lattice-windowed rooms began to be home. There was a jolly old-fashioned garden, with grass paths, and no end of hollyhocks and sunflowers, and big lilies. From the window you could see the marsh-pastures, and beyond them the blue, thin line of the sea. We were as happy as the summer was glorious, and settled down into work sooner than we ourselves expected. I was never tired of sketching the view and the wonderful cloud effects from the open lattice, and Laura would sit at the table and write verses about them, in which I mostly played the part of foreground.

We got a tall old peasant woman to do for us. Her face and figure were good, though her cooking was of the homeliest; but she understood all about gardening, and told us all the old names of the coppices and cornfields, and the stories of the smugglers and highwaymen, and, better still, of the 'things that walked', and of the 'sights' which met one in lonely glens of a starlight night. She was a great comfort to us, because Laura hated housekeeping as much as I loved folklore, and we soon came to leave all the domestic business to Mrs Dorman, and to use her legends in little magazine stories which brought in the jingling guinea.

We had three months of married happiness, and did not have a single quarrel. One October evening I had been down to smoke a pipe with the doctor – our only neighbour – a pleasant young Irishman. Laura had stayed at home to finish a comic sketch of a village episode for the *Monthly Marplot*. I left her laughing over her own jokes, and came in to find her a crumpled heap of pale muslin weeping on the window seat.

'Good heavens, my darling, what's the matter?' I cried, taking her in my arms. She leaned her little dark head against my shoulder and went on crying. I had never seen her cry before – we had always been so happy, you see – and I felt sure some frightful misfortune had happened.

'What is the matter? Do speak.'

'It's Mrs Dorman,' she sobbed.

'What has she done?' I inquired, immensely relieved.

'She says she must go before the end of the month, and she says her niece is ill; she's gone down to see her now, but I don't believe that's the reason, because her niece is always ill. I believe someone has been setting her against us. Her manner was so queer –'

'Never mind, Pussy,' I said; 'whatever you do, don't cry, or I shall have to cry too, to keep you in countenance, and then you'll never respect your man again!'

She dried her eyes obediently on my handkerchief, and even smiled faintly.

'But you see,' she went on, 'it is really serious, because these village people are so sheepy, and if one won't do a thing you may be quite sure none of the others will. And I shall have to cook the dinners, and wash up the hateful greasy plates; and you'll have to carry cans of water about, and clean the boots and knives – and we shall never have any time for work, or earn any money, or anything. We shall have to work all day, and only be able to rest when we are waiting for the kettle to boil!'

I represented to her that even if we had to perform these duties, the day would still present some margin for other toils and recreations. But she refused to see the matter in any but the greyest light. She was very unreasonable, my Laura, but I could not have loved her any more if she had been as reasonable as Whately.

'I'll speak to Mrs Dorman when she comes back, and see if I can't come to terms with her,' I said. 'Perhaps she wants a rise in her screw. It will be all right. Let's walk up to the church.'

The church was a large and lonely one, and we loved to go there, especially upon bright nights. The path skirted a wood, cut through it once, and ran along the crest of the hill through two meadows, and round the churchyard wall, over which the old yews loomed in black masses of shadow. This path, which was partly paved, was called 'the bier-balk', for it had long been the way by which the corpses had been carried to burial. The churchyard was richly treed, and was shaded by great elms which stood just outside and stretched their majestic arms in benediction over the happy dead. A large, low porch let one into the building by a Norman doorway and a heavy oak door studded with iron. Inside, the arches rose into darkness, and between them the reticulated windows, which stood out white in the moonlight. In the chancel, the windows were of rich glass, which showed in faint light their noble colouring, and made the black oak of the choir pews hardly more solid than the shadows. But on each side of the altar lay a grey marble figure of a knight in full plate armour lying upon a low slab, with hands held up in everlasting prayer, and these figures, oddly enough, were always to be seen if there was any glimmer of light in the church. Their names were lost, but the peasants told of them that they had been fierce and wicked men, marauders by land and sea, who had been the scourge of their time, and had been guilty of deeds so foul that the house they had lived in – the big house, by the way, that had stood on the site of our cottage – had been stricken by lightning and the vengeance of Heaven. But for all that, the gold of their heirs had bought them a place in the church. Looking at the bad hard faces reproduced in the marble, this story was easily believed.

The church looked at its best and weirdest on that night, for the shadows of the yew trees fell through the windows upon the floor of the nave and touched the pillars with tattered shade. We sat down together without speaking, and watched the solemn beauty of the old church, with some of that awe which inspired its early builders. We walked to the chancel and looked at the sleeping warriors. Then we rested some time on the stone seat in the porch, looking out over the stretch of quiet moonlit meadows, feeling in every fibre of our being the peace of the night and of our happy love; and came away at last with a sense that even scrubbing and blackleading were but small troubles at their worst.

Mrs Dorman had come back from the village, and I at once invited her to a *tête-à-tête*.

'Now, Mrs Dorman,' I said, when I had got her into my painting room, 'what's all this about your not staying with us?'

'I should be glad to get away, sir, before the end of the month,' she answered, with her usual placid dignity.

'Have you any fault to find, Mrs Dorman?'

'None at all, sir; you and your lady have always been most kind, I'm sure –'

'Well, what is it? Are your wages not high enough?'

'No, sir, I gets quite enough.'

'Then why not stay?'

'I'd rather not' – with some hesitation – 'my niece is ill.'

'But your niece has been ill ever since we came.'

No answer. There was a long and awkward silence. I broke it.

'Can't you stay for another month?' I asked.

'No, sir. I'm bound to go by Thursday.'

And this was Monday!

'Well, I must say, I think you might have let us know before. There's no time now to get any one else, and your mistress is not fit to do heavy housework. Can't you stay till next week?'

'I might be able to come back next week.'

I was now convinced that all she wanted was a brief holiday, which we should have been willing enough to let her have, as soon as we could get a substitute.

'But why must you go this week?' I persisted. 'Come, out with it.'

Mrs Dorman drew the little shawl, which she always wore, tightly across her bosom, as though she were cold. Then she said, with a sort of effort –

'They say, sir, as this was a big house in Catholic times, and there was a many deeds done here.'

The nature of the 'deeds' might be vaguely inferred from the inflection of Mrs Dorman's voice – which was enough to make one's blood run cold. I was glad that Laura was not in the room. She was always nervous, as highly-strung natures are, and I felt that these tales about our house, told by this old peasant woman, with her impressive manner and contagious credulity, might have made our home less dear to my wife.

'Tell me all about it, Mrs Dorman,' I said; 'you needn't mind about telling me. I'm not like the young people who make fun of such things.'

Which was partly true.

'Well, sir' – she sank her voice – 'you may have seen in the church, beside the altar, two shapes.'

'You mean the effigies of the knights in armour,' I said cheerfully.

'I mean them two bodies, drawed out man-size in marble,' she returned, and I had to admit that her description was a thousand times more graphic than mine, to say nothing of a certain weird force and uncanniness about the phrase 'drawed out man-size in marble'.

'They do say, as on All Saints' Eve them two bodies sits up on their slabs, and gets off of them, and then walks down the aisle, *in their marble*' – (another good phrase, Mrs Dorman) – 'and as the church clock strikes eleven they walks out of the church door, and over the graves, and along the bier-balk, and if it's a wet night there's the marks of their feet in the morning.'

'And where do they go?' I asked, rather fascinated.

'They comes back here to their home, sir, and if any one meets them –'

'Well, what then?' I asked.

But no – not another word could I get from her, save that her niece was ill and she must go. After what I had heard I scorned to discuss the niece, and tried to get from Mrs Dorman more details of the legend. I could get nothing but warnings.

'Whatever you do, sir, lock the door early on All Saints' Eve, and make the cross-sign over the doorstep and on the windows.'

'But has any one ever seen these things?' I persisted.

'That's not for me to say. I know what I know, sir.'

'Well, who was here last year?'

'No one, sir; the lady as owned the house only stayed here in summer, and she always went to London a full month afore the night. And I'm sorry to inconvenience you and your lady, but my niece is ill and I must go on Thursday.'

I could have shaken her for her absurd reiteration of that obvious fiction, after she had told me her real reasons.

She was determined to go, nor could our united entreaties move her in the least.

I did not tell Laura the legend of the shapes that 'walked in their marble', partly because a legend concerning our house might perhaps trouble my wife, and partly, I think, from some more occult reason. This was not quite the same to me as any other story, and I did not want to talk about it till the day was over. I had very soon ceased to think of the legend, however. I was painting a portrait of Laura, against the lattice window, and I could not think of much else. I had got a splendid background of yellow and grey sunset, and was working away with enthusiasm at her lace. On Thursday Mrs Dorman went. She relented, at parting, so far as to say –

'Don't you put yourself about too much, ma'am, and if there's any little thing I can do next week, I'm sure I shan't mind.'

From which I inferred that she wished to come back to us after Hallowe'en. Up to the last she adhered to the fiction of the niece with touching fidelity.

Thursday passed off pretty well. Laura showed marked ability in the matter of steak and potatoes, and I confess that my knives, and the plates, which I insisted upon washing, were better done than I had dared to expect.

Friday came. It is about what happened on that Friday that this is written. I wonder if I should have believed it, if anyone had told it to me. I will write the story of it as quickly and plainly as I can. Everything that happened on that day is burnt into my brain. I shall not forget anything, nor leave anything out.

I got up early, I remember, and lighted the kitchen fire, and had just achieved a smoky success, when my little wife came running down, as sunny and sweet as the clear October morning itself. We prepared breakfast together, and found it very good fun. The housework was soon done, and when brushes and brooms and pails were quiet again, the house was still indeed. It is wonderful what a difference one makes in a house. We really missed Mrs Dorman, quite apart from considerations concerning pots and pans. We spent the day in dusting our books and putting them straight, and dined gaily on cold steak and coffee. Laura was, if possible, brighter and gayer and sweeter than usual, and I began to think that a little domestic toil was really good for her. We had never been so merry since we were married, and the walk we had that afternoon was, I think, the happiest time of all my life. When we had watched the deep scarlet clouds slowly pale into leaden grey against a pale-green sky, and saw the white mists curl up along the hedgerows in the distant marsh, we came back to the house, silently, hand in hand.

'You are sad, my darling,' I said, half-jestingly, as we sat down together in our little parlour. I expected a disclaimer, for my own silence had been the silence of complete happiness. To my surprise she said –

'Yes. I think I am sad, or rather I am uneasy. I don't think I'm very well. I have shivered three or four times since we came in, and it is not cold, is it?'

'No,' I said, and hoped it was not a chill caught from the treacherous mists that roll up from the marshes in the dying light. No – she said, she did not think so. Then, after a silence, she spoke suddenly –

'Do you ever have presentiments of evil?'

'No,' I said, smiling, 'and I shouldn't believe in them if I had.'

'I do,' she went on; 'the night my father died I knew it, though he was right away in the north of Scotland.' I did not answer in words.

She sat looking at the fire for some time in silence, gently stroking my hand. At last she sprang up, came behind me, and, drawing my head back, kissed me.

'There, it's over now,' she said. 'What a baby I am! Come, light the candles, and we'll have some of these new Rubinstein duets.'

And we spent a happy hour or two at the piano.

At about half-past ten I began to long for the good-night pipe, but Laura looked so white that I felt it would be brutal of me to fill our sitting-room with the fumes of strong cavendish.

'I'll take my pipe outside,' I said.

'Let me come, too.'

'No, sweetheart, not to-night; you're much too tired. I shan't be long. Get to bed, or I shall have an invalid to nurse to-morrow as well as the boots to clean.'

I kissed her and was turning to go, when she flung her arms round my neck, and held me as if she would never let me go again. I stroked her hair.

'Come, Pussy, you're over-tired. The housework has been too much for you.'

She loosened her clasp a little and drew a deep breath.

'No. We've been very happy to-day, Jack, haven't we? Don't stay out too long.'

'I won't, my dearie.'

I strolled out of the front door, leaving it unlatched. What a night it was! The jagged masses of heavy dark cloud were rolling at intervals from horizon to horizon, and thin white wreaths covered the stars. Through all the rush of the cloud river, the moon swam, breasting the waves and disappearing again in the darkness. When now and again her light reached the woodlands they seemed to be slowly and noiselessly waving in time to the swing of the clouds above them. There was a strange grey light over all the earth; the fields had that shadowy bloom over them which only comes from the marriage of dew and moonshine, or frost and starlight.

I walked up and down, drinking in the beauty of the quiet earth and the changing sky. The night was absolutely silent. Nothing seemed to be abroad. There was no skurrying of rabbits, or twitter of the half-asleep birds. And though the clouds went sailing across the sky, the wind that drove them never came low enough to rustle the dead leaves in the woodland paths. Across the meadows I could see the church tower standing out black and grey against the sky. I walked there thinking over our three months of happiness – and of my wife, her dear eyes, her loving ways. Oh, my little girl! my own little girl; what a vision came then of a long, glad life for you and me together!

I heard a bell-beat from the church. Eleven already! I turned to go in, but the night held me. I could not go back into our little warm rooms yet. I would go up to the church. I felt vaguely that it would be good to carry my love and thankfulness to the sanctuary whither so many loads of sorrow and gladness had been borne by the men and women of the dead years.

I looked in at the low window as I went by. Laura was half lying on her chair in front of the fire. I could not see her face, only her little head showed dark against the pale blue wall. She was quite still. Asleep, no doubt. My heart reached out to her, as I went on. There must be a God, I thought, and a God who was good. How otherwise could anything so sweet and dear as she have ever been imagined?

I walked slowly along the edge of the wood. A sound broke

the stillness of the night, it was a rustling in the wood. I stopped and listened. The sound stopped too. I went on, and now distinctly heard another step than mine answer mine like an echo. It was a poacher or a wood-stealer, most likely, for these were not unknown in our Arcadian neighbourhood. But whoever it was, he was a fool not to step more lightly. I turned into the wood, and now the footstep seemed to come from the path I had just left. It must be an echo, I thought. The wood looked perfect in the moonlight. The large dying ferns and the brushwood showed where through thinning foliage the pale light came down. The tree trunks stood up like Gothic columns all around me. They reminded me of the church, and I turned into the bier-balk, and passed through the corpse-gate between the graves to the low porch. I paused for a moment on the stone seat where Laura and I had watched the fading landscape. Then I noticed that the door of the church was open, and I blamed myself for having left it unlatched the other night. We were the only people who ever cared to come to the church except on Sundays, and I was vexed to think that through our carelessness the damp autumn airs had had a chance of getting in and injuring the old fabric. I went in. It will seem strange, perhaps, that I should have gone half-way up the aisle before I remembered – with a sudden chill, followed by as sudden a rush of self-contempt – that this was the very day and hour when, according to tradition, the 'shapes drawed out man-size in marble' began to walk.

Having thus remembered the legend, and remembered it with a shiver, of which I was ashamed, I could not do otherwise than walk up towards the altar, just to look at the figures – as I said to myself; really what I wanted was to assure myself, first, that I did not believe the legend, and, secondly, that it was not true. I was rather glad that I had come. I thought now I could tell Mrs Dorman how vain her fancies were, and how peacefully the marble figures slept on through the ghastly hour. With my hands in my pockets I passed up the aisle. In the grey dim light the eastern end of the church looked larger than usual, and the arches above the two tombs looked larger too. The moon came out and showed me the reason. I stopped short, my heart gave a leap that nearly choked me, and then sank sickeningly.

The 'bodies drawed out man-size' *were gone*, and their marble slabs lay wide and bare in the vague moonlight that slanted through the east window.

Were they really gone? or was I mad? Clenching my nerves, I stooped and passed my hand over the smooth slabs, and felt their flat unbroken surface. Had someone taken the things away? Was it some vile practical joke? I would make sure, anyway. In an instant I had made a torch of a newspaper, which happened to be in my pocket, and lighting it held it high above my head. Its yellow glare illumined the dark arches and those slabs. The figures were gone. And I was alone in the church; or was I alone?

And then a horror seized me, a horror indefinable and indescribable – an overwhelming certainty of supreme and accomplished calamity. I flung down the torch and tore along the aisle and out through the porch, biting my lips as I ran to keep myself from shrieking aloud. Oh, was I mad – or what was this that possessed me? I leaped the churchyard wall and took the straight cut across the fields, led by the light from our windows. Just as I got over the first stile, a dark figure seemed to spring out of the ground. Mad still with that certainty of misfortune, I made for the thing that stood in my path, shouting, 'Get out of the way, can't you!'

But my push met with a more vigorous resistance than I had expected. My arms were caught just above the elbow and held as in a vice, and the raw-boned Irish doctor actually shook me.

'Would ye?' he cried, in his own unmistakable accents – 'would ye, then?'

'Let me go, you fool,' I gasped. 'The marble figures have gone from the church; I tell you they've gone.'

He broke into a ringing laugh. 'I'll have to give ye a draught to-morrow, I see. Ye've bin smoking too much and listening to old wives' tales.'

'I tell you, I've seen the bare slabs.'

'Well, come back with me. I'm going up to old Palmer's – his daughter's ill; we'll look in at the church and let me see the bare slabs.'

'You go, if you like,' I said, a little less frantic for his laughter; 'I'm going home to my wife.'

'Rubbish, man,' said he; 'd'ye think I'll permit of that? Are ye to go saying all yer life that ye've seen solid marble endowed with vitality, and me to go all me life saying ye were a coward? No, sir – ye shan't do ut.'

The night air – a human voice – and I think also the physical contact with this six feet of solid common sense, brought me back a little to my ordinary self, and the word 'coward' was a mental shower-bath.

'Come on, then,' I said sullenly; 'perhaps you're right.'

He still held my arm tightly. We got over the stile and back to the church. All was still as death. The place smelt very damp and earthy. We walked up the aisle. I am not ashamed to confess that I shut my eyes: I knew the figures would not be there. I heard Kelly strike a match.

'Here they are, ye see, right enough; ye've been dreaming or drinking, asking yer pardon for the imputation.'

I opened my eyes. By Kelly's expiring vesta I saw two shapes lying 'in their marble' on their slabs. I drew a deep breath, and caught his hand.

'I'm awfully indebted to you,' I said. 'It must have been some trick of light, or I have been working rather hard, perhaps that's it. Do you know, I was quite convinced they were gone.'

'I'm aware of that,' he answered rather grimly; 'ye'll have to be careful of that brain of yours, my friend, I assure ye.'

He was leaning over and looking at the right-hand figure, whose stony face was the most villainous and deadly in expression.

'By Jove,' he said, 'something has been afoot here – this hand is broken.'

And so it was. I was certain that it had been perfect the last time Laura and I had been there.

'Perhaps someone has *tried* to remove them,' said the young doctor.

'That won't account for my impression,' I objected.

'Too much painting and tobacco will account for that, well enough.'

'Come along,' I said, 'or my wife will be getting anxious. You'll come in and have a drop of whisky and drink confusion to ghosts and better sense to me.'

'I ought to go up to Palmer's, but it's so late now I'd best leave it till the morning,' he replied. 'I was kept late at the Union, and I've had to see a lot of people since. All right, I'll come back with ye.'

I think he fancied I needed him more than did Palmer's girl, so, discussing how such an illusion could have been possible, and deducing from this experience large generalities concerning ghostly apparitions, we walked up to our cottage. We saw, as we walked up the garden-path, that bright light streamed out of the front door, and presently saw that the parlour door was open too. Had she gone out?

'Come in,' I said, and Dr Kelly followed me into the parlour. It was all ablaze with candles, not only the wax ones, but at least a dozen guttering, glaring tallow dips, stuck in vases and ornaments in unlikely places. Light, I knew, was Laura's remedy for nervousness. Poor child! Why had I left her? Brute that I was.

We glanced round the room, and at first we did not see her. The window was open, and the draught set all the candles flaring one way. Her chair was empty and her handkerchief and book lay on the floor. I turned to the window. There, in the recess of the window, I saw her. Oh, my child, my love, had she gone to that window to watch for me? And what had come into the room behind her? To what had she turned with that look of frantic fear and horror? Oh, my little one, had she thought that it was I whose step she heard, and turned to meet – what?

She had fallen back across a table in the window, and her body lay half on it and half on the window-seat, and her head hung down over the table, the brown hair loosened and fallen to the carpet. Her lips were drawn back, and her eyes wide, wide open. They saw nothing now. What had they seen last?

The doctor moved towards her, but I pushed him aside and sprang to her; caught her in my arms and cried –

'It's all right, Laura! I've got you safe, wifie.'

She fell into my arms in a heap. I clasped her and kissed her, and called her by all her pet names, but I think I knew all the time that she was dead. Her hands were tightly clenched. In one of them she held something fast. When I was quite sure that she was dead, and that nothing mattered at all any more, I let him open her hand to see what she held.

It was a grey marble finger.

2 No-Man's-Land

BY JOHN BUCHAN (1900)

I The Shieling of Farawa

It was with a light heart and a pleasing consciousness of holiday that I set out from the inn at Allermuir to tramp my fifteen miles into the unknown. I walked slowly, for I carried my equipment on my back – my basket, fly-books and rods, my plaid of Grant tartan (for I boast myself a distant kinsman of that house), and my great staff, which had tried ere then the front of the steeper Alps. A small valise with books and some changes of linen clothing had been sent on ahead in the shepherd's own hands. It was yet early April, and before me lay four weeks of freedom – twenty-eight blessed days in which to take fish and smoke the pipe of idleness. The Lent term had pulled me down, a week of modest enjoyment thereafter in town had finished the work; and I drank in the sharp moorish air like a thirsty man who has been forwandered among deserts.

I am a man of varied tastes and a score of interests. As an undergraduate I had been filled with the old mania for the complete life. I distinguished myself in the Schools, rowed in my college eight, and reached the distinction of practising for three weeks in the Trials. I had dabbled in a score of learned activities, and when the time came that I won the inevitable St Chad's fellowship on my chaotic acquirements, and I found myself compelled to select if I would pursue a scholar's life, I had some toil in finding my vocation. In the end I resolved that the ancient life of the North, of the Celts and the Northmen and the unknown Pictish tribes, held for me the chief fascination. I had acquired a smattering of

Gaelic, having been brought up as a boy in Lochaber, and now I set myself to increase my store of languages. I mastered Erse and Icelandic, and my first book – a monograph on the probable Celtic elements in the Eddic songs – brought me the praise of scholars and the deputy-professor's chair of Northern Antiquities. So much for Oxford. My vacations had been spent mainly in the North – in Ireland, Scotland, and the Isles, in Scandinavia and Iceland, once even in the far limits of Finland. I was a keen sportsman of a sort, an old-experienced fisher, a fair shot with gun and rifle, and in my hillcraft I might well stand comparison with most men. April has ever seemed to me the finest season of the year even in our cold northern altitudes, and the memory of many bright Aprils had brought me up from the South on the night before to Allerfoot, whence a dogcart had taken me up Glen Aller to the inn at Allermuir; and now the same desire had set me on the heather with my face to the cold brown hills.

You are to picture a sort of plateau, benty and rock-strewn, running ridge-wise above a chain of little peaty lochs and a vast tract of inexorable bog. In a mile the ridge ceased in a shoulder of hill, and over this lay the head of another glen, with the same doleful accompaniment of sunless lochs, mosses, and a shining and resolute water. East and west and north, in every direction save the south, rose walls of gashed and serrated hills. It was a grey day with blinks of sun, and when a ray chanced to fall on one of the great dark faces, lines of light and colour sprang into being which told of mica and granite. I was in high spirits, as on the eve of holiday; I had breakfasted excellently on eggs and salmon-steaks; I had no cares to speak of, and my prospects were not uninviting. But in spite of myself the landscape began to take me in thrall and crush me. The silent vanished peoples of the hills seemed to be stirring; dark primeval faces seemed to stare at me from behind boulders and jags of rock. The place was so still, so free from the cheerful clamour of nesting birds, that it seemed a temenos sacred to some old-world god. At my feet the lochs lapped ceaselessly; but the waters were so dark that one could not see bottom a foot from the edge. On my right the links of green told of snakelike mires waiting to crush the unwary wanderer. It seemed to me for the moment a land of death, where the tongues of the dead cried aloud for recognition.

My whole morning's walk was full of such fancies. I lit a pipe to cheer me, but the things would not be got rid of. I thought of the Gaels who had held those fastnesses; I thought of the Britons before them, who yielded to their advent. They were all strong peoples in their day, and now they had gone the way of the earth. They had left their mark on the levels of the glens and on the more habitable uplands, both in names and in actual forts, and graves where men might still dig curios. But the hills – that black stony amphitheatre before me – it seemed strange that the hills bore no traces of them. And then with some uneasiness I reflected on that older and stranger race who were said to have held the hill-tops. The Picts, the Picti – what in the name of goodness were they? They had troubled me in all my studies, a sort of blank wall to put an end to speculation. We knew nothing of them save certain strange names which men called Pictish, the names of those hills in front of me – the Muneraw, the Yirnie, the Calmarton. They were the *corpus vile* for learned experiment; but Heaven alone knew what dark abyss of savagery once yawned in the midst of the desert.

And then I remembered the crazy theories of a pupil of mine at St Chad's, the son of a small landowner on the Aller, a young gentleman who had spent his substance too freely at Oxford, and was now dreeing his weird in the backwoods. He had been no scholar; but a certain imagination marked all his doings, and of a Sunday night he would come and talk to me of the North. The Picts were his special subject, and his ideas were mad. 'Listen to me,' he would say, when I had mixed him toddy and given him one of my cigars; 'I believe there are traces – ay, and more than traces – of an old culture lurking in those hills and waiting to be discovered. We never hear of the Picts being driven from the hills. The Britons drove them from the lowlands, the Gaels from Ireland did the same for the Britons; but the hills were left unmolested. We hear of no one going near them except outlaws and tinklers. And in that very place you have the strangest mythology. Take the story of the Brownie. What is that but the story of a little swart man of uncommon strength and cleverness, who does good and ill indiscriminately, and then disappears. There are many scholars, as you yourself confess, who think that the origin of the Brownie was in some mad belief in the old race of the Picts, which still survived somewhere in the hills. And do we not hear of the Brownie in authentic records right down to the year 1756? After that, when people grew more incredulous, it is natural that the belief should have begun to die out; but I do not see why stray traces should not have survived till late.'

'Do you not see what that means?' I had said in mock gravity. 'Those same hills are, if anything, less known now than they were a hundred years ago. Why should not your Picts or Brownies be living to this day?'

'Why not, indeed?' he had rejoined, in all seriousness.

I laughed, and he went to his rooms and returned with a large leather-bound book. It was lettered, in the rococo style of a young man's taste, *Glimpses of the Unknown*, and some of the said glimpses he proceeded to impart to me. It was not pleasant reading; indeed, I had rarely heard anything so well fitted to shatter sensitive nerves. The early part consisted of folk-tales and folk-sayings, some of them wholly obscure, some of them with a glint of meaning, but all of them with some hint of a mystery in the hills. I heard the Brownie story in countless versions. Now the thing was a friendly little man, who wore grey breeches and lived on brose; now he was a twisted being, the sight of which made the ewes miscarry in the lambing-time. But the second part was the stranger, for it was made up of actual tales, most of them with date and place appended. It was a most Bedlamite catalogue of horrors, which, if true, made the wholesome moors a place instinct with tragedy. Some told of children carried away from villages, even from towns, on the verge of the uplands. In almost every case they were girls, and the strange fact was their utter disappearance. Two little girls would be coming home from school, would be seen last by a neighbour just where the road crossed a patch of heath or entered a wood, and then – no human eye ever saw them again. Children's cries had startled outlying shepherds in the night, and when they had rushed to the door they could hear nothing but the night wind. The instances of such disappearances were not very common – perhaps once in twenty years – but they were confined to this one tract of country, and came in a sort of fixed progression from the middle of last century, when the record began. But this was only one side of the history. The latter part was all devoted to a chronicle of crimes which had gone unpunished, seeing that no hand had ever been traced. The list was fuller in the last century;[1] in the earlier years of the present it had dwindled; then came a revival about the 'fifties; and now again in our own time it had sunk low. At the little cottage of Auchterbrean, on the roadside in Glen Aller, a labourer's wife had been found pierced to the heart. It was thought to be a case of a woman's jealousy, and her neighbour was accused, convicted, and hanged. The woman, to be sure, denied the charge with her last breath; but circumstantial evidence seemed sufficiently strong against her. Yet some

---

1 The narrative of Mr Graves was written in the year 1898.

people in the glen believed her guiltless. In particular, the carrier who had found the dead woman declared that the way in which her neighbour received the news was a sufficient proof of innocence; and the doctor who was first summoned professed himself unable to tell with what instrument the wound had been given. But this was all before the days of expert evidence, so the woman had been hanged without scruple. Then there had been another story of peculiar horror, telling of the death of an old man at some little lonely shieling called Carrickfey. But at this point I had risen in protest, and made to drive the young idiot from my room.

'It was my grandfather who collected most of them,' he said. 'He had theories,[2] but people called him mad, so he was wise enough to hold his tongue. My father declares the whole thing mania; but I rescued the book, had it bound, and added to the collection. It is a queer hobby; but, as I say, I have theories, and there are more things in heaven and earth –'

But at this he heard a friend's voice in the Quad, and dived out, leaving the banal quotation unfinished.

2   In the light of subsequent events I have jotted down the materials to which I refer. The last authentic record of the Brownie is in the narrative of the shepherd of Clachlands, taken down towards the close of last century by the Reverend Mr Gillespie, minister of Allerkirk, and included by him in his 'Songs and Legends of Glen Aller'. The authorities on the strange carrying-away of children are to be found in a series of articles in a local paper, the *Allerfoot Advertiser*, September and October 1878, and a curious book published anonymously at Edinburgh in 1848, entitled *The Weathergaw*. The records of the unexplained murders in the same neighbourhood are all contained in Mr Fordoun's *Theory of Expert Evidence*, and an attack on the book in the *Law Review* for June 1881. The Carrickfey case has a pamphlet to itself – now extremely rare – a copy of which was recently obtained in a bookseller's shop in Dumfries by a well-known antiquary, and presented to the library of the Supreme Court in Edinburgh.

Strange though it may seem, this madness kept coming back to me as I crossed the last few miles of moor. I was now on a rough tableland, the watershed between two lochs, and beyond and above me rose the stony backs of the hills. The burns fell down in a chaos of granite boulders, and huge slabs of grey stone lay flat and tumbled in the heather. The full waters looked prosperously for my fishing, and I began to forget all fancies in anticipation of sport.

Then suddenly in a hollow of land I came on a ruined cottage. It had been a very small place, but the walls were still half-erect, and the little moorland garden was outlined on the turf. A lonely apple-tree, twisted and gnarled with winds, stood in the midst.

From higher up on the hill I heard a loud roar, and I knew my excellent friend the shepherd of Farawa, who had come thus far to meet me. He greeted me with the boisterous embarrassment which was his way of prefacing hospitality. A grave reserved man at other times, on such occasions he thought it proper to relapse into hilarity. I fell into step with him, and we set off for his dwelling. But first I had the curiosity to look back to the tumble-down cottage and ask him its name.

A queer look came into his eyes. 'They ca' the place Carrickfey,' he said. 'Naebody has daured to bide there this twenty year sin' – but I see ye ken the story.' And, as if glad to leave the subject, he hastened to discourse on fishing.

II   Tells of an evening's talk

The shepherd was a masterful man; tall, save for the stoop which belongs to all moorland folk, and active as a wild goat. He was not a new importation, nor did he belong to the place; for his people had lived in the remote Borders, and he had come as a boy to this shieling of Farawa. He was unmarried, but an elderly sister lived with him and cooked his meals. He was reputed to be extraordinarily skilful in his trade; I know for a fact that he was in his way a keen sportsman; and his few neighbours gave him credit for a sincere piety. Doubtless this last report was due in part to his silence, for after his first greeting he was wont to relapse into a singular taciturnity. As we strode across the heather he gave me a short outline of his year's lambing. 'Five pair o' twins yestreen, twae this morn; that makes thirty-five yowes that hae lambed since the Sabbath. I'll dae weel if God's willin'.' Then, as I looked towards the hill-tops whence the thin mist of morn was trailing, he followed my gaze. 'See,' he said with uplifted crook – 'see that sicht. Is that no what is written of in the Bible when it says, "The mountains do smoke".' And with this piece of exegesis he finished his talk, and in a little we were at the cottage.

It was a small enough dwelling in truth, and yet large for a moorland house, for it had a garret below the thatch, which was given up to my sole enjoyment. Below was the wide kitchen with box-beds, and next to it the inevitable second room, also with its cupboard sleeping-places. The interior was very clean, and yet I remember to have been struck with the faint musty smell which is inseparable from moorland dwellings. The kitchen pleased me best, for there the great rafters were black with peat-reek, and the uncovered stone floor, on which the fire gleamed dully, gave an air of primeval simplicity. But the walls spoiled all, for tawdry things of to-day had penetrated even there. Some grocers' almanacs – years old – hung in places of honour, and an extraordinary lithograph of the Royal Family in its youth. And this, mind you, between crooks and fishing-rods and old guns, and horns of sheep and deer.

The life for the first day or two was regular and placid. I was up early, breakfasted on porridge (a dish which I detest), and then off to the lochs and streams. At first my sport prospered mightily. With a drake-wing I killed a salmon of seventeen pounds, and the next day had a fine basket of trout from a hill-burn. Then for no earthly reason the weather changed. A bitter wind came out of the north-east, bringing showers of snow and stinging hail, and lashing the waters into storm. It was now farewell to fly-fishing. For a day or two I tried trolling with the minnow on the lochs, but it was poor sport, for I had no boat, and the edges were soft and mossy. Then in disgust I gave up the attempt, went back to the cottage, lit my biggest pipe, and sat down with a book to await the turn of the weather.

The shepherd was out from morning till night at his work, and when he came in at last, dog-tired, his face would be set and hard, and his eyes heavy with sleep. The strangeness of the man grew upon me. He had a shrewd brain beneath his thatch of hair, for I had tried him once or twice, and found him abundantly intelligent. He had some smattering of an education, like all Scottish peasants, and, as I have said, he was deeply religious. I set him down as a fine type of his class, sober, serious, keenly critical, free from the bondage of superstition. But I rarely saw him, and our talk was chiefly in monosyllables – short interjected accounts of the number of lambs dead or alive on the hill. Then he would produce a pencil and notebook, and be immersed in some calculation; and finally he would be revealed sleeping heavily in his chair, till his sister wakened him, and he stumbled off to bed.

So much for the ordinary course of life; but one day – the second I think of the bad weather – the extraordinary happened. The storm had passed in the afternoon into a resolute and blinding snow, and the shepherd, finding it hopeless on the hill, came home about three o'clock. I could make out from his way of entering that he was in a great temper. He kicked his feet savagely against the door-post.

Then he swore at his dogs, a thing I had never heard him do before. 'Hell!' he cried, 'can ye no keep out o' my road, ye britts?' Then he came sullenly into the kitchen, thawed his numbed hands at the fire, and sat down to his meal.

I made some aimless remark about the weather.

'Death to man and beast,' he grunted. 'I hae got the sheep doun frae the hill, but the lambs will never thole this. We maun pray that it will no last'.

His sister came in with some dish. 'Margit,' he cried, 'three lambs away this morning, and three deid wi' the hole in the throat.'

The woman's face visibly paled. 'Guid help us, Adam; that hasna happened this three year.'

'It has happened noo,' he said, surlily. 'But, by God! if it happens again I'll gang mysel' to the Scarts o' the Muneraw.'

'O Adam!' the woman cried shrilly, 'haud your tongue. Ye kenna wha hears ye.' And with a frightened glance at me she left the room.

I asked no questions, but waited till the shepherd's anger should cool. But the cloud did not pass so lightly. When he had finished his dinner he pulled his chair to the fire and sat staring moodily. He made some sort of apology to me for his conduct. 'I'm sore troubled, sir; but I'm vexed ye should see me like this. Maybe things will be better the morn.' And then, lighting his short black pipe, he resigned himself to his meditations.

But he could not keep quiet. Some nervous unrest seemed to have possessed the man. He got up with a start and went to the window, where the snow was drifting, unsteadily past. As he stared out into the storm I heard him mutter to himself, 'Three away, God help me, and three wi' the hole in the throat.'

Then he turned round to me abruptly. I was jotting down notes for an article I contemplated in the *Revue Celtique*, so my thoughts were far away from the present. The man recalled me by demanding fiercely. 'Do ye believe in God?'

I gave him some sort of answer in the affirmative.

'Then do ye believe in the Devil?' he asked.

The reply must have been less satisfactory, for he came forward, and flung himself violently into the chair before me.

'What do ye ken about it?' he cried. 'You that bides in a southern toun, what can ye ken o' the God that works in thae hills and the Devil – ay, the manifold devils – that He suffers to bide here? I tell ye, man, that if ye had seen what I have seen ye wad be on your knees at this moment praying to God to pardon your unbelief. There are devils at the back o' every stane and hidin' in every cleuch, and it's by the grace o' God alone that a man is alive upon the earth.' His voice had risen high and shrill, and then suddenly he cast a frightened glance towards the window and was silent.

I began to think that the man's wits were unhinged, and the thought did not give me satisfaction. I had no relish for the prospect of being left alone in this moorland dwelling with the cheerful company of a maniac. But his next movements reassured me. He was clearly only dead-tired, for he fell sound asleep in his chair, and by the time his sister brought tea and wakened him, he seemed to have got the better of his excitement.

When the window was shuttered and the lamp lit, I set myself again to the completion of my notes. The shepherd had got out his Bible, and was solemnly reading with one great finger travelling down the lines. He was smoking, and whenever some text came home to him with power he would make pretence to underline it with the end of the stem. Soon I had finished the work I desired, and, my mind being full of my pet hobby, I fell into an inquisitive frame of mind, and began to question the solemn man opposite on the antiquities of the place.

He stared stupidly at me when I asked him concerning monuments or ancient weapons.

'I kenna,' said he. 'There's a heap o' queer things in the hills.'

'This place should be a centre for such relics. You know that the name of the hill behind the house, as far as I can make it out, means the 'Place of the Little Men'. It is a good Gaelic word, though there is some doubt about its exact interpretation. But clearly the Gaelic peoples did not speak of themselves when they gave the name; they must have referred to some older and stranger population.'

The shepherd looked at me dully, as not understanding.

'It is partly this fact – besides the fishing, of course – which interests me in this countryside,' said I, gaily.

Again he cast the same queer frightened glance towards the window. 'If ye'll tak the advice of an aulder man,' he said, slowly, 'ye'll let well alane and no meddle wi' uncanny things.'

I laughed pleasantly, for at last I had found out my hard-headed host in a piece of childishness. 'Why, I thought that you of all men would be free from superstition.'

'What do ye call supersteetion?' he asked.

'A belief in old wives' tales,' said I, 'a trust in the crude supernatural and the patently impossible.'

He looked at me beneath his shaggy brows. 'How do ye ken what is impossible? Mind ye, sir, ye're no in the toun just now, but in the thick of the wild hills.'

'But, hang it all, man,' I cried, 'you don't mean to say that you believe in that sort of thing? I am prepared for many things up here, but not for the Brownie – though, to be sure, if one could meet him in the flesh, it would be rather pleasant than otherwise, for he was a companionable sort of fellow.'

'When a thing pits the fear o' death on a man he aye speaks well of it.'

It was true – the Eumenides and the Good Folk over again; and I awoke with interest to the fact that the conversation was getting into strange channels.

The shepherd moved uneasily in his chair. 'I am a man that fears God, and has nae time for daft stories; but I havena traivelled the hills for twenty years wi' my een shut. If I say that I could tell ye stories o' faces seen in the mist, and queer things that have knocked against me in the snaw, wad ye believe me? I wager ye wadna. Ye wad say I had been drunk, and yet I am a God-fearing temperate man.'

He rose and went to a cupboard, unlocked it, and brought out something in his hand, which he held out to me. I took it with some curiosity, and found that it was a flint arrow-head.

Clearly a flint arrow-head, and yet like none that I had ever seen in any collection. For one thing it was larger, and the barb less clumsily thick. More, the chipping was new, or comparatively so; this thing had not stood the wear of fifteen hundred years among the stones of the hillside. Now there are, I regret to say, institutions which manufacture primitive relics; but it is not hard for a practised eye to see the difference. The chipping has either a regularity and a balance which is unknown in the real thing, or the rudeness has been overdone, and the result is an implement incapable of harming a mortal creature. But this was the real thing if it ever existed; and yet – I was prepared to swear on my reputation that it was not half a century old.

'Where did you get this?' I asked with some nervousness.

'I hae a story about that,' said the shepherd. 'Outside the door there ye can see a muckle flat stane aside the buchts. One simmer nicht I was sitting there smoking till the dark, and I wager there was naething on the stane then. But that same nicht I awoke wi' a queer thocht, as if there were folk moving around the hoose – folk that didna mak' muckle noise. I mind o' lookin' out o' the windy, and I could hae sworn I saw something black movin' amang the heather and intil the buchts. Now I had maybe threescore o' lambs there that nicht, for I had to tak' them many miles off in the early morning. Weel, when I gets up about four o'clock and gangs out, as I am passing the muckle stane I finds this bit errow. 'That's come here in the nicht,' says I, and I wunnered a wee and put it in my pouch. But when I came to my faulds what did I see? Five o' my best hoggs were away, and three mair were lying deid wi' a hole in their throat.'

'Who in the world –?' I began.

Dinna ask,' said he. 'If I aince sterted to speir about thae maitters, I wadna keep my reason.'

'Then that was what happened on the hill this morning?'

'Even sae, and it has happened mair than aince sin' that time. It's the most uncanny slaughter, for sheep-stealing I can understand, but no this pricking o' the puir beasts' wizands. I kenna how they dae't either, for it's no wi' a knife or ony common tool.'

'Have you never tried to follow the thieves?'

'Have I no?' he asked, grimly. 'If it had been common sheep-stealers I wad hae had them by the heels, though I had followed them a hundred miles. But this is no common. I've tracked them, and it's ill they are to track; but I never got beyond ae place, and that was the Scarts o' the Muneraw that ye've heard me speak o'.'

'But who in Heaven's name are the people? Tinklers or poachers or what?'

'Ay,' said he, drily. 'Even so. Tinklers and poachers whae wark wi' stane errows and kill sheep by a hole in their throat. Lord, I kenna what they are, unless the Muckle Deil himsel'.'

The conversation had passed beyond my comprehension. In this prosaic hard-headed man I had come on the dead-rock of superstition and blind fear.

'That is only the story of the Brownie over again, and he is an exploded myth,' I said, laughing.

'Are ye the man that exploded it?' said the shepherd, rudely. 'I trow no, neither you nor ony ither. My bonny man, if ye lived a twalmonth in thae hills, ye wad sing safter about exploded myths, as ye call them.'

'I tell you what I would do,' said I. 'If I lost sheep as you lose them, I would go up the Scarts of the Muneraw and never rest till I had settled the question once and for all.' I spoke hotly, for I was vexed by the man's childish fear.

'I daresay ye wad,' he said, slowly. 'But then I am no you, and maybe I ken mair o' what is in the Scarts o' the Muneraw. Maybe I ken that whilk, if ye kenned it, wad send ye back to the South Country wi' your hert in your mouth. But, as I say, I am no sae brave as you, for I saw something in the first year o' my herding here which put the terror o' God on me, and makes me a fearfu' man to this day. Ye ken the story o' the gudeman o' Carrickfey?'

I nodded.

'Weel, I was the man that fand him. I had seen the deid afore and I've seen them since. But never have I seen aucht like the look in that man's een. What he saw at his death I may see the morn, so I walk before the Lord in fear.'

Then he rose and stretched himself. 'It's bedding-time, for I maun be up at three,' and with a short good night he left the room.

III   The Scarts of the Muneraw

The next morning was fine, for the snow had been intermittent, and had soon melted except in the high corries. True, it was deceptive weather, for the wind had gone to the rainy south-west, and the masses of cloud on that horizon boded ill for the afternoon. But some days' inaction had made me keen for a chance of sport, so I rose with the shepherd and set out for the day.

He asked me where I proposed to begin.

I told him the tarn called the Loch o' the Threshes, which lies over the back of the Muneraw on another watershed. It is on the ground of the Rhynns Forest, and I had fished it of old from the Forest House. I knew the merits of the trout, and I knew its virtues in a south-west wind, so I had resolved to go thus far afield.

The shepherd heard the name in silence. 'Your best road will be ower that rig, and syne on to the water o' Caulds. Keep abune the moss till ye come to the place they ca' the Nick o' the Threshes. That will take ye to the very lochside, but it's a lang road and a sair.'

The morning was breaking over the bleak hills. Little clouds drifted athwart the corries, and wisps of haze fluttered from the peaks. A great rosy flush lay over one side of the glen, which caught the edge of the sluggish bog-pools and turned them to fire. Never before had I seen the mountain-land so clear, for far back into the east and west I saw mountain-tops set as close as flowers in a border, black crags seamed with silver lines which I knew for mighty waterfalls, and below at my feet the lower slopes fresh with the dewy green of spring. A name stuck in my memory from the last night's talk.

'Where are the Scarts of the Muneraw?' I asked.

The shepherd pointed to the great hill which bears the name, and which lies, a huge mass, above the watershed.

'D'ye see yon corrie at the east that runs straucht up the side? It looks a bit scart, but it's sae deep that it's aye derk at the bottom o't. Weel, at the tap o' the rig it meets anither corrie that runs doun the ither side, and that one they ca' the Scarts. There is a sort o' burn in it that flows intil the Dule and sae intil the Aller, and, indeed, if ye were gaun there it wad be from Aller Glen that your best road wad lie. But it's an ill bit, and ye'll be sair guidit if ye try't.'

There he left me and went across the glen, while I struck upwards over the ridge. At the top I halted and looked down on the wide glen of the Caulds, which there is little better than a bog, but lower down grows into a green pastoral valley. The great Muneraw still dominated the landscape, and the black scaur on its side seemed blacker than before. The place fascinated me, for in that fresh morning air the shepherd's fears seemed monstrous. 'Some day,' said I to myself, 'I will go and explore the whole of that mighty hill.' Then I descended and struggled over the moss, found the Nick, and in two hours' time was on the loch's edge.

I have little in the way of good to report of the fishing. For perhaps one hour the trout took well; after that they sulked steadily for the day. The promise, too, of fine weather had been deceptive. By midday the rain was falling in that soft soaking fashion which gives no hope of clearing. The mist was down to the edge of the water, and I cast my flies into a blind sea of white. It was hopeless work, and yet from a sort of ill-temper I stuck to it long after my better judgment had warned me of its folly. At last, about three in the afternoon, I struck my camp, and prepared myself for a long and toilsome retreat.

And long and toilsome it was beyond anything I had ever encountered. Had I had a vestige of sense I would have followed the burn from the loch down to the Forest House. The place was shut up, but the keeper would gladly have given me shelter for the night. But foolish pride was too strong in me. I had found my road in mist before, and could do it again.

Before I got to the top of the hill I had repented my decision; when I got there I repented it more. For below me was a dizzy chaos of grey; there was no landmark visible; and before me

I knew was the bog through which the Caulds Water twined. I had crossed it with some trouble in the morning, but then I had light to pick my steps. Now I could only stumble on, and in five minutes I might be in a bog-hole, and in five more in a better world.

But there was no help to be got from hesitation, so with a rueful courage I set off. The place was if possible worse than I had feared. Wading up to the knees with nothing before you but a blank wall of mist and the cheerful consciousness that your next step may be your last–such was my state for one weary mile. The stream itself was high, and rose to my armpits, and once and again I only saved myself by a violent leap backwards from a pitiless green slough. But at last it was past, and I was once more on the solid ground of the hillside.

Now, in the thick weather I had crossed the glen much lower down than in the morning, and the result was that the hill on which I stood was one of the giants which, with the Muneraw for centre, guard the watershed. Had I taken the proper way, the Nick o' the Threshes would have led me to the Caulds, and then once over the bog a little ridge was all that stood between me and the glen of Farawa. But instead I had come a wild cross-country road, and was now, though I did not know it, nearly as far from my destination as at the start.

Well for me that I did not know, for I was wet and dispirited, and had I not fancied myself all but home, I should scarcely have had the energy to make this last ascent. But soon I found it was not the little ridge I had expected. I looked at my watch and saw that it was five o'clock. When, after the weariest climb, I lay on a piece of level ground which seemed the top, I was not surprised to find that it was now seven. The darkening must be at hand, and sure enough the mist seemed to be deepening into a greyish black. I began to grow desperate. Here was I on the summit of some infernal mountain, without any certainty where my road lay. I was lost with a vengeance, and at the thought I began to be acutely afraid.

I took what seemed to me the way I had come, and began to descend steeply. Then something made me halt, and the next instant I was lying on my face trying painfully to retrace my steps. For I had found myself slipping, and before I could stop, my feet were dangling over a precipice with Heaven alone knows how many yards of sheer mist between me and the bottom. Then I tried keeping the ridge, and took that to the right, which I thought would bring me nearer home. It was no good trying to think out a direction, for in the fog my brain was running round, and I seemed to stand on a pin-point of space where the laws of the compass had ceased to hold.

It was the roughest sort of walking, now stepping warily over acres of loose stones, now crawling down the face of some battered rock, and now wading in the long dripping heather. The soft rain had begun to fall again, which completed my discomfort. I was now seriously tired, and, like all men who in their day have bent too much over books, I began to feel it in my back. My spine ached, and my breath came in short broken pants. It was a pitiable state of affairs for an honest man who had never encountered much grave discomfort. To ease myself I was compelled to leave my basket behind me, trusting to return and find it, if I should ever reach safety and discover on what pathless hill I had been strayed. My rod I used as a staff, but it was of little use, for my fingers were getting too numb to hold it.

Suddenly from the blankness I heard a sound as of human speech. At first I thought it mere craziness – the cry of a weasel or a hill-bird distorted by my ears. But again it came, thick and faint, as through acres of mist, and yet clearly the sound of 'articulate-speaking men'. In a moment I lost my despair and cried out in answer. This was some forwandered traveller like myself, and between us we could surely find some road to safety. So I yelled back at the pitch of my voice and waited intently.

But the sound ceased, and there was utter silence again. Still I waited, and then from some place much nearer came the same soft mumbling speech. I could make nothing of it. Heard in that drear place it made the nerves tense and the heart timorous. It was the strangest jumble of vowels and consonants I had ever met.

A dozen solutions flashed through my brain. It was some maniac talking Jabberwock to himself. It was some belated traveller whose wits had given out in fear. Perhaps it was only some shepherd who was amusing himself thus, and whiling the way with nonsense. Once again I cried out and waited.

Then suddenly in the hollow trough of mist before me, where things could still be half discerned, there appeared a figure. It was little and squat and dark; naked, apparently, but so rough with hair that it wore the appearance of a skin-covered being. It crossed my line of vision, not staying for a moment, but in its face and eyes there seemed to lurk an elder world of mystery and barbarism, a troll-like life which was too horrible for words.

The shepherd's fear came back on me like a thunderclap. For one awful instant my legs failed me, and I had almost fallen. The next I had turned and ran shrieking up the hill.

If he who may read this narrative has never felt the force of an overmastering terror, then let him thank his Maker and pray that he never may. I am no weak child, but a strong grown man, accredited in general with sound sense and little suspected of hysterics. And yet I went up that brae-face with my heart fluttering like a bird and my throat aching with fear. I screamed in short dry gasps; involuntarily, for my mind was beyond any purpose. I felt that beast-like clutch at my throat;

those red eyes seemed to be staring at me from the mist; I heard ever behind and before and on all sides the patter of those inhuman feet.

Before I knew I was down, slipping over a rock and falling some dozen feet into a soft marshy hollow. I was conscious of lying still for a second and whimpering like a child. But as I lay there I awoke to the silence of the place. There was no sound of pursuit; perhaps they had lost my track and given up. My courage began to return, and from this it was an easy step to hope. Perhaps after all it had been merely an illusion, for folk do not see clearly in the mist, and I was already done with weariness.

But even as I lay in the green moss and began to hope, the faces of my pursuers grew up through the mist. I stumbled madly to my feet; but I was hemmed in, the rock behind and my enemies before. With a cry I rushed forward, and struck wildly with my rod at the first dark body. It was as if I had struck an animal, and the next second the thing was wrenched from my grasp. But still they came no nearer. I stood trembling there in the centre of those malignant devils, my brain a mere weathercock, and my heart crushed shapeless with horror. At last the end came, for with the vigour of madness I flung myself on the nearest, and we rolled on the ground. Then the monstrous things seemed to close over me, and with a choking cry I passed into unconsciousness.

IV   The Darkness that is Under the Earth

There is an unconsciousness that is not wholly dead, where a man feels numbly and the body lives without the brain. I was beyond speech or thought, and yet I felt the upward or downward motion as the way lay in hill or glen, and I most assuredly knew when the open air was changed for the close underground. I could feel dimly that lights were flared in my face, and that I was laid in some bed on the earth. Then with the stopping of movement the real sleep of weakness seized me, and for long I knew nothing of this mad world.

※

Morning came over the moors with bird-song and the glory of fine weather. The streams were still rolling in spate, but the hill-pastures were alight with dawn, and the little seams of snow glistened like white fire. A ray from the sunrise cleft its path somehow into the abyss, and danced on the wall above my couch. It caught my eye as I wakened, and for long I lay crazily wondering what it meant. My head was splitting with pain, and in my heart was the same fluttering nameless fear. I did not wake to full consciousness; not till the twinkle of sun from the clean bright out-of-doors caught my senses did I realise that I lay in a great dark place with a glow of dull firelight in the middle.

In time things rose and moved around me, a few ragged shapes of men, without clothing, shambling with their huge feet and looking towards me with curved beast-like glances. I tried to marshal my thoughts, and slowly, bit by bit, I built up the present. There was no question to my mind of dreaming; the past hours had scored reality upon my brain. Yet I cannot say that fear was my chief feeling. The first crazy terror had subsided, and now I felt mainly a sickened disgust with just a tinge of curiosity. I found that my knife, watch, flask, and money had gone, but they had left me a map of the countryside. It seemed strange to look at the calico, with the name of a London printer stamped on the back, and lines of railway and highroad running through every shire. Decent and comfortable civilisation! And here was I a prisoner in this den of nameless folk, and in the midst of a life which history knew not.

Courage is a virtue which grows with reflection and the absence of the immediate peril. I thought myself into some sort of resolution, and lo! when the Folk approached me and bound my feet I was back at once in the most miserable terror. They tied me all but my hands with some strong cord, and carried me to the centre, where the fire was glowing. Their soft touch was the acutest torture to my nerves, but I stifled my cries lest some one should lay his hand on my mouth. Had that happened, I am convinced my reason would have failed me.

So there I lay in the shine of the fire, with the circle of unknown things around me. There seemed but three or four, but I took no note of number. They talked huskily among themselves in a tongue which sounded all gutturals. Slowly my fear became less an emotion than a habit, and I had room for the smallest shade of curiosity. I strained my ear to catch a word, but it was a mere chaos of sound. The thing ran and thundered in my brain as I stared dumbly into the vacant air. Then I thought that unless I spoke I should certainly go crazy, for my head was beginning to swim at the strange cooing noise.

I spoke a word or two in my best Gaelic, and they closed round me inquiringly. Then I was sorry I had spoken, for my words had brought them nearer, and I shrank at the thought. But as the faint echoes of my speech hummed in the rock-chamber, I was struck by a curious kinship of sound. Mine was sharper, more distinct, and staccato; theirs was blurred, formless, but still with a certain root-resemblance.

Then from the back there came an older being, who seemed to have heard my words. He was like some foul grey badger, his red eyes sightless, and his hands trembling on a stump of bog-oak. The others made way for him with such deference as they were capable of, and the thing squatted down by me and spoke.

To my amazement his words were familiar. It was some manner of speech akin to the Gaelic, but broadened, lengthened, coarsened. I remembered an old book-tongue, commonly supposed to be an impure dialect once used in Brittany, which I had met in the course of my researches. The words recalled it, and as far as I could remember the thing, I asked him who he was and where the place might be.

He answered me in the same speech – still more broadened, lengthened, coarsened. I lay back with sheer amazement. I had found the key to this unearthly life.

For a little an insatiable curiosity, the ardour of the scholar, prevailed. I forgot the horror of the place, and thought only of the fact that here before me was the greatest find that scholarship had ever made. I was precipitated into the heart of the past. Here must be the fountainhead of all legends, the chrysalis of all beliefs. I actually grew light-hearted. This strange folk around me were now no more shapeless things of terror, but objects of research and experiment. I almost came to think them not unfriendly.

For an hour I enjoyed the highest of earthly pleasures. In that strange conversation I heard – in fragments and suggestions – the history of the craziest survival the world has ever seen. I heard of the struggles with invaders, preserved as it were in a sort of shapeless poetry. There were bitter words against the Gaelic oppressor, bitterer words against the Saxon stranger, and for a moment ancient hatreds flared into life. Then there came the tale of the hill-refuge, the morbid hideous existence preserved for centuries amid a changing world. I heard fragments of old religions, primeval names of god and goddess, half-understood by the Folk, but to me the key to a hundred puzzles. Tales which survive to us in broken disjointed riddles were intact here in living form. I lay on my elbow and questioned feverishly. At any moment they might become morose and refuse to speak. Clearly it was my duty to make the most of a brief good fortune.

And then the tale they told me grew more hideous. I heard of the circumstances of the life itself and their daily shifts for existence. It was a murderous chronicle – a history of lust and rapine and unmentionable deeds in the darkness. One thing they had early recognised – that the race could not be maintained within itself; so that ghoulish carrying away of little girls from the lowlands began, which I had heard of but never credited. Shut up in those dismal holes, the girls soon died, and when the new race had grown up the plunder had been repeated. Then there were bestial murders in lonely cottages, done for God knows what purpose. Sometimes the occupant had seen more than was safe, sometimes the deed was the mere exuberance of a lust of slaying. As they gabbled their tales my heart's blood froze, and I lay back in the agonies of fear. If they had used the others thus, what way of escape was open for myself? I had been brought to this place, and not murdered on the spot. Clearly there was torture before death in store for me, and I confess I quailed at the thought.

But none molested me. The elders continued to jabber out their stories, while I lay tense and deaf. Then to my amazement food was brought and placed beside me – almost with respect. Clearly my murder was not a thing of the immediate future. The meal was some form of mutton – perhaps the shepherd's lost ewes – and a little smoking was all the cooking it had got. I strove to eat, but the tasteless morsels choked me. Then they set drink before me in a curious cup, which I seized on eagerly, for my mouth was dry with thirst. The vessel was of gold, rudely formed, but of the pure metal, and a coarse design in circles ran round the middle. This surprised me enough, but a greater wonder awaited me. The liquor was not water, as I had guessed, but a sort of sweet ale, a miracle of flavour. The taste was curious, but somehow familiar; it was like no wine I had ever drunk, and yet I had known that flavour all my life. I sniffed at the brim, and there rose a faint fragrance of thyme and heather honey and the sweet things of the moorland. I almost dropped the thing in my surprise; for here in this rude place I had stumbled upon that lost delicacy of the North, the heather ale.

For a second I was entranced with my discovery, and then the wonder of the cup claimed my attention. Was it a mere relic of pillage, or had this folk some hidden mine of the precious metal? Gold had once been common in these hills. There were the traces of mines on Cairnsmore; shepherds had found it in the gravel of the Gled Water; and the name of a house at the head of the Clachlands meant the 'Home of Gold.'

Once more I began my questions, and they answered them willingly. There and then I heard that secret for which many had died in old time, the secret of the heather ale. They told of the gold in the hills, of corries where the sand gleamed and abysses where the rocks were veined. All this they told me, freely, without a scruple. And then, like a clap, came the awful thought that this, too, spelled death. These were secrets which this race aforetime had guarded with their lives; they told them generously to me because there was no fear of betrayal. I should go no more out from this place.

The thought put me into a new sweat of terror – not at death, mind you, but at the unknown horrors which might precede the final suffering. I lay silent, and after binding my hands they began to leave me and go off to other parts of the cave. I dozed in the horrible half-swoon of fear, conscious only of my shaking limbs, and the great dull glow of the fire in the centre. Then I became calmer. After all, they had treated me with tolerable kindness: I had spoken their language, which few of their victims could have done for many a century; it might be that I found favour in their eyes. For a little I comforted myself with this delusion, till I caught sight of a wooden box in a corner. It was of modern make, one such as grocers use to pack provisions in. It had some address nailed on it, and an aimless curiosity compelled me to creep thither and read it. A torn and weather-stained scrap of paper, with the nails at the corner rusty with age; but something of the address might still be made out. Amid the stains my feverish eyes read, 'To Mr M–, Carrickfey, by Allerfoot Station.'

The ruined cottage in the hollow of the waste with the single gnarled apple-tree was before me in a twinkling. I remembered the shepherd's shrinking from the place and the name, and his wild eyes when he told me of the thing that had happened there. I seemed to see the old man in his moorland cottage, thinking no evil; the sudden entry of the nameless things; and then the eyes glazed in unspeakable terror. I felt my lips dry and burning. Above me was the vault of rock; in the distance I saw the fire-glow and the shadows of shapes moving around it. My fright was too great for inaction, so I crept from the couch, and silently, stealthily, with tottering steps and bursting heart, I began to reconnoitre.

But I was still bound, my arms tightly, my legs more loosely, but yet firm enough to hinder flight. I could not get my hands at my leg-straps, still less could I undo the manacles. I rolled on the floor, seeking some sharp edge of rock, but all had been worn smooth by the use of centuries. Then suddenly an idea came upon me like an inspiration. The sounds from the fire seemed to have ceased, and I could hear them repeated from another and more distant part of the cave. The Folk had left their orgy round the blaze, and at the end of the long tunnel I saw its glow fall unimpeded upon the floor. Once there, I might burn off my fetters and be free to turn my thoughts to escape.

I crawled a little way with much labour. Then suddenly I came abreast an opening in the wall, through which a path went. It was a long straight rock-cutting, and at the end I saw a gleam of pale light. It must be the open air; the way of escape was prepared for me; and with a prayer I made what speed I could towards the fire.

I rolled on the verge, but the fuel was peat, and the warm ashes would not burn the cords. In desperation I went farther, and my clothes began to singe, while my face ached beyond endurance. But yet I got no nearer my object. The strips of hide warped and cracked, but did not burn. Then in a last effort I thrust my wrists bodily into the glow and held them there. In an instant I drew them out with a groan of pain, scarred and sore, but to my joy with the band snapped in one place. Weak as I was, it was now easy to free myself, and then came the untying of my legs. My hands trembled, my eyes were dazed with hurry, and I was longer over the job than need have been. But at length I had loosed my cramped knees and stood on my feet, a free man once more.

I kicked off my boots, and fled noiselessly down the passage to the tunnel mouth. Apparently it was close on evening, for the white light had faded to a pale yellow. But it was daylight, and that was all I sought, and I ran for it as eagerly as ever runner ran to a goal. I came out on a rock-shelf, beneath which a moraine of boulders fell away in a chasm to a dark loch. It was all but night, but I could see the gnarled and fortressed rocks rise in ramparts above, and below the unknown screes and cliffs which make the side of the Muneraw a place only for foxes and the fowls of the air.

The first taste of liberty is an intoxication, and assuredly I was mad when I leaped down among the boulders. Happily at the top of the gully the stones were large and stable, else the noise would certainly have discovered me. Down I went, slipping, praying, my charred wrists aching, and my stockinged feet wet with blood. Soon I was in the jaws of the cleft, and a pale star rose before me. I have always been timid in the face of great rocks, and now, had not an awful terror been dogging my footsteps, no power on earth could have driven me to that descent. Soon I left the boulders behind, and came to long spouts of little stones, which moved with me till the hillside seemed sinking under my feet. Sometimes I was face downwards, once and again I must have fallen for yards. Had there been a cliff at the foot, I should have gone over it without resistance; but by the providence of God the spout ended in a long curve into the heather of the bog.

When I found my feet once more on soft boggy earth, my strength was renewed within me. A great hope of escape sprang up in my heart. For a second I looked back. There was a great line of shingle with the cliffs beyond, and above all the unknown blackness of the cleft. There lay my terror, and I set off running across the bog for dear life. My mind was clear enough to know my road. If I held round the loch in front I should come to a burn which fed the Farawa stream, on whose banks stood the shepherd's cottage. The loch could not be far; once at the Farawa I would have the light of the shieling clear before me.

Suddenly I heard behind me, as if coming from the hillside, the patter of feet. It was the sound which white hares make in the winter-time on a noiseless frosty day as they patter over the snow. I have heard the same soft noise from a herd of deer when they changed their pastures. Strange that so kindly a sound should put the very fear of death in my heart. I ran madly, blindly, yet thinking shrewdly. The loch was before me. Somewhere I had read or heard, I do not know where, that the brutish aboriginal races of the North could not swim. I myself swam powerfully; could I but cross the loch I should save two miles of a desperate country.

There was no time to lose, for the patter was coming nearer, and I was almost at the loch's edge. I tore off my coat and rushed in. The bottom was mossy, and I had to struggle far before I found any depth. Something plashed in the water before me, and then something else a little behind. The thought that I was a mark for unknown missiles made me crazy with fright, and I struck fiercely out for the other shore. A gleam of moonlight was on the water at the burn's exit, and thither I guided myself. I found the thing difficult enough in itself, for my hands ached, and I was numb with my bonds. But my fancy raised a thousand phantoms to vex me. Swimming in that black bog water, pursued by those nameless things, I seemed to be in a world of horror far removed from the kindly world of men. My strength seemed inexhaustible from my terror. Monsters at the bottom of the water seemed to bite at my feet, and the pain of my wrists made me believe that the loch was boiling hot, and that I was in some hellish place of torment.

I came out on a spit of gravel above the burn mouth, and set off down the ravine of the burn. It was a strait place, strewn with rocks; but now and then the hill turf came in stretches, and eased my wounded feet. Soon the fall became more abrupt, and I was slipping down a hillside, with the water on my left making great cascades in the granite. And then I was out in the wider vale where the Farawa water flowed among links of moss.

Far in front, a speck in the blue darkness shone the light of the cottage. I panted forward, my breath coming in gasps and my back shot with fiery pains. Happily the land was easier for the feet as long as I kept on the skirts of the bog. My ears were sharp as a wild beast's with fear, as I listened for the noise of pursuit. Nothing came but the rustle of the gentlest hill-wind and the chatter of the falling streams.

Then suddenly the light began to waver and move athwart the window. I knew what it meant. In a minute or two the household at the cottage would retire to rest, and the lamp would be put out. True, I might find the place in the dark, for there was a moon of sorts and the road was not desperate. But somehow in that hour the lamplight gave a promise of safety which I clung to despairingly.

And then the last straw was added to my misery. Behind me came the pad of feet, the pat–patter, soft, eerie, incredibly swift. I choked with fear, and flung myself forward in a last effort. I give my word it was sheer mechanical shrinking that drove me on. God knows I would have lain down to die in the heather, had the things behind me been a common terror of life.

I ran as man never ran before, leaping hags, scrambling through green well-heads, straining towards the fast-dying light. A quarter of a mile and the patter sounded nearer. Soon I was not two hundred yards off, and the noise seemed almost at my elbow. The light went out, and the black mass of the cottage loomed in the dark.

Then, before I knew, I was at the door, battering it wearily and yelling for help. I heard steps within and a hand on the bolt. Then something shot past me with lightning force and buried itself in the wood. The dreadful hands were almost at my throat, when the door was opened and I stumbled in, hearing with a gulp of joy the key turn and the bar fall behind me.

V   The Troubles of a Conscience

My body and senses slept, for I was utterly tired, but my brain all the night was on fire with horrid fancies. Again I was in that accursed cave; I was torturing my hands in the fire; I was slipping barefoot among jagged boulders; and then with bursting heart I was toiling the last mile with the cottage light – now grown to a great fire in the heavens – blazing before me.

It was broad daylight when I awoke, and I thanked God for the comfortable rays of the sun. I had been laid in a box-bed off the inner room, and my first sight was the shepherd sitting with folded arms in a chair regarding me solemnly. I rose and began to dress, feeling my legs and arms still tremble with weariness. The shepherd's sister bound up my scarred wrists and put an ointment on my burns; and limping like an old man, I went into the kitchen.

I could eat little breakfast, for my throat seemed dry and narrow; but they gave me some brandy-and-milk, which put strength into my body. All the time the brother and sister sat in silence, regarding me with covert glances.

'Ye have been delivered from the jaws o' the Pit,' said the man at length. 'See that,' and he held out to me a thin shaft of flint. 'I fand that in the door this morning.'

I took it, let it drop, and stared vacantly at the window. My nerves had been too much tried to be roused by any new terror. Out of doors it was fair weather, flying gleams of April sunlight and the soft colours of spring. I felt dazed, isolated, cut off from my easy past and pleasing future, a companion of horrors and the sport of nameless things. Then suddenly my eye fell on my books heaped on a table, and the old distant civilisation seemed for the moment inexpressibly dear.

'I must go – at once. And you must come too. You cannot stay here. I tell you it is death. If you knew what I know you would be crying out with fear. How far is it to Allermuir? Eight, fifteen miles; and then ten down Glen Aller to Allerfoot, and then the railway. We must go together while it is daylight, and perhaps we may be untouched. But quick, there is not a moment to lose.' And I was on my shaky feet, and bustling among my possessions.

'I'll gang wi' ye to the station,' said the shepherd, 'for ye're clearly no fit to look after yourself. My sister will bide and keep the house. If naething has touched us this ten year, naething will touch us the day.'

'But you cannot stay. You are mad,' I began; but he cut me short with the words, 'I trust in God.'

'In any case let your sister come with us. I dare not think of a woman alone in this place.'

'I'll bide,' said she. 'I'm no feared as lang as I'm indoors and there's steeks on the windies.'

So I packed my few belongings as best I could, tumbled my books into a haversack, and, gripping the shepherd's arm nervously, crossed the threshold. The glen was full of sunlight. There lay the long shining links of the Farawa burn, the rough hills tumbled beyond, and far over all the scarred and distant forehead of the Muneraw. I had always looked on moorland country as the freshest on earth – clean, wholesome, and homely. But now the fresh uplands seemed like a horrible pit. When I looked to the hills my breath choked in my throat, and the feel of soft heather below my feet set my heart trembling.

It was a slow journey to the inn at Allermuir. For one thing, no power on earth would draw me within sight of the shieling of Carrickfey, so we had to cross a shoulder of hill and make our way down a difficult glen, and then over a treacherous moss. The lochs were now gleaming like fretted silver, but to me, in my dreadful knowledge, they seemed more eerie than on that grey day when I came. At last my eyes were cheered by the sight of a meadow and a fence; then we were on a little by-road; and soon the fir-woods and cornlands of Allercleuch were plain before us.

The shepherd came no farther, but with brief good-bye turned his solemn face hillwards. I hired a trap and a man to drive, and down the ten miles of Glen Aller I struggled to keep my thoughts from the past. I thought of the kindly

South Country, of Oxford, of anything comfortable and civilised. My driver pointed out the objects of interest as in duty bound, but his words fell on unheeding ears. At last he said something which roused me indeed to interest – the interest of the man who hears the word he fears most in the world. On the left side of the river there suddenly sprang into view a long gloomy cleft in the hills, with a vista of dark mountains behind, down which a stream of considerable size poured its waters.

'That is the Water o' Dule,' said the man in a reverent voice. 'A graund water to fish, but dangerous to life, for it's a' linns. Awa' at the heid they say there's a terrible wild place called the Scarts o' Muneraw – that's a shouther o' the muckle hill itsel' that ye see – but I've never been there, and I never kent ony man that had either.'

At the station, which is a mile from the village of Allerfoot, I found I had some hours to wait on my train for the south. I dared not trust myself for one moment alone, so I hung about the goods-shed, talked vacantly to the porters, and when one went to the village for tea I accompanied him, and to his wonder entertained him at the inn. When I returned I found on the platform a stray bagman who was that evening going to London. If there is one class of men in the world which I heartily detest it is this; but such was my state that I hailed him as a brother, and besought his company. I paid the difference for a first-class fare, and had him in the carriage with me. He must have thought me an amiable maniac, for I talked in fits and starts, and when he fell asleep I would wake him up and beseech him to speak to me. At wayside stations I would pull down the blinds in case of recognition, for to my unquiet mind the world seemed full of spies sent by that terrible Folk of the Hills. When the train crossed a stretch of moor I would lie down on the seat in case of shafts fired from the heather. And then at last with utter weariness I fell asleep, and woke screaming about midnight to find myself well down in the cheerful English midlands, and red blast-furnaces blinking by the railway-side.

In the morning I breakfasted in my rooms at St Chad's with a dawning sense of safety. I was in a different and calmer world. The lawn-like quadrangles, the great trees, the cawing of rooks, and the homely twitter of sparrows – all seemed decent and settled and pleasing. Indoors the oak-panelled walls, the shelves of books, the pictures, the faint fragrance of tobacco, were very different from the gimcrack adornments and the accursed smell of peat and heather in that deplorable cottage. It was still vacation-time, so most of my friends were down; but I spent the day hunting out the few cheerful pedants to whom term and vacation were the same. It delighted me to hear again their precise talk, to hear them make a boast of their work, and narrate the childish little accidents of their life. I yearned for the childish once more; I craved for women's drawing-rooms, and women's chatter, and everything which makes life an elegant game. God knows I had had enough of the other thing for a lifetime!

That night I shut myself in my rooms, barred my windows, drew my curtains, and made a great destruction. All books or pictures which recalled to me the moorlands were ruthlessly doomed. Novels, poems, treatises I flung into an old box, for sale to the second-hand bookseller. Some prints and water-colour sketches I tore to pieces with my own hands. I ransacked my fishing-book, and condemned all tackle for moorland waters to the flames. I wrote a letter to my solicitors, bidding them to go no further in the purchase of a place in Lorne I had long been thinking of. Then, and not till then, did I feel the bondage of the past a little loosed from my shoulders. I made myself a night-cap of rum-punch instead of my usual whisky-toddy, that all associations with that dismal land might be forgotten, and to complete the renunciation I returned to cigars and flung my pipe into a drawer.

But when I woke in the morning I found that it is hard to get rid of memories. My feet were still sore and wounded, and when I felt my arms cramped and reflected on the causes, there was that black memory always near to vex me.

In a little, term began, and my duties – as deputy-professor of Northern Antiquities – were once more clamorous. I can well believe that my hearers found my lectures strange, for instead of dealing with my favourite subjects and matters, which I might modestly say I had made my own, I confined myself to recondite and distant themes, treating even these cursorily and dully. For the truth is, my heart was no more in my subject. I hated – or I thought that I hated – all things Northern with the virulence of utter fear. My reading was confined to science of the most recent kind, to abstruse philosophy, and to foreign classics. Anything which savoured of romance or mystery was abhorrent; I pined for sharp outlines and the tangibility of a high civilisation.

All the term I threw myself into the most frivolous life of the place. My Harrow schooldays seemed to have come back to me. I had once been a fair cricketer, so I played again for my college, and made decent scores. I coached an indifferent crew on the river. I fell into the slang of the place, which I had hitherto detested. My former friends looked on me askance, as if some freakish changeling had possessed me. Formerly I had been ready for pedantic discussion, I had been absorbed in my work, men had spoken of me as a rising scholar. Now I fled the very mention of things I had once delighted in. The Professor of Northern Antiquities, a scholar of European reputation, meeting me once in the parks, embarked on an account of certain novel rings recently found in Scotland, and to his horror found that, when he had got well under weigh, I had slipped off unnoticed. I heard afterwards that the good old man was found by a friend walking disconsolately with bowed head in the middle of the High Street. Being rescued from among the horses' feet, he could only murmur, 'I am thinking of Graves, poor man! And a year ago he was as sane as I am!'

✕

But a man may not long deceive himself. I kept up the illusion valiantly for the term; but I felt instinctively that the fresh schoolboy life, which seemed to me the extreme opposite to the ghoulish North, and as such the most desirable of things, was eternally cut off from me. No cunning affectation could ever dispel my real nature or efface the memory of a week. I realised miserably that sooner or later I must fight it out with my conscience. I began to call myself a coward. The chief thoughts of my mind began to centre themselves more and more round that unknown life waiting to be explored among the unfathomable wilds.

One day I met a friend – an official in the British Museum – who was full of some new theory about primitive habitations. To me it seemed inconceivably absurd; but he was strong in his confidence, and without flaw in his evidence. The man irritated me, and I burned to prove him wrong, but I could think of no argument which was final against his. Then it flashed upon me that my own experience held the disproof; and without more words I left him, hot, angry with myself, and tantalised by the unattainable.

I might relate my bona-fide experience, but would men believe me? I must bring proofs, I must complete my researches, so as to make them incapable of disbelief. And there in those deserts was waiting the key. There lay the greatest discovery of the century – nay, of the millennium. There, too, lay the road to wealth such as I had never dreamed of. Could I succeed, I should be famous for ever. I would revolutionise history and anthropology; I would systematise folk-lore; I would show the world of men the pit whence they were digged and the rock whence they were hewn.

And then began a game of battledore between myself and my conscience.

'You are a coward,' said my conscience.

'I am sufficiently brave,' I would answer. 'I have seen things and yet lived. The terror is more than mortal, and I cannot face it.'

'You are a coward,' said my conscience.

'I am not bound to go there again. It would be purely for my own aggrandisement if I went, and not for any matter of duty.'

'Nevertheless you are a coward,' said my conscience.

'In any case the matter can wait.'

'You are a coward.'

※

Then came one awful midsummer night, when I lay sleepless and fought the thing out with myself. I knew that the strife was hopeless, that I should have no peace in this world again unless I made the attempt. The dawn was breaking when I came to the final resolution; and when I rose and looked at my face in a mirror, lo! it was white and lined and drawn like a man of sixty.

VI Summer on the Moors

The next morning I packed a bag with some changes of clothing and a collection of notebooks, and went up to town. The first thing I did was to pay a visit to my solicitors. 'I am about to travel,' said I, 'and I wish to have all things settled in case any accident should happen to me.' So I arranged for the disposal of my property in case of death, and added a codicil which puzzled the lawyers. If I did not return within six months, communications were to be entered into with the shepherd at the shieling of Farawa – post-town Allerfoot. If he could produce any papers, they were to be put into the hands of certain friends, published, and the cost charged to my estate. From my solicitors, I went to a gunmaker's in Regent Street and bought an ordinary six-chambered revolver, feeling much as a man must feel who proposed to cross the Atlantic in a skiff and purchased a small life-belt as a precaution.

I took the night express to the North, and, for a marvel, I slept. When I woke about four we were on the verge of Westmoreland, and stony hills blocked the horizon. At first I hailed the mountain-land gladly; sleep for the moment had caused forgetfulness of my terrors. But soon a turn of the line brought me in full view of a heathery moor, running far to a confusion of distant peaks. I remembered my mission and my fate, and if ever condemned criminal felt a more bitter regret I pity his case. Why should I alone among the millions of this happy isle be singled out as the repository of a ghastly secret, and be cursed by a conscience which would not let it rest?

I came to Allerfoot early in the forenoon, and got a trap to drive me up the valley. It was a lowering grey day, hot and yet sunless. A sort of heat-haze cloaked the hills, and every now and then a smurr of rain would meet us on the road, and in a minute be over. I felt wretchedly dispirited; and when at last the whitewashed kirk of Allermuir came into sight and the broken-backed bridge of Aller, man's eyes seemed to have looked on no drearier scene since time began.

I ate what meal I could get, for, fears or no, I was voraciously hungry. Then I asked the landlord to find me some man who would show me the road to Farawa. I demanded company, not for protection – for what could two men do against such brutish strength? – but to keep my mind from its own thoughts.

The man looked at me anxiously.

'Are ye acquaint wi' the folks, then?' he asked.

I said I was, that I had often stayed in the cottage.

'Ye ken that they've a name for being queer. The man never comes here forbye once or twice a-year, and he has few dealings wi' other herds. He's got an ill name, too, for losing sheep. I dinna like the country ava. Up by yon Muneraw – no that I've ever been there, but I've seen it afar off – is enough to put a man daft for the rest o' his days. What's taking ye thereaways? It's no the time for the fishing?'

I told him that I was a botanist going to explore certain hill-crevices for rare ferns. He shook his head, and then after some delay found me an ostler who would accompany me to the cottage.

The man was a shock-headed, long-limbed fellow, with fierce red hair and a humorous eye. He talked sociably about his life, answered my hasty questions with deftness, and beguiled me for the moment out of myself. I passed the melancholy lochs, and came in sight of the great stony hills without the trepidation I had expected. Here at my side was one who found some humour even in those uplands. But one thing I noted which brought back the old uneasiness. He took the road which led us farthest from Carrickfey, and when to try him I proposed the other, he vetoed it with emphasis.

After this his good spirits departed, and he grew distrustful.

'What mak's ye a freend o' the herd at Farawa?' he demanded a dozen times.

Finally, I asked him if he knew the man, and had seen him lately.

'I dinna ken him, and I hadna seen him for years till a fortnicht syne, when a' Allermuir saw him. He cam doun one afternoon to the public-hoose, and begood to drink. He had aye been kenned for a terrible godly kind o' a man, so ye may believe folk wondered at this. But when he had stuck to the drink for twae days, and filled himsel' blind-fou half-a-dozen o' times, he took a fit o' repentance, and raved and blethered about siccan a life as he led in the muirs. There was some said he was speakin' serious, but maist thocht it was juist daftness.'

'And what did he speak about?' I asked sharply.

'I canna verra weel tell ye. It was about some kind o' bogle that lived in the Muneraw – that's the shouthers o't ye see yonder – and it seems that the bogle killed his sheep and frichted himsel'. He was aye bletherin', too, about something or somebody ca'd Grave; but oh! The man wasna wise.' And my companion shook a contemptuous head.

And then below us in the valley we saw the shieling, with a thin shaft of smoke rising into the rainy grey weather. The man left me, sturdily refusing any fee. 'I wantit my legs stretched as weel as you. A walk in the hills is neither here nor there to a stoot man. When will ye be back, sir?'

The question was well-timed. 'To-morrow fortnight,' I said, 'and I want somebody from Allermuir to come out here in the morning and carry some baggage. Will you see to that?'

He said 'Ay,' and went off, while I scrambled down the hill to the cottage. Nervousness possessed me, and though it was broad daylight and the whole place lay plain before me, I ran pell-mell, and did not stop till I reached the door.

The place was utterly empty. Unmade beds, unwashed dishes, a hearth strewn with the ashes of peat, and dust thick on everything, proclaimed the absence of inmates. I began to be horribly frightened. Had the shepherd and his sister, also, disappeared? Was I left alone in the bleak place, with a dozen lonely miles between me and human dwellings? I could not return alone; better this horrible place than the unknown perils of the out-of-doors. Hastily I barricaded the door, and to the best of my power shuttered the windows; and then with dreary forebodings I sat down to wait on fortune.

In a little I heard a long swinging step outside and the sound of dogs. Joyfully I opened the latch, and there was the shepherd's grim face waiting stolidly on what might appear.

At the sight of me he stepped back. 'What in the Lord's name are ye daein' here?' he asked. 'Didna ye get enough afore?'

'Come in,' I said, sharply. 'I want to talk.'

In he came with those blessed dogs – what a comfort it was to look on their great honest faces! He sat down on the untidy bed and waited.

'I came because I could not stay away. I saw too much to give me any peace elsewhere. I must go back, even though I risk my life for it. The cause of scholarship demands it as well as the cause of humanity.'

'Is that a' the news ye hae?' he said. 'Weel, I've mair to tell ye. Three weeks syne my sister Margit was lost, and I've never seen her mair.'

My jaw fell, and I could only stare at him.

'I cam hame from the hill at nightfa' and she was gone. I lookit for her up hill and doun, but I couldna find her. Syne I think I went daft. I went to the Scarts and huntit them up and doun, but no sign could I see. The folk can bide quiet enough when they want. Syne I went to Allermuir and drank mysel' blind – me, that's a God-fearing man and a saved soul; but the Lord help me, I didna ken what I was at. That's my news, and day and nicht I wander thae hills, seekin' for what I canna find.'

'But, man, are you mad?' I cried. 'Surely there are neighbours to help you. There is a law in the land, and you had only to find the nearest police-office and compel them to assist you.'

'What guid can man dae?' he asked. 'An army o' sodgers couldna find that hidy-hole. Forby, when I went into Allermuir wi' my story the folk thocht me daft. It was that set me drinking for – the Lord forgive me! – I wasna my ain maister. I threepit till I was hairse, but the bodies just lauch'd.'

And he lay back on the bed like a man mortally tired.

Grim though the tidings were, I can only say that my chief feeling was of comfort. Pity for the new tragedy had swallowed up my fear. I had now a purpose, and a purpose, too, not of curiosity but of mercy.

'I go to-morrow morning to the Muneraw. But first I want to give you something to do.' And I drew roughly a chart of the place on the back of a letter. 'Go into Allermuir tomorrow, and give this paper to the landlord at the inn. The letter will tell him what to do. He is to raise at once all the men he can get, and come to the place on the chart marked with a cross. Tell him life depends on his hurry.'

The shepherd nodded. 'D'ye ken the Folk are watching for you? They let me pass without trouble, for they've nae use for me, but I see fine they're seeking you. Ye'll no gang half a mile the morn afore they grip ye.'

'So much the better,' I said. 'That will take me quicker to the place I want to be at.'

'And I'm to gang to Allemuir the morn,' he repeated, with the air of a child conning a lesson. 'But what if they'll no believe me?'

'They'll believe the letter.'

'Maybe,' he said, and relapsed into a doze.

I set myself to put that house in order, to rouse the fire, and prepare some food. It was dismal work; and meantime outside the night darkened, and a great wind rose, which howled round the walls and lashed the rain on the windows.

VII   *In tuas manus, Domine!*

I had not got twenty yards from the cottage door ere I knew I was watched. I had left the shepherd still dozing, in the half-conscious state of a dazed and broken man. All night the wind had wakened me at intervals, and now in the half-light of morn the weather seemed more vicious than ever. The wind cut my ears, the whole firmament was full of the rendings and thunders of the storm. Rain fell in blinding sheets, the heath was a marsh, and it was the most I could do to struggle against the hurricane which stopped my breath. And all the while I knew I was not alone in the desert.

All men know – in imagination or in experience – the sensation of being spied on. The nerves tingle, the skin grows hot and prickly, and there is a queer sinking of the heart. Intensify this common feeling a hundredfold, and you get a tenth part of what I suffered. I am telling a plain tale, and record bare physical facts. My lips stood out from my teeth as I heard, or felt, a rustle in the heather, a scraping among stones. Some subtle magnetic link seemed established between my body and the mysterious world around. I became sick – acutely sick – with the ceaseless apprehension.

My fright became so complete that when I turned a corner of rock, or stepped in deep heather, I seemed to feel a body rub against me. This continued all the way up the Farawa water, and then up its feeder to the little lonely loch. It kept me from looking forward; but it likewise kept me in such a sweat of fright that I was ready to faint. Then the notion came upon me to test this fancy of mine. If I was tracked thus closely, clearly the trackers would bar my way if I turned back. So I wheeled round and walked a dozen paces down the glen.

Nothing stopped me. I was about to turn again, when something made me take six more paces. At the fourth something rustled in the heather, and my neck was gripped as in a vice. I had already made up my mind on what I would do. I would be perfectly still, I would conquer my fear, and let them do as they pleased with me so long as they took me to their dwelling. But at the touch of the hands my resolutions fled. I struggled and screamed. Then something was clapped on my mouth, speech and strength went from me, and once more I was back in the maudlin childhood of terror.

※

In the cave it was always a dusky twilight. I seemed to be lying in the same place, with the same dull glare of firelight far off, and the same close stupefying smell. One of the creatures was standing silently at my side, and I asked him some trivial question. He turned and shambled down the passage, leaving me alone.

Then he returned with another, and they talked their guttural talk to me. I scarcely listened till I remembered that in a sense I was here of my own accord, and on a definite mission. The purport of their speech seemed to be that, now I had returned, I must beware of a second flight. Once I had been spared; a second time I should be killed without mercy.

I assented gladly. The Folk, then, had some use for me. I felt my errand prospering.

Then the old creature which I had seen before crept out of some corner and squatted beside me. He put a claw on my shoulder, a horrible, corrugated, skeleton thing, hairy to the finger-tips and nailless. He grinned, too, with toothless gums, and his hideous old voice was like a file on sandstone.

I asked questions, but he would only grin and jabber, looking now and then furtively over his shoulder towards the fire.

I coaxed and humoured him, till he launched into a narrative of which I could make nothing. It seemed a mere string of names, with certain words repeated at fixed intervals. Then it flashed on me that this might be a religious incantation. I had discovered remnants of a ritual and a mythology among them. It was possible that these were sacred days, and that I had stumbled upon some rude celebration.

I caught a word or two and repeated them. He looked at me

curiously. Then I asked him some leading question, and he replied with clearness. My guess was right. The midsummer week was the holy season of the year, when sacrifices were offered to the gods.

The notion of sacrifices disquieted me, and I would fain have asked further. But the creature would speak no more. He hobbled off, and left me alone in the rock-chamber to listen to a strange sound which hung ceaselessly about me. It must be the storm without, like a pack of artillery rattling among the crags. A storm of storms surely, for the place echoed and hummed, and to my unquiet eye the very rock of the roof seemed to shake!

Apparently my existence was forgotten, for I lay long before any one returned. Then it was merely one who brought food, the same strange meal as before, and left hastily. When I had eaten I rose and stretched myself. My hands and knees still quivered nervously; but I was strong and perfectly well in body. The empty, desolate, tomb-like place was eerie enough to scare anyone; but its emptiness was comfort when I thought of its inmates. Then I wandered down the passage towards the fire which was burning in loneliness. Where had the Folk gone? I puzzled over their disappearance.

Suddenly sounds began to break on my ear, coming from some inner chamber at the end of that in which the fire burned. I could scarcely see for the smoke; but I began to make my way towards the noise, feeling along the sides of rock. Then a second gleam of light seemed to rise before me, and I came to an aperture in the wall which gave entrance to another room.

This in turn was full of smoke and glow – a murky orange glow, as if from some strange flame of roots. There were the squat moving figures, running in wild antics round the fire. I crouched in the entrance, terrified and yet curious, till I saw something beyond the blaze which held me dumb. Apart from the others and tied to some stake in the wall was a woman's figure, and the face was the face of the shepherd's sister.

My first impulse was flight. I must get away and think – plan, achieve some desperate way of escape. I sped back to the silent chamber as if the gang were at my heels. It was still empty, and I stood helplessly in the centre, looking at the impassable walls of rock as a wearied beast may look at the walls of its cage. I bethought me of the way I had escaped before and rushed thither, only to find it blocked by a huge contrivance of stone. Yards and yards of solid rock were between me and the upper air, and yet through it all came the crash and whistle of the storm. If I were at my wits' end in this inner darkness, there was also high commotion among the powers of the air in that upper world.

As I stood I heard the soft steps of my tormentors. They seemed to think I was meditating escape, for they flung themselves on me and bore me to the ground. I did not struggle, and when they saw me quiet, they squatted round and began to speak. They told me of the holy season and its sacrifices. At first I could not follow them; then when I caught familiar words I found some clue, and they became intelligible. They spoke of a woman, and I asked, 'What woman?' With all frankness they told me of the custom which prevailed – how every twentieth summer a woman was sacrificed to some devilish god, and by the hand of one of the stranger race. I said nothing, but my whitening face must have told them a tale, though I strove hard to keep my composure. I asked if they had found the victims. 'She is in this place,' they said; 'and as for the man, thou art he.' And with this they left me.

I had still some hours; so much I gathered from their talk, for the sacrifice was at sunset. Escape was cut off for ever. I have always been something of a fatalist, and at the prospect of the irrevocable end my cheerfulness returned. I had my pistol, for they had taken nothing from me. I took out the little weapon and fingered it lovingly. Hope of the lost, refuge of the vanquished, ease to the coward – blessed be he who first conceived it!

The time dragged on, the minutes grew to hours, and still I was left solitary. Only the mad violence of the storm broke the quiet. It had increased in violence, for the stones at the mouth of the exit by which I had formerly escaped seemed to rock with some external pressure, and cutting shafts of wind slipped past and cleft the heat of the passage. What a sight the ravine outside must be, I thought, set in the forehead of a great hill, and swept clean by every breeze! Then came a crashing, and the long hollow echo of a fall. The rocks are splitting, said I; the road down the corrie will be impassable now and for evermore.

I began to grow weak with the nervousness of the waiting, and by-and-by I lay down and fell into a sort of doze. When I next knew consciousness I was being roused by two of the Folk, and bidden get ready. I stumbled to my feet, felt for the pistol in the hollow of my sleeve, and prepared to follow.

When we came out into the wider chamber the noise of the storm was deafening. The roof rang like a shield which has been struck. I noticed, perturbed as I was, that my guards cast anxious eyes around them, alarmed, like myself, at the murderous din. Nor was the world quieter when we entered the last chamber, where the fire burned and the remnant of the Folk waited. Wind had found an entrance from somewhere or other, and the flames blew here and there, and the smoke gyrated in odd circles. At the back, and apart from the rest, I saw the dazed eyes and the white old drawn face of the woman.

They led me up beside her to a place where there was a rude flat stone, hollowed in the centre, and on it a rusty iron knife, which seemed once to have formed part of a scythe-blade. Then I saw the ceremonial which was marked out for me. It was the very rite which I had dimly figured as current among a rude people, and even in that moment I had something of the scholar's satisfaction.

The oldest of the Folk, who seemed to be a sort of priest, came to my side and mumbled a form of words. His fetid breath sickened me; his dull eyes, glassy like a brute's with age, brought my knees together. He put the knife in my hands, dragged the terror-stricken woman forward to the altar, and bade me begin.

I began by sawing her bonds through. When she felt herself free she would have fled back, but stopped when I bade her. At that moment there came a noise of rending and crashing as if the hills were falling, and for one second the eyes of the Folk were averted from the frustrated sacrifice.

Only for a moment. The next they saw what I had done, and with one impulse rushed towards me. Then began the last scene in the play. I sent a bullet through the right eye of the first thing that came on. The second shot went wide; but the third shattered the hand of an elderly ruffian with a cruel club. Never for an instant did they stop, and now they were clutching at me. I pushed the woman behind, and fired three rapid shots in blind panic, and then, clutching the scythe, I struck right and left like a madman.

Suddenly I saw the foreground sink before my eyes. The roof sloped down, and with a sickening hiss a mountain of rock and earth seemed to precipitate itself on my assailants. One, nipped in the middle by a rock, caught my eye by his hideous writhings. Two only remained in what was now a little suffocating chamber, with embers from the fire still smoking on the floor.

The woman caught me by the hand and drew me with her, while the two seemed mute with fear. 'There's a road at the back,' she screamed. 'I ken it. I fand it out.' And she pulled me up a narrow hole in the rock.

※

How long we climbed I do not know. We were both fighting for air, with the tightness of throat and chest, and the craziness of limb which mean suffocation. I cannot tell when we first came to the surface, but I remember the woman, who seemed to have the strength of extreme terror, pulling me from the edge of a crevasse and laying me on a flat rock. It seemed to be the depth of winter, with sheer-falling rain and a wind that shook the hills.

Then I was once more myself and could look about me. From my feet yawned a sheer abyss, where once had been a hill-shoulder. Some great mass of rock on the brow of the mountain had been loosened by the storm, and in its fall had caught the lips of the ravine and swept the nest of dwellings into a yawning pit. Beneath a mountain of rubble lay buried that life on which I had thought to build my fame.

My feeling – Heaven help me! – was not thankfulness for God's mercy and my escape, but a bitter mad regret. I rushed frantically to the edge, and when I saw only the blackness of darkness I wept weak tears. All the time the storm was tearing at my body, and I had to grip hard by hand and foot to keep my place.

Suddenly on the brink of the ravine I saw a third figure. We two were not the only fugitives. One of the Folk had escaped.

The thought put new life into me, for I had lost the first fresh consciousness of terror. There still remained a relic of the vanished life. Could I but make the thing my prisoner, there would be proof in my hands to overcome a sceptical world.

I ran to it, and to my surprise the thing as soon as it saw me rushed to meet me. At first I thought it was with some instinct of self-preservation, but when I saw its eyes I knew the purpose of fight. Clearly one or other should go no more from the place.

We were some ten yards from the brink when I grappled with it. Dimly I heard the woman scream with fright, and saw her scramble across the hillside. Then we were tugging in a death-throe, the hideous smell of the thing in my face, its red eyes burning into mine, and its hoarse voice muttering. Its strength seemed incredible; but I, too, am no weakling. We tugged and strained, its nails biting into my flesh, while I choked its throat unsparingly. Every second I dreaded lest we should plunge together over the ledge, for it was thither my adversary tried to draw me. I caught my heel in a nick of rock, and pulled madly against it.

And then, while I was beginning to glory with the pride of conquest, my hope was dashed in pieces. The thing seemed to break from my arms, and, as if in despair, cast itself headlong into the impenetrable darkness. I stumbled blindly after it, saved myself on the brink, and fell back, sick and ill, into a merciful swoon.

VIII   Note in conclusion by the Editor

At this point the narrative of my unfortunate friend, Mr Graves of St Chad's, breaks off abruptly. He wrote it shortly before his death, and was prevented from completing it by the shock of apoplexy which carried him off. In accordance with the instructions in his will, I have prepared it for publication, and now in much fear and hesitation give it to the world. First, however, I must supplement it by such facts as fall within my knowledge.

The shepherd seems to have gone to Allermuir and by the help of the letter convinced the inhabitants. A body of men was collected under the landlord, and during the afternoon set out for the hills. But unfortunately the great midsummer storm – the most terrible of recent climatic disturbances – had filled the mosses and streams, and they found themselves unable to proceed by any direct road. Ultimately late in the evening they arrived at the cottage of Farawa, only to find there a raving woman, the shepherd's sister, who seemed crazy with brain-fever. She told some rambling story about her escape, but her narrative said nothing of Mr Graves. So they treated her with what skill they possessed, and sheltered for the night in and around the cottage. Next morning the storm had abated a little, and the woman had recovered something of her wits. From her they learned that Mr Graves was lying in a ravine on the side of the Muneraw in imminent danger of his life. A body set out to find him; but so immense was the landslip, and so dangerous the whole mountain, that it was nearly evening when they recovered him from the ledge of rock. He was alive, but unconscious, and on bringing him back to the cottage it was clear that he was, indeed, very ill. There he lay for three months, while the best skill that could be got was procured for him. By dint of an uncommon toughness of constitution he survived; but it was an old and feeble man who returned to Oxford in the early winter.

The shepherd and his sister immediately left the countryside, and were never more heard of, unless they are the pair of unfortunates who are at present in a Scottish pauper asylum, incapable of remembering even their names. The people who last spoke with them declared that their minds seemed weakened by a great shock, and that it was hopeless to try to get any connected or rational statement.

The career of my poor friend from that hour was little short of a tragedy. He awoke from his illness to find the world incredulous; even the countryfolk of Allermuir set down the story to the shepherd's craziness and my friend's credulity. In Oxford his argument was received with polite scorn. An account of his experiences which he drew up for the *Times* was refused by the editor; and an article on 'Primitive Peoples of the North,' embodying what he believed to be the result of his discoveries, was unanimously rejected by every responsible journal in Europe. At first he bore the treatment bravely. Reflection convinced him that the colony had not been destroyed. Proofs were still awaiting his hand, and with courage and caution he might yet triumph over his enemies. But unfortunately, though the ardour of the scholar burned more fiercely than ever and all fear seemed to have been purged from his soul, the last adventure had grievously sapped his bodily strength. In the spring following his accident he made an effort to reach the spot – alone, for no-one could be persuaded to follow him in what was regarded as a childish madness. He slept at the now deserted cottage of Farawa, but in the morning found himself unable to continue, and with difficulty struggled back to the shepherd's cottage at Allercleuch, where he was confined to bed for a fortnight. Then it became necessary for him to seek health abroad, and it was not till the following autumn that he attempted the journey again. He fell sick a second time at the inn of Allermuir, and during his convalescence had himself carried to a knoll in the inn garden, where a glimpse can be obtained of the shoulder of the Muneraw. There he would sit for hours with his eyes fixed on the horizon, and at times he would be found weeping with weakness and vexation. The last attempt was made but two months before his last illness. On this occasion he got no farther than Carlisle, where he was taken ill with what proved to be a premonition of death. After that he shut his lips tightly, as though recognising the futility of his hopes. Whether he had been soured by the treatment he received, or whether his brain had already been weakened, he had become a morose silent man, and for the two years before his death had few friends and no society. From the obituary notice in the *Times* I take the following paragraph, which shows in what light the world had come to look upon him:

'At the outset of his career he was regarded as a rising scholar in one department of archaeology, and his Taffert lectures were a real contribution to an obscure subject. But in after-life he was led into fantastic speculations; and when he found himself unable to convince his colleagues, he gradually retired into himself, and lived practically a hermit's life till his death. His career, thus broken short, is a sad instance of the fascination which the recondite and the quack can exercise even on men of approved ability.'

And now his own narrative is published, and the world can judge as it pleases about the amazing romance. The view which will doubtless find general acceptance is that the whole is a figment of the brain, begotten of some harmless moorland adventure and the company of such religious maniacs as the shepherd and his sister. But some who knew the former sobriety and calmness of my friend's mind may be disposed timorously and with deep hesitation to another verdict. They may accept the narrative, and believe that somewhere in those moorlands he met with a horrible primitive survival, passed through the strangest adventure, and had his finger on an epoch-making discovery. In this case they will be inclined to sympathise with the loneliness and misunderstanding of his latter days. It is not for me to decide the question. Though a fellow-historian, the Picts are outside my period, and I dare not advance an opinion on a matter with which I am not fully familiar. But I would point out that the means of settling the question are still extant, and I would call upon some young archaeologist, with a reputation to make, to seize upon the chance of the century. Most of the expresses for the North stop at Allerfoot; a ten-miles' drive will bring him to Allermuir; and then with a fifteen-miles' walk he is at Farawa and on the threshold of discovery. Let him follow the burn and cross the ridge and ascend the Scarts of the Muneraw, and, if he return at all, it may be with a more charitable judgement of my unfortunate friend.

3 The Willows

BY ALGERNON BLACKWOOD (1907)

1

After leaving Vienna, and long before you come to Budapest, the Danube enters a region of singular loneliness and desolation, where its waters spread away on all sides regardless of a main channel, and the country becomes a swamp for miles upon miles, covered by a vast sea of low willow-bushes. On the big maps this deserted area is painted in a fluffy blue, growing fainter in colour as it leaves the banks, and across it may be seen in large straggling letters the word *Sümpfe*, meaning marshes.

In high flood this great acreage of sand, shingle-beds, and willow-grown islands is almost topped by the water, but in normal seasons the bushes bend and rustle in the free winds, showing their silver leaves to the sunshine in an ever-moving plain of bewildering beauty. These willows never attain to the dignity of trees; they have no rigid trunks; they remain humble bushes, with rounded tops and soft outline, swaying on slender stems that answer to the least pressure of the wind; supple as grasses, and so continually shifting that they somehow give the impression that the entire plain is moving and *alive*. For the wind sends waves rising and falling over the whole surface, waves of leaves instead of waves of water, green swells like the sea, too, until the branches turn and lift, and then silvery white as their underside turns to the sun.

Happy to slip beyond the control of the stern banks, the Danube here wanders about at will among the intricate network of channels intersecting the islands everywhere with broad avenues down which the waters pour with a shouting sound; making whirlpools, eddies, and foaming rapids;

tearing at the sandy banks; carrying away masses of shore and willow-clumps; and forming new islands innumerably which shift daily in size and shape and possess at best an impermanent life, since the flood-time obliterates their very existence.

Properly speaking, this fascinating part of the river's life begins soon after leaving Pressburg, and we, in our Canadian canoe, with gipsy tent and frying-pan on board, reached it on the crest of a rising flood about mid-July. That very same morning, when the sky was reddening before sunrise, we had slipped swiftly through still-sleeping Vienna, leaving it a couple of hours later a mere patch of smoke against the blue hills of the Wienerwald on the horizon; we had breakfasted below Fischeramend under a grove of birch trees roaring in the wind; and had then swept on the tearing current past Orth, Hainburg, Petronell (the old Roman Carnuntum of Marcus Aurelius), and so under the frowning heights of Thelsen on a spur of the Carpathians, where the March steals in quietly from the left and the frontier is crossed between Austria and Hungary.

Racing along at twelve kilometres an hour soon took us well into Hungary, and the muddy waters – sure sign of flood – sent us aground on many a shingle-bed, and twisted us like a cork in many a sudden belching whirlpool before the towers of Pressburg (Hungarian, Poszóny) showed against the sky; and then the canoe, leaping like a spirited horse, flew at top speed under the grey walls, negotiated safely the sunken chain of the Fliegende Brücke ferry, turned the corner sharply to the left, and plunged on yellow foam into the wilderness of islands, sandbanks, and swamp-land beyond – the land of the willows.

The change came suddenly, as when a series of bioscope pictures snaps down on the streets of a town and shifts without warning into the scenery of lake and forest. We entered the land of desolation on wings, and in less than half an hour there was neither boat nor fishing-hut nor red roof, nor any single sign of human habitation and civilisation within sight. The sense of remoteness from the world of humankind, the utter isolation, the fascination of this singular world of willows, winds, and waters, instantly laid its spell upon us both, so that we allowed laughingly to one another that we ought by rights to have held some special kind of passport to admit us, and that we had, somewhat audaciously, come without asking leave into a separate little kingdom of wonder and magic – a kingdom that was reserved for the use of others who had a right to it, with everywhere unwritten warnings to trespassers for those who had the imagination to discover them.

Though still early in the afternoon, the ceaseless buffetings of a most tempestuous wind made us feel weary, and we at once began casting about for a suitable camping-ground for the night. But the bewildering character of the islands made landing difficult; the swirling flood carried us in shore and then swept us out again; the willow branches tore our hands as we seized them to stop the canoe, and we pulled many a yard of sandy bank into the water before at length we shot with a great sideways blow from the wind into a backwater and managed to beach the bows in a cloud of spray. Then we lay panting and laughing after our exertions on the hot yellow sand, sheltered from the wind, and in the full blaze of a scorching sun, a cloudless blue sky above, and an immense army of dancing, shouting willow bushes, closing in from all sides, shining with spray and clapping their thousand little hands as though to applaud the success of our efforts.

'What a river!' I said to my companion, thinking of all the way we had travelled from the source in the Black Forest, and how he had often been obliged to wade and push in the upper shallows at the beginning of June.

'Won't stand much nonsense now, will it?' he said, pulling the canoe a little farther into safety up the sand, and then composing himself for a nap.

I lay by his side, happy and peaceful in the bath of the elements – water, wind, sand, and the great fire of the sun – thinking of the long journey that lay behind us, and of the great stretch before us to the Black Sea, and how lucky I was to have such a delightful and charming traveling companion as my friend, the Swede.

We had made many similar journeys together, but the Danube, more than any other river I knew, impressed us from the very beginning with its *aliveness*. From its tiny bubbling entry into the world among the pinewood gardens of Donaueschingen, until this moment when it began to play the great river-game of losing itself among the deserted swamps, unobserved, unrestrained, it had seemed to us like following the grown of some living creature. Sleepy at first, but later developing violent desires as it became conscious of its deep soul, it rolled, like some huge fluid being, through all the countries we had passed, holding our little craft on its mighty shoulders, playing roughly with us sometimes, yet always friendly and well-meaning, till at length we had come inevitably to regard it as a Great Personage.

How, indeed, could it be otherwise, since it told us so much of its secret life? At night we heard it singing to the moon as we lay in our tent, uttering that odd sibilant note peculiar to itself and said to be caused by the rapid tearing of the pebbles along its bed, so great is its hurrying speed. We knew, too, the voice of its gurgling whirlpools, suddenly bubbling up on a surface previously quite calm; the roar of its shallows and swift rapids; its constant steady thundering below all mere surface sounds; and that ceaseless tearing of its icy waters at the banks. How it stood up and shouted when the rains fell flat upon its face! And how its laughter roared out when the wind blew up-stream and tried to stop its growing speed! We knew all its sounds and voices, its tumblings and foamings, its unnecessary splashing against the bridges; that self-conscious chatter when there were hills to look on; the affected dignity of its speech when it passed through the little towns, far too important to laugh; and all these faint, sweet whisperings when the sun caught it fairly in some slow curve and poured down upon it till the steam rose.

It was full of tricks, too, in its early life before the great world knew it. There were places in the upper reaches among the Swabian forests, when yet the first whispers of its destiny had not reached it, where it elected to disappear through holes in the ground, to appear again on the other side of the porous limestone hills and start a new river with another name; leaving, too, so little water in its own bed that we had to climb out and wade and push the canoe through miles of shallows.

And a chief pleasure, in those early days of its irresponsible youth, was to lie low, like Brer Fox, just before the little turbulent tributaries came to join it from the Alps, and to refuse to acknowledge them when in, but to run for miles side by side, the dividing line well marked, the very levels different, the Danube utterly declining to recognise the newcomer. Below Passau, however, it gave up this particular trick, for there the Inn comes in with a thundering power impossible to ignore, and so pushes and incommodes the parent river that there is hardly room for them in the long twisting gorge that follows, and the Danube is shoved this way and that against the cliffs, and forced to hurry itself with great waves and much dashing to and fro in order to get through in time. And during the fight our canoe slipped down from its shoulder to its breast, and had the time of its life among the struggling waves. But the Inn taught the old river a lesson, and after Passau it no longer pretended to ignore new arrivals.

This was many days back, of course, and since then we had come to know other aspects of the great creature, and across the Bavarian wheat plain of Straubing she wandered so slowly under the blazing June sun that we could well imagine only the surface inches were water, while below there moved, concealed as by a silken mantle, a whole army of Undines, passing silently and unseen down to the sea, and very leisurely too, lest they be discovered.

Much, too, we forgave her because of her friendliness to the birds and animals that haunted the shores. Cormorants lined the banks in lonely places in rows like short black palings; grey crows crowded the shingle-beds; storks stood fishing in the vistas of shallower water that opened up between the islands, and hawks, swans, and marsh birds of all sorts filled the air with glinting wings and singing, petulant cries. It was impossible to feel annoyed with the river's vagaries after seeing a deer leap with a splash into the water at sunrise and swim past the bows of the canoe; and often we saw fawns peering at us from the underbrush, or looked straight into the brown eyes of a stag as we charged full tilt round a corner and entered another reach of the river. Foxes, too, everywhere haunted the banks, tripping daintily among the driftwood and disappearing so suddenly that it was impossible to see how they managed it.

But now, after leaving Pressburg, everything changed a little, and the Danube became more serious. It ceased trifling. It was half-way to the Black Sea, within seeming distance almost of other, stranger countries where no tricks would be permitted or understood. It became suddenly grown-up, and claimed our respect and even our awe. It broke out into three arms, for one thing, that only met again a hundred kilometres farther down, and for a canoe there were no indications which one was intended to be followed.

'If you take a side channel,' said the Hungarian officer we met in the Pressburg shop while buying provisions, 'you may find yourselves, when the flood subsides, forty miles from anywhere, high and dry, and you may easily starve. There are no people, no farms, no fishermen. I warn you not to continue. The river, too, is still rising, and this wind will increase.'

The rising river did not alarm us in the least, but the matter of being left high and dry by a sudden subsidence of the waters might be serious, and we had consequently laid in an extra stock of provisions. For the rest, the officer's prophecy held true, and the wind, blowing down a perfectly clear sky, increased steadily till it reached the dignity of a westerly gale.

It was earlier than usual when we camped, for the sun was a good hour or two from the horizon, and leaving my friend still asleep on the hot sand, I wandered about in desultory examination of our hotel. The island, I found, was less than an acre in extent, a mere sandy bank standing some two or three feet above the level of the river. The far end, pointing into the sunset, was covered with flying spray which the tremendous wind drove off the crests of the broken waves. It was triangular in shape, with the apex up stream.

I stood there for several minutes, watching the impetuous crimson flood bearing down with a shouting roar, dashing in waves against the bank as though to sweep it bodily away, and then swirling by in two foaming streams on either side. The ground seemed to shake with the shock and rush, while the furious movement of the willow bushes as the wind poured over them increased the curious illusion that the island itself actually moved. Above, for a mile or two, I could see the great river descending upon me; it was like looking up the slope of a sliding hill, white with foam, and leaping up everywhere to show itself to the sun.

The rest of the island was too thickly grown with willows to make walking pleasant, but I made the tour, nevertheless. From the lower end the light, of course, changed, and the river looked dark and angry. Only the backs of the flying waves were visible, streaked with foam, and pushed forcibly by the great puffs of wind that fell upon them from behind. For a short mile it was visible, pouring in and out among the islands, and then disappearing with a huge sweep into the willows, which closed about it like a herd of monstrous antediluvian creatures crowding down to drink. They made me think of gigantic sponge-like growths that sucked the river up into themselves. They caused it to vanish from sight. They herded there together in such overpowering numbers.

Altogether it was an impressive scene, with its utter loneliness, its bizarre suggestion; and as I gazed, long and curiously, a singular emotion began to stir somewhere in the depths of me. Midway in my delight of the wild beauty, there crept, unbidden and unexplained, a curious feeling of disquietude, almost of alarm.

A rising river, perhaps, always suggests something of the ominous; many of the little islands I saw before me would probably have been swept away by the morning; this resistless, thundering flood of water touched the sense of awe. Yet I was aware that my uneasiness lay deeper far than the emotions of awe and wonder. It was not that I felt. Nor had it directly to do with the power of the driving wind – this shouting hurricane that might almost carry up a few acres of willows into the air and scatter them like so much chaff over the landscape. The wind was simply enjoying itself, for nothing rose out of the flat landscape to stop it, and I was conscious of sharing its great game with a kind of pleasurable excitement. Yet this novel emotion had nothing to do with the wind. Indeed, so vague was the sense of distress I experienced, that it was impossible to trace it to its source and deal with it accordingly, though I was aware somehow that it had to do with my realisation of our utter insignificance before this unrestrained power of the elements about me. The huge-grown river had something to do with it too – a vague, unpleasant idea that we had somehow trifled with these great elemental forces in whose power we lay helpless every hour of the day and night. For here, indeed, they were gigantically at play together, and the sight appealed to the imagination.

But my emotion, so far as I could understand it, seemed to attach itself more particularly to the willow bushes, to these acres and acres of willows, crowding, so thickly growing there, swarming everywhere the eye could reach, pressing upon the river as though to suffocate it, standing in dense array mile after mile beneath the sky, watching, waiting, listening. And, apart quite from the elements, the willows connected themselves subtly with my malaise, attacking the mind insidiously somehow by reason of their vast numbers, and contriving in some way or other to represent to the imagination a new and mighty power, a power, moreover, not altogether friendly to us.

Great revelations of nature, of course, never fail to impress in one way or another, and I was no stranger to moods of the kind. Mountains overawe and oceans terrify, while the mystery of great forests exercises a spell peculiarly its own. But all these, at one point or another, somewhere link on intimately with human life and human experience. They stir comprehensible, even if alarming, emotions. They tend on the whole to exalt.

With this multitude of willows, however, it was something far different, I felt. Some essence emanated from them that besieged the heart. A sense of awe awakened, true, but of awe touched somewhere by a vague terror. Their serried ranks, growing everywhere darker about me as the shadows deepened, moving furiously yet softly in the wind, woke in me the curious and unwelcome suggestion that we had trespassed here upon the borders of an alien world, a world where we were intruders, a world where we were not wanted or invited to remain–where we ran grave risks perhaps!

The feeling, however, though it refused to yield its meaning entirely to analysis, did not at the time trouble me by passing into menace. Yet it never left me quite, even during the very practical business of putting up the tent in a hurricane of wind and building a fire for the stew-pot. It remained, just enough to bother and perplex, and to rob a most delightful camping-ground of a good portion of its charm. To my companion, however, I said nothing, for he was a man I considered devoid of imagination. In the first place, I could never have explained to him what I meant, and in the second, he would have laughed stupidly at me if I had.

There was a slight depression in the centre of the island, and here we pitched the tent. The surrounding willows broke the wind a bit.

'A poor camp,' observed the imperturbable Swede when at last the tent stood upright, 'no stones and precious little firewood. I'm for moving on early tomorrow – eh? This sand won't hold anything.'

But the experience of a collapsing tent at midnight had taught us many devices, and we made the cozy gipsy house as safe as possible, and then set about collecting a store of wood to last till bed-time. Willow bushes drop no branches, and driftwood was our only source of supply. We hunted the shores pretty thoroughly. Everywhere the banks were crumbling as the rising flood tore at them and carried away great portions with a splash and a gurgle.

'The island's much smaller than when we landed,' said the accurate Swede. 'It won't last long at this rate. We'd better drag the canoe close to the tent, and be ready to start at a moment's notice. I shall sleep in my clothes.'

He was a little distance off, climbing along the bank, and I heard his rather jolly laugh as he spoke.

'By Jove!' I heard him call, a moment later, and turned to see what had caused his exclamation. But for the moment he was hidden by the willows, and I could not find him.

'What in the world's this?' I heard him cry again, and this time his voice had become serious.

I ran up quickly and joined him on the bank. He was looking over the river, pointing at something in the water.

'Good Heavens, it's a man's body!' he cried excitedly. 'Look!'

A black thing, turning over and over in the foaming waves, swept rapidly past. It kept disappearing and coming up to the surface again. It was about twenty feet from the shore, and just as it was opposite to where we stood it lurched round and looked straight at us. We saw its eyes reflecting the sunset, and gleaming an odd yellow as the body turned over. Then it gave a swift, gulping plunge, and dived out of sight in a flash.

'An otter, by gad!' we exclaimed in the same breath, laughing.

It *was* an otter, alive, and out on the hunt; yet it had looked exactly like the body of a drowned man turning helplessly in the current. Far below it came to the surface once again, and we saw its black skin, wet and shining in the sunlight.

Then, too, just as we turned back, our arms full of driftwood, another thing happened to recall us to the river bank. This time it really was a man, and what was more, a man in a boat. Now a small boat on the Danube was an unusual sight at any time, but here in this deserted region, and at flood time, it was so unexpected as to constitute a real event. We stood and stared.

Whether it was due to the slanting sunlight, or the refraction from the wonderfully illumined water, I cannot say, but, whatever the cause, I found it difficult to focus my sight properly upon the flying apparition. It seemed, however, to be a man standing upright in a sort of flat-bottomed boat, steering with a long oar, and being carried down the opposite shore at a tremendous pace. He apparently was looking across in our direction, but the distance was too great and the light too uncertain for us to make out very plainly what he was about. It seemed to me that he was gesticulating and making signs at us. His voice came across the water to us shouting something furiously, but the wind drowned it so that no single word was audible. There was something curious about the whole appearance – man, boat, signs, voice – that made an impression on me out of all proportion to its cause.

'He's crossing himself!' I cried. 'Look, he's making the sign of the Cross!'

'I believe you're right,' the Swede said, shading his eyes with his hand and watching the man out of sight. He seemed to be gone in a moment, melting away down there into the sea of willows where the sun caught them in the bend of the river and turned them into a great crimson wall of beauty. Mist, too, had begun to rise, so that the air was hazy.

'But what in the world is he doing at night-fall on this flooded river?' I said, half to myself. 'Where is he going at such a time, and what did he mean by his signs and shouting? D'you think he wished to warn us about something?'

'He saw our smoke, and thought we were spirits probably,' laughed my companion. 'These Hungarians believe in all sorts of rubbish; you remember the shopwoman at Pressburg warning us that no one ever landed here because it belonged to some sort of beings outside man's world! I suppose they believe in fairies and elementals, possibly demons, too. That peasant in the boat saw people on the islands for the first time in his life,' he added, after a slight pause, 'and it scared him, that's all.'

The Swede's tone of voice was not convincing, and his manner lacked something that was usually there. I noted the change instantly while he talked, though without being able to label it precisely.

'If they had enough imagination,' I laughed loudly – I remember trying to make as much *noise* as I could – 'they might well people a place like this with the old gods of antiquity. The Romans must have haunted all this region more or less with their shrines and sacred groves and elemental deities.'

The subject dropped and we returned to our stew-pot, for my friend was not given to imaginative conversation as a rule. Moreover, just then I remember feeling distinctly glad that he was not imaginative; his stolid, practical nature suddenly seemed to me welcome and comforting. It was an admirable temperament, I felt; he could steer down rapids like a red Indian, shoot dangerous bridges and whirlpools better than any white man I ever saw in a canoe. He was a grand fellow for an adventurous trip, a tower of strength when untoward things happened. I looked at his strong face and light curly hair as he staggered along under his pile of driftwood (twice the size of mine!), and I experienced a feeling of relief. Yes, I was distinctly glad just then that the Swede was – what he was, and that he never made remarks that suggested more than they said.

'The river's still rising, though,' he added, as if following out some thoughts of his own, and dropping his load with a gasp. 'This island will be under water in two days if it goes on.'

'I wish the *wind* would go down,' I said. 'I don't care a fig for the river.'

The flood, indeed, had no terrors for us; we could get off at ten minutes' notice, and the more water the better we liked it. It meant an increasing current and the obliteration of the treacherous shingle-beds that so often threatened to tear the bottom out of our canoe.

Contrary to our expectations, the wind did not go down with the sun. It seemed to increase with the darkness, howling overhead and shaking the willows round us like straws. Curious sounds accompanied it sometimes, like the explosion of heavy guns, and it fell upon the water and the island in great flat blows of immense power. It made me think of the sounds a planet must make, could we only hear it, driving along through space.

But the sky kept wholly clear of clouds, and soon after supper the full moon rose up in the east and covered the river and the plain of shouting willows with a light like the day.

We lay on the sandy patch beside the fire, smoking, listening to the noises of the night round us, and talking happily of the journey we had already made, and of our plans ahead. The map lay spread in the door of the tent, but the high wind made it hard to study, and presently we lowered the curtain and extinguished the lantern. The firelight was enough to smoke and see each other's faces by, and the sparks flew about overhead like fireworks. A few yards beyond, the river gurgled and hissed, and from time to time a heavy splash announced the falling away of further portions of the bank.

Our talk, I noticed, had to do with the faraway scenes and incidents of our first camps in the Black Forest, or of other subjects altogether remote from the present setting, for neither of us spoke of the actual moment more than was necessary – almost as though we had agreed tacitly to avoid discussion of the camp and its incidents. Neither the otter nor the boatman, for instance, received the honour of a single mention, though ordinarily these would have furnished discussion for the greater part of the evening. They were, of course, distinct events in such a place.

The scarcity of wood made it a business to keep the fire going, for the wind, that drove the smoke in our faces wherever we sat, helped at the same time to make a forced draught. We took it in turn to make some foraging expeditions into the darkness, and the quantity the Swede brought back always made me feel that he took an absurdly long time finding it; for the fact was I did not care much about being left alone, and yet it always seemed to be my turn to grub about among the bushes or scramble along the slippery banks in the moonlight. The long day's battle with wind and water – such wind and such water! – had tired us both, and an early bed was the obvious programme. Yet neither of us made the move for the tent. We lay there, tending the fire, talking in desultory fashion, peering about us into the dense willow bushes, and listening to the thunder of wind and river. The loneliness of the place had entered our very bones, and silence seemed natural, for after a bit the sound of our voices became a trifle unreal and forced; whispering would have been the fitting mode of communication, I felt, and the human voice, always rather absurd amid the roar of the elements, now carried with it something almost illegitimate. It was like talking out loud in church, or in some place where it was not lawful, perhaps not quite *safe*, to be overheard.

The eeriness of this lonely island, set among a million willows, swept by a hurricane, and surrounded by hurrying deep waters, touched us both, I fancy. Untrodden by man, almost unknown to man, it lay there beneath the moon, remote from human influence, on the frontier of another world, an alien world, a world tenanted by willows only and the souls of willows. And we, in our rashness, had dared to invade it, even to make use of it! Something more than the power of its mystery stirred in me as I lay on the sand, feet to fire, and peered up through the leaves at the stars. For the last time I rose to get firewood.

'When this has burnt up,' I said firmly, 'I shall turn in,' and my companion watched me lazily as I moved off into the surrounding shadows.

For an unimaginative man I thought he seemed unusually receptive that night, unusually open to suggestion of things other than sensory. He too was touched by the beauty and loneliness of the place. I was not altogether pleased, I remember, to recognise this slight change in him, and instead of immediately collecting sticks, I made my way to the far point of the island where the moonlight on plain and river could be seen to better advantage. The desire to be alone had come suddenly upon me; my former dread returned in force; there was a vague feeling in me I wished to face and probe to the bottom.

When I reached the point of sand jutting out among the waves, the spell of the place descended upon me with a positive shock. No mere 'scenery' could have produced such an effect. There was something more here, something to alarm.

I gazed across the waste of wild waters; I watched the whispering willows; I heard the ceaseless beating of the tireless wind; and, one and all, each in its own way, stirred in me this sensation of a strange distress. But the *willows* especially; for ever they went on chattering and talking among themselves, laughing a little, shrilly crying out, sometimes sighing – but what it was they made so much to-do about belonged to the secret life of the great plain they inhabited. And it was utterly alien to the world I knew, or to that of the wild yet kindly elements. They made me think of a host of beings from another plane of life, another evolution altogether, perhaps, all discussing a mystery known only to themselves. I watched them moving busily together, oddly shaking their big bushy heads, twirling their myriad leaves even when there was no wind. They moved of their own will as though alive, and they touched, by some incalculable method, my own keen sense of the *horrible*.

There they stood in the moonlight, like a vast army surrounding our camp, shaking their innumerable silver spears defiantly, formed all ready for an attack.

The psychology of places, for some imaginations at least, is very vivid; for the wanderer, especially, camps have their 'note' either of welcome or rejection. At first it may not always be apparent, because the busy preparations of tent and cooking prevent, but with the first pause – after supper usually – it comes and announces itself. And the note of this willow-camp now became unmistakably plain to me; we were interlopers, trespassers; we were not welcomed. The sense of unfamiliarity grew upon me as I stood there watching. We touched the frontier of a region where our presence was resented. For a night's lodging we might perhaps be tolerated; but for a prolonged and inquisitive stay – No! by all the gods of the trees and wilderness, no! We were the first human influences upon this island, and we were not wanted. *The willows were against us.*

Strange thoughts like these, bizarre fancies, borne I know not whence, found lodgment in my mind as I stood listening. What, I thought, if, after all, these crouching willows proved to be alive; if suddenly they should rise up, like a swarm of living creatures, marshalled by the gods whose territory we had invaded, sweep towards us off the vast swamps, booming overhead in the night – and then *settle down*! As I looked it was so easy to imagine they actually moved, crept nearer, retreated a little, huddled together in masses, hostile, waiting for the great wind that should finally start them a-running. I could have sworn their aspect changed a little, and their ranks deepened and pressed more closely together.

The melancholy shrill cry of a night-bird sounded overhead, and suddenly I nearly lost my balance as the piece of bank I stood upon fell with a great splash into the river, undermined by the flood. I stepped back just in time, and went on hunting for firewood again, half laughing at the odd fancies that crowded so thickly into my mind and cast their spell upon me. I recalled the Swede's remark about moving on next day, and I was just thinking that I fully agreed with him, when I turned with a start and saw the subject of my thoughts standing immediately in front of me. He was quite close. The roar of the elements had covered his approach.

'You've been gone so long,' he shouted above the wind, 'I thought something must have happened to you.'

But there was that in his tone, and a certain look in his face as well, that conveyed to me more than his usual words, and in a flash I understood the real reason for his coming. It was because the spell of the place had entered his soul too, and he did not like being alone.

'River still rising,' he cried, pointing to the flood in the moonlight, 'and the wind's simply awful.'

He always said the same things, but it was the cry for companionship that gave the real importance to his words.

'Lucky,' I cried back, 'our tent's in the hollow. I think it'll hold all right.' I added something about the difficulty of finding wood, in order to explain my absence, but the wind caught my words and flung them across the river, so that he did not hear, but just looked at me through the branches, nodding his head.

'Lucky if we get away without disaster!' he shouted, or words to that effect; and I remember feeling half angry with him for putting the thought into words, for it was exactly what I felt myself. There was disaster impending somewhere, and the sense of presentiment lay unpleasantly upon me.

We went back to the fire and made a final blaze, poking it up with our feet. We took a last look round. But for the wind the heat would have been unpleasant. I put this thought into words, and I remember my friend's reply struck me oddly: that he would rather have the heat, the ordinary July weather, than this 'diabolical wind'.

Everything was snug for the night; the canoe lying turned over beside the tent, with both yellow paddles beneath her;

the provision sack hanging from a willow-stem, and the washed-up dishes removed to a safe distance from the fire, all ready for the morning meal.

We smothered the embers of the fire with sand, and then turned in. The flap of the tent door was up, and I saw the branches and the stars and the white moonlight. The shaking willows and the heavy buffetings of the wind against our taut little house were the last things I remembered as sleep came down and covered all with its soft and delicious forgetfulness.

II

Suddenly I found myself lying awake, peering from my sandy mattress through the door of the tent. I looked at my watch pinned against the canvas, and saw by the bright moonlight that it was past twelve o'clock – the threshold of a new day – and I had therefore slept a couple of hours. The Swede was asleep still beside me; the wind howled as before; something plucked at my heart and made me feel afraid. There was a sense of disturbance in my immediate neighbourhood.

I sat up quickly and looked out. The trees were swaying violently to and fro as the gusts smote them, but our little bit of green canvas lay snugly safe in the hollow, for the wind passed over it without meeting enough resistance to make it vicious. The feeling of disquietude did not pass, however, and I crawled quietly out of the tent to see if our belongings were safe. I moved carefully so as not to waken my companion. A curious excitement was on me.

I was half-way out, kneeling on all fours, when my eye first took in that the tops of the bushes opposite, with their moving tracery of leaves, made shapes against the sky. I sat back on my haunches and stared. It was incredible, surely, but there, opposite and slightly above me, were shapes of some indeterminate sort among the willows, and as the branches swayed in the wind they seemed to group themselves about these shapes, forming a series of monstrous outlines that shifted rapidly beneath the moon. Close, about fifty feet in front of me, I saw these things.

My first instinct was to waken my companion, that he too might see them, but something made me hesitate – the sudden realisation, probably, that I should not welcome corroboration; and meanwhile I crouched there staring in amazement with smarting eyes. I was wide awake. I remember saying to myself that I was *not* dreaming.

They first became properly visible, these huge figures, just within the tops of the bushes – immense, bronze-coloured, moving, and wholly independent of the swaying of the branches. I saw them plainly and noted, now I came to examine them more calmly, that they were very much larger than human, and indeed that something in their appearance proclaimed them to be *not human* at all. Certainly they were not merely the moving tracery of the branches against the moonlight. They shifted independently. They rose upwards in a continuous stream from earth to sky, vanishing utterly as soon as they reached the dark of the sky. They were interlaced one with another, making a great column, and I saw their limbs and huge bodies melting in and out of each other, forming this serpentine line that bent and swayed and twisted spirally with the contortions of the wind-tossed trees. They were nude, fluid shapes, passing up the bushes, *within* the leaves almost – rising up in a living column into the heavens. Their faces I never could see. Unceasingly they poured upwards, swaying in great bending curves, with a hue of dull bronze upon their skins.

I stared, trying to force every atom of vision from my eyes. For a long time I thought they *must* every moment disappear and resolve themselves into the movements of the branches and prove to be an optical illusion. I searched everywhere for a proof of reality, when all the while I understood quite well that the standard of reality had changed. For the longer I looked the more certain I became that these figures were real and living, though perhaps not according to the standards that the camera and the biologist would insist upon.

Far from feeling fear, I was possessed with a sense of awe and wonder such as I have never known. I seemed to be gazing at the personified elemental forces of this haunted and primeval region. Our intrusion had stirred the powers of the place into activity. It was we who were the cause of the disturbance, and my brain filled to bursting with stories and legends of the spirits and deities of places that have been acknowledged and worshipped by men in all ages of the world's history. But, before I could arrive at any possible explanation, something impelled me to go farther out, and I crept forward on the sand and stood upright. I felt the ground still warm under my bare feet; the wind tore at my hair and face; and the sound of the river burst upon my ears with a sudden roar. These things, I knew, were real, and proved that my senses were acting normally. Yet the figures still rose from earth to heaven, silent, majestically, in a great spiral of grace and strength that overwhelmed me at length with a genuine deep emotion of worship. I felt that I must fall down and worship – absolutely worship.

Perhaps in another minute I might have done so, when a gust of wind swept against me with such force that it blew me sideways, and I nearly stumbled and fell. It seemed to shake the dream violently out of me. At least it gave me another point of view somehow. The figures still remained, still ascended into heaven from the heart of the night, but my reason at last began to assert itself. It must be a subjective experience, I argued – none the less real for that, but still subjective. The moonlight and the branches combined to work out these pictures upon the mirror of my imagination, and for some reason I projected them outwards and made them appear objective. I knew this must be the case, of course. I took courage, and began to move forward across the open patches of sand. By Jove, though, was it all hallucination? Was it merely subjective? Did not my reason argue in the old futile way from the little standard of the known?

I only know that great column of figures ascended darkly into the sky for what seemed a very long period of time, and with a very complete measure of reality as most men are accustomed to gauge reality. Then suddenly they were gone!

And, once they were gone and the immediate wonder of their great presence had passed, fear came down upon me with a cold rush. The esoteric meaning of this lonely and haunted region suddenly flamed up within me, and I began to tremble dreadfully. I took a quick look round – a look of horror that came near to panic – calculating vainly ways of escape; and then, realising how helpless I was to achieve anything really effective, I crept back silently into the tent and lay down again upon my sandy mattress, first lowering the door-curtain to shut out the sight of the willows in the moonlight, and then burying my head as deeply as possible beneath the blankets to deaden the sound of the terrifying wind.

III

As though further to convince me that I had not been dreaming, I remember that it was a long time before I fell again into a troubled and restless sleep; and even then only the upper crust of me slept, and underneath there something that never quite lost consciousness, but lay alert and on the watch.

But this second time I jumped up with a genuine start of terror. It was neither the wind nor the river that woke me, but the slow approach of something that caused the sleeping portion of me to grow smaller and smaller till at last it vanished altogether, and I found myself sitting bolt upright – listening.

Outside there was a sound of multitudinous little patterings. They had been coming, I was aware, for a long time, and in my sleep they had first become audible. I sat there nervously wide awake as though I had not slept at all. It seemed to me that my breathing came with difficulty, and that there was a great weight upon the surface of my body. In spite of the hot night, I felt clammy with cold and shivered. Something surely was pressing steadily against the sides of the tent and weighing down upon it from above. Was it the body of the wind? Was this the pattering rain, the dripping of the leaves? The spray blown from the river by the wind and gathering in big drops? I thought quickly of a dozen things.

Then suddenly the explanation leaped into my mind: a bough from the poplar, the only large tree on the island, had fallen with the wind. Still half caught by the other branches, it would fall with the next gust and crush us, and meanwhile its leaves brushed and tapped upon the tight canvas surface of the tent. I raised a loose flap and rushed out, calling to the Swede to follow.

But when I got out and stood upright I saw that the tent was free. There was no hanging bough; there was no rain or spray; nothing approached.

A cold, grey light filtered down through the bushes and lay on the faintly gleaming sand. Stars still crowded the sky directly overhead, and the wind howled magnificently, but the fire no longer gave out any glow, and I saw the east reddening in streaks through the trees. Several hours must have passed since I stood there before watching the ascending figures, and the memory of it now came back to me horribly, like an evil dream. Oh, how tired it made me feel, that ceaseless raging wind! Yet, though the deep lassitude of a sleepless night was on me, my nerves were tingling with the activity of an equally tireless apprehension, and all idea of repose was out of the question. The river I saw had risen further. Its thunder filled the air, and a fine spray made itself felt through my thin sleeping shirt.

Yet nowhere did I discover the slightest evidence of anything to cause alarm. This deep, prolonged disturbance in my heart remained wholly unaccounted for.

My companion had not stirred when I called him, and there was no need to waken him now. I looked about me carefully, noting everything; the turned-over canoe; the yellow paddles – two of them, I'm certain; the provision sack and the extra lantern hanging together from the tree; and, crowding everywhere about me, enveloping all, the willows, those endless, shaking willows. A bird uttered its morning cry, and a string of duck passed with whirring flight overhead in the twilight. The sand whirled, dry and stinging, about my bare feet in the wind.

I walked round the tent and then went out a little way into the bush, so that I could see across the river to the farther landscape, and the same profound yet indefinable emotion of distress seized upon me again as I saw the interminable sea of bushes stretching to the horizon, looking ghostly and unreal in the wan light of dawn. I walked softly here and there, still puzzling over that odd sound of infinite pattering, and of that pressure upon the tent that had wakened me. It *must* have been the wind, I reflected – the wind bearing upon the loose, hot sand, driving the dry particles smartly against the taut canvas – the wind dropping heavily upon our fragile roof.

Yet all the time my nervousness and malaise increased appreciably.

I crossed over to the farther shore and noted how the coastline had altered in the night, and what masses of sand the river had torn away. I dipped my hands and feet into the cool current, and bathed my forehead. Already there was a glow of sunrise in the sky and the exquisite freshness of coming day. On my way back I passed purposely beneath the very bushes where I had seen the column of figures rising into the air, and midway among the clumps I suddenly found myself overtaken by a sense of vast terror. From the shadows a large figure went swiftly by. Someone passed me, as sure as ever man did …

It was a great staggering blow from the wind that helped me forward again, and once out in the more open space, the sense of terror diminished strangely. The winds were about and walking, I remember saying to myself, for the winds often move like great presences under the trees. And altogether the fear that hovered about me was such an unknown and immense kind of fear, so unlike anything I had ever felt before, that it woke a sense of awe and wonder in me that did much to counteract its worst effects; and when I reached a high point in the middle of the island from which I could see the wide stretch of river, crimson in the sunrise, the whole magical beauty of it all was so overpowering that a sort of wild yearning woke in me and almost brought a cry up into the throat.

But this cry found no expression, for as my eyes wandered from the plain beyond to the island round me and noted our little tent half hidden among the willows, a dreadful discovery leaped out at me, compared to which my terror of the walking winds seemed as nothing at all.

For a change, I thought, had somehow come about in the arrangement of the landscape. It was not that my point of vantage gave me a different view, but that an alteration had apparently been effected in the relation of the tent to the willows, and of the willows to the tent. Surely the bushes now crowded much closer – unnecessarily, unpleasantly close.

They had moved nearer.

Creeping with silent feet over the shifting sands, drawing imperceptibly nearer by soft, unhurried movements, the willows had come closer during the night. But had the wind moved them, or had they moved of themselves? I recalled the sound of infinite small patterings and the pressure upon the tent and upon my own heart that caused me to wake in terror. I swayed for a moment in the wind like a tree, finding it hard to keep my upright position on the sandy hillock. There was a suggestion here of personal agency, of deliberate intention, of aggressive hostility, and it terrified me into a sort of rigidity.

Then the reaction followed quickly. The idea was so bizarre, so absurd, that I felt inclined to laugh. But the laughter came no more readily than the cry, for the knowledge that my mind was so receptive to such dangerous imaginings brought the additional terror that it was through our minds and not through our physical bodies that the attack would come, and was coming.

The wind buffeted me about, and, very quickly it seemed, the sun came up over the horizon, for it was after four o'clock, and I must have stood on that little pinnacle of sand longer than I knew, afraid to come down to close quarters with the willows. I returned quietly, creepily, to the tent, first taking another exhaustive look round and – yes, I confess it – making a few measurements. I paced out on the warm sand the distances between the willows and the tent, making a note of the shortest distance particularly.

I crawled stealthily into my blankets. My companion, to all appearances, still slept soundly, and I was glad that this was so. Provided my experiences were not corroborated, I could find strength somehow to deny them, perhaps. With the daylight I could persuade myself that it was all a subjective hallucination, a fantasy of the night, a projection of the excited imagination.

Nothing further came in to disturb me, and I fell asleep almost at once, utterly exhausted, yet still in dread of hearing again that weird sound of multitudinous pattering, or of feeling the pressure upon my heart that had made it difficult to breathe.

IV

The sun was high in the heavens when my companion woke me from a heavy sleep and announced that the porridge was cooked and there was just time to bathe. The grateful smell of frizzling bacon entered the tent door.

'River still rising,' he said, 'and several islands out in midstream have disappeared altogether. Our own island's much smaller.'

'Any wood left?' I asked sleepily.

'The wood and the island will finish tomorrow in a dead heat,' he laughed, 'but there's enough to last us till then.'

I plunged in from the point of the island, which had indeed altered a lot in size and shape during the night, and was swept down in a moment to the landing-place opposite the tent. The water was icy, and the banks flew by like the country from an express train. Bathing under such conditions was an exhilarating operation, and the terror of the night seemed cleansed out of me by a process of evaporation in the brain. The sun was blazing hot; not a cloud showed itself anywhere; the wind, however, had not abated one little jot.

Quite suddenly then the implied meaning of the Swede's words flashed across me, showing that he no longer wished to leave post-haste, and had changed his mind. 'Enough to last till tomorrow'—he assumed we should stay on the island another night. It struck me as odd. The night before he was so positive the other way. How had the change come about?

Great crumblings of the banks occurred at breakfast,

with heavy splashings and clouds of spray which the wind brought into our frying-pan, and my fellow-traveller talked incessantly about the difficulty the Vienna-Pesth steamers must have to find the channel in flood. But the state of his mind interested and impressed me far more than the state of the river or the difficulties of the steamers. He had changed somehow since the evening before. His manner was different— a trifle excited, a trifle shy, with a sort of suspicion about his voice and gestures. I hardly know how to describe it now in cold blood, but at the time I remember being quite certain of one thing, viz. that he had become frightened?

He ate very little breakfast, and for once omitted to smoke his pipe. He had the map spread open beside him, and kept studying its markings.

'We'd better get off sharp in an hour,' I said presently, feeling for an opening that must bring him indirectly to a partial confession at any rate. And his answer puzzled me uncomfortably: 'Rather! If they'll let us.'

'Who'll let us? The elements?' I asked quickly, with affected indifference.

'The powers of this awful place, whoever they are,' he replied, keeping his eyes on the map. 'The gods are here, if they are anywhere at all in the world.'

'The elements are always the true immortals,' I replied, laughing as naturally as I could manage, yet knowing quite well that my face reflected my true feelings when he looked up gravely at me and spoke across the smoke:

'We shall be fortunate if we get away without further disaster.'

This was exactly what I had dreaded, and I screwed myself up to the point of the direct question. It was like agreeing to allow the dentist to extract the tooth; it *had* to come anyhow in the long run, and the rest was all pretence.

'Further disaster! Why, what's happened?'

'For one thing – the steering paddle's gone,' he said quietly.

'The steering paddle gone!' I repeated, greatly excited, for this was our rudder, and the Danube in flood without a rudder was suicide. 'But what –'

'And there's a tear in the bottom of the canoe,' he added, with a genuine little tremor in his voice.

I continued staring at him, able only to repeat the words in his face somewhat foolishly. There, in the heat of the sun, and on this burning sand, I was aware of a freezing atmosphere descending round us. I got up to follow him, for he merely nodded his head gravely and led the way towards the tent a few yards on the other side of the fireplace. The canoe still lay there as I had last seen her in the night, ribs uppermost, the paddles, or rather, *the* paddle, on the sand beside her.

'There's only one,' he said, stooping to pick it up. 'And here's the rent in the base-board.'

It was on the tip of my tongue to tell him that I had clearly noticed *two* paddles a few hours before, but a second impulse made me think better of it, and I said nothing. I approached to see.

There was a long, finely made tear in the bottom of the canoe where a little slither of wood had been neatly taken clean out; it looked as if the tooth of a sharp rock or snag had eaten down her length, and investigation showed that the hole went through. Had we launched out in her without observing it we must inevitably have foundered. At first the water would have made the wood swell so as to close the hole, but once out in mid-stream the water must have poured in, and the canoe, never more than two inches above the surface, would have filled and sunk very rapidly.

'There, you see an attempt to prepare a victim for the sacrifice,' I heard him saying, more to himself than to me, 'two victims rather,' he added as he bent over and ran his fingers along the slit.

I began to whistle – a thing I always do unconsciously when utterly nonplussed – and purposely paid no attention to his words. I was determined to consider them foolish.

'It wasn't there last night,' he said presently, straightening up from his examination and looking anywhere but at me.

'We must have scratched her in landing, of course,' I stopped whistling to say. 'The stones are very sharp.'

I stopped abruptly, for at that moment he turned round and met my eye squarely. I knew just as well as he did how impossible my explanation was. There were no stones, to begin with.

'And then there's this to explain too,' he added quietly, handing me the paddle and pointing to the blade.

A new and curious emotion spread freezingly over me as I took and examined it. The blade was scraped down all over, beautifully scraped, as though someone had sand-papered it with care, making it so thin that the first vigorous stroke must have snapped it off at the elbow.

'One of us walked in his sleep and did this thing,' I said feebly, 'or – or it has been filed by the constant stream of sand particles blown against it by the wind, perhaps.'

'Ah,' said the Swede, turning away, laughing a little, 'you can explain everything.'

'The same wind that caught the steering paddle and flung it so near the bank that it fell in with the next lump that crumbled,' I called out after him, absolutely determined to find an explanation for everything he showed me.

'I see,' he shouted back, turning his head to look at me before disappearing among the willow bushes.

Once alone with these perplexing evidences of personal agency, I think my first thoughts took the form of 'One of us must have done this thing, and it certainly was not I.' But my second thought decided how impossible it was to suppose, under all the circumstances, that either of us had done it. That my companion, the trusted friend of a dozen similar expeditions, could have knowingly had a hand in it, was a suggestion not to be entertained for a moment. Equally absurd seemed the explanation that this imperturbable and densely practical nature had suddenly become insane and was busied with insane purposes.

Yet the fact remained that what disturbed me most, and kept my fear actively alive even in this blaze of sunshine and wild beauty, was the clear certainty that some curious alteration had come about in his *mind* – that he was nervous, timid, suspicious, aware of goings on he did not speak about, watching a series of secret and hitherto unmentionable events – waiting, in a word, for a climax that he expected, and, I thought, expected very soon. This grew up in my mind intuitively – I hardly knew how.

I made a hurried examination of the tent and its surroundings, but the measurements of the night remained the same. There were deep hollows formed in the sand I now noticed for the first time, basin-shaped and of various depths and sizes, varying from that of a tea-cup to a large bowl. The wind, no doubt, was responsible for these miniature craters, just as it was for lifting the paddle and tossing it towards the water. The rent in the canoe was the only thing that seemed quite inexplicable; and, after all, it was conceivable that a sharp point had caught it when we landed. The examination I made of the shore did not assist this theory, but all the same I clung to it with that diminishing portion of my intelligence which I called my 'reason'. An explanation of some kind was an absolute necessity, just as some working explanation of the universe is necessary – however absurd – to the happiness of every individual who seeks to do his duty in the world and face the problems of life. The simile seemed to me at the time an exact parallel.

I at once set the pitch melting, and presently the Swede joined me at the work, though under the best conditions in the world the canoe could not be safe for traveling till the following day. I drew his attention casually to the hollows in the sand.

'Yes,' he said, 'I know. They're all over the island. But *you* can explain them, no doubt!'

'Wind, of course,' I answered without hesitation. 'Have you never watched those little whirlwinds in the street that twist and twirl everything into a circle? This sand's loose enough to yield, that's all.'

He made no reply, and we worked on in silence for a bit. I watched him surreptitiously all the time, and I had an idea he was watching me. He seemed, too, to be always listening attentively to something I could not hear, or perhaps for something that he expected to hear, for he kept turning about and staring into the bushes, and up into the sky, and out across the water where it was visible through the openings among the willows. Sometimes he even put his hand to his ear and held it there for several minutes. He said nothing to me, however, about it, and I asked no questions. And meanwhile, as he mended that torn canoe with the skill and address of a red Indian, I was glad to notice his absorption in the work, for there was a vague dread in my heart that he would speak of the changed aspect of the willows. And, if he had noticed *that*, my imagination could no longer be held a sufficient explanation of it.

At length, after a long pause, he began to talk.

'Queer thing,' he added in a hurried sort of voice, as though he wanted to say something and get it over. 'Queer thing. I mean, about that otter last night.'

I had expected something so totally different that he caught me with surprise, and I looked up sharply.

'Shows how lonely this place is. Otters are awfully shy things –'

'I don't mean that, of course,' he interrupted. 'I mean – do you think – did you think it really was an otter?'

'What else, in the name of Heaven, what else?'

'You know, I saw it before you did, and at first it seemed – so *much* bigger than an otter.'

'The sunset as you looked up-stream magnified it, or something,' I replied.

He looked at me absently a moment, as though his mind were busy with other thoughts.

'It had such extraordinary yellow eyes,' he went on half to himself.

'That was the sun too,' I laughed, a trifle boisterously. 'I suppose you'll wonder next if that fellow in the boat –'

I suddenly decided not to finish the sentence. He was in the act again of listening, turning his head to the wind, and something in the expression of his face made me halt. The subject dropped, and we went on with our caulking. Apparently he had not noticed my unfinished sentence. Five minutes later, however, he looked at me across the canoe, the smoking pitch in his hand, his face exceedingly grave.

'I *did* rather wonder, if you want to know,' he said slowly, 'what that thing in the boat was. I remember thinking at the time it was not a man. The whole business seemed to rise quite suddenly out of the water.'

I laughed again boisterously in his face, but this time there was impatience, and a strain of anger too, in my feeling.

'Look here now,' I cried, 'this place is quite queer enough without going out of our way to imagine things! That boat was an ordinary boat, and the man in it was an ordinary man, and they were both going down-stream as fast as they could lick. And that otter *was* an otter, so don't let's play the fool about it!'

He looked steadily at me with the same grave expression. He was not in the least annoyed. I took courage from his silence.

'And, for Heaven's sake,' I went on, 'don't keep pretending you hear things, because it only gives me the jumps, and there's nothing to hear but the river and this cursed old thundering wind.'

'You *fool!*' he answered in a low, shocked voice, 'you utter fool. That's just the way all victims talk. As if you didn't understand just as well as I do!' he sneered with scorn in his voice, and a sort of resignation. 'The best thing you can do is to keep quiet and try to hold your mind as firm as possible. This feeble attempt at self-deception only makes the truth harder when you're forced to meet it.'

My little effort was over, and I found nothing more to say, for I knew quite well his words were true, and that I was the fool, not *he*. Up to a certain stage in the adventure he kept ahead of me easily, and I think I felt annoyed to be out of it, to be thus proved less psychic, less sensitive than himself to these extraordinary happenings, and half ignorant all the time of what was going on under my very nose. *He knew* from the very beginning, apparently. But at the moment I wholly missed the point of his words about the necessity of there being a victim, and that we ourselves were destined to satisfy the want. I dropped all pretence thenceforward, but thenceforward likewise my fear increased steadily to the climax.

'But you're quite right about one thing,' he added, before the subject passed, 'and that is that we're wiser not to talk about it, or even to think about it, because what one *thinks* finds expression in words, and what one *says*, happens.'

That afternoon, while the canoe dried and hardened, we spent trying to fish, testing the leak, collecting wood, and watching the enormous flood of rising water. Masses of driftwood swept near our shores sometimes, and we fished for them with long willow branches. The island grew perceptibly smaller as the banks were torn away with great gulps and splashes. The weather kept brilliantly fine till about four o'clock, and then for the first time for three days the wind showed signs of abating. Clouds began to gather in the south-west, spreading thence slowly over the sky.

This lessening of the wind came as a great relief, for the incessant roaring, banging, and thundering had irritated our nerves. Yet the silence that came about five o'clock with its sudden cessation was in a manner quite as oppressive. The booming of the river had everything in its own way then; it filled the air with deep murmurs, more musical than the wind noises, but infinitely more monotonous. The wind held many notes, rising, falling always beating out some sort of great elemental tune; whereas the river's song lay between three notes at most – dull pedal notes, that held a lugubrious quality foreign to the wind, and somehow seemed to me, in my then nervous state, to sound wonderfully well the music of doom.

It was extraordinary, too, how the withdrawal suddenly of bright sunlight took everything out of the landscape that made for cheerfulness; and since this particular landscape had already managed to convey the suggestion of something sinister, the change of course was all the more unwelcome and noticeable. For me, I know, the darkening outlook became distinctly more alarming, and I found myself more than once calculating how soon after sunset the full moon would get up in the east, and whether the gathering clouds would greatly interfere with her lighting of the little island.

With this general hush of the wind – though it still indulged in occasional brief gusts – the river seemed to me to grow blacker, the willows to stand more densely together.

The latter, too, kept up a sort of independent movement of their own, rustling among themselves when no wind stirred, and shaking oddly from the roots upwards. When common objects in this way become charged with the suggestion of horror, they stimulate the imagination far more than things of unusual appearance; and these bushes, crowding huddled about us, assumed for me in the darkness a bizarre *grotesquerie* of appearance that lent to them somehow the aspect of purposeful and living creatures. Their very ordinariness, I felt, masked what was malignant and hostile to us. The forces of the region drew nearer with the coming of night. They were focusing upon our island, and more particularly upon ourselves. For thus, somehow, in the terms of the imagination, did my really indescribable sensations in this extraordinary place present themselves.

I had slept a good deal in the early afternoon, and had thus recovered somewhat from the exhaustion of a disturbed night, but this only served apparently to render me more susceptible than before to the obsessing spell of the haunting. I fought against it, laughing at my feelings as absurd and childish, with very obvious physiological explanations, yet, in spite of every effort, they gained in strength upon me so that I dreaded the night as a child lost in a forest must dread the approach of darkness.

The canoe we had carefully covered with a waterproof sheet during the day, and the one remaining paddle had been securely tied by the Swede to the base of a tree, lest the wind should rob us of that too. From five o'clock onwards I busied myself with the stew-pot and preparations for dinner, it being my turn to cook that night. We had potatoes, onions, bits of bacon fat to add flavor, and a general thick residue from former stews at the bottom of the pot; with black bread broken up into it the result was most excellent, and it was followed by a stew of plums with sugar and a brew of strong tea with dried milk. A good pile of wood lay close at hand, and the absence of wind made my duties easy. My companion sat lazily watching me, dividing his attentions between cleaning his pipe and giving useless advice – an admitted privilege of the off-duty man. He had been very quiet all the afternoon, engaged in re-caulking the canoe, strengthening the tent ropes, and fishing for driftwood while I slept. No more talk about undesirable things had passed between us, and I think his only remarks had to do with the gradual destruction of the island, which he declared was not fully a third smaller than when we first landed.

The pot had just begun to bubble when I heard his voice calling to me from the bank, where he had wandered away without my noticing. I ran up.

'Come and listen,' he said, 'and see what you make of it.' He held his hand cupwise to his ear, as so often before.

'*Now* do you hear anything?' he asked, watching me curiously.

We stood there, listening attentively together. At first I heard only the deep note of the water and the hissings rising from its turbulent surface. The willows, for once, were motionless and silent. Then a sound began to reach my ears faintly, a peculiar sound – something like the humming of a distant gong. It seemed to come across to us in the darkness from the waste of swamps and willows opposite. It was repeated at regular intervals, but it was certainly neither the sound of a bell nor the hooting of a distant steamer. I can liken it to nothing so much as to the sound of an immense gong, suspended far up in the sky, repeating incessantly its muffled metallic note, soft and musical, as it was repeatedly struck. My heart quickened as I listened.

'I've heard it all day,' said my companion. 'While you slept this afternoon it came all round the island. I hunted it down, but could never get near enough to see – to localise it correctly. Sometimes it was overhead, and sometimes it seemed under the water. Once or twice, too, I could have sworn it was not outside at all, but *within myself* – you know – the way a sound in the fourth dimension is supposed to come.'

I was too much puzzled to pay much attention to his words. I listened carefully, striving to associate it with any known familiar sound I could think of, but without success. It changed in the direction, too, coming nearer, and then sinking utterly away into remote distance. I cannot say that it was ominous in quality, because to me it seemed distinctly musical, yet I must admit it set going a distressing feeling that made me wish I had never heard it.

'The wind blowing in those sand-funnels,' I said determined to find an explanation, 'or the bushes rubbing together after the storm perhaps.'

'It comes off the whole swamp,' my friend answered. 'It comes from everywhere at once.' He ignored my explanations. 'It comes from the willow bushes somehow –'

'But now the wind has dropped,' I objected. 'The willows can hardly make a noise by themselves, can they?'

His answer frightened me, first because I had dreaded it, and secondly, because I knew intuitively it was true.

'It is *because* the wind has dropped we now hear it. It was drowned before. It is the cry, I believe, of the –'

I dashed back to my fire, warned by the sound of bubbling that the stew was in danger, but determined at the same time to escape further conversation. I was resolute, if possible, to avoid the exchanging of views. I dreaded, too, that he would begin about the gods, or the elemental forces, or something else disquieting, and I wanted to keep myself well in hand for what might happen later. There was another night to be faced before we escaped from this distressing place, and there was no knowing yet what it might bring forth.

'Come and cut up bread for the pot,' I called to him, vigorously stirring the appetising mixture. That stew-pot held sanity for us both, and the thought made me laugh.

He came over slowly and took the provision sack from the tree, fumbling in its mysterious depths, and then emptying the entire contents upon the ground-sheet at his feet.

'Hurry up!' I cried; 'it's boiling.'

The Swede burst out into a roar of laughter that startled me. It was forced laughter, not artificial exactly, but mirthless.

'There's nothing here!' he shouted, holding his sides.

'Bread, I mean.'

'It's gone. There is no bread. They've taken it!'

I dropped the long spoon and ran up. Everything the sack had contained lay upon the ground-sheet, but there was no loaf.

The whole dead weight of my growing fear fell upon me and shook me. Then I burst out laughing too. It was the only thing to do: and the sound of my laughter also made me understand his. The stain of psychical pressure caused it – this explosion of unnatural laughter in both of us; it was an effort of repressed forces to seek relief; it was a temporary safety-valve. And with both of us it ceased quite suddenly.

'How criminally stupid of me!' I cried, still determined to be consistent and find an explanation. 'I clean forgot to buy a loaf at Pressburg. That chattering woman put everything out of my head, and I must have left it lying on the counter or –'

'The oatmeal, too, is much less than it was this morning,' the Swede interrupted.

Why in the world need he draw attention to it? I thought angrily.

'There's enough for tomorrow,' I said, stirring vigorously, 'and we can get lots more at Komorn or Gran. In twenty-four hours we shall be miles from here.'

'I hope so – to God,' he muttered, putting the things back into the sack, 'unless we're claimed first as victims for the sacrifice,' he added with a foolish laugh. He dragged the sack into the tent, for safety's sake, I suppose, and I heard him mumbling to himself, but so indistinctly that it seemed quite natural for me to ignore his words.

Our meal was beyond question a gloomy one, and we ate it almost in silence, avoiding one another's eyes, and keeping the fire bright. Then we washed up and prepared for the night, and, once smoking, our minds unoccupied with any definite duties, the apprehension I had felt all day long became more and more acute. It was not then active fear, I think, but the very vagueness of its origin distressed me far more that if I had been able to ticket and face it squarely. The curious sound I have likened to the note of a gong became now almost incessant, and filled the stillness of the night with a faint, continuous ringing rather than a series of distinct notes. At one time it was behind and at another time in front of us. Sometimes I fancied it came from the bushes on our left, and then again from the clumps on our right. More often it hovered directly overhead like the whirring of wings. It was really everywhere at once, behind, in front, at our sides and over our heads, completely surrounding us. The sound really defies description. But nothing within my knowledge is like that ceaseless muffled humming rising off the deserted world of swamps and willows.

We sat smoking in comparative silence, the strain growing every minute greater. The worst feature of the situation seemed to me that we did not know what to expect, and could therefore make no sort of preparation by way of defense. We could anticipate nothing. My explanations made in the sunshine, moreover, now came to haunt me with their foolish and wholly unsatisfactory nature, and it was more and more clear to us that some kind of plain talk with my companion was inevitable, whether I liked it or not. After all, we had to spend the night together, and to sleep in the same tent side by side. I saw that I could not get along much longer without the support of his mind, and for that, of course, plain talk was imperative. As long as possible, however, I postponed this little climax, and tried to ignore or laugh at the occasional sentences he flung into the emptiness.

Some of these sentences, moreover, were confoundedly disquieting to me, coming as they did to corroborate much that I felt myself; corroboration, too – which made it so much more convincing – from a totally different point of view. He composed such curious sentences, and hurled them at me in such an inconsequential sort of way, as though his main line of thought was secret to himself, and these fragments were mere bits he found it impossible to digest. He got rid of them by uttering them. Speech relieved him. It was like being sick.

'There are things about us, I'm sure, that make for disorder, disintegration, destruction, *our* destruction,' he said once, while the fire blazed between us. 'We've strayed out of a safe line somewhere.'

And, another time, when the gong sounds had come nearer, ringing much louder than before, and directly over our heads, he said as though talking to himself:

'I don't think a phonograph would show any record of that. The sound doesn't come to me by the ears at all. The vibrations reach me in another manner altogether, and seem to be within me, which is precisely how a fourth dimensional sound might be supposed to make itself heard.'

I purposely made no reply to this, but I sat up a little closer to the fire and peered about me into the darkness. The clouds were massed all over the sky, and no trace of moonlight came through. Very still, too, everything was, so that the river and the frogs had things all their own way.

'It has that about it,' he went on, 'which is utterly out of common experience. It is *unknown*. Only one thing describes it really; it is a non-human sound; I mean a sound outside humanity.'

Having rid himself of this indigestible morsel, he lay quiet for a time, but he had so admirably expressed my own feeling that it was a relief to have the thought out, and to have confined it by the limitation of words from dangerous wandering to and fro in the mind.

The solitude of that Danube camping-place, can I ever forget it? The feeling of being utterly alone on an empty planet! My thoughts ran incessantly upon cities and the haunts of men. I would have given my soul, as the saying is, for the 'feel' of those Bavarian villages we had passed through by the score; for the normal, human commonplaces; peasants drinking beer, tables beneath the trees, hot sunshine, and a ruined castle on the rocks behind the red-roofed church. Even the tourists would have been welcome.

Yet what I felt of dread was no ordinary ghostly fear. It was infinitely greater, stranger, and seemed to arise from some dim ancestral sense of terror more profoundly disturbing than anything I had known or dreamed of. We had 'strayed', as the Swede put it, into some region or some set of conditions where the risks were great, yet unintelligible to us; where the frontiers of some unknown world lay close about us. It was a spot held by the dwellers in some outer space, a sort of peep-hole whence they could spy upon the earth, themselves unseen, a point where the veil between had worn a little thin. As the final result of too long a sojourn here, we should be carried over the border and deprived of what we called 'our lives', yet by mental, not physical, processes. In that sense, as he said, we should be the victims of our adventure – a sacrifice.

It took us in different fashion, each according to the measure of his sensitiveness and powers of resistance. I translated it vaguely into a personification of the mightily disturbed elements, investing them with the horror of a deliberate and malefic purpose, resentful of our audacious intrusion into their breeding-place; whereas my friend threw it into the unoriginal form at first of a trespass on some ancient shrine, some place where the old gods still held sway, where the emotional forces of former worshippers still clung, and the ancestral portion of him yielded to the old pagan spell.

At any rate, here was a place unpolluted by men, kept clean by the winds from coarsening human influences, a place where spiritual agencies were within reach and aggressive. Never, before or since, have I been so attacked by indescribable suggestions of a 'beyond region', of another scheme of life, another revolution not parallel to the human. And in the end our minds would succumb under the weight of the awful spell, and we should be drawn across the frontier into *their* world.

Small things testified to the amazing influence of the place, and now in the silence round the fire they allowed themselves to be noted by the mind. The very atmosphere had proved itself a magnifying medium to distort every indication: the otter rolling in the current, the hurrying boatman making signs, the shifting willows, one and all had been robbed of its natural character, and revealed in something of its other aspect – as it existed across the border to that other region. And this changed aspect I felt was now not merely to me, but to the race. The whole experience whose verge we touched was unknown to humanity at all. It was a new order of experience, and in the true sense of the word *unearthly*.

'It's the deliberate, calculating purpose that reduces one's courage to zero,' the Swede said suddenly, as if he had been actually following my thoughts. 'Otherwise imagination might count for much. But the paddle, the canoe, the lessening food –'

'Haven't I explained all that once?' I interrupted viciously.

'You have,' he answered dryly; 'you have indeed.'

He made other remarks too, as usual, about what he called the 'plain determination to provide a victim'; but, having now arranged my thoughts better, I recognised that this was simply the cry of his frightened soul against the knowledge that he was being attacked in a vital part, and that he would be somehow taken or destroyed. The situation called for a courage and calmness of reasoning that neither of us could compass, and I have never before been so clearly conscious of two persons in me – the one that explained everything, and the other that laughed at such foolish explanations, yet was horribly afraid.

Meanwhile, in the pitchy night the fire died down and the wood pile grew small. Neither of us moved to replenish the stock, and the darkness consequently came up very close to our faces. A few feet beyond the circle of firelight it was inky black. Occasionally a stray puff of wind set the willows shivering about us, but apart from this not very welcome sound a deep and depressing silence reigned, broken only by the gurgling of the river and the humming in the air overhead.

We both missed, I think, the shouting company of the winds.

At length, at a moment when a stray puff prolonged itself as though the wind were about to rise again, I reached the point for me of saturation, the point where it was absolutely necessary to find relief in plain speech, or else to betray myself by some hysterical extravagance that must have been far worse in its effect upon both of us. I kicked the fire into a blaze, and turned to my companion abruptly. He looked up with a start.

'I can't disguise it any longer,' I said; 'I don't like this place, and the darkness, and the noises, and the awful feelings I get. There's something here that beats me utterly. I'm in a blue funk, and that's the plain truth. If the other shore was – different, I swear I'd be inclined to swim for it!'

The Swede's face turned very white beneath the deep tan of sun and wind. He stared straight at me and answered quietly, but his voice betrayed his huge excitement by its unnatural calmness. For the moment, at any rate, he was the strong man of the two. He was more phlegmatic, for one thing.

'It's not a physical condition we can escape from by running away,' he replied, in the tone of a doctor diagnosing some grave disease; 'we must sit tight and wait. There are forces close here that could kill a herd of elephants in a second as easily as you or I could squash a fly. Our only chance is to keep perfectly still. Our insignificance perhaps may save us.'

I put a dozen questions into my expression of face, but found no words. It was precisely like listening to an accurate description of a disease whose symptoms had puzzled me.

'I mean that so far, although aware of our disturbing presence, they have not *found* us – not 'located' us, as the Americans say,' he went on. 'They're blundering about like men hunting for a leak of gas. The paddle and canoe and provisions prove that. I think they *feel* us, but cannot actually see us. We must keep our minds quiet – it's our minds they feel. We must control our thoughts, or it's all up with us.'

'Death, you mean?' I stammered, icy with the horror of his suggestion.

'Worse – by far,' he said. 'Death, according to one's belief, means either annihilation or release from the limitations of the senses, but it involves no change of character. *You* don't suddenly alter just because the body's gone. But this means a radical alteration, a complete change, a horrible loss of oneself by substitution – far worse than death, and not even annihilation. We happen to have camped in a spot where their region touches ours, where the veil between has worn thin' – horrors! he was using my very own phrase, my actual words – 'so that they are aware of our being in their neighbourhood.'

'But *who* are aware?' I asked.

I forgot the shaking of the willows in the windless calm, the humming overhead, everything except that I was waiting for an answer that I dreaded more than I can possibly explain.

He lowered his voice at once to reply, leaning forward a little over the fire, an indefinable change in his face that made me avoid his eyes and look down upon the ground.

'All my life,' he said, 'I have been strangely, vividly conscious of another region – not far removed from our own world in one sense, yet wholly different in kind – where great things go on unceasingly, where immense and terrible personalities hurry by, intent on vast purposes compared to which earthly affairs, the rise and fall of nations, the destinies of empires, the fate of armies and continents, are all as dust in the balance; vast purposes, I mean, that deal directly with the soul, and not indirectly with more expressions of the soul – '

'I suggest just now –' I began, seeking to stop him, feeling as though I was face to face with a madman. But he instantly overbore me with his torrent that *had* to come.

'You think,' he said, 'it is the spirit of the elements, and I thought perhaps it was the old gods. But I tell you now it is – *neither*. These would be comprehensible entities, for they have relations with men, depending upon them for worship or sacrifice, whereas these beings who are now about us have absolutely nothing to do with mankind, and it is mere chance that their space happens just at this spot to touch our own.'

The mere conception, which his words somehow made so

convincing, as I listened to them there in the dark stillness of that lonely island, set me shaking a little all over. I found it impossible to control my movements.

'And what do you propose?' I began again.

'A sacrifice, a victim, might save us by distracting them until we could get away,' he went on, 'just as the wolves stop to devour the dogs and give the sleigh another start. But – I see no chance of any other victim now.'

I stared blankly at him. The gleam in his eye was dreadful. Presently he continued.

'It's the willows, of course. The willows *mask* the others, but the others are feeling about for us. If we let our minds betray our fear, we're lost, lost utterly.' He looked at me with an expression so calm, so determined, so sincere, that I no longer had any doubts as to his sanity. He was as sane as any man ever was. 'If we can hold out through the night,' he added, 'we may get off in the daylight unnoticed, or rather, *undiscovered*.'

'But you really think a sacrifice would –'

That gong-like humming came down very close over our heads as I spoke, but it was my friend's scared face that really stopped my mouth.

'Hush!' he whispered, holding up his hand. 'Do not mention them more than you can help. Do not refer to them *by name*. To name is to reveal; it is the inevitable clue, and our only hope lies in ignoring them, in order that they may ignore us.'

'Even in thought?' He was extraordinarily agitated.

'Especially in thought. Our thoughts make spirals in their world. We must keep them *out of our minds* at all costs if possible.'

I raked the fire together to prevent the darkness having everything its own way. I never longed for the sun as I longed for it then in the awful blackness of that summer night.

'Were you awake all last night?' he went on suddenly.

'I slept badly a little after dawn,' I replied evasively, trying to follow his instructions, which I knew instinctively were true, 'but the wind, of course —'

'I know. But the wind won't account for all the noises.'

'Then you heard it too?'

'The multiplying countless little footsteps I heard,' he said, adding, after a moment's hesitation, 'and that other sound —'

'You mean above the tent, and the pressing down upon us of something tremendous, gigantic?'

He nodded significantly.

'It was like the beginning of a sort of inner suffocation?' I said.

'Partly, yes. It seemed to me that the weight of the atmosphere had been altered — had increased enormously, so that we should have been crushed.'

'And *that*,' I went on, determined to have it all out, pointing upwards where the gong-like note hummed ceaselessly, rising and falling like wind. 'What do you make of that?'

'It's *their* sound,' he whispered gravely. 'It's the sound of their world, the humming in their region. The division here is so thin that it leaks through somehow. But, if you listen carefully, you'll find it's not above so much as around us. It's in the willows. It's the willows themselves humming, because here the willows have been made symbols of the forces that are against us.'

I could not follow exactly what he meant by this, yet the thought and idea in my mind were beyond question the thought and idea in his. I realised what he realised, only with less power of analysis than his. It was on the tip of my tongue to tell him at last about my hallucination of the ascending figures and the moving bushes, when he suddenly thrust his face again close into mine across the firelight and began to speak in a very earnest whisper. He amazed me by his calmness and pluck, his apparent control of the situation.

This man I had for years deemed unimaginative, stolid!

'Now listen,' he said. 'The only thing for us to do is to go on as though nothing had happened, follow our usual habits, go to bed, and so forth; pretend we feel nothing and notice nothing. It is a question wholly of the mind, and the less we think about them the better our chance of escape. Above all, don't *think*, for what you think happens!'

'All right,' I managed to reply, simply breathless with his words and the strangeness of it all; 'all right, I'll try, but tell me one more thing first. Tell me what you make of those hollows in the ground all about us, those sand-funnels?'

'No!' he cried, forgetting to whisper in his excitement. 'I dare not, simply dare not, put the thought into words. If you have not guessed I am glad. Don't try to. *They* have put it into my mind; try your hardest to prevent their putting it into yours.'

He sank his voice again to a whisper before he finished, and I did not press him to explain. There was already just about as much horror in me as I could hold. The conversation came to an end, and we smoked our pipes busily in silence.

Then something happened, something unimportant apparently, as the way is when the nerves are in a very great state of tension, and this small thing for a brief space gave me an entirely different point of view. I chanced to look down at my sand-shoe – the sort we used for the canoe – and something to do with the hole at the toe suddenly recalled to me the London shop where I had bought them, the difficulty the man had in fitting me, and other details of the uninteresting but practical operation. At once, in its train, followed a wholesome view of the modern sceptical world I was accustomed to move in at home. I thought of roast beef, and ale, motor-cars, policemen, brass bands, and a dozen other things that proclaimed the soul of ordinariness or utility. The effect was immediate and astonishing even to myself. Psychologically, I suppose, it was simply a sudden and violent reaction after the strain of living in an atmosphere of things that to the normal consciousness must seem impossible and incredible. But, whatever the cause, it momentarily lifted the spell from my heart, and left me for the short space of a minute feeling free and utterly unafraid. I looked up at my friend opposite.

'You damned old pagan!' I cried, laughing aloud in his face. 'You imaginative idiot! You superstitious idolater! You –'

I stopped in the middle, seized anew by the old horror. I tried to smother the sound of my voice as something sacrilegious. The Swede, of course, heard it too – the strange cry overhead in the darkness – and that sudden drop in the air as though something had come nearer.

He had turned ashen white under the tan. He stood bolt upright in front of the fire, stiff as a rod, staring at me.

'After that,' he said in a sort of helpless, frantic way, 'we must go! We can't stay now; we must strike camp this very instant and go on – down the river.'

He was talking, I saw, quite wildly, his words dictated by abject terror – the terror he had resisted so long, but which had caught him at last.

'In the dark?' I exclaimed, shaking with fear after my hysterical outburst, but still realising our position better than he did. 'Sheer madness! The river's in flood, and we've only got a single paddle. Besides, we only go deeper into their country! There's nothing ahead for fifty miles but willows, willows, willows!'

He sat down again in a state of semi-collapse. The positions, by one of those kaleidoscopic changes nature loves, were suddenly reversed, and the control of our forces passed over into my hands. His mind at last had reached the point where it was beginning to weaken.

'What on earth possessed you to do such a thing?'

he whispered with the awe of genuine terror in his voice and face.

I crossed round to his side of the fire. I took both his hands in mine, kneeling down beside him and looking straight into his frightened eyes.

'We'll make one more blaze,' I said firmly, 'and then turn in for the night. At sunrise we'll be off full speed for Komorn. Now, pull yourself together a bit, and remember your own advice about *not thinking fear!*'

He said no more, and I saw that he would agree and obey. In some measure, too, it was a sort of relief to get up and make an excursion into the darkness for more wood. We kept close together, almost touching, groping among the bushes and along the bank. The humming overhead never ceased, but seemed to me to grow louder as we increased our distance from the fire. It was shivery work!

We were grubbing away in the middle of a thickish clump of willows where some driftwood from a former flood had caught high among the branches, when my body was seized in a grip that made me half drop upon the sand. It was the Swede. He had fallen against me, and was clutching me for support. I heard his breath coming and going in short gasps.

'Look! By my soul!' he whispered, and for the first time in my experience I knew what it was to hear tears of terror in a human voice. He was pointing to the fire, some fifty feet away. I followed the direction of his finger, and I swear my heart missed a beat.

There, in front of the dim glow, *something was moving.*

I saw it through a veil that hung before my eyes like the gauze drop-curtain used at the back of a theatre – hazily a little. It was neither a human figure nor an animal. To me it gave the strange impression of being as large as several animals grouped together, like horses, two or three, moving slowly. The Swede, too, got a similar result, though expressing it differently, for he thought it was shaped and sized like a clump of willow bushes, rounded at the top, and moving all over upon its surface – 'coiling upon itself like smoke,' he said afterwards.

'I watched it settle downwards through the bushes,' he sobbed at me. 'Look, by God! It's coming this way! Oh, oh!' – he gave a kind of whistling cry. *'They've found us.'*

I gave one terrified glance, which just enabled me to see that the shadowy form was swinging towards us through the bushes, and then I collapsed backwards with a crash into the branches. These failed, of course, to support my weight, so that with the Swede on top of me we fell in a struggling heap upon the sand. I really hardly knew what was happening. I was conscious only of a sort of enveloping sensation of icy fear that plucked the nerves out of their fleshly covering, twisted them this way and that, and replaced them quivering. My eyes were tightly shut; something in my throat choked me; a feeling that my consciousness was expanding, extending out into space, swiftly gave way to another feeling that I was losing it altogether, and about to die.

An acute spasm of pain passed through me, and I was aware that the Swede had hold of me in such a way that he hurt me abominably. It was the way he caught at me in falling.

But it was the pain, he declared afterwards, that saved me; it caused me to *forget them* and think of something else at the very instant when they were about to find me. It concealed my mind from them at the moment of discovery, yet just in time to evade their terrible seizing of me. He himself, he says, actually swooned at the same moment, and that was what saved him.

I only know that at a later date, how long or short is impossible to say, I found myself scrambling up out of the slippery network of willow branches, and saw my companion standing in front of me holding out a hand to assist me. I stared at him in a dazed way, rubbing the arm he had twisted for me. Nothing came to me to say, somehow.

'I lost consciousness for a moment or two,' I heard him say. 'That's what saved me. It made me stop thinking about them.'

'You nearly broke my arm in two,' I said, uttering my only connected thought at the moment. A numbness came over me.

'That's what saved *you!*' he replied. 'Between us, we've managed to set them off on a false tack somewhere. The humming has ceased. It's gone – for the moment at any rate!'

A wave of hysterical laughter seized me again, and this time spread to my friend too – great healing gusts of shaking laughter that brought a tremendous sense of relief in their train. We made our way back to the fire and put the wood on so that it blazed at once. Then we saw that the tent had fallen over and lay in a tangled heap upon the ground.

We picked it up, and during the process tripped more than once and caught our feet in sand.

'It's those sand-funnels,' exclaimed the Swede, when the tent was up again and the firelight lit up the ground for several yards about us. 'And look at the size of them!'

All round the tent and about the fireplace where we had seen the moving shadows there were deep funnel-shaped hollows in the sand, exactly similar to the ones we had already found over the island, only far bigger and deeper, beautifully formed, and wide enough in some instances to admit the whole of my foot and leg.

Neither of us said a word. We both knew that sleep was the safest thing we could do, and to bed we went accordingly without further delay, having first thrown sand on the fire and taken the provision sack and the paddle inside the tent with us. The canoe, too, we propped in such a way at the end of the tent that our feet touched it, and the least motion would disturb and wake us.

In case of emergency, too, we again went to bed in our clothes, ready for a sudden start.

V

It was my firm intention to lie awake all night and watch, but the exhaustion of nerves and body decreed otherwise, and sleep after a while came over me with a welcome blanket of oblivion. The fact that my companion also slept quickened its approach. At first he fidgeted and constantly sat up, asking me if I 'heard this' or 'heard that'. He tossed about on his cork mattress, and said the tent was moving and the river had risen over the point of the island, but each time I went out to look I returned with the report that all was well, and finally he grew calmer and lay still. Then at length his breathing became regular and I heard unmistakable sounds of snoring– the first and only time in my life when snoring has been a welcome and calming influence.

This, I remember, was the last thought in my mind before dozing off.

A difficulty in breathing woke me, and I found the blanket over my face. But something else besides the blanket was pressing upon me, and my first thought was that my companion had rolled off his mattress on to my own in his sleep. I called to him and sat up, and at the same moment it came to me that the tent was *surrounded*. That sound of multitudinous soft pattering was again audible outside, filling the night with horror.

I called again to him, louder than before. He did not answer, but I missed the sound of his snoring, and also noticed that the flap of the tent was down. This was the unpardonable sin. I crawled out in the darkness to hook it back securely, and it was then for the first time I realised positively that the Swede was not here. He had gone.

I dashed out in a mad run, seized by a dreadful agitation, and the moment I was out I plunged into a sort of torrent of humming that surrounded me completely and came out of every quarter of the heavens at once. It was that same familiar humming – gone mad! A swarm of great invisible bees might have been about me in the air. The sound seemed to thicken the very atmosphere, and I felt that my lungs worked with difficulty.

But my friend was in danger, and I could not hesitate.

The dawn was just about to break, and a faint whitish light spread upwards over the clouds from a thin strip of clear horizon. No wind stirred. I could just make out the bushes and river beyond, and the pale sandy patches. In my excitement I ran frantically to and fro about the island, calling him by name, shouting at the top of my voice the first words that came into my head. But the willows smothered my voice, and the humming muffled it, so that the sound only travelled a few feet round me. I plunged among the bushes, tripping headlong, tumbling over roots, and scraping my face as I tore this way and that among the preventing branches.

Then, quite unexpectedly, I came out upon the island's point and saw a dark figure outlined between the water and the sky. It was the Swede. And already he had one foot in the river! A moment more and he would have taken the plunge.

I threw myself upon him, flinging my arms about his waist and dragging him shorewards with all my strength. Of course he struggled furiously, making a noise all the time just like that cursed humming, and using the most outlandish phrases in his anger about 'going *inside* to Them', and 'taking the way of the water and the wind', and God only knows what more besides, that I tried in vain to recall afterwards, but which turned me sick with horror and amazement as I listened. But in the end I managed to get him into the comparative safety of the tent, and flung him breathless and cursing upon the mattress where I held him until the fit had passed.

I think the suddenness with which it all went and he grew calm, coinciding as it did with the equally abrupt cessation of the humming and pattering outside – I think this was almost the strangest part of the whole business perhaps. For he had just opened his eyes and turned his tired face up to me so that the dawn threw a pale light upon it through the doorway, and said, for all the world just like a frightened child:

'My life, old man – it's my life I owe you. But it's all over now anyhow. They've found a victim in our place!'

Then he dropped back upon his blankets and went to sleep literally under my eyes. He simply collapsed, and began to snore again as healthily as though nothing had happened and he had never tried to offer his own life as a sacrifice by drowning. And when the sunlight woke him three hours later – hours of ceaseless vigil for me – it became so clear to me that he remembered absolutely nothing of what he had attempted to do, that I deemed it wise to hold my peace and ask no dangerous questions.

He woke naturally and easily, as I have said, when the sun was already high in a windless hot sky, and he at once got up and set about the preparation of the fire for breakfast. I followed him anxiously at bathing, but he did not attempt to plunge in, merely dipping his head and making some remark about the extra coldness of the water.

'River's falling at last,' he said, 'and I'm glad of it.'

'The humming has stopped too,' I said.

He looked up at me quietly with his normal expression. Evidently he remembered everything except his own attempt at suicide.

'Everything has stopped,' he said, 'because –'

He hesitated. But I knew some reference to that remark he

had made just before he fainted was in his mind, and I was determined to know it.

'Because "they've found another victim"?' I said, forcing a little laugh.

'Exactly,' he answered, 'exactly! I feel as positive of it as though – as though – I feel quite safe again, I mean,' he finished.

He began to look curiously about him. The sunlight lay in hot patches on the sand. There was no wind. The willows were motionless. He slowly rose to feet.

'Come,' he said; 'I think if we look, we shall find it.'

He started off on a run, and I followed him. He kept to the banks, poking with a stick among the sandy bays and caves and little back-waters, myself always close on his heels.

'Ah!' he exclaimed presently, 'ah!'

The tone of his voice somehow brought back to me a vivid sense of the horror of the last twenty-four hours, and I hurried up to join him. He was pointing with his stick at a large black object that lay half in the water and half on the sand. It appeared to be caught by some twisted willow roots so that the river could not sweep it away. A few hours before the spot must have been under water.

'See,' he said quietly, 'the victim that made our escape possible!'

And when I peered across his shoulder I saw that his stick rested on the body of a man. He turned it over. It was the corpse of a peasant, and the face was hidden in the sand. Clearly the man had been drowned, but a few hours before, and his body must have been swept down upon our island somewhere about the hour of the dawn – *at the very time the fit had passed*.

'We must give it a decent burial, you know.'

'I suppose so,' I replied. I shuddered a little in spite of myself, for there was something about the appearance of that poor drowned man that turned me cold.

The Swede glanced up sharply at me, an undecipherable expression on his face, and began clambering down the bank. I followed him more leisurely. The current, I noticed, had torn away much of the clothing from the body, so that the neck and part of the chest lay bare.

Halfway down the bank my companion suddenly stopped and held up his hand in warning; but either my foot slipped, or I had gained too much momentum to bring myself quickly to a halt, for I bumped into him and sent him forward with a sort of leap to save himself. We tumbled together on to the hard sand so that our feet splashed into the water. And, before anything could be done, we had collided a little heavily against the corpse.

The Swede uttered a sharp cry. And I sprang back as if I had been shot.

At the moment we touched the body there rose from its surface the loud sound of humming – the sound of several hummings – which passed with a vast commotion as of winged things in the air about us and disappeared upwards into the sky, growing fainter and fainter till they finally ceased in the distance. It was exactly as though we had disturbed some living yet invisible creatures at work.

My companion clutched me, and I think I clutched him, but before either of us had time properly to recover from the unexpected shock, we saw that a movement of the current was turning the corpse round so that it became released from the grip of the willow roots. A moment later it had turned completely over, the dead face uppermost, staring at the sky. It lay on the edge of the main stream. In another moment it would be swept away.

The Swede started to save it, shouting again something

I did not catch about a 'proper burial' – and then abruptly dropped upon his knees on the sand and covered his eyes with his hands. I was beside him in an instant.

I saw what he had seen.

For just as the body swung round to the current the face and the exposed chest turned full towards us, and showed plainly how the skin and flesh were indented with small hollows, beautifully formed, and exactly similar in shape and kind to the sand-funnels that we had found all over the island.

'Their mark!' I heard my companion mutter under his breath. 'Their awful mark!'

And when I turned my eyes again from his ghastly face to the river, the current had done its work, and the body had been swept away into mid-stream and was already beyond our reach and almost out of sight, turning over and over on the waves like an otter.

4 Caterpillars

BY E F BENSON (1912)

I saw a month or two ago in an Italian paper that the Villa
Cascana, in which I once stayed, had been pulled down, and
that a manufactory of some sort was in process of erection on
its site. There is therefore no longer any reason for refraining
from writing of those things which I myself saw (or imagined
I saw) in a certain room and on a certain landing of the villa
in question, nor from mentioning the circumstances which
followed, which may or may not (according to the opinion
of the reader) throw some light on or be somehow connected
with this experience.

The Villa Cascana was in all ways but one a perfectly
delightful house, yet, if it were standing now, nothing in the
world – I use the phrase in its literal sense – would induce me
to set foot in it again, for I believe it to have been haunted in
a very terrible and practical manner. Most ghosts, when all
is said and done, do not do much harm; they may perhaps
terrify, but the person whom they visit usually gets over their
visitation. They may on the other hand be entirely friendly
and beneficent. But the appearances in the Villa Cascana
were not beneficent, and had they made their 'visit' in a very
slightly different manner, I do not suppose I should have got
over it any more than Arthur Inglis did.

✳

The house stood on an ilex-clad hill not far from Sestri di
Levante on the Italian Riviera, looking out over the iridescent
blues of that enchanted sea, while behind it rose the pale
green chestnut woods that climb up the hillsides till they give
place to the pines that, black in contrast with them, crown

the slopes. All round it the garden in the luxuriance of mid-spring bloomed and was fragrant, and the scent of magnolia and rose, borne on the salt freshness of the winds from the sea, flowed like a stream through the cool vaulted rooms.

On the ground floor a broad pillared *loggia* ran round three sides of the house, the top of which formed a balcony for certain rooms of the first floor. The main staircase, broad and of grey marble steps, led up from the hall to the landing outside these rooms, which were three in number, namely, two big sitting-rooms and a bedroom arranged *en suite*. The latter was unoccupied, the sitting-rooms were in use. From these the main staircase was continued to the second floor, where were situated certain bedrooms, one of which I occupied, while from the other side of the first-floor landing some half-dozen steps led to another suite of rooms, where, at the time I am speaking of, Arthur Inglis, the artist, had his bedroom and studio. Thus the landing outside my bedroom at the top of the house commanded both the landing of the first floor and also the steps that led to Inglis' rooms. Jim Stanley and his wife, finally (whose guest I was), occupied rooms in another wing of the house, where also were the servants' quarters.

I arrived just in time for lunch on a brilliant noon of mid-May. The garden was shouting with colour and fragrance, and not less delightful after my broiling walk up from the *marina*, should have been the coming from the reverberating heat and blaze of the day into the marble coolness of the villa. Only (the reader has my bare word for this, and nothing more), the moment I set foot in the house I felt that something was wrong. This feeling, I may say, was quite vague, though very strong, and I remember that when I saw letters waiting for me on the table in the hall I felt certain that the explanation was here: I was convinced that there was bad news of some sort for me. Yet when I opened them I found no such explanation of my premonition: my correspondents all reeked of prosperity. Yet this clear miscarriage of a presentiment did not dissipate my uneasiness. In that cool fragrant house there was something wrong.

I am at pains to mention this because to the general view it may explain that though I am as a rule so excellent a sleeper that the extinction of my light on getting into bed is apparently contemporaneous with being called on the following morning, I slept very badly on my first night in the Villa Cascana. It may also explain the fact that when I did sleep (if it was indeed in sleep that I saw what I thought I saw) I dreamed in a very vivid and original manner, original, that is to say, in the sense that something that, as far as I knew, had never previously entered into my consciousness, usurped it then. But since, in addition to this evil premonition, certain words and events occurring during the rest of the day might have suggested something of what I thought happened that night, it will be well to relate them.

After lunch, then, I went round the house with Mrs Stanley, and during our tour she referred, it is true, to the unoccupied bedroom on the first floor, which opened out of the room where we had lunched.

'We left that unoccupied,' she said, 'because Jim and I have a charming bedroom and dressing-room, as you saw, in the wing, and if we used it ourselves we should have to turn the dining-room into a dressing-room and have our meals downstairs. As it is, however, we have our little flat there, Arthur Inglis has his little flat in the other passage; and I remembered (aren't I extraordinary?) that you once said that the higher up you were in a house the better you were pleased. So I put you at the top of the house, instead of giving you that room.'

It is true, that a doubt, vague as my uneasy premonition, crossed my mind at this. I did not see why Mrs Stanley should have explained all this, if there had not been more to explain. I allow, therefore, that the thought that there was something to explain about the unoccupied bedroom was momentarily present to my mind.

The second thing that may have borne on my dream was this.

At dinner the conversation turned for a moment on ghosts. Inglis, with the certainty of conviction, expressed his belief that anybody who could possibly believe in the existence of supernatural phenomena was unworthy of the name of an ass. The subject instantly dropped. As far as I can recollect, nothing else occurred or was said that could bear on what follows.

We all went to bed rather early, and personally I yawned my way upstairs, feeling hideously sleepy. My room was rather hot, and I threw all the windows wide, and from without poured in the white light of the moon, and the love-song of many nightingales. I undressed quickly, and got into bed, but though I had felt so sleepy before, I now felt extremely wide-awake. But I was quite content to be awake: I did not toss or turn, I felt perfectly happy listening to the song and seeing the light. Then, it is possible, I may have gone to sleep, and what follows may have been a dream. I thought, anyhow, that after a time the nightingales ceased singing and the moon sank. I thought also that if, for some unexplained reason, I was going to lie awake all night, I might as well read, and I remembered that I had left a book in which I was interested in the dining-room on the first floor. So I got out of bed, lit a candle, and went downstairs. I went into the room, saw on a side-table the book I had come to look for, and then, simultaneously, saw that the door into the unoccupied bedroom was open. A curious grey light, not of dawn nor of moonshine, came out of it, and I looked in. The bed stood just opposite the door, a big four-poster, hung with tapestry at the head. Then I saw that the greyish light of the bedroom came from the bed, or rather from what was on the bed. For it was covered with great caterpillars, a foot or more in length, which crawled over it. They were faintly luminous, and it was the light from them that showed me the room. Instead of the sucker-feet of ordinary caterpillars they had rows of pincers like crabs, and they moved by grasping what they lay on with their pincers, and then sliding their bodies forward. In colour these dreadful insects were yellowish-grey, and they were covered with irregular lumps and swellings. There must have been hundreds of them, for they formed a sort of writhing, crawling pyramid on the bed. Occasionally one fell off on to the floor, with a soft fleshy thud, and though the floor was of hard concrete, it yielded to the pincerfeet as if it had been putty, and, crawling back, the caterpillar would mount on to the bed again, to rejoin its fearful companions. They appeared to have no faces, so to speak, but at one end of them there was a mouth that opened sideways in respiration.

Then, as I looked, it seemed to me as if they all suddenly became conscious of my presence. All the mouths, at any rate, were turned in my direction, and next moment they began dropping off the bed with those soft fleshy thuds on to the floor, and wriggling towards me. For one second a paralysis as of a dream was on me, but the next I was running upstairs again to my room, and I remember feeling the cold of the marble steps on my bare feet. I rushed into my bedroom, and slammed the door behind me, and then – I was certainly wide awake now – I found myself standing by my bed with the sweat of terror pouring from me. The noise of the banged door still rang in my ears. But, as would have been more usual, if this had been mere nightmare, the terror that had been mine when I saw those foul beasts crawling about the bed or dropping softly on to the floor did not cease then. Awake, now, if dreaming before, I did not at all recover from the horror of dream: it did not seem to me that I had dreamed. And until dawn, I sat or stood, not daring to lie down, thinking that every rustle or movement that I heard was the approach of the caterpillars. To them and the claws that bit into the cement the wood of the door was child's play: steel would not keep them out.

But with the sweet and noble return of day the horror vanished: the whisper of wind became benignant again: the nameless fear, whatever it was, was smoothed out and terrified me no longer. Dawn broke, hueless at first; then it grew dove-coloured, then the flaming pageant of light spread over the sky.

✕

The admirable rule of the house was that everybody had breakfast where and when he pleased, and in consequence it was not till lunch-time that I met any of the other members of our party, since I had breakfast on my balcony, and wrote letters and other things till lunch. In fact, I got down to that meal rather late, after the other three had begun. Between my knife and fork there was a small pill-box of cardboard, and as I sat down Inglis spoke.

'Do look at that,' he said, 'since you are interested in natural history. I found it crawling on my counterpane last night, and I don't know what it is.'

I think that before I opened the pill-box I expected something of the sort which I found in it. Inside it, anyhow, was a small caterpillar, greyish-yellow in colour, with curious bumps and excrescences on its rings. It was extremely active, and hurried round the box, this way and that. Its feet were unlike the feet of any caterpillar I ever saw: they were like the pincers of a crab. I looked, and shut the lid down again.

'No, I don't know it,' I said, 'but it looks rather unwholesome. What are you going to do with it?'

'Oh, I shall keep it,' said Inglis. 'It has begun to spin: I want to see what sort of a moth it turns into.'

I opened the box again, and saw that these hurrying movements were indeed the beginning of the spinning of the web of its cocoon. Then Inglis spoke again.

'It has got funny feet, too,' he said. 'They are like crabs' pincers. What's the Latin for crab? Oh, yes, Cancer. So in case it is unique, let's christen it: "Cancer Inglisensis".'

Then something happened in my brain, some momentary piecing together of all that I had seen or dreamed. Something in his words seemed to me to throw light on it all, and my own intense horror at the experience of the night before linked itself on to what he had just said. In effect, I took the box and threw it, caterpillar and all, out of the window. There was a gravel path just outside, and beyond it, a fountain playing into a basin. The box fell on to the middle of this.

Inglis laughed.

'So the students of the occult don't like solid facts,' he said. 'My poor caterpillar!'

The talk went off again at once on to other subjects, and I have only given in detail, as they happened, these trivialities in order to be sure myself that I have recorded everything that could have borne on occult subjects or on the subject of caterpillars. But at the moment when I threw the pill-box into the fountain, I lost my head: my only excuse is that, as is probably plain, the tenant of it was, in miniature, exactly what I had seen crowded on to the bed in the unoccupied room. And though this translation of those phantoms into flesh and blood – or whatever it is that caterpillars are made of – ought perhaps to have relieved the horror of the night, as a matter of fact it did nothing of the kind. It only made the crawling pyramid that covered the bed in the unoccupied room more hideously real.

※

After lunch we spent a lazy hour or two strolling about the garden or sitting in the *loggia*, and it must have been about four o'clock when Stanley and I started off to bathe, down the path that led by the fountain into which I had thrown the pill-box. The water was shallow and clear, and at the bottom of it I saw its white remains. The water had disintegrated the cardboard, and it had become no more than a few strips and shreds of sodden paper. The centre of the fountain was a marble Italian Cupid which squirted the water out of a wine-skin held under its arm. And crawling up its leg was the caterpillar. Strange and scarcely credible as it seemed, it must have survived the falling-to-bits of its prison, and made its way to shore, and there it was, out of arm's reach, weaving and waving this way and that as it evolved its cocoon.

Then, as I looked at it, it seemed to me again that, like the caterpillar I had seen last night, it saw me, and breaking out of the threads that surrounded it, it crawled down the marble leg of the Cupid and began swimming like a snake across the water of the fountain towards me. It came with extraordinary speed (the fact of a caterpillar being able to swim was new to me), and in another moment was crawling up the marble lip of the basin. Just then Inglis joined us.

'Why, if it isn't old "Cancer Inglisensis" again,' he said, catching sight of the beast. 'What a tearing hurry it is in.'

We were standing side by side on the path, and when the caterpillar had advanced to within about a yard of us, it stopped, and began waving again as if in doubt as to the direction in which it should go. Then it appeared to make up its mind, and crawled on to Inglis' shoe.

'It likes me best,' he said, 'but I don't really know that I like it. And as it won't drown I think perhaps –'

He shook it off his shoe on to the gravel path and trod on it.

※

All afternoon the air got heavier and heavier with the Sirocco that was without doubt coming up from the south, and that night again I went up to bed feeling very sleepy; but below my drowsiness, so to speak, there was the consciousness, stronger than before, that there was something wrong in the house, that something dangerous was close at hand. But I fell asleep at once, and – how long after I do not know – either woke or dreamed I awoke, feeling that I must get up at once, *or I should be too late.* Then (dreaming or awake) I lay and fought this fear, telling myself that I was but the prey of my own nerves disordered by Sirocco or what not, and at the same time quite clearly knowing in another part of my mind, so to speak, that every moment's delay added to the danger. At last this second feeling became irresistible, and I put on coat and trousers and went out of my room on to the landing. And then I saw that I had already delayed too long, and that I was now too late.

The whole of the landing of the first floor below was invisible under the swarm of caterpillars that crawled there. The folding doors into the sitting-room from which opened the bedroom where I had seen them last night were shut, but they were squeezing through the cracks of it and dropping one by one through the keyhole, elongating themselves into mere string as they passed, and growing fat and lumpy again on emerging. Some, as if exploring, were nosing about the steps into the passage at the end of which were Inglis' rooms, others were crawling on the lowest steps of the staircase that led up to where I stood. The landing, however, was completely covered with them: I was cut off. And of the frozen horror that seized me when I saw that I can give no idea in words.

※

Then at last a general movement began to take place, and they grew thicker on the steps that led to Inglis' room. Gradually, like some hideous tide of flesh, they advanced along the passage, and I saw the foremost, visible by the pale grey luminousness that came from them, reach his door. Again and again I tried to shout and warn him, in terror all the time that they would turn at the sound of my voice and mount my stair instead, but for all my efforts I felt that no sound came from my throat. They crawled along the hinge-crack of his door, passing through as they had done before, and still I stood there, making impotent efforts to shout to him, to bid him escape while there was time.

✳

At last the passage was completely empty: they had all gone, and at that moment I was conscious for the first time of the cold of the marble landing on which I stood barefooted. The dawn was just beginning to break in the eastern sky.

✳

Six months after I met Mrs Stanley in a country house in England. We talked on many subjects and at last she said:

'I don't think I have seen you since I got that dreadful news about Arthur Inglis a month ago.'

'I haven't heard,' said I.

'No? He has got cancer. They don't even advise an operation, for there is no hope of a cure: he is riddled with it, the doctors say.'

Now during all these six months I do not think a day had passed on which I had not had in my mind the dreams (or whatever you like to call them) which I had seen in the Villa Cascana.

'It is awful, is it not?' she continued, 'and I feel I can't help feeling, that he may have —'

'Caught it at the villa?' I asked.

She looked at me in blank surprise.

'Why did you say that?' she asked. 'How did you know?' Then she told me. In the unoccupied bedroom a year before there had been a fatal case of cancer. She had, of course, taken the best advice and had been told that the utmost dictates of prudence would be obeyed so long as she did not put anybody to sleep in the room, which had also been thoroughly disinfected and newly white-washed and painted. But –

5 The Bad Lands

BY JOHN METCALFE (1920)

It is now perhaps fifteen years ago that Brent Ormerod, seeking the rest and change of scene that should help him to slay the demon neurosis, arrived in Todd towards the close of a mid-October day. A decrepit fly bore him to the one hotel, where his rooms were duly engaged, and it is this vision of himself sitting in the appalling vehicle that makes him think it was October or thereabouts, for he distinctly remembers the determined settling down of the dusk that forced him to drive when he would have preferred to follow his luggage on foot.

He decided immediately that five o'clock was an unsuitable time to arrive in Todd. The atmosphere, as it were, was not receptive. There was a certain repellent quality about the frore autumn air, and something peculiarly shocking in the way in which desultory little winds would spring up in darkening streets to send the fallen leaves scurrying about in hateful, furtive whirlpools.

Dinner, too, at the hotel hardly brought the consolation he had counted on. The meal itself was unexceptionable, and the room cheerful and sufficiently well filled for that time of year, yet one trivial circumstance was enough to send him upstairs with his temper ruffled and his nerves on edge. They had put him to a table with a one-eyed man, and that night the blank eye haunted all his dreams.

But for the first eight or nine days at Todd things went fairly well with him. He took frequent cold baths and regular exercise and made a point of coming back to the hotel so physically tired that to get into bed was usually to drop immediately into sleep. He wrote back to his sister Joan, at

Kensington, that his nerves were already much improved and that only another fortnight seemed needed to complete the cure. 'Altogether a highly satisfactory week.'

Those who have been to Todd remember it as a quiet, secretive watering-place, couched watchfully in a fold of a long range of low hills along the Norfolk coast. It has been pronounced 'restful' by those in high authority, for time there has a way of passing dreamily as if the days, too, were being blown past like the lazy clouds on the wings of wandering breezes. At the back, the look of the land is somehow strangely forbidding, and it is wiser to keep to the shore and the more neighbouring villages. Salterton, for instance, has been found quite safe and normal.

There are long stretches of sand dunes to the west, and by their side a nine-hole golf-course. Here, at the time of Brent's visit, stood an old and crumbling tower, an enigmatic structure which he found interesting from its sheer futility. Behind it an inexplicable road seemed to lead with great decision most uncomfortably to nowhere … Todd, he thought, was in many ways a nice spot, but he detected in it a tendency to grow on one unpleasantly.

He came to this conclusion at the end of the ninth day, for it was then that he became aware of a peculiar uneasiness, an indescribable malaise.

This feeling of disquiet he at first found himself quite unable to explain or analyse. His nerves he had thought greatly improved since he had left Kensington, and his general health was good. He decided, however, that perhaps yet more exercise was necessary, and so he walked along the links and the sand dunes to the queer tower and the inexplicable road that lay behind it three times a day instead of twice.

His discomfort rapidly increased. He would become conscious, as he set out for his walk, of a strange sinking at his heart and of a peculiar moral disturbance which was very difficult to describe. These sensations attained their maximum when he had reached his goal upon the dunes, and he suffered then what something seemed to tell him was very near the pangs of spiritual dissolution.

It was on the eleventh day that some faint hint of the meaning of these peculiar symptoms crossed his mind. For the first time he asked himself why it was that of all the many rambles he had taken in Todd since his arrival each one seemed inevitably to bring him to the same place – the yellow sand dunes with the mysterious looking tower in the background. Something in the bland foolishness of the structure seemed to have magnetised him, and in the unaccountable excitement which the sight of it invariably produced, he had found himself endowing it with almost human characteristics.

With its white nightcap dome and its sides of pale yellow stucco it might seem at one moment to be something extravagantly ridiculous, a figure of fun at which one should laugh and point. Then, as likely as not, its character would change a little, and it would take on the abashed and crestfallen look of a jester whose best joke has fallen deadly flat, while finally, perhaps, it would develop with startling rapidity into a jovial old gentleman laughing madly at Ormerod from the middle distance out of infinite funds of merriment.

Now Brent was well aware of the dangers of an obsession such as this, and he immediately resolved to rob the tower of its unwholesome fascination by simply walking straight up to it, past it, and onwards along the road that stretched behind it.

It was on the morning of one of the last October days that he set out from the hotel with this intention in his mind. He reached the dunes at about ten, and plodded with some difficulty across them in the direction of the tower. As he neared it his accustomed sensations became painfully apparent, and presently increased to such a pitch that it was all he could do to continue on his way.

He remembered being struck again with the peculiar character of the winding road that stretched before him into a hazy distance where everything seemed to melt and swim in shadowy vagueness. On his left the gate stood open, to his right the grotesque form of the tower threatened …

Now he had reached it, and its shadow fell straight across his path. He did not halt to examine it, but strode forward through the open gate and entered upon the winding road. At the same moment he was astonished to notice that the painful clutch at his heart was immediately lifted, and that with it, too, all the indescribable uneasiness which he had characterised to himself as 'moral' had utterly disappeared.

He had walked on for some little distance before another rather remarkable fact struck his attention. The country was no longer vague; rather, it was peculiarly distinct, and he was able to see for long distances over what seemed considerable stretches of park-like land, grey, indeed, in tone and somehow sad with a most poignant melancholy, yet superficially, at least, well cultivated and in some parts richly timbered. He looked behind him to catch a glimpse of Todd and of the sea, but was surprised to find that in that direction the whole landscape was become astonishingly indistinct and shadowy.

It was not long before the mournful aspect of the country about him began so to depress him and work upon his nerves that he debated with himself the advisability of returning at once to the hotel. He found that the ordinary, insignificant things about him were becoming charged with sinister suggestion and that the scenery on all sides was rapidly developing an unpleasant tendency to the *macabre*. Moreover his watch told him that it was now half-past eleven – and lunch was at one. Almost hastily he turned about and began to descend the winding road.

It was about an hour later that he again reached the tower and saw the familiar dunes stretching once more before him. For some reason or other he seemed to have found the way back much longer and more difficult than the outward journey, and it was with a feeling of distinct relief that he actually passed through the gate and set his face towards Todd.

He did not go out again that afternoon, but sat smoking and thinking in the hotel. In the lounge he spoke to a man who sat in a chair beside him.

'What a queer place that is all at the back there behind the dunes!'

His companion's only comment was a somewhat drowsy grunt.

'Behind the tower,' pursued Ormerod, 'the funny tower at the other end of the links. The most God-forsaken, dismal place you can imagine. And simply miles of it!'

The other, roused to coherence much against his will, turned slowly round.

'Don't know it,' he said. 'There's a large farm where you say, and the other side of that is a river, and then you come to Harkaby or somewhere.'

He closed his eyes and Ormerod was left to ponder the many difficulties of his remarks.

At dinner he found a more sympathetic listener. Mr Stanton-Boyle had been in Todd a week when Brent arrived, and his sensitive, young-old face with the eager eyes and the quick, nervous contraction of the brows had caught the newcomer's attention from the first. Up to now, indeed, they had only exchanged commonplaces, but to-night each seemed more disposed towards intimacy. Ormerod began.

'I suppose you've walked around the country at the back here a good deal?' he said.

'No,' replied the other. 'I never go there now. I went there once or twice and that was enough.'

'Why?'

'Oh, it gets on my nerves, that's all. Do you get any golf here …?'

The conversation passed to other subjects, and it was not until both were smoking together over liqueur brandies in the lounge that it returned to the same theme. And then they came to a remarkable conclusion.

'The country at the back of this place,' said Brent's companion, 'is somehow abominable. It ought to be blown up or something. I don't say it was always like that. Last year, for instance, I don't remember noticing it at all. I fancy it may have been depressing enough, but it was not – not abominable. It's gone abominable since then, particularly to the south-west!'

They said good-night after agreeing to compare notes on Todd, SW, and Ormerod had a most desolating dream wherein he walked up and up into a strange dim country, full of sighs and whisperings and crowding, sombre trees, where hollow breezes blew fitfully, and a queer house set with lofty pine shone out white against a lurid sky …

On the next day he walked again past the tower and through the gate and along the winding road. As he left Todd behind him and began the slow ascent among the hills he became conscious of some strange influence that hung over the country like a brooding spirit. The clearness of the preceding day was absent; instead, all seemed nebulous and indistinct, and the sad landscape dropped behind and below him in the numb, unreal recession of a dream.

It was about four o'clock, and as he slowly ascended into the mournful tracts the greyness of the late autumn day was deepening into dusk. All the morning, clouds had been gathering in the west, and now the dull ache of the damp sky gave the uneasy sense of impending rain. Here a fitful wind blew the gold flame of a sere leaf athwart the November gloom, and out along the horizon great leaden masses were marching out to sea.

A terrible sense of loneliness fell upon the solitary walker trudging up into the sighing country, and even the sight of scattered habitations, visible here and there among the shadows, seemed only to intensify his feeling of dream and unreality. Everywhere the uplands strained in the moist wind, and the lines of gaunt firs that marched against the horizon gloom pointed ever out to sea. The wan crowding on of the weeping heavens, the settled pack of those leaning firs, and the fitful scurry of the leaves in the chill blast down the lane smote upon his spirit as something unutterably sad and terrible. On his right a skinny blackthorn shot up hard and wiry towards the dull, grey sky; there ahead trees in a wood fluttered ragged, yellow flags against the dimness.

A human figure appeared before him, and presently he saw that it was a man, apparently a labourer. He carried tools upon his shoulders, and his head was bent so that it was only when Ormerod addressed him that he looked up and showed a withered countenance. 'What is the name of all this place?' said Brent, with a wide sweep of his arm.

'This,' said the labourer, in a voice so thin and tired that it seemed almost like the cold breath of the wind that drove beside them, 'is Hayes-in-the-Up. Of course, though, it'll be a mile further on for you before you get to Fennington.' He pointed in the direction from which he had just come, turned his sunken eyes again for a moment upon Ormerod, and then quickly faded down the descending path.

Brent looked after him wondering, but as he swept his gaze about him much of his wonder vanished. All around, the wan country seemed to rock giddily beneath those lowering skies, so heavy with the rain that never fell; all around, the sailing uplands seemed to heave and yearn under the sad tooting of the damp November wind. Oh, he could well imagine that the men of this weary, twilight region would be worn and old before their time, with its sinister stare in their eyes and its haggard gloom abroad in their pinched faces!

Thinking thus, he walked on steadily, and it was not long before certain words of the man he had met rose with uneasy suggestion to the surface of his mind. What, he asked himself, was Fennington? Somehow he did not think that the name stood for another village; rather, the word seemed to connect itself ominously with the dream he had had some little time ago. He shuddered, and had not walked many paces further before he found that his instinct was correct.

Opposite him, across a shallow valley, stood that white house, dimly set in giant pines. Here the winds seemed almost visible as they strove in those lofty trees and the constant rush by of the weeping sky behind made all the view seem to tear giddily through some unreal, watery medium. A striking resemblance of the pines to palm-trees and a queer effect of light which brought the white facade shaking bright against the sailing cloud-banks gave the whole a strangely exotic look.

Gazing at it across the little valley, Ormerod felt somehow that this, indeed, was the centre and hub of the wicked country, the very kernel and essence of this sad, unwholesome land that he saw flung wide in weariness about him. This abomination was it that magnetised him, that attracted him from afar with fatal fascination, and threatened him with untold disaster. Almost sobbing, he descended his side of the valley and then rose again to meet the house.

Park-like land surrounded the building, and from the smooth turf arose the pines and some clusters of shrubs. Amongst these Ormerod walked carefully till he was suddenly so near that he could look into a small room through its open window whilst he sheltered in a large yew whose dusky skirts swept the ground.

The room seemed strangely bare and deserted. A small table was pushed to one side, and dust lay thick upon it. Nearer Ormerod a chair or two appeared, and, opposite, a great black mantelpiece glowered in much gloom. In the centre of the floor was set the object that seemed to dominate the whole.

This was a large and cumbrous spinning-wheel of forbidding mien. It glistened foully in the dim light, and its many moulded points pricked the air in very awful fashion. Waiting there in the close stillness, the watcher fancied he could see the treadle stir. Quickly, with beating heart, beset by sudden dread, he turned away, retraced his steps among the sheltering shrubs, and descended to the valley bottom.

He climbed up the other side, and was glad to walk rapidly away down the winding path till, on turning his head, it was no longer possible to see the evil house he had just left.

It must have been near six o'clock when, on approaching the gate and tower, weary from his walk and anxious to reach the familiar and reassuring atmosphere of the hotel, he came suddenly upon a man walking through the darkness in the same direction as himself. It was Stanton-Boyle.

Ormerod quickly overtook him and spoke. 'You have no idea,' he said, 'how glad I am to see you. We can walk back together now.'

As they strolled to the hotel Brent described his walk, and he saw the other trembling. Presently Stanton-Boyle looked at him earnestly and spoke. 'I've been there too,' he said, 'and I feel just as you do about it. I feel that that place Fennington is the centre of the rottenness. I looked through the window, too, and saw the spinning-wheel and' He stopped suddenly. 'No,' he went on quietly a moment later, 'I won't tell you what else I saw!'

'It ought to be destroyed!' shouted Ormerod. A curious excitement tingled in his blood. His voice was loud, so that people passing them in the street turned and gazed after them. His eyes were very bright. He went on, pulling Stanton-Boyle's arm impressively. 'I shall destroy it!' he said. 'I shall burn it and I shall most assuredly smash that old spinning-wheel and break off its horrid spiky points!' He had a vague sense of saying curious and unusual things, but this increased rather than moderated his unaccountable elation.

Stanton-Boyle seemed somewhat abnormal too. He seemed to be gliding along the pavement with altogether unexampled smoothness and nobility as he turned his glowing eyes on Brent. 'Destroy it!' he said. 'Burn it! Before it is too late and it destroys you. Do this and you will be an unutterably brave man!'

When they reached the hotel Ormerod found a telegram awaiting him from Joan. He had not written to her for some time and she had grown anxious and was coming down herself on the following day. He must act quickly, before she came, for her mind in this matter would be unsympathetic. That night as he parted from Stanton-Boyle his eyes blazed in a high resolve. 'Tomorrow,' he said, as he shook the other's hand, 'I shall attempt it.'

The following morning found the neurotic as good as his word. He carried matches and a tin of oil. His usually pale cheeks were flushed and his eyes sparkled strangely. Those who saw him leave the hotel remembered afterwards how his limbs had trembled and his speech halted. Stanton-Boyle, who was to see him off at the tower, reflected these symptoms in a less degree. Both men were observed to set out arm-in-arm engaged in earnest conversation.

At about noon Stanton-Boyle returned. He had walked with Ormerod to the sand dunes, and there left him to continue on his strange mission alone. He had seen him pass the tower, strike the fatal gate in the slanting morning sun, and then dwindle up the winding path till he was no more than an intense, pathetic dot along that way of mystery.

As he returned he was aware of companionship along the street. He looked round and noticed a policeman strolling in much abstraction some fifty yards behind him. Again at the hotel-entrance he turned about. The same figure in blue uniform was visible, admiring the houses opposite from the shade of an adjacent lamp-post. Stanton-Boyle frowned and withdrew to lunch.

At half-past two Joan arrived. She inquired nervously for Ormerod, and was once addressed by Stanton-Boyle, who had waited for her in the entrance hall as desired by Brent. 'Mr Ormerod,' he told her, 'is out. He is very sorry. Will you allow me the impropriety of introducing myself? My name is Stanton-Boyle …'

Joan tore open the note which had been left for her by Ormerod. She seemed to find the contents unsatisfactory, for she proceeded to catechise Stanton-Boyle upon her brother's health and general habit of life at Todd. Following this she left the hotel hastily after ascertaining the direction from which Ormerod might be expected to return.

Stanton-Boyle waited. The moments passed, heavy, anxious, weighted with the sense of coming trouble. He sat and smoked. Discreet and muffled noises from within the hotel seemed full somehow of uneasy suggestion and foreboding. Outside, the street looked very gloomy in the November darkness. Something, assuredly, would happen directly.

It came, suddenly. A sound of tramping feet and excited cries that grew rapidly in volume and woke strange echoes in the reserved autumnal roads. Presently the tumult lessened abruptly, and only broken, fitful shouts and staccato ejaculations stabbed the silence. Stanton-Boyle jumped to his feet and walked hurriedly to the entrance hall.

Here there were cries and hustlings and presently strong odours and much suppressed excitement. He saw Joan talking very quickly to the manager of the hotel. She seemed to be developing a Point-of-View, and it was evident that it was not the manager's. For some time the press of people prevented him from discovering the cause of the commotion, but here and there he could make out detached sentences:

'Tried to set old Hackney's farm on fire.' – 'But they'd seen him before and another man too, so …' – 'Asleep in the barn several times.'

Before long, all but the hotel residents had dispersed, and in the centre of the considerable confusion which still remained it was now possible to see Ormerod supported by two policemen. A third hovered in the background with a large notebook. As Stanton-Boyle gazed, Brent lifted his bowed head so that their eyes met. 'I have done it,' he said. 'I smashed it up. I brought back one of its points in my pocket … Overcoat, left hand … as a proof.' Having pronounced which words Mr Ormerod fainted very quietly.

For some time there was much disturbance. The necessary arrangements for the temporary pacification of the Law and of the Hotel had to be earned through, and after that Ormerod had to be got to bed. It was only after the initial excitement had in large measure abated that Stanton-Boyle ventured to discuss the matter over the after-dinner coffee. He had recognised one of the three policemen as the man whom he had noticed in the morning, and had found it well to retire from observation until he and his companions had left the hotel. Now, however, he felt at liberty to explain his theories of the situation to such as chose to listen.

He held forth with peculiar vehemence and with appropriate gestures. He spoke of a new kind of *terre-mauvaise*, of strange regions, connected, indeed, with definite geographical limits upon the earth, yet somehow apart from them and beyond them. 'The relation,' he said, 'is rather one of parallelism and correspondence than of actual connection. I honestly believe that these regions do exist, and are quite as "real" in their way as the ordinary world we know. We might say they consist in a special and separated set of stimuli to which only certain minds in certain conditions are able to respond. Such a district seems to be superimposed upon the country to the south-west of this place.'

A laugh arose. 'You won't get the magistrate to believe that,' said someone. 'Why, all where you speak of past that gate by the dunes is just old Hackney's farm and nothing else.'

'Of course,' said another. 'It was one of old Hackney's barns he was setting alight, I understand. I was speaking to one of the policemen about it. He said that fellow Ormerod had always been fossicking around there, and had gone to sleep in the barn twice. I expect it's all bad dreams.'

A third spoke derisively. 'Surely,' he said, 'you don't really expect us to believe in your Bad Lands. It's like Jack-in-the-Beanstalk.'

'All right!' said Stanton-Boyle. 'Have it your own way! I know my use of the term "Bad Lands" may be called incorrect, because it usually means that bit in the States, you know – but that's a detail. I tell you I've run up against things like this before. There was the case of Dolly Wishart, but no, I won't say anything about that – you wouldn't believe it.'

The group around looked at him oddly. Suddenly there was a stir, and a man appeared in the doorway. He carried Ormerod's overcoat.

'This may settle the matter,' he said. 'I heard him say he'd put something in the pocket. He said –'

Stanton-Boyle interrupted him excitedly. 'Why, yes,' he said. 'I'd forgotten that. What I was telling you about the spinning-wheel. It will be interesting to see if –' He stopped and fumbled in the pockets. In another moment he brought out something which he held in his extended hand for all to see.

It was part of the handle of a patent separator – an object familiar enough to any who held even meagre acquaintance with the life of farms, and upon it could still be discerned the branded letters G P H.

'George Philip Hackney,' interpreted the unbelievers with many smiles.

6 Randalls Round

BY ELEANOR SCOTT (1929)

'Of course, I don't pretend to be aesthetic and all that,' said Heyling in that voice of half contemptuous indifference that often marks the rivalry between Science and Art, 'but I must say that this folk-song and dance business strikes me as pretty complete rot. I dare say there may be some arguments in favour of it for exercise and that, but I'm dashed if I can see why a chap need leap about in fancy braces because he wants to train down his fat.'

He lit a cigarette disdainfully.

'All revivals are a bit artificial, I expect,' said Mortlake in his quiet, pleasant voice, 'but it's not a question of exercise only in this case, you know. People who know say that it's the remains of a religious cult – sacrificial rites and that. There certainly are some very odd things done in out-of-the-way places.'

'How d'you mean?' asked Heyling, unconvinced. 'You can't really think that there's any kind of heathen cult still practised in this country?'

'Well,' said Mortlake, 'there's not much left now. More in Wales, I believe, and France, than here. But I believe that if we could find a place where people had never lost the cult, we might run into some queer things. There are a few places like that,' he went on, 'places where they're said to perform their own rite occasionally. I mean to look it up some time. By the way,' he added, suddenly sitting upright, 'didn't you say you were going to a village called Randalls for the weekend?'

'Yes – little place in the Cotswolds somewhere. Boney gave me an address.'

'Going to work, or for an easy?'

'Not to work. Boney's afraid of my precious health. He thinks I'm overworking my delicate constitution.'

'Well, if you've the chance, I wish you'd take a look at the records in the old Guildhall there and see if you can find any references to folk customs. Randalls is believed to be one of the places where there is a genuine survival. They have a game I think, or a dance, called Randalls Round. I'd very much like to know if there are any written records – anything definite. Not if you're bored you know, or don't want to. Just if you're at a loose end.'

'Right, I will,' said Heyling; and there the talk ended.

It is unusual for Oxford undergraduates to take a long weekend off in the Michaelmas term with the permission of the college authorities; but Heyling, from whom his tutor expected great things, had certainly been reading too hard. The weather that autumn was unusually close and clammy, even for Oxford; and Heyling was getting into such a state of nerves that he was delighted to take the chance of getting away from Oxford for the weekend.

The weather, as he cycled out along the Woodstock Road, was moist and warm; but as the miles slipped by and the ground rose, he became aware of the softness of the air, the pleasant lines of the bare, sloping fields, the quiet of the low, rolling clouds. Already he felt calmer, more at ease.

The lift of the ground became more definite, and the character of the country changed. It became more open, bleaker; it had something of the quality of moorland, and the little scattered stone houses had that air of being one with the earth that is the right of moorland houses.

Randalls was, as Heyling's tutor had told him, quite a small place, though it had once boasted a market. Round a little square space, grass-grown now, where once droves of patient cattle and flocks of shaggy Cotswold sheep had stood to be sold, were grouped houses, mostly of the seventeenth or early eighteenth century, made of the beautiful mellow stone of the Cotswolds; and Heyling noticed among these one building of exceptional beauty, earlier in date than the others, long and low, with a deep square porch and mullioned windows.

'That's the Guildhall Mortlake spoke of I expect,' he said to himself as he made his way to the Flaming Hand Inn, where his quarters were booked. 'Quite a good place to look up town records. Queer how that sort of vague rot gets hold of quite sensible men.'

Heyling received a hearty welcome at the inn. Visitors were not very frequent at that time of year, for Randalls is rather far from the good hunting country. Even a chance weekender was something of an event. Heyling was given a quite exceptionally nice room (or rather, a pair of rooms – for two communicated with one another) on the ground floor. The front one, looking out on to the old square, was furnished as a sitting-room; the other gave onto the inn yard, a pleasant cobbled place surrounded by a moss-grown wall and barns with beautiful lichened roofs. Heyling began to feel quite cheerful and vigorous as he lit his pipe and prepared to spend a lazy evening.

As he was settling down in his chair with one of the inn's scanty supply of very dull novels, he was mildly surprised to hear children's voices chanting outside. He reflected that Guy Fawkes' Day was not due yet, and that in any case the tune they sang was not the formless huddle usually produced on that august occasion. This was a real melody – rather an odd, plaintive air, ending with an abrupt drop that pleased his ear. Little as he knew folk-lore, and much as he despised it, Heyling could not but recognise that this was a genuine folk air, and a very attractive one.

The children did not appear to be begging; their song finished, they simply went away; but Heyling was surprised when some minutes later he heard the same air played again, this time on a flute or flageolet. There came also the sound of many feet in the market square. It was evident that the whole population had turned out to see some sight. Mildly interested, Heyling rose and lounged across to the bay window of his room.

The tiny square was thronged with villagers, all gazing at an empty space left in the centre. At one end of this space stood a man playing on a long and curiously sweet pipe: he played the same haunting plaintive melody again and again. In the very centre stood a pole, as a maypole stands in some villages; but instead of garlands and ribbons, this pole had flung over it the shaggy hide of some creature like an ox. Heyling could just see the blunt heavy head with its short thick horns. Then, without a word or a signal, men came out from among the watchers and began a curious dance.

Heyling had seen folk-dancing done in Oxford, and he recognised some of the features of the dance; but it struck him as being a graver, more barbaric affair than the performances he had seen before. It was almost solemn.

As he watched, the dancers began a figure that he recognised. They took hands in a ring, facing outwards; then, with their hands lifted, they began to move slowly round, counter-clockwise. Memory stirred faintly, and two things came drifting into Heyling's mind: one, the sound of Mortlake's voice as the two men had stood watching a performance of the Headington Mummers – 'That's the Back Ring. It's supposed to be symbolic of death – a survival of a time when a dead victim lay in the middle and the dancers turned away from him.' The other memory was dimmer, for he could not remember who had told him that to move in a circle counter-clockwise was unlucky. It must have been a Scot, though, for he remembered the word 'widdershins.'

These faint stirrings of memory were snapped off by a sudden movement in the dance going on outside. Two new figures advanced – one a man, whose head was covered by a mask made in the rough likeness of a bull; the other shrouded from head to foot in a white sheet, so that even the sex was indistinguishable. Without a sound these two came into the space left in the centre of the dance. The bull-headed man placed the second figure with its back to the pole where hung the hide. The dancers moved more and more slowly. Evidently some crisis of the dance was coming.

Suddenly the bull-headed man jerked the pole so that the shaggy hide fell outspread on the shrouded figure standing before it. It gave a horrid impression – as if the creature hanging limp on the pole had suddenly come to life, and with one swift, terrible movement had engulfed and devoured the helpless victim standing passively before it.

Heyling felt quite shocked – startled, as if he ought to do something. He even threw the window open, as though he meant to spring out and stop the horrid rite. Then he drew back, laughing a little at his own folly. The dance had come to an end: the bull-headed man had lifted the hide from the shrouded figure and thrown it carelessly over his shoulder. The flute-player had stopped his melody, and the crowd was melting away.

'What a queer performance!' said Heyling to himself. 'I see now what old Mortlake means. It does look like a survival of some sort. Where's that book of his?'

He rummaged in his rucksack and produced a book that Mortlake had lent him – one volume of a very famous book on folk-lore. There were many accounts of village games and 'feasts', all traced in a sober and scholarly fashion to some barbaric, primitive rite. He was interested to see how often mention was made of animal masks, or of the hides or tails of animals being worn by performers in these odd revels. There was nothing fantastic or strained in these accounts – nothing of the romantic type that Heyling scornfully dubbed 'aesthetic'. They were as careful and well authenticated as the facts in a scientific treatise. Randalls was mentioned, and the dance described – rather scantily, Heyling thought, until, reading on, he found that the author acknowledged that he had not himself seen it, but was indebted to a friend for the account of it. But Heyling found something that interested him.

'The origin of this dance,' he read, 'is almost certainly sacrificial. Near Randalls is one of those 'banks' or mounds, surrounded by a thicket, which the villagers refuse to approach. These mounds are not uncommon in the Cotswolds, though few seem to be regarded with quite as much awe as Randalls Bank, which the country people avoid scrupulously. The bank is oval in shape, and is almost certainly formed by a long barrow of the Paleolithic age. This theory is borne out by the fact that at one time the curious Randalls Round was danced about the mound, the 'victim' being led into the fringe of the thicket that surrounds it.' (A footnote added, 'Whether this is still the case I cannot be certain.') 'Permission to open the tumulus has always been most firmly refused.'

'That's amusing,' thought Heyling, as he laid down the book and felt for a match. 'Jove, what a lark it would be to get into that barrow!' he went on, drawing at his pipe. 'Wonder if I could get leave? The villagers seem to have changed their ways a bit – they do their show in the village now. They mayn't be so set on their blessed mound as they used to be. Where exactly is the place?'

He drew out an ordnance map, and soon found it – a field about a mile and a half north-west of the village, with the word 'Tumulus' in Gothic characters.

'I'll have a look at that tomorrow,' Heyling told himself, folding up the map. 'I must find out who owns the field, and get leave to investigate a bit. The landlord would know who the owner is, I expect.'

Unfortunately for Heyling's plans, the next day dawned wet, although occasional gleams gave hope that the weather would clear later. His interest had not faded during the night, and he determined that as soon as the weather was a little better he would cycle out to Randalls Bank and have a look at it. Meanwhile, it might not be a bad plan to see whether the Guildhall held any records that might throw a light on his search as Mortlake had suggested. He accordingly hunted out a worthy who was, among many other offices, Town Clerk, and was led by him to the fifteenth century building he had noticed on his way to the Flaming Hand.

It was very cool and dark inside the old Guildhall. The atmosphere of the place pleased Heyling; he liked the simple groining of the roof and the worn stone stair that led up to the Record Room. This was a low, pleasant place, with deep windows and a singularly beautiful ceiling; Heyling noticed that it also served the purpose of a small reference library.

While the Town Clerk pottered with keys in the locks of chests and presses, Heyling idly examined the titles of the books ranged decorously on the shelves about the room. His eye was caught by the title, 'Prehistoric Remains in the Cotswolds'. He took the volume down. There was an opening chapter dealing with prehistoric remains in general, and, glancing through it, he saw mentions of long and round barrows. He kept the book in his hand for closer inspection. He really knew precious little about barrows, and it would be just as well to find out a little before beginning his exploration. In fact, when the Town Clerk left him alone in the Record Room, that book was the first thing he studied.

It was a mere text-book, after all, but to Heyling's ignorance it revealed a few facts of interest. Long barrows, he gathered, were older than round, and more uncommon, and were often objects of superstitious awe among the country folk of the district, who generally opposed any effort to explore them;

but the whole chapter was very brief and skimpy, and Heyling had soon exhausted its interest.

The town records, however, were more amusing, for he very soon found references to his particular field. There was a lawsuit in the early seventeenth century which concerned it, and the interest to Heyling was redoubled by the vagueness of certain evidence. A certain Beale brought charges of witchcraft against 'diuers Persouns of ys Towne'. He had reason for alarm, for apparently his son, 'a yong and comely Lad of 20ann', had completely disappeared: 'wherefore ye sd. Jno. Beale didd openlie declare and state yt ye sd. Son Frauncis hadd been led away by Warlockes in ye Daunce (for yt his Ringe, ye wh. he hadd long worne, was found in ye Fielde wh. ye wot of) and hadd by ym beene done to Deathe in yr Abhominable Practicinges'. The case seemed to have been hushed up, although several people cited by 'ye sd. Jno. Beale' admitted having been in the company of the missing youth on the night of his disappearance – which, Heyling was interested to notice, was that very day, 31st October.

Another document, of a later date, recorded the attempted sale of the 'field wh. ye wot of' – (no name was ever given to the place) – and the refusal of the purchaser to fulfil his contract owing to 'ye ill repute of the place, the wh. was unknowen to Himm when he didd entre into his Bargayn'.

The only other documents of interest to Heyling were some of the seventeenth century, wherein the authorities of the Commonwealth inveighed against 'ye Lewd Games and Dauncyng, ye wh. are Seruice to Sathanas and a moste strong Abhominatioun to ye Lorde'. These spoke openly of devil worship and 'loathlie Ceremonie at ye Banke in ye Fielde'. It seemed that more than one person had stood trial for conducting these ceremonies, and against one case (dated 7th November, 1659) was written, *'Conuicti et combusti.'*

'Good Lord – burnt!' exclaimed Heyling aloud. 'What an

appalling business! I suppose the poor beggars were only doing much the same thing as those chaps I saw yesterday.'

He sat lost in thought for some time. He thought how that odd tune and dance had gone on in this remote village for centuries; had there been more to it once, he wondered? Did that queer business with the hide mean – well, some real devilry? Pictures floated into his mind – odd, squat little men, broad of shoulder and long of arm, naked and hairy, dancing in solemn, ghastly worship, dim ages ago ... This business was getting a stronger hold of him than he would have thought possible.

'Strikes me that if there is anything of the old devilry left, it'll be in that field,' he concluded at last. 'The dance they do now is all open and above board; but if they still avoid the field, as that book of Mortlake's seems to think, that might be a clue. I'll find out.'

He rose and went down to inform the Town Clerk that his researches were over, and then went back to the inn in a comfortable frame of mind. Certainly his weekend was bringing him distraction from his work: no thought of it had entered his head since he first heard the children singing outside the inn.

The landlord of the Flaming Hand was a solid man who gave the impression of honesty and sense. Heyling felt that he could depend upon him for a reasonable account of 'the fielde which ye wot of'. He accordingly tackled him after lunch, and was at once amused, surprised and annoyed to find that the man hedged as soon as he was questioned on the subject. He quite definitely opposed any idea of exploration.

'I'm not like some on 'em, sir,' he said. 'I wouldn't go for to say that it'd do any 'arm for you to take a turn in the field while it was light, like. But it ain't 'ealthy after dark, sir, that field aren't. Nor it ain't no sense to go a-diggin' and a-delvin' in that there bank. I've lived in this 'ere place a matter of forty year, man and boy, and I know what I'm a-sayin' of.'

'But why isn't it healthy? Is it marshy?'

'No, sir, it ain't not to say marshy.'

'Don't the farmers ever cultivate it?'

'Well, sir, all I can say is I been in this place forty year, man and boy, and it ain't never been dug nor ploughed nor sown nor reaped in my mem'ry. Nor yet in my father's, nor in my grandfather's. Crops wouldn' do, sir, not in that field.'

'Well, I want to go and examine the mound. Who's the owner? – I ought to get his leave, I suppose.'

'You won't do that, sir.'

'Why not?'

"Cause I'm the owner, sir, and I won't 'ave anyone, not the King 'isself nor yet the King's son, a-diggin' in that bank. Not for a waggon-load of gold, I won't.'

Heyling saw it was useless.

'Oh, all right! If you feel like that about it!' he said carelessly.

The stubborn, half-frightened look left the host's eyes.

'Thank you, sir,' he said, quite gratefully.

But he had not really gained the victory. Heyling was as obstinate as he, and he had determined that before he left Randalls he would have investigated that barrow. If he could not get permission, he would go without.

He decided that as soon as darkness fell he would go out on the quiet and explore in earnest. He would borrow a spade from the open cart-shed of the inn – a spade and a pick, if he could find one. He began to feel some of the enthusiasm of the explorer. He decided that he would spend part of the afternoon in examining the outside of the mound. It was not more than a ten minutes' ride to the field, which lay on the road. It was, as the landlord had said, uncultivated. Almost in the middle of it rose a mass of stunted trees and bushes – a thick mass of intertwining boughs that would certainly take some strength to penetrate. Was it really a tomb, Heyling wondered? And he thought with some awe of the strange prehistoric being who might lie there, his rude jewels and arms about him.

He returned to the inn, his interest keener than ever. He would most certainly get into that barrow as soon as it was dark enough to try. He felt restless now, as one always does when one is looking forward with some excitement to an event a few hours distant. He fidgeted about the room, one eye constantly on his watch.

He wanted to get to the field as soon as possible after dark, for his casual inspection of the afternoon had shown him that the task of pushing through the bushes, tangled and interwoven as they were, would be no light one; and then there was the opening of the tumulus to be done – that soil, untouched by spade or plough for centuries, to be broken by the pick until an entrance was forced into the chamber within. He ought to be off as soon as he could safely secure the tools he wanted to borrow.

But Fate was against him. There seemed to be a constant flow of visitors to the Flaming Hand that evening – not ordinary labourers dropping in for a drink, but private visitors to the landlord, who went through to his parlour behind the bar and left by the yard at the side of the inn. It really did seem like some silly mystery story, thought Heyling impatiently; the affair in the marketplace, the landlord's odd manner over the question of the field, and now this hushed coming and going from the landlord's room!

He went to his bedroom window and looked out into the yard. He wanted to make quite sure that the pick and spade were still in the open cart-shed. To his relief they were; but as he looked he got yet another shock. A man slipped out from the door of the inn kitchen and slipped across the yard into the lane that lay behind the inn. Another followed him, and a little later another; and all three had black faces. Their hands showed light, and their necks; but their faces were covered with soot, so that the features were quite indistinguishable.

'This is too mad!' exclaimed Heyling half aloud. 'Jove, I didn't expect to run into this sort of farce when I came here. Wonder if all old Cross's mysterious visitors have had black faces? Anyway, I wish they'd buck up and clear out. I may not have another chance to go to that mound if I don't get off soon.'

The queer happenings at the inn now appeared to him solely as obstacles to his own movements. If their import came into his mind at all, it was to make him wonder whether there were any play like a mummers' show which the village kept up; or games, perhaps, like those played in Scotland at Hallowe'en ... By Jove! That probably was the explanation. It was All Hallows' Eve! Why couldn't they buck up and get on with it, anyhow?

His patience was not to be tried much longer. Soon after nine the noises ceased; but to make doubly sure, Heyling did not leave his room till ten had struck from Randalls church.

He got cautiously out of his bedroom window and landed softly on the cobbles of the yard. The tools still leaned against the wall of the open shed – trusting man, Mr Cross, of the Flaming Hand! The shed where his cycle stood was locked, though, and he swore softly at the loss of time this would mean in getting to the field. It would take him twenty-five minutes to walk.

As a matter of fact, it did not take him quite so long, for impatience gave him speed. The country looked very beautiful under the slow-rising hunter's moon. The long bare lines of the fields swept up to the ridges, black against the dark serene blue of the night sky. The air was cool and clean, with the smell of frost in it. Heyling, hurrying along the rough white road, was dimly conscious of the purity and peace of the night. At last the field came in sight, empty and still in the cold moonlight. Only the mound, black as a tomb, broke the flood of light. The gate was wide open, and even in his haste this struck Heyling as odd.

'I could have sworn I shut that gate,' he said to himself. 'I remember thinking I must, in case anyone spotted I'd been in. It just shows that people don't avoid the place as much as old Cross would like me to believe.'

He decided to attack the barrow on the side away from the road, lest any belated labourer should pass by. He walked round the mound, looking for a thin spot in its defence of thorn and hazel bushes; but there was none. The scrub formed a thick belt all round the barrow, and was so high that he could not see the top of the mound at all. The confounded stuff might grow half-way up the tumulus for all he could see.

He abandoned any idea of finding an easy spot to begin operations. It was obviously just a question of breaking through. Then, just as he was about to take this heroic course, he stopped short, listening. It sounded to him as if some creature were moving within the bushes – something heavy and bulky, breaking the smaller branches of the undergrowth.

'Must be a fox, I suppose,' he thought, 'but he must be a monster. It sounds more like a cow, though of course it can't be. Well, here goes.'

He turned his back to the belt of thick undergrowth, ducked his head forward, and was just about to force his backwards way through the bushes when again he stopped to listen. This time it was a very different sound that arrested him – it was the distant playing of a pipe. He recognised it – the plaintive melody of Randalls Round.

He paused, listening. Yes – feet were coming up the road – many feet, pattering unevenly. There was some village game afoot, then!

The words of Mortlake's book came back to his mind. The author had said that at one time the barrow was the centre of the dance. Was it possible that it was so still – that there was a second form, less decorous perhaps, which took place at night?

Anyhow, he mustn't be seen, that was certain. Lucky the mound was between him and the road. He stole cautiously towards the hedge on the far side of the field. Thank goodness it was a hedge and not one of those low stone walls that surround most fields in the Cotswolds.

As he took cautious cover he couldn't help feeling a very complete fool. Was it really necessary to take this precaution? And then he remembered the look of stubborn determination on the landlord's face. Yes, if he were to investigate the barrow he must keep dark. Besides, there might be something to see in this business – something to delight old Mortlake's heart.

The tune came nearer, and the sound of footsteps was muffled. They were in the grassy field, then. Heyling cautiously raised his head from the ditch where he lay; but the mound blocked his view as yet. What luck that he'd happened to go to Randalls just at that time – Hallowe'en! He remembered the documents in the Guildhall, and Jno. Beale's indictment of the men who, he averred, had made away with his son at Hallowe'en. Heyling's blood tingled with excitement.

The playing came closer, and now Heyling could see the figures of men moving into the circle they formed for Randalls Round. Again he was struck by the queer barbaric look of the thing and by the gravity of their movements; and then his heart gave a sudden heavy thump. The dancers had all the blackened mask-like faces of the men he had seen leaving the inn. How odd! thought Heyling. They perform quite openly in the village square, and then steal away at night, disguising their faces …

The dance was extraordinarily impressive, seen in that empty field under the quiet moon. There was no sound but the whispering of their feet on the long dry grass and the melancholy music of the pipe. Then, quite suddenly, Heyling heard again the cracking, rustling sound from the dense bushes about the mound. It was exactly like the stirring of some big clumsy animal. The dancers heard it too; there came a sort of shuddering gasp; Heyling saw one man glance at his neighbour, and his eyes shone light and terrified in his blackened face.

The melody came slower, and with a kind of horror Heyling knew that the crisis of the dance was near. Slowly the dancers formed the ring, their faces turned away from the mound; then from outside the circle came a shrouded figure led by a man wearing a mask like a bull's head. The veiled form was led into the ring. The pipe mourned on.

Again, shattering the quiet, came a snapping, crashing noise from the inmost recesses of the bushes about the barrow. There was some big animal in there, crashing his way out …

Then he saw it, bulky and black in the pure white light – some horrible primitive creature, with heavy lowered head. The dancers circled slowly; the air of the flute grew faint.

Heyling felt cold and sick. This was loathsome, devilish … He buried his head in his arms and tried to drown the sound of that mourning melody.

Sounds came through the muffling hands over his ears – a crunching, tearing sound, and then a horrible noise like an animal lapping. Sweat broke out on Heyling's back. It sounded like bones … He could not think, or move, or pray … The haunting music still crooned on …

The crashing, snapping noise again as the branches broke. It, whatever it was, was going back into its lair. The tune grew fainter and fainter. Steps sounded again on the road – slow steps, with no life in them. The horrible rite was over.

Very cautiously Heyling got to his feet. His knees trembled, and his breath came short and rough. He felt sick with horror and with personal fear as he skirted the mound. His fascinated eyes saw the break in the hazels and thorns; then they fell upon a dark mark on the ground – dark and wet, soaking into the dry grass. A white rag, dappled with dark stains, lay near ...

Heyling could bear no more. He gave a strangled cry as he rushed, blindly stumbling, falling sometimes, out of the field and down the road.

7 Lost Keep

BY L A LEWIS (1934)

Peter Hunt was barely seventeen when news reached him of his Aunt Kate's death in a north London hospital, and, knowing that she was almost penniless, he entertained no expectation of benefits as her only surviving relative. It was with some surprise, therefore, that he read in the Matron's letter of the despatch of a small, locked box, recently brought from a safe-deposit to her bed-side, to which she had evidently attached great importance. By the same post there also arrived a package from his Aunt herself addressed in the weak, spidery calligraphy of extreme age, enclosing a key and a brief note which read: 'To my nephew, Peter Hunt. Open the box and make what use Fate wills of its contents.'

The box arrived by delivery van in the evening of the same day, and was carried upstairs by Peter himself to his mean back bedroom in a Tilbury lodging-house. It was not very heavy, and any hope of hoarded coin vanished as soon as he lifted it, though there remained, of course, the slender chance of banknotes or bearer bonds. He cut the cords with which its lock had been reinforced and, taking the key from his pocket, opened it. It contained three objects only – a small-scale model of a stone fortress mounted on a pedestal shaped to resemble a rocky hill, a folded sheet of paper, and something which looked like a silver-framed magnifying glass, except that its lens was opaque – almost black, in fact – and nearly impervious to light.

Peter drew the miniature towards him – it was no more than three inches high – and examined it as closely as the poor light from the dirty window would allow. It was too early to use the gas. The meter was always ravenous for his pennies.

Even to his untutored eyes the workmanship of the model was exquisite, the degree of finish seeming to represent a lifetime's labour. Every single stone block – and there were thousands – in the structure of the building had been faithfully reproduced, and even such details as patches of lichen had not been overlooked. With luck the thing would be worth several pounds as a curiosity. Perhaps he would have it valued by Christie's; it wouldn't do to trust 'Uncle' Abe at the corner shop. He pushed it aside and reached for the folded paper, recognising his father's characteristic handwriting as he smoothed it out. It related to the contents of the box, and read as follows –

I, Vernon John Hunt, having been given by the doctors three months to live, have determined to put in writing what is known of 'Lost Keep' of which this scale model has been handed down from parent to child for many generations.

Tradition has it that the miniature was made under pain of death by an Italian craftsman condemned by an early ancestor to imprisonment in the original stronghold until such time as he should complete the task. That he *did* complete it the miniature itself testifies, but history does not relate whether his release followed or whether, with the callousness of Feudal days, he was left to rot in his prison. There is, I regret to say, some ground for the latter supposition, for he is credited in the Latin manuscript, now destroyed, with having laid some kind of curse on this piece of craftsmanship. A peculiarity of the whole matter is that there have been so many female heirs that the name of the original title holders is forgotten, the heirloom having passed haphazard from male to female issue and so transferred itself to various different families. Even the locality of the original site is unrecorded – hence its name of 'Lost Keep' – and the curse of the modeller is concerned with this fact. The old fortress, if it still stands, may be in Iceland, Scandinavia, Russia, or, for that matter, any part of the world; but, translating from the Latin script, it is supposed to be rediscoverable by any one who has *'the wit or fortune to combine glass and facsimile with understanding.'* Whoever solves the riddle, however, is threatened with *'greater temptations of the Devil than have beset any other of Adam's descendants,'* and, if he succumbs, will find *'death in the home of his fathers at the hand of his son.'* Doubtless each successive holder of the heirloom has attacked the problem, though there is no rumoured instance of its solution. I in my turn have wasted hours in speculation as to the purpose of the dark glass shaped so like a lens, yet so obviously useless as such, and have examined every point of the model's surface with a normal reading-glass for signs of engraved lettering, but have learned no more than to marvel at the delicacy of the work. On the latter count the model would probably be of considerable value among collectors, but its secret, if it really possesses one, is well hidden.

So, being under sentence of death, I entrust this sole heirloom of a family whose fortunes are at ebb to my sister Kate, requesting her to hold it for my son Peter until her death or his majority.

The document was neither dated nor signed.

Peter leaned back and looked with a distaste that familiarity had never conquered round the shabby room. So his *father* had believed the model to be of value too? So much the better. He'd have no false sentiment about parting with it since he'd never even heard of it till to-day, and he'd certainly get it valued at an early opportunity. It ought to fetch enough to pay for a course of night classes at a technical school, or – with great luck –a real college career for which he could drop his present uncongenial job as warehouse packer and fit himself to enter those higher spheres that his hereditary instinct craved. Meanwhile his day's work was finished and he could not afford to go out looking for amusement. He might as well have a shot at the dark glass problem.

Picking the apparently useless thing up, he studied it closely. It certainly *looked* like a lens, being a circle of some vitreous composition thick at the centre, thin at the sides, and mounted in a metal ring. Lighting the gas-jet – an old-fashioned fish-tail burner – he held the thing to the light, but through its opacity could distinguish only a shapeless blur. Perhaps distance, either from the eyes or the object to be focused, would sharpen its outline. He experimented thus, standing at arm's length from the jet, and gradually advancing the glass towards the flame. At really close quarters it *did* seem to let through a little more light, and he was so occupied with this discovery that he never thought of the effect which the accompanying heat might have on the glass until a sharp snap followed by a tinkle on the linoleum informed him that he had cracked it.

With a muttered expletive the boy turned it over, and at once noticed an interesting fact. The glass appeared to be built up in layers, and the heat had split off a piece of the outer one, revealing a second and seemingly undamaged surface beneath.

He pursed his lips in a whistle. The discovery might have some bearing on the apparent uselessness of the object. It was a natural conclusion that a perfect lens might be hidden under the dark covering, though the purpose of all the secrecy and mystery woven around glass and miniature was more than

Peter could guess. He found his pen-knife, and, carefully inserting it under the broken edge, split off another fragment. Once started, the remainder came away so easily that in a few minutes he had completely exposed the underlying surface, the layer on the other side flaking away with equal facility after a light rap with the handle of the knife. The now transparent lens – tinted, as far as he could judge against the twilight with his back to the gas, a kind of smoky blue – possessed an astounding power of magnification when he tried it on the back of his hand. The hand, as such, in fact, completely disappeared, and the circle of glass showed only a portion of the skin enlarged to a degree which he would have thought only a microscope could achieve. As he watched, the enlarging process seemed to continue as though concentric rings of the tissue were rolling out from the centre and vanishing through the rim. He had a sickening sensation of being about to sink bodily into the glass, and, hastily shutting his eyes, put it down on the table. The queer sensation passed off rapidly, but left him with a mixed feeling of giddiness, excitement, and fear. There was something *uncanny* about the lens – *damned* uncanny – but his faults did not include cowardice, and he resolved to complete his experiments single-handed. With this decision he proceeded to lock the door, and, pulling the table as near as he could to the gas-jet, sat down to test the effect of the lens on the miniature.

※

The grey, perpetual twilight had neither brightened nor darkened by one iota when Peter completed his seventh circuit of the mighty battlements. Dizzily far below him the waves of an apparently tideless sea broke and hissed back along the same bank of shingle, neither advancing nor retiring, each followed by an interminable succession of troughs and crests sweeping in from a vague horizon that seemed infinitely distant from the high eminence upon which he stood. But for their maddeningly regular beat no sound whatever broke the silence, no breeze moved the cold and stagnant air, and throughout the gigantic mass of masonry he was the only thing that lived. Above him the sky was a leaden monotony broken at one place alone by a mere pin-point of light which appeared to be a far-off beacon. It shone where the diminishing thread of a titanic causeway merged into the sky-line.

Peter drew a clammy hand across his eyes and leaned wearily against the ramparts. *Was he mad?* Or had some unbelievable miracle literally transported him in a flash of time from his dingy back-room to this far distant and eerie place? That he was not dreaming his sore knuckles proved, where he had struck them hard against unyielding stone in the panic frenzy of his incredible translation. He said aloud, 'O God!' in a meaningless sort of way, and repeated it several times, partly for the love of any sound other than that of the waves, and partly to focus his attention. Though he could not then have put it into words, the panorama, to his rather limited mind accustomed to concrete surroundings, savoured alarmingly of the Abstract.

Resolutely directing his gaze at the nearest buttress of the ramparts, he went over in his mind, perhaps for the twentieth time, the series of his sensations from the moment when he had held the lens over the model. Through the glass the tiny castle had appeared to grow and grow in swiftly overlapping rings from its centre, there had been a feeling of suction as though he were being dragged violently towards it, and then a moment – or an hour – of complete black-out from which he had emerged to a realisation of standing in an immense copy of the miniature courtyard looking up at the terrific mass of the Keep. Appalled by its sickening height and crushed by his own proportional sense of smallness, he had nevertheless been impelled to enter the open door and climb endlessly up flight after flight of stone steps till he came out weak and trembling on the roof. And then the feverish pacing of its periphery, a prey to wonder, fear, and a horrible giddiness each time he looked down towards the sea. And all the time the grey, unnatural twilight had persisted, tormenting him with the half-knowledge that he was not even on the Earth at all, but in some incredible place utterly divorced from all things human and alive.

It was healthy, physical hunger that eventually restored his mental balance to something near normality. In whatever nightmare realm he had landed himself, it clearly contained no possible source of food, and he must find his way out before starvation overtook him. The castle was sea-girt, and the interminable causeway that stretched from the shore towards the horizon was the only apparent means of exit. He felt a trifle fortified at the prospect of escape, and eagerly began the long descent of the stairways.

✳

'The glass,' Mrs Stebbings repeated defiantly, 'ain't here, and I ain't took it. Them bits in the 'earth might be it – broke – but that don't tell me where young 'Unt 'as 'opped orf to.' She tossed her head. 'And 'im owing me a week's rent,' she added with meaning. The Police Sergeant turned from his inspection of the broken lock and gave her an expressionless glance. 'That's all right,' he replied 'I'm not accusing you of taking it, but it certainly isn't in this room. No doubt Hunt has it with him – that's to say if there *is* a glass, as this writing states.

'Now, Mrs S,' he went on pacifically, 'please see if your other lodger is in the house. We shall want him to confirm your account of breaking into this room – not that we doubt your word,' he added hastily, 'just as a matter of form.' As the landlady's footsteps died away on the rickety stairs he turned to the constable who accompanied him.

'Another mare's nest, I fancy,' he remarked, 'lodger owes week's rent and can't pay, so leaves quietly. Can't smuggle his stuff out 'cause she's too sharp-eyed. Clothes aren't worth much, anyway. Hard on the lady, of course, but scarcely one of the cases where we call in the Yard.' He paused, and looked thoughtfully around him. 'All the same,' he continued, 'it *is* a bit queer how he got out with the door locked inside. The window's too big a drop, the roof's out of reach, and there are no marks on the key to show he turned it from outside with forceps.'

'How long's he been missing?' asked the Constable. The Sergeant consulted his watch. 'About forty-two hours. She saw him coming upstairs with a parcel – probably this,' he indicated the box and model on the table,' about five pm on Saturday, left him to sleep, as she supposed, all yesterday, and got the other fellow to break the lock when he didn't come down to breakfast this morning, and she found the door fastened. Yes, it looks like a case of convenient disappearance, seeing that he's not turned up at his job. Well, she ought to get her rent and a bit over on the price of this miniature if he doesn't come back to claim it after a reasonable interval. But I doubt if she'll see Master Hunt again in *this* house,' he concluded.

'For God's sake water – and food,' said a hoarse, feeble voice behind them, and they swung round in amazement to see the missing lodger, pale and haggard, sprawled across the bed!

✳

That familiarity breeds contempt is a proverb of some antiquity and more than a little justification and although contempt was the last sentiment Peter Hunt felt with regard to Lost Keep it was not long before his initial fear of the unknown was transmuted into a complacent acceptance of his heritage and of the supernatural powers it conveyed. His circumstances at the age of thirty differed vastly from those in which the arrival of the remarkable miniature had found him. He now possessed a house in Park Lane, a country-seat down in Dorset, three cars, a large staff of servants for the upkeep of his establishments, and, above all, a very charming but neglected wife among whose many contributions to his well-being was a son and heir also named Peter, but generally known as Pete for purposes of distinction.

It was in the library of his Park Lane mansion that Peter was sitting one August evening when a telephone call informed him that Lord Knifton proposed calling on him for a private interview in half an hour's time, and Peter's thin lips twisted into a grimace of satisfaction as he hung up the receiver. Knifton was his co-director in many of the big commercial enterprises from which his income was derived, and he had lately been behaving in a most obstructive way by refusing to approve certain conversion schemes which he – Peter – had evolved for their joint enrichment at the expense of the shareholders. He was one of the few financial magnates sufficiently powerful to interfere seriously with Peter's activities, and the time had come when one or the other must definitely take second place. Well, Knifton might indulge in whatever ideals he chose, but Peter *knew* which of them that one would be.

He opened the drawer of his desk and took out the miniature fortress. The hard circle of the lens pressed comfortingly against his abdomen in the inner pocket where it always reposed. A thousand Kniftons could not dominate the master of Lost Keep.

With half an hour's leisure, Peter's thoughts wandered back to the day when he had discovered the trick of the model and so nearly lost his life in the discovery. Even now he shuddered to recall that unending march along the rocky causeway that seemed to lead on eternally towards an horizon that never grew a mile nearer. How that unchanging grey twilight had mocked him with its denial of Time after he had dropped his watch into the sea and had no means of counting the passage of the hours. The sullen waves had lapped on with changeless rhythm either side of him, raising and lowering their fringe of decaying weed with never a variation in the limit of their lift – until he had screamed aloud at their inexorable monotony. He remembered how he had tramped on mile after mile towards the ever-receding sky-line till sheer exhaustion had dropped him in his tracks, and how, as he fell, his hand doubled under him, had come in contact with the lens which he then recollected having slipped into his pocket just as unconsciousness was claiming him in the Tilbury bedroom. With tired fingers he had drawn it out and held it, by some inner prompting, between his dim eyes and the distant beacon, to find himself, an instant later, lying across his bed with two policemen in the room and the tread of his landlady's feet ascending the stairs. Even then, with no formulated ideas of the value of his discovery, instinct had warned him to slip the lens again into his pocket, and to their excited queries about where he had been and the manner of his return he had reiterated foolishly that he had been asleep. They had given him water – that of the strange ocean had been too brackish to drink – and bread, which he had devoured wolfishly, but to all their questions he had answered, 'I don't know. I was asleep,' until they finally left him, evidently much mystified, and whispering together.

It was during the ensuing night that, unable to sleep for thinking about the model fortress, he began to realise the almost unlimited possibilities it contained. In whatever uncharted spot the original was situated, he felt sure that its whereabouts remained undiscovered by man, and it followed logically that he would have unquestioned dominion there. True, there were no inhabitants upon whom to exercise it – but suppose he could find a way of transporting other people to the place? He had assured himself that the whole thing was not feverish delirium by making several more brief visits to the Keep, always being careful to maintain a tight hold on the lens when the period of black-out arrived. Reference to the alarum clock by his bed showed him that, whatever might be the distance from the model to the real fortress, the transit occupied no measurable time at all; and this fact alone, should he choose to defy mankind, would provide a perfect *alibi*, since no jury would admit that he could travel hundreds – maybe thousands – of miles in a fraction of a second. Any breach of law or convention would have to be carried out at the *real* place at a time when he was known to be at home, and this arrangement would safeguard him against its very discovery. He reverted to the problem of getting his victims – veritable slaves they would be – to the island of his sovereignty, and concluded that the lens was large enough for two people to look through it at once, if it were held at the right distance.

Peter awoke from a half-dream and smiled at the model. To this day he had never come an inch nearer to solving the location of Lost Keep itself, but the miniature had served him well, and he loved those early memories. How scornfully disbelieving his foreman had been when he had hinted at the acquisition of something with magical properties! It had required a lot of restraint and tact to persuade him round to the lodging-house for a demonstration after he had brusquely sacked Peter for failing to be at work on that memorable Monday, but Peter had feigned cheerful indifference, supporting his attitude with talk of a quite mythical better job waiting for him, and the mention of a bottle of whiskey, bought out of his slender savings, had clinched the matter. After a few drinks Peter had brought out the miniature, and, inviting the foreman to sit beside him and concentrate upon it, had focused it with the lens. The usual enlargement of the image and the subsequent black-out had duly occurred, but this time, on coming to his senses in the great courtyard, he had seen beside him another figure – a figure with dropped jaw and blank eyes staring up at the colossal pile overhanging them. He had thereupon directed the lens at the beacon and translated himself back to Tilbury – alone.

It was only fair to himself, Peter always reflected at this point, to remember that he had been in ignorance of the man's alcoholic heart. He had intended only to punish him by leaving him marooned for a day, and it was with no little horror – for his autocratic power was still new – that he found him lying dead at the gateway on the following morning. Assurance of immunity, however, had gone far to overcome any remorse he had felt, and the six pounds odd which he had found in the man's pockets had consoled him in his unemployment. Those six pounds had, in fact, been the foundation of his present fortune, for from that chance windfall the acquisition of other and larger sums had been a rational and easy step, and he had found that anything he carried on his person was translated with him on his journeys be-tween Lost Keep and the everyday world. Other advantages, too, were afforded by his unique possession; there had been, for instance, women who had denied him.

※

On one thing Peter had always congratulated himself. He had never allowed any of his bond-slaves to escape from Lost Keep. Once, indeed, he had been tempted to bring back a girl, for whom he had felt an unusually lasting passion, into the warm world of sunlight and blue skies, but he had realised in time the danger of having his secret betrayed, and had left her to pine in the cold, grey twilight where none it seemed could survive more than a few months. He had taken her food and drink in plenty, for it had hurt him to visualise her in the agonies of starvation, but he had seen the lovely face grow wan, and eyes lose a spark more of their lustre on each successive visit, and at the end he had stayed away for many days rather than face more of her pleadings for release.

Peter shook himself, and glanced at the clock. Knifton was nearly due. He had been sitting dreaming in his shirt-sleeves, for the evening was oppressively hot, and now he rose and donned a heavy silk dressing gown that was hung over the back of his chair. It was a highly coloured affair, the fabric of which had been especially woven for him in a unique pattern of interlacing circles.

※

Lord Knifton was a man some fifty years of age, who possessed both personality and tact. Though he frankly disagreed with many of Peter's principles, and never hesitated to tell him so, when their joint affairs were involved, he had considerable respect for his business acumen, and liked him well enough socially. Thus it was that, on being shown into the library, he made no immediate attempt to introduce the subject of their recent dispute, but shook hands and accepted a cigar while chatting of generalities. He soon noticed the model fortress and remarked upon its brilliant workmanship.

'Yes,' Peter agreed, 'a marvellous example of miniature craft – but its wonders show up better when viewed through this glass. Just sit still and keep the model in focus. Don't look away even if it makes your head swim for a second. There's no danger to the eyes, and you'll find the effect amazing.' He leaned over the back of Lord Knifton's chair, and held the lens so that both could see the fortress through it.

'And now, Knifton,' he said stridently, 'I've got you just where I want you.'

His companion rubbed his eyes and looked about him in bewilderment. A moment ago he had been sitting in Hunt's luxuriously furnished library on a hot August night, looking at a miniature on the desk. Now, by some miracle, he found himself in a gigantic, stone-flagged court, high-walled, and fronted by a fortress of staggering dimensions, while, under a dead grey sky that cast no shadows, the windless air struck coldly through his thin evening suit. The stench of a charnel-house assailed his nostrils, and he saw with revulsion that the ground was strewn with human remains in all stages of decomposition from bare, bleached skeletons to gory carcasses of the freshly slain, and the less recently alive – hideously distended.

He cried out sharply, and recoiled several paces, slewing round with upraised arms as he collided with someone behind him.

'Only your host,' said the voice of Peter Hunt, with a chilly suavity from which all trace of friendliness had vanished, 'please make yourself *quite* at home. It *is* your home, now, you know – that is, until you realise that I'm bound to win in the end, and sign this concession you so smugly discountenanced yesterday.'

He produced an impressive looking document, stiff with seals, and opened it with a flourish, then, seeing that his guest remained tongue-tied, went on bitingly, 'Framing a spate of questions, I suppose? What's this place? How did I get here? And so forth. Well, you may save your breath. *Where* you are I know no better than you. What I do know is, that I have been absolutely monarch of it for many years. Peter Hunt of Park Lane, pillar of Society, political leader, supporter of the Constitution, deferring to the wishes of a dozen pettifogging public bodies – and enjoying the farce because I know that I can, at will, take any man to whose opinion I pretend to bow, and bring him here and *rule* him as *you* can rule a dog!' He laughed unpleasantly. 'You damned fool! Do you think it's for the money that I want your signature? I can get enough to pay the National Debt by bringing the rich to Lost Keep and stripping them of their wealth. There's one in there,' he muttered, as a despairing moan echoed from behind a barred grating in the stonework, 'he's trying to decide whether it's worthwhile to sign a cheque and write home to say how much he's enjoying his holiday – in Portugal! No, my esteemed and scrupulous partner, one grows weary of ruling over subjects a few at a time in this gloomy place. I want to come out into the open and rule a country – and when this concession goes through I can do it!'

At last Lord Knifton spoke, and in his tones were neither fear nor anger. Only an abiding sorrow.

'Peter Hunt,' he replied solemnly, 'by some diabolical means which I do not even wish to fathom you wield a power that no man is ready to possess. I can only say: God take that power from you before more evil is done!'

As he spoke a swift shadow blotted out half the sky, and Hunt threw back his head in amazement. In the whole course of his association with this weird retreat he had never known anything to break the canopy of twilight, and his hands fell nervelessly to his sides as there burst on his vision a mass of shining metal, so huge as almost to dwarf the Keep, miraculously suspended in space above it. For a few seconds its great spatulate point hovered over the turrets. Then, it darted down and rushed at then, its lower edge grinding and roaring along the paving stones.

※

'Uncle, you promised to show me your new microscope. May I see it now?' Pete demanded with a sidelong glance at his mother.

'But it's bedtime, dear,' said Lydia Hunt, 'and you can see Uncle Harry's reading. Run upstairs now like a good boy and you shall see it to-morrow.'

Pete drooped a pathetic lower lip. He was a sunny-natured child, though a trifle spoilt.

'Oh, but Uncle *did* promise. He *said* to-day, and I've been looking forward to it all school-time. I told the other chaps in our form about it, and they'll want to hear what I've seen with it to-morrow. Won't you show me something to-night *please*, Uncle Harry?'

Lydia's brother looked up from his evening paper with a whimsical smile. 'Well,' he laughed, 'I've promised to take it round to Dr Pruden's to-morrow to check over some of his cultures, so perhaps the boy had better see it to-night. It won't take long. All right, Pete. The 'mike's' in Daddy's library, and I believe he's got Lord Knifton there with him, but we'll see if they'll let us have it.'

Pete clutched one of his hands with the enthusiasm of the ten-year-old, and danced across the hall at his side. They came to the library door and knocked, but there was no reply. Pete pushed it open and looked in. 'Come on, Uncle Harry,' he cried, 'they must have gone out. Where's the microscope?'

His uncle crossed over to a cupboard, lifted out something large and shiny, and stood it on the desk. It was an expensive instrument, covered with exciting little brass knobs, and Pete's eyes gleamed when they saw it. 'Coo, what a beauty!' he exclaimed rapturously, 'wish I had one! ... Oh, and look, Uncle! Here's daddy's model fortress! I've never seen it properly before. Can we look at *that* through the microscope?'

'No, of course not, you silly kid. They're for examining very tiny things like grains of dust, and you have to put them between the glass plates so as to light them from behind. If you just stood the end of the barrel against a lump of solid stuff you'd see nothing at all. Now then, here's a slide,' he went on, handing the boy two little oblongs of glass, 'just get a wee flake of dirt on the tip of that silver paper-knife and park it between these. Then I'll show you how the world looks to an influenza germ.'

Pete giggled, and scraped up a speck of dust from the courtyard of the model fortress, wiped the knife on the slide, and obediently passed it across. His uncle fitted it into a frame at the lower end of the barrel, bent down to the eye-piece and began manipulating the brass knobs. Pete watched him, fascinated, and chafed at the time it took to get the adjustment right. He was on the point of asking how soon he might be allowed to have a look when he heard his uncle give a low whistle.

'Pete,' he said, in a funny unsteady voice, and without lifting his head from the eye-piece, 'go and ask Mummy to come here, will you. And then hang on in the drawing-room till we call you, there's a good chap. I've got something I want her to see first, and after that you shall have the microscope to yourself till you go to bed.'

Though crestfallen at this further delay, Pete understood from the tone that it was not the time to argue, and presently Mrs Hunt had taken his place by the desk. Her brother rose, and gave her searching glance.

'Take a look at that, old girl,' he suggested, indicating the microscope, 'and tell me if I'm dreaming.' Lydia sat down in the chair. 'Why, Harry,' she exclaimed, 'they're miniature skeletons! But how on earth can they be modelled so perfectly on such a scale?'

Her brother shook his head. 'Pete certainly scraped that bit of dust off the miniature,' he answered. 'But they are *not* models! Take a grip on yourself, and shift the slide from right to left. This is the button that operates it!'

Lydia obeyed the instruction and then broke out again in a tone of astonishment: 'But it's unbelievable! A pigmy race no bigger than bacilli, and shaped in the exact pattern of humans! … Why,' she added, 'there are even buckles and bits of cloth just like we wear. But they *must* be models!'

'Move the slide a bit further,' said Harry quietly, and then gripped her by the shoulders as she thrust her chair backwards from the desk with a cry of horror, cheeks blanched and eyes dilated.

'Harry! Harry!' she gasped, 'I can't bear it! It's Peter and Lord Knifton! That dressing-gown. There's not another like it in the world! … Oh, that horrible mess of blood … And the limbs were – were still *twitching*! What does it *mean*?'

Her brother poured some whiskey into a glass and held it to her lips. 'It means, I think, that there was truth in the legend of Lost Keep, and that Peter found the key. It would account for his mysterious disappearances – and other things!' he concluded grimly.

Lydia drained the tumbler and straightened up in the chair. 'You mean that the original castle really exists, and that, in some beastly fashion, its happenings are mirrored in the model? … Then tell me, Harry. How can we find the real place? There may still be life in them. We must send help. We *must*!'

Her brother sighed. 'There is no journey to make. How such a thing can be, God knows – but that thing *is* Lost Keep, and there they are locked – *multum in parvo* – Ugh! It makes me sick!'

Suddenly Lydia was galvanised into action. She began to turn out the drawers of the desk, scattering their contents on the carpet. 'The lens, Harry. The lens!' she cried hysterically. 'We can go ourselves and find out!'

Harry took her gently by the arm. 'No, dear,' he replied with finality, 'Peter has the lens.'

8 N

BY ARTHUR MACHEN (1934)

1

They were talking about old days and old ways and all the changes that have come on London in the last weary years; a little party of three of them, gathered for a rare meeting in Perrott's rooms.

One man, the youngest of the three, a lad of fifty-five or so, had begun to say: 'I know every inch of that neighbourhood, and I tell you there's no such place.'

His name was Harliss; and he was supposed to have something to do with chemicals and carboys and crystals.

They had been recalling many London vicissitudes, these three; and it must be noted that the boy of the party, Harliss, could remember very well the Strand as it used to be, before they spoilt it all. Indeed, if he could not have gone as far back as the years of those doings, it is doubtful whether Perrott would have let him into the meeting in Mitre Place, an alley which was an entrance of the inn by day, but was blind after nine o'clock at night, when the iron gates were shut, and the pavement grew silent. The rooms were on the second floor, and from the front windows could be seen the elms in the inn garden, where the rooks used to build before the war. Within, the large, low room was softly, deeply carpeted from wall to wall; the winter night, with a bitter dry wind rising, and moaning even in the heart of London, was shut out by thick crimson curtains, and the three then sat about a blazing fire in an old fireplace, a fireplace that stood high from the hearth, with hobs on each side of it, and a big kettle beginning to murmur on one of them. The armchairs on which the three sat were of the sort that Mr Pickwick sits on for ever in his frontispiece. The round table of dark mahogany stood on one leg, very deeply and profusely carved, and Perrott said it was a George IV table, though the third friend, Arnold, held that William IV, or even very early Victoria, would have been nearer the mark. On the dark red wall-paper there were eighteenth-century engravings of Durham Cathedral and Peterborough Cathedral, which showed that, in spite of Horace Walpole and his friend Mr Gray, the eighteenth century couldn't draw a Gothic building when its towers and traceries were before its eyes: 'because they couldn't see it,' Arnold had insisted, late one night, when the gliding signs were far on in their course, and the punch in the jar had begun to thicken a little on its spices. There were other engravings of a later date about the walls, things of the thirties and forties by forgotten artists, known well enough in their day; landscapes of the Valley of the Usk, and the Holy Mountain, and Llanthony: all with a certain enchantment and vision about them, as if their domed hills and solemn woods were more of grace than of nature. Over the hearth was *Bolton Abbey in the Olden Time.*

Perrott would apologise for it.

'I know,' he would say. 'I know all about it. It is a pig, and a goat, and a dog, and a damned nonsense' – he was quoting a Welsh story – 'but it used to hang over the fire in the dining-room at home. And I often wish I had brought along *Te Deum Laudamus* as well.'

'What's that?' Harliss asked.

'Ah, you're too young to have lived with it. It depicts three choir-boys in surplices; one singing for his life, and the other two looking about them – just like choir-boys. And we were always told that the busy boy was hanged at last. The companion picture showed three charity girls, also singing. This was called *Te Dominum Confitemur.* I never heard their story.'

'I know.' Harliss brightened. 'I came upon them both in lodgings near the station at Brighton, in Mafeking year. And, a year or two later, I saw *Sherry, Sir* in an hotel at Tenby.'

'The finest wax fruit I ever saw,' Arnold joined in, 'was in a window in the King's Cross Road.'

So they would maunder along, about the old-fashioned rather than the old. And so on this winter night of the cold wind they lingered about the London streets of forty, forty-five, fifty-five years ago.

One of them dilated on Bloomsbury, in the days when the bars were up, and the Duke's porters had boxes beside the gates, and all was peace, not to say profound dullness, within those solemn boundaries. Here was the high vaulted church of a strange sect, where, they said, while the smoke of incense fumed about a solemn rite, a wailing voice would suddenly rise up with the sound of an incantation in magic. Here, another church, where Christina Rossetti bowed her head; all about, dim squares where no-one walked, and the leaves of the trees were dark with smoke and soot.

'I remember one spring,' said Arnold, 'when they were the brightest green I ever saw. In Bloomsbury Square. Long ago.'

'That wonderful little lion stood on the iron posts in the pavement in front of the British Museum,' Perrott put in. 'I believe they have kept a few and hidden them in museums. That's one of the reasons why the streets grow duller and duller. If there is anything curious, anything beautiful in a street, they take it away and stick it in a museum. I wonder what has become of that odd little figure, I think it was in a cocked hat, that stood by the bar-parlour door in the courtyard of the Bell in Holborn.'

They worked their way down by Fetter Lane, and lamented Dryden's house – 'I think it was in 87 that they pulled it down' – and lingered on the site of Clifford's Inn – 'you could walk into the seventeenth century' – and so at last into the Strand.

'Someone said it was the finest street in Europe.'

'Yes, no doubt – in a sense. Not at all in the obvious sense; it wasn't *belle architecture de ville*. It was of all ages and all sizes and heights and styles: a unique enchantment of a street; an incantation, full of words that meant nothing to the uninitiated.'

A sort of Litany followed.

'The Shop of the Pale Puddings, where little David Copperfield might have bought his dinner.'

'That was close to Bookseller's Row – sixteenth-century houses.'

'And "Chocolate as in Spain"; opposite Charing Cross.'

'The *Globe* office, where one sent one's early turnovers.'

'The narrow alleys with steps going down to the river.'

'The smell of making soap from the scent shop.'

'Nutt's bookshop, near the Welsh mutton butcher's, where the street was narrow.'

'The *Family Herald* office; with a picture in the window of an early type-setting machine, showing the operator working a contraption with long arms, that hovered over the case.'

'And Garden House in the middle of a lawn, in Clement's Inn.'

'And the flicker of those old yellow gas-lamps, when the wind blew up the street, and the people were packing into that passage that led to the Lyceum pit.'

One of them, his ear caught by a phrase that another had used, began to murmur verses from 'Oh, plump head waiter at the Cock.'

'What chops they were!' sighed Perrott. And he began to make the punch, grating first of all the lumps of sugar against the lemons; drawing forth thereby the delicate, aromatic oils from the rind of the Mediterranean fruit. Matters were brought forth from cupboards at the dark end of the room: rum from the Jamaica Coffee House in the City, spices in blue china boxes, one or two old bottles containing secret essences. The kettle boiled, the ingredients were dusted in and poured into the red-brown jar, which was then muffled and set to digest on the hearth, in the heat of the fire.

'*Misce, fiat mistura*,' said Harliss.

'Very well,' answered Arnold. 'But remember that all the true matters of the work are invisible.'

Nobody minded him or his alchemy; and after a due interval, the glasses were held over the fragrant steam of the jar, and then filled. The three sat round the fire, drinking and sipping with grateful hearts.

2

Let it be noted that the glasses in question held no great quantity of the hot liquor. Indeed, they were what used to be called rummers; round, and of a bloated aspect, but of comparatively small capacity. Therefore, nothing injurious to the clearness of those old heads is to be inferred, when it is said that between the third and fourth filling, the talk drew away from central London and the lost, beloved Strand and began to go farther afield, into stranger, less-known territories. Perrott began it, by tracing a curious passage he had once made northward, dodging by the Globe and the Olympic theatres into the dark labyrinth of Clare Market, under arches and by alleys, till he came into Great Queen Street, near the Freemason's Tavern and Inigo Jones's red pilasters. Another took up the tale, and drifting into Holborn by Whetstone's Park, and going astray a little to visit Kingsgate Street – 'just like Phiz's plate: mean, low, deplorable; but I wish they hadn't pulled it down' – finally reached Theobald's Road. There, they delayed a little, to consider curiously decorated leaden water-cisterns that were once to be seen in the areas of a few of the older houses, and also to speculate on the legend that an ancient galleried inn, now used as a warehouse, had survived till quite lately at the back of Tibbles Road – for so they called it. And thence, northward and eastward, up the Gray's Inn Road, crossing the King's Cross Road, and going up the hill. 'And here,' said Arnold, 'we begin to touch on the conjectured. We have left the known world behind us.'

Indeed, it was he who now had the party in charge.

'Do you know,' said Perrott, 'that sounds awful rot, but it's true; at least so far as I am concerned. I don't think I ever went beyond Holborn Town Hall, as it used to be – I mean walking. Of course, I've driven in a hansom to King's Cross Railway Station, and I went once or twice to the Military Tournament, when it was at the Agricultural Hall, in Islington; but I don't remember how I got there.'

Harliss said he had been brought up in North London, but much farther north – Stoke Newington way.

'I once knew a man,' said Perrott, 'who knew all about Stoke Newington; at least he ought to have known about it. He was a Poe enthusiast, and he wanted to find out whether the school where Poe boarded when he was a little boy was still standing. He went again and again; and the odd thing is that, in spite of his interest in the matter, he didn't seem to know whether the school was still there, or whether he had seen it. He spoke of certain survivals of the Stoke Newington that Poe indicates in a phrase or two in "William Wilson": the dreamy village, the misty trees, the old rambling red-brick houses, standing in their gardens, with high walls all about them. But though he declared that he had gone so far as to interview the vicar, and could describe the old church with the dormer windows, he could never make up his mind whether he had seen Poe's school.'

'I never heard of it when I lived there,' said Harliss. 'But I came of business stock. We didn't gossip much about authors. I have a vague sort of notion that I once heard somebody

speak of Poe as a notorious drunkard – and that's about all I
ever heard of him till a good deal later.'

'It is queer, but it's true,' Arnold broke in, 'that there's a
general tendency to seize on the accidental, and ignore the
essential. You may be vague enough about the treble works,
the vast designs of the laboured rampart lines; but at least
you knew that the Duke of Wellington had a very big nose. I
remember it on the tins of knife polish.'

'But that fellow I was speaking of,' said Perrott, going back
to his topic, 'I couldn't make him out. I put it to him; "Surely
you know one way or the other: this old school is still standing
– or was still standing – or not: you either saw it or you didn't:
there can't be any doubt about the matter." But we couldn't
get to negative or positive. He confessed that it was strange;
"But upon my word I don't know. I went once, I think, about
95, and then, again, in 99 – that was the time I called on the
vicar; and I have never been since." He talked like a man who
had gone into a mist, and could not speak with any certainty
of the shapes he had seen in it.

'And that reminds me. Long after my talk with Hare – that
was the man who was interested in Poe – a distant cousin
of mine from the country came up to town to see about
the affairs of an old aunt of his who had lived all her life
somewhere Stoke Newington way, and had just died. He
came in here one evening to look me up – we had not met for
many years – and he was saying, truly enough, I am sure, how
little the average Londoner knew of London, when you once
took him off his beaten track. "For example," he said to me,
"have you ever been in Stoke Newington?" I confessed that I
hadn't, that I had never had any reason to go there. "Exactly;
and I don't suppose you've ever even heard of Canon's Park?"
I confessed ignorance again. He said it was an extraordinary
thing that such a beautiful place as this, within four or five
miles of the centre of London, seemed absolutely unknown

and unheard of by nine Londoners out of ten.'

'I know every inch of that neighbourhood,' broke in Harliss. 'I was born there and lived there till I was sixteen. There's no such place anywhere near Stoke Newington.'

'But, look here, Harliss,' said Arnold. 'I don't know that you're really an authority.'

'Not an authority on a place I knew backwards for sixteen years? Besides, I represented Crosbies in that district later, soon after I went into business.'

'Yes, of course. But – I suppose you know the Haymarket pretty well, don't you?'

'Of course I do; both for business and pleasure. Everybody knows the Haymarket.'

'Very good. Then tell me the way to St James's Market.'

'There's no such market.'

'We have him,' said Arnold, with bland triumph. 'Literally, he is correct: I believe it's all pulled down now. But it was standing during the war: a small open space with old, low buildings in it, a stone's throw from the back of the tube station. You turned to the right, as you walked down the Haymarket.'

'Quite right,' confirmed Perrott. 'I went there, only once, on the business of an odd magazine that was published in one of those low buildings. But I was talking of Canon's Park, Stoke Newington –'

'I beg your pardon,' said Harliss. 'I remember now. There is a park in Stoke Newington or near it called Canon's Park. But it isn't a park at all; nothing like a park. That's only a builder's name. It's just a lot of streets. I think there's a Canon's Square, and a Park Crescent, and an Esplanade: there are some decent shops there. But it's all quite ordinary; there's nothing beautiful about it.'

'But my cousin said it was an amazing place. Not a bit like the ordinary London parks or anything of the kind he'd seen abroad. You go in through a gateway, and he said it was like finding yourself in another country. Such trees, that must have been brought from the end of the world: there were none like them in England, though one or two reminded him of trees in Kew Gardens; deep hollows with streams running from the rocks; lawns all purple and gold with flowers, and golden lilies too, towering up into the trees, and mixing with the crimson of the flowers that hung from the boughs. And here and there, there were little summer-houses and temples, shining white in the sun, like a view in China, as he put it.'

Harliss did not fail with his response, 'I tell you there's no such place.'

And he added: 'And, anyhow, it all sounds a bit too flowery. But perhaps your cousin was that sort of man: ready to be enthusiastic over a patch of dandelions in a back-garden. A friend of mine once sent me a wire to "come at once: most important: meet me St John's Wood Station". Of course I went, thinking it must be really important; and what he wanted was to show me the garden of a house to let in Grove End Road, which was a blaze of dandelions.'

'And a very beautiful sight,' said Arnold, with fervour.

'It was a fine sight; but hardly a thing to wire a man about. And I should think that's the secret of all this stuff your cousin told you, Perrott. There used to be one or two big well-kept gardens at Stoke Newington; and I suppose he strolled into one of them by mistake, and then got rather wildly enthusiastic about what he saw.'

'It's possible, of course,' said Perrott, 'but in a general way he wasn't that sort of man. He had an experimental farm, not far from Wells, and bred new kinds of wheat, and improved grasses. I have heard him called stodgy, though I always found him pleasant enough when we met.'

'Well, I tell you there's no such place in Stoke Newington or anywhere near it. I ought to know.'

'How about St James's Market?' asked Arnold.

Then, they 'left it at that'. Indeed, they had felt for some time that they had gone too far away from their known world, and from the friendly tavern fires of the Strand, into the wild no man's land of the north. To Harliss, of course, those regions had once been familiar, common, and uninteresting: he could not revisit them in talk with any glow of feeling. The other two held them unfriendly and remote; as if one were to discourse of Arctic explorations, and lands of everlasting darkness.

They all returned with relief to their familiar hunting-grounds, and saw the play in theatres that had been pulled down for thirty-five years or more, and had steaks and strong ale afterwards, in the box by the fire, by the fire that had been finally raked out soon after the new law courts were opened.

3

So, at least, it appeared at the time; but there was something in the tale of this suburban park that remained with Arnold and beset him, and sent him at last to the remote north of the story. For, as he was meditating on this vague attraction, he chanced to light on a shabby brown book on his untidy shelves; a book gathered from a stall in Farringdon Street, where the manuscript of Traherne's *Centuries of Meditations* had been found. So far, Arnold had scarcely glanced at it. It was called, *A London Walk: Meditations in the Streets of the Metropolis*. The author was the Reverend Thomas Hampole, and the book was dated 1853. It consisted for the most part of moral and obvious reflections, such as might be expected from a pious and amiable clergyman of the day. In the middle of the nineteenth century, the relish of moralising which flourished so in the age of Addison and Pope and Johnson, which made the *Rambler* a popular book, and gave fortunes to the publishers of sermons, had still a great deal of vigour. People liked to be warned of the consequences of their actions, to have lessons in punctuality, to learn about the importance of little things, to hear sermons from stones, and to be taught that there were gloomy reflections to be drawn from almost everything. So then, the Reverend Thomas Hampole stalked the London streets with a moral and monitory glance in his eye: saw Regent Street in its early splendour and thought of the ruins of mighty Rome, preached on the text of solitude in a multitude as he viewed what he called the teeming myriads, and allowed a desolate, half-ruinous house 'in Chancery' to suggest thoughts of the happy Christmas parties that had once thoughtlessly revelled behind the crumbling walls and broken windows.

But here and there, Mr Hampole became less obvious, and perhaps more really profitable. For example, there is a passage – it has already been quoted, I think, by some modern author – which seems curious enough.

Has it ever been your fortune, courteous reader [Mr Hampole inquired] to rise in the earliest dawning of a summer day, ere yet the radiant beams of the sun have done more than touch with light the domes and spires of the great city? ... If this has been your lot, have you not observed that magic powers have apparently been at work? The accustomed scene has lost its familiar appearance. The houses which you have passed daily, it may be for years, as you have issued forth on your business or on your pleasure, now seem as if you beheld them for the first time. They have suffered a mysterious change, into something rich and strange. Though they may have been designed with no extraordinary exertion of the art of architecture ... yet you have been ready to admit that they now 'stand in glory, shine like stars, apparelled in a light serene'. They have become magical habitations, supernal dwellings, more desirable to the eye than the fabled pleasure dome of the Eastern potentate, or the bejewelled hall built by the Genie for Aladdin in the Arabian tale.

A good deal in this vein; and then, when one expected the obvious warning against putting trust in appearances, both transitory and delusory, there came a very odd passage:

> Some have declared that it lies within our own choice to gaze continually upon a world of equal or even greater wonder and beauty. It is said by these that the experiments of the alchemists of the Dark Ages ... are, in fact, related, not to the transmutation of metals, but to the transmutation of the entire Universe ... This method, or art, or science, or whatever we choose to call it (supposing it to exist, or to have ever existed), is simply concerned to restore the delights of the primal Paradise; to enable men, if they will, to inhabit a world of joy and splendour. It is perhaps possible that there is such an experiment, and that there are some who have made it.

The reader was referred to a note – one of several – at the end of the volume, and Arnold, already a good deal interested by this unexpected vein in the Reverend Thomas, looked it up. And thus it ran:

> I am aware that these speculations may strike the reader as both singular and (I may, perhaps, add) chimerical; and, indeed, I may have been somewhat rash and ill-advised in committing them to the printed page. If I have done wrong, I hope for pardon; and, indeed, I am far from advising anyone who may read these lines to

engage in the doubtful and difficult experiment which they adumbrate. Still; we are bidden to be seekers of the truth: *veritas contra mundum.*

I am strengthened in my belief that there is at least some foundation for the strange theories at which I have hinted, by an experience that befell me in the early days of my ministry. Soon after the termination of my first curacy, and after I had been admitted to Priest's Orders, I spent some months in London, living with relations in Kensington. A college friend of mine, whom I will call the Reverend Mr S–, was, I was aware, a curate in a suburb of the north of London, SN. I wrote to him, and afterwards called at his lodgings at his invitation. I found S– in a state of some perturbation. He was threatened, it seemed, with an affection of the lungs and his medical adviser was insistent that he should leave London for a while, and spend the four months of the winter in the more genial climate of Devonshire. Unless this were done, the doctor declared, the consequences to my friend's health might be of a very serious kind. S– was very willing to act on this advice, and indeed, anxious to do so; but, on the other hand, he did not wish to resign his curacy, in which, as he said, he was both happy and, he trusted, useful. On hearing this, I at once proffered my services, telling him that if his Vicar approved, I should be happy to do his duty till the end of the ensuing March; or even later, if the physicians considered a longer stay in the south would be advisable. S– was overjoyed. He took me at once to see the Vicar; the fitting inquiries were made, and I entered on my temporary duties in the course of a fortnight.

It was during this brief ministry in the environs of London, that I became acquainted with a very singular person, whom I shall call Glanville. He was a regular attendant at our services, and, in the course of my duty, I called on him, and expressed my gratification at his evident attachment to the Liturgy of the Church of England. He replied with due politeness, asked me to sit down and partake with him of the soothing cup, and we soon found ourselves engaged in conversation. I discovered early in our association that he was conversant with the reveries of the German Theosophist, Behmen, and the later works of his English disciple, William Law; and it was clear to me that he looked on these labyrinths of mystical theology with a friendly eye. He was a middle-aged man, spare of habit, and of a dark complexion; and his face was illuminated in a very impressive manner, as he discussed the speculations which had evidently occupied his thoughts for many years. Based as these theories were on the doctrines (if we may call them by that name) of Law and Behmen, they struck me as of an extremely fantastic, I would even say fabulous, nature, but I confess that I listened with a considerable degree of interest, while making it evident that as a Minister of the Church of England I was far from giving my free assent to the propositions that were placed before me. They were not, it is true, manifestly and certainly opposed to orthodox belief, but they were assuredly strange, and as such to be received with salutary caution. As an example of the ideas which beset a mind which was ingenious, and I may say, devout, I may mention that Mr Glanville often dwelt on a consequence, not generally acknowledged, of the Fall of Man. 'When man yielded,' he would say, 'to the mysterious temptation intimated by the figurative language of Holy Writ, the universe, originally fluid and the servant of his spirit, became solid, and crashed down upon him overwhelming him beneath its weight and its dead mass.' I requested him to furnish me with more light on this remarkable belief; and I found that in his opinion that which we now regard as stubborn matter was, primally, to use his singular phraseology, the Heavenly Chaos, a soft and ductile substance, which could be moulded by the imagination of uncorrupted man into whatever forms he chose it to assume. 'Strange as it may seem,' he added, 'the wild inventions (as we consider them) of the Arabian Tales give us some notion of the powers of the *homo protoplastus*. The prosperous city becomes a lake, the carpet transports us in an instant of time, or rather without time, from one end of the earth to another, the palace rises at a word from nothingness. Magic, we call all this, while we deride the possibility of any such feats; but this magic of the East is but a confused and fragmentary recollection of operations which were of the first nature of man, and of the fiat which was then entrusted to him.'

I listened to this and other similar expositions of Mr Glanville's extraordinary beliefs with some interest, as I have remarked. I could not but feel that such opinions were in many respects more in accordance with the doctrine I had undertaken to expound than much of the teaching of the philosophers of the day, who seemed to exalt rationalism at the expense of Reason, as that divine faculty was exhibited by Coleridge. Still, when I assented, I made it clear to Glanville that my assent was qualified by my firm adherence to the principles which I had solemnly professed at my ordination.

The months went by in the peaceful performance of the pastoral duties of my office. Early in March, I received a letter from my friend Mr S–, who informed me that he had greatly benefited by the air of Torquay, and that his medical adviser had assured him that he need no longer hesitate to resume his duties in London. Consequently, S– proposed to return at once, and, after warmly expressed thanks for my extreme kindness, as he called it, he announced his wish to perform his part in the Church services on the following Sunday. Accordingly, I paid my final visits to those of the parishioners with whom I had more particularly associated, reserving my call on Mr Glanville for the last day of my residence at SN. He was sorry, I think, to hear of my impending departure, and told me that he would always recollect our conversational exchanges with much pleasure.

'I, too, am leaving SN,' he added. 'Early next week I sail for the East, where my stay may be prolonged for a considerable period.'

After mutual expressions of polite regret, I rose from my chair, and was about to make my farewells, when I observed that Glanville was gazing at me with a fixed and singular regard.

'One moment,' he said, beckoning me to the window, where he was standing. 'I want to show you the view. I don't think you have seen it.'

The suggestion struck me as peculiar, to say the least of it. I was, of course, familiar with the street in which Glanville resided, as with most of the SN streets; and he on his side must have been well aware that no prospect that his window might command could show me anything that I had not seen many times during my four months' stay in the parish. In addition to this, the streets of our London suburbs do not often offer a spectacle to engage the amateur of landscape and the picturesque. I was hesitating, hardly knowing whether to comply with Glanville's request, or to treat it as a piece of pleasantry, when it struck me that it was possible that his first-floor window might afford a distant view of St Paul's Cathedral;

I accordingly stepped to his side, and waited for him to indicate the scene which he, presumably, wished me to admire.

His features still wore the odd expression which I have already remarked.

'Now,' said he, 'look out and tell me what you see.'

Still bewildered, I looked through the window, and saw exactly that which I had expected to see: a row or terrace of neatly designed residences, separated from the highway by a parterre or miniature park, adorned with trees and shrubs. A road, passing to the right of the terrace, gave a view of streets and crescents of more recent construction, and of some degree of elegance. Still, in the whole of the familiar spectacle I saw nothing to warrant any particular attention; and, in a more or less jocular manner, I said as much to Glanville.

By way of reply, he touched me lightly with his finger-tips on the shoulder, and said:

'Look again.'

I did so. For a moment, my heart stood still, and I gasped for breath. Before me, in place of the familiar structures, there was disclosed a panorama of unearthly, of astounding beauty. In deep dells, bowered by overhanging trees, there bloomed flowers such as only dreams can show; such deep purples that yet seemed to glow like precious stones with a hidden but ever-present radiance, roses whose hues outshone any that are to be seen in our gardens, tall lilies alive with light, and blossoms that were as beaten gold. I saw well-shaded walks that went down to green hollows bordered with thyme; and here and there the grassy eminence above, and the bubbling well below, were crowned with architecture of fantastic and unaccustomed beauty, which seemed to speak of fairyland itself. I might almost say that my soul was ravished by the spectacle displayed before me. I was possessed by a degree of rapture and delight such as I had never experienced. A sense of beatitude pervaded my whole being; my bliss was such as cannot be expressed by words. I uttered an inarticulate cry of joy and wonder. And then, under the influence of a swift revulsion of terror, which even now I cannot explain, I turned and rushed from the room and from the house, without one word of comment or farewell to the extraordinary man who had done – I knew not what.

In great perturbation and confusion of mind, I made my way into the street. Needless to say, no trace of the phantasmagoria that had been displayed before me remained. The familiar street had resumed its usual aspect, the terrace stood as I had always seen it, and the newer buildings beyond, where I had seen oh! what dells of delight, what blossoms of glory, stood as before in their neat, though unostentatious order. Where I had seen valleys embowered in green leafage, waving gently in the sunshine and the summer breeze, there were now boughs bare and black, scarce showing so much as a single bud. As I have mentioned, the season was early in March, and a black frost which had set in ten days or a fortnight before still constrained the earth and its vegetation.

I walked hurriedly away to my lodgings, which were some distance from the abode of Glanville. I was sincerely glad to think that I was leaving the neighbourhood on the following day. I may say that up to the present moment I have never revisited SN.

Some months later I encountered my friend Mr S–, and under cover of asking about the affairs of the parish in which he still ministered, I inquired after Glanville, with whom (I said) I had made acquaintance. It seemed he had fulfilled his intention of leaving the neighbourhood

within a few days of my own departure. He had not
confided his destination or his plans for the future to
anyone in the parish.

'My acquaintance with him,' said S–, 'was of the
slightest, and I do not think that he made any friends in
the locality, though he had resided in SN for more than
five years.'

It is now some fifteen years since this most strange
experience befell me; and during that period I have heard
nothing of Glanville. Whether he is still alive in the
distant Orient, or whether he is dead, I am completely
ignorant.

4

Arnold was generally known as an idle man; and, as he said
himself, he hardly knew what the inside of an office was
like. But he was laborious in his idleness, and always ready
to take any amount of pains, over anything in which he was
interested. And he was very much interested in this Canon's
Park business. He felt sure that there was a link between Mr
Hampole's odd story – 'more than odd,' he meditated – and
the experience of Perrott's cousin, the wheat-breeder from
the west country. He made his way to Stoke Newington, and
strolled up and down it, looking about him with an inquisitive
eye. He found Canon's Park, or what remained of it, without
any trouble. It was pretty well as Harliss had described it:
a neighbourhood laid out in the twenties or thirties of the
last century for City men of comfortable down to tolerable
incomes.

Some of these houses remained, and there was an attractive
row of old-fashioned shops still surviving. Again, in one place
there was the modest cot of late Georgian or early Victorian
design, with its trellised porch of faded blue-green paint, its

patterned iron balcony, not displeasing, its little garden in the front, and its walled garden at the back; a small coach-house, a small stable. In another, something more exuberant and on a much larger scale: ambitious pilasters and stucco, broad lawns and sweeping drives, towering shrubs, and grass in the back premises. But on all the territory modernism had delivered its assault. The big houses remaining had been made into maisonettes, the small ones were down-at-heel, no longer objects of love; and everywhere there were blocks of flats in wicked red brick, as if Mrs Todgers had given Mr Pecksniff her notion of an up-to-date gaol, and he had worked out her design. Opposite Canon's Park, and occupying the site on which Mr Glanville's house must have stood, was a technical college; next to it a school of economics. Both buildings curdled the blood: in their purpose and in their architecture. They looked as if Mr H G Wells's bad dreams had come true.

In none of this, whether moderately ancient or grossly modern, could Arnold see anything to his purpose. In the period of which Mr Hampole wrote, Canon's Park may have been tolerably pleasant; it was now becoming intolerably unpleasant. But at its best, there could not have been anything in its aspect to suggest the wonderful vision which the clergyman thought he had seen from Glanville's window. And suburban gardens, however well kept, could not explain the farmer's rhapsodies. Arnold repeated the sacred words of the explanation formula: telepathy, hallucination, hypnotism; but felt very little easier. Hypnotism, for example: that was commonly used to explain the Indian rope trick. There was no such trick, and in any case, hypnotism could not explain that or any other marvel seen by a number of people at once, since hypnotism could only be applied to individuals, and with their full knowledge, consent, and conscious attention. Telepathy might have taken place between Glanville and Hampole; but whence did Perrott's cousin receive the impression that he not only saw a sort of Kubla Khan, or Old Man of the Mountain paradise, but actually walked abroad in it? The S P R had, one might say, discovered telepathy, and had devoted no small part of their energies for the last forty-five years or more to a minute and thoroughgoing investigation of it; but, to the best of his belief, their recorded cases gave no instance of anything so elaborate as this business of Canon's Park. And again; so far as he could remember, the appearances ascribed to a telepathic agency were all personal; visions of people, not of places: there were no telepathic landscapes. And as for hallucination: that did not carry one far. That stated a fact, but offered no explanation of it. Arnold had suffered from liver trouble: he had come down to breakfast one morning and had been vexed to see the air all dancing with black specks. Though he did not smell the nauseous odour of a smoky chimney, he made no doubt at first that the chimney had been smoking, or that the black specks were floating soot. It was some time before he realised that, objectively, there were no black specks, that they were optical illusions, and that he had been hallucinated. And no doubt the parson and the farmer had been hallucinated: but the cause, the motive power, was to seek. Dickens told how, waking one morning, he saw his father sitting by his bedside, and wondered what he was doing there. He addressed the old man, and got no answer, put out his hand to touch him: and there was no such thing. Dickens was hallucinated; but since his father was perfectly well at the time, and in no sort of trouble, the mystery remained insoluble, unaccountable. You had to accept it; but there was no rationale of it. It was a problem that had to be given up.

But Arnold did not like giving problems up. He beat the coverts of Stoke Newington, and dived into pubs of promising aspect, hoping to meet talkative old men, who might remember their fathers' stories and repeat them. He found a few, for though London has always been a place of restless, migratory tribes, and shifting populations; and now more than ever before; yet there still remains in many places, and above all in the remoter northern suburbs, an old fixed element, which can go back in memory sometimes for a hundred, even a hundred and fifty years. So in a venerable tavern – it would have been injurious and misleading to call it a pub – on the borders of Canon's Park he found an ancient circle that gathered nightly for an hour or two in a snug, if dingy, parlour. They drank little and that slowly, and went early home. They were small tradesmen of the neighbourhood, and talked their business and the changes they had seen, the curse of multiple shops, the poor stuff sold in them, and the cutting of prices and profits. Arnold edged into the conversation by degrees, after one or two visits – 'Well, sir, I am very much obliged to you, and I won't refuse' – and said that he thought of settling in the neighbourhood: it seemed quiet. 'Best wishes, I'm sure. Quiet; well it was, once; but not much of that now in Stoke Newington. All pride and dress and bustle now; and the people that had the money and spent it, they're gone, long ago.'

'There were well-to-do people here?' asked Arnold, treading cautiously, feeling his way, inch by inch.

'There were, I assure you. Sound men – warm men, my father used to call them. There was Mr Tredegar, head of Tredegar's Bank. That was amalgamated with the City and National many years ago: nearer fifty than forty, I suppose. He was a fine gentleman, and grew beautiful pineapples. I remember his sending us one, when my wife was poorly all one summer. You can't buy pineapples like that now.'

'You're right, Mr Reynolds, perfectly right. I have to stock what they call pineapples, but I wouldn't touch them myself. No scent, no flavour. Tough and hard; you can't compare a crabapple with a Cox's pippin.'

There was a general assent to this proposition; and Arnold felt that it was slow work.

And even when he got to his point, there was not much gained. He said he had heard that Canon's Park was a quiet part; off the main track.

'Well, there's something in that,' said the ancient who had accepted the half-pint. 'You don't get very much traffic there, it's true: no trams or buses or motor coaches. But they're pulling it all to pieces; building new blocks of flats every few months. Of course, that might suit your views. Very popular these flats are, no doubt, with many people; most economical, they tell me. But I always liked a house of my own, myself.'

'I'll tell you one way a flat is economical,' the greengrocer said with a preparatory chuckle. 'If you're fond of the wireless, you can save the price and the licence. You'll hear the wireless on the floor above, and the wireless on the floor below, and one or two more besides when they've got their windows open on summer evenings.'

'Very true, Mr Batts, very true. Still, I must say, I'm rather partial to the wireless myself. I like to listen to a cheerful tune, you know, at tea time.'

'You don't tell me, Mr Potter, that you like that horrible jazz, as they call it?'

'Well, Mr Dickson, I must confess ...' and so forth, and so forth. It became evident that there were modernists even here: Arnold thought that he heard the term 'hot blues' distinctly uttered. He forced another half-pint – 'very kind of you; mild this time, if you don't mind' – on his neighbour, who turned out to be Mr Reynolds, the pharmaceutical chemist, and tried back.

'So you wouldn't recommend Canon's Park as a desirable residence.'

'Well, no, sir; not to a gentleman who wants quiet, I

should not. You can't have quiet when a place is being pulled down about your ears, as you may say. It certainly was quiet enough in former days. Wouldn't you say so, Mr Batts?' – breaking in on the musical discussion – 'Canon's Park was quiet enough in our young days, wasn't it? It would have suited this gentleman then, I'm sure.'

'Perhaps so,' said Mr Batts. 'Perhaps so, and perhaps not. There's quiet, and quiet.'

And a certain stillness fell upon the little party of old men. They seemed to ruminate, to drink their beer in slower sips.

'There was always something about the place I didn't altogether like,' said one of them at last. 'But I'm sure I don't know why.'

'Wasn't there some tale of a murder there, a long time ago? Or was it a man that killed himself, and was buried at the crossroads by the green, with a stake through his heart?'

'I never heard of that, but I've heard my father say that there was a lot of fever about there formerly.'

'I think you're all wide of the mark, gentlemen, if you'll excuse my saying so' – this from an elderly man in a corner, who had said very little hitherto. 'I wouldn't say Canon's Park had a bad name, far from it. But there certainly was something about it that many people didn't like; fought shy of, you may say. And it's my belief that it was all on account of the lunatic asylum that used to be there, awhile ago.'

'A lunatic asylum was there?' Arnold's particular friend asked. 'Well, I think I remember hearing something to that effect in my very young days, now you recall the circumstances. I know we boys used to be very shy of going through Canon's Park after dark. My father used to send me on errands that way now and again, and I always got another boy to come along with me if I could. But I don't remember that we were particularly afraid of the lunatics either. In fact, I hardly know what we were afraid of, now I come to think of it.'

'Well, Mr Reynolds, it's a long time ago; but I do think it was that madhouse put people off Canon's Park in the first place. You know where it was, don't you?'

'I can't say I do.'

'Well, it was that big house right in the middle of the park, that had been empty years and years – forty years, I dare say, and going to ruin.'

'You mean the place where Empress Mansions are now? Oh, yes, of course. Why they pulled it down more than twenty years ago, and then the land was lying idle all through the war and long after. A dismal-looking old place it was; I remember it well: the ivy growing over the chimney-pots, and the windows smashed, and the "To Let" boards smothered in creepers. Was that house an asylum in its day?'

'That was the very house, sir. Himalaya House, it was called. In the first place it was built on to an old farmhouse by a rich gentleman from India, and when he died, having no children, his relations sold the property to a doctor. And he turned it into a madhouse. And as I was saying, I think people didn't much like the idea of it. You know, those places weren't so well looked after as they say they are now, and some very unpleasant stories got about; I'm not sure if the doctor didn't get mixed up in a lawsuit over a gentleman, of good family, I believe, who had been shut up in Himalaya House by his relations for years, and as sensible as you or me all the time. And then there was that young fellow that managed to escape: that was a queer business. Though there was no doubt that he was mad enough for anything.'

'One of them got away, did he?' Arnold inquired, wishing to break the silence that again fell on the circle.

'That was so. I don't know how he managed it, as they were said to be very strictly kept, but he contrived to climb out or creep out somehow or other, one evening about tea time, and walked as quietly as you please up the road, and took lodgings close by here, in that row of old red-brick houses that stood where the technical college is now. I remember well hearing Mrs Wilson that kept the lodgings – she lived to be a very old woman – telling my mother that she never saw a nice-looking, better-spoken young man than this Mr Valiance – I think he called himself: not his real name, of course. He told her a proper story enough about coming from Norwich, and having to be very quiet on account of his studies and all that. He had his carpetbag in his hand, and said the heavy luggage was coming later, and paid a fortnight in advance, quite regular. Of course, the doctor's men were after him directly and making inquiries in all directions, but Mrs Wilson never thought for a moment that this quiet young lodger of hers was the missing madman. Not for some time, that is.'

Arnold took advantage of a rhetorical pause in the story. He leaned forward to the landlord, who was leaning over the bar, and listening like the rest. Presently orders round were solicited, and each of the circle voted for a small drop of gin, feeling 'mild' or even 'bitter' to be inadequate to the crisis of such a tale. And then, with courteous expressions, they drank the health of 'our friend sitting by our friend Mr Reynolds'. And one of them said:

'So she found out, did she?'

'I believe,' the narrator continued, 'that it was a week or thereabouts before Mrs Wilson saw there was something wrong. It was when she was clearing away his tea, he suddenly spoke up, and says:

'"What I like about these apartments of yours, Mrs Wilson, is the amazing view you have from your windows."

'Well, you know, that was enough to startle her. We all of us know what there was to see from the windows of Rodman's Row: Fothergill Terrace, and Chatham Street, and Canon's Park: very nice properties, no doubt, all of them, but nothing to write home about, as the young people say. So Mrs Wilson didn't know how to take it quite, and thought it might be a joke. She put down the tea-tray, and looked the lodger straight in the face.

"'What is it, sir, you particularly admire, if I might ask?'"

"'What do I admire?' said he. "Everything.'" And then, it seems, he began to talk the most outrageous nonsense about golden and silver and purple flowers, and the bubbling well, and the walk that went under the trees right into the wood, and the fairy house on the hill; and I don't know what. He wanted Mrs Wilson to come to the window and look at it all. She was frightened, and took up her tray, and got out of the room as quick as she could; and I don't wonder at it. And that night, when she was going up to bed, she passed her lodger's door, and heard him talking out loud, and she stopped to listen. Mind you, I don't think you can blame the woman for listening. I dare say she wanted to know who and what she had got in her house. At first she couldn't make out what he was saying. He was jabbering in what sounded like a foreign language; and then he cried out in plain English as if he were talking to a young lady, and making use of very affectionate expressions.

'That was too much for Mrs Wilson, and she went off to bed with her heart in her boots, and hardly got to sleep all through the night. The next morning the gentleman seemed quiet enough, but Mrs Wilson knew he wasn't to be trusted, and directly after breakfast she went round to the neighbours, and began to ask questions. Then, of course, it came out who her lodger must be, and she sent word round to Himalaya House. And the doctor's men took the young fellow back. And, bless my soul, gentlemen; it's close on ten o'clock.'

The meeting broke up in a kind of cordial bustle. The old man who had told the story of the escaped lunatic had remarked, it appeared, the very close attention that Arnold had given to the tale. He was evidently gratified. He shook

Arnold warmly by the hand, remarking: 'So you see, sir, the grounds I have for my opinion that it was that madhouse that gave Canon's Park rather a bad name in our neighbourhood.'

And Arnold, revolving many things, set out on the way back to London. Much seemed heavily obscure, but he wondered whether Mrs Wilson's lodger was a madman at all; any madder than Mr Hampole, or the farmer from Somerset or Charles Dickens, when he saw the appearance of his father by his bed.

5

Arnold told the story of his researches and perplexities at the next meeting of the three old friends in the quiet court leading into the inn. The scene had changed into a night in June, with the trees in the inn garden fluttering in a cool breeze, that wafted a vague odour of hayfields far away into the very heart of London. The liquor in the brown jar smelt of Gascon vineyards and herb-gardens, and ice had been laid about it, but not for too long a time.

Harliss's word all through Arnold's tale was: 'I know every inch of that neighbourhood, and I told you there was no such place.'

Perrott was judicial. He allowed that the history was a remarkable one: 'You have three witnesses,' Arnold had pointed out.

'Yes,' said Perrott, 'but have you allowed for the marvellous operation of the law of coincidences? There's a case, trivial enough, perhaps you may think, that made a deep impression on me when I read it, a few years ago. Forty years before, a man had bought a watch in Singapore – or Hong Kong, perhaps. The watch went wrong, and he took it to a shop in Holborn to be seen to. The man who took it from him over the counter was the man who had sold him the watch in the

East all those years before. You can never put coincidence out of court, and dismiss it as an impossible solution. Its possibilities are infinite.'

Then Arnold told the last broken, imperfect chapter of the story.

'After that night at the King of Jamaica,' he began, 'I went home and thought it all over. There seemed no more to be done. Still, I felt as if I would like to have another look at this singular park, and I went up there one dark afternoon. And then and there I came upon the young man who had lost his way, and had lost – as he said – the one who lived in the white house on the hill. And I am not going to tell you about her, or her house, or her enchanted gardens. But I am sure that the young man was lost also – and for ever.'

And after a pause, he added:

'I believe that there is a *perichoresis*, an interpenetration. It is possible, indeed, that we three are now sitting among desolate rocks, by bitter streams.

'… And with what companions?'

9 Mappa Mundi

BY MARY BUTTS

I

Paris is not a safe City. It is never supposed to be, but so often for the wrong reasons. Perhaps the only place in the world that is really and truly both a sink of iniquity and a Fountain of Life at one and the same time; in the same quarter, in the same place, at the same hour, with the same properties – to even the same person.

It is no use, or not much use, to know it only as a spree, or as an aesthetic jolt, returning very sophisticated about it. Like all the great feminine places, behind its first dazzling the free display, you come quickly upon profound reserves. After the spree a veil is drawn, a sober, *noli me tangere* veil. Isis, whose face swift initiation you think you have seen, even to the colour of her eyes, Isis you believe you have kissed, withdraws, well wrapped-up, grown instantly to her own height – as is the property of a Goddess. Colossal, as Apuleius saw Hecate, and made of stone which is goddess's material; and for lover and mistress you are left with an image, remote as St Geneviève where she stands looking upstream, an inviolable city behind her.

Probably snubbed, or enchanted, if you remain, above all if you live there, you learn that the delights of that first spree are repeated and confirmed as pleasure does not often repeat itself. Not only these, you find that there are others, possibilities of thrilling ways of life that do not depend on wealth or sex or the excitements between midnight and dawn; vistas of well-being that touch the commonest acts with the service of the goddess and her law, the quality of sheer living, sufficient in itself, as Tamar Karsavina tells in her book.

That is as far as most people get. Wise men stay there; more than the ghosts of good Americans settle down to the bliss of it. Only remember we are dealing with the goddess Isis. Her forbidding veil is off and not for a long time replaced. She moves now in transparencies. Only do not pretend to yourself that you have seen her eyes. Still less her smile. Least of all perhaps, do not ask what she is smiling about.

If you do you must be prepared for other things about to happen.

There are people who do. That is how I account for the what became of Currer Mileson, the American boy I met outside the Café des Deux Magots. Who was seen, who was seen less, who was not seen. Until he was never seen again. It was a business people explained in various ways – so far as it was explained at all. Until they gave it up. For he had come to Europe, so I gathered, all by himself out of the Middle West; and there one supposes were a few people who said: 'that wicked Paris got him'. Which about sums up, perhaps omitting the adjective, all that was ever said.

Yet American boys usually take some killing – if Currer Mileson is dead. As nuts they are tough, and as eggs hard-boiled. Their imaginations having less historic exercise than ones over here, they are inclined to be superficial – that is, romantic. Or, their national culture not yet achieved, when they do not despise they gobble. Or, anxious to assert their capacity, become culture-fans.

Enough about American boys. As rare and no rarer than rarity the world over, there are some of them who do not fit into any conversation of their land.

I knew he was a rare one when I saw him, sitting along on the round-the-corner part of the *terrasse*. The beautiful lean body, immense strength the generations had fined, even to over-fineness. All length that old age would make gaunt, and wild bright hunter's eyes. Eyes that were looking east, towards the shabby end of the Boulevard St Germain where behind the Boul' Miche rises the Sorbonne, and behind the Sorbonne, the Rue du Cardinal Lemoine, where Strindberg ran away from two crossed sticks when he was finding the philosopher's stone.

We had met before. I sat down beside him and we each looked. The spring made one's senses ache as they ache nowhere but in Paris.

'Have you ever thought?' we both began at once. Both meaning the same question, but it was he who explained.

'Have you ever thought what lies behind this city – above all behind the ancient part we're sitting looking at? What, if you go at it long enough, comes through, comes *out*, what you walk into when you're awake and when you're asleep?' I stared at him. He went on:

'It's easiest on the Quai Notre-Dame, by the little old shop where they sell books on how to raise the devil. There it's pretty well done for you.'

'What about when you're asleep?' said I.

He turned half round to have a good look at me, as though to be sure of my face for the first time:

'So you go there too?' he said. I nodded.

'Here? In Paris? But I might have seen you.'

'Here and other places – places I have really known, got inside of, worked into myself.'

Like him I sat, my face lifted towards the quarter which is the womb of Paris, where her young still go and her secret poor. Down the street where the broken bits of Julian's baths lie about, which he built when the legions occupied the little city of the Parisii called Lutetia. Stones cluttering the grass railed off from the pavement, round the house full of symbols of the real story, the Cluny Museum. All the Parises were about us, behind us, on our right and our left. Only before me invisible behind the high roofs, stood the matrix of Isis' temple, the darkened shrine. He went on suddenly: –

'What do you think is the meaning of it? What do you see there when you go? What is it, that kind of sheep?'

'Well,' I said, 'I think, I'm nearly sure that then, in *that* way, we are seeing, or even being shown, as much as we can see of what is really there.'

'Why do you say "sometimes"?'

I hesitated.

'You know what dreams are – even these sometimes begin and fade away into quite ordinary dreamstuff.'

'Mine don't. They're as sharp and separate as two kinds of being alive. But this other thing that happens when we're awake, that we're watching here right now, sitting on the edge of the Boulevard St Germain – that's different, that's another thing, isn't it?'

'Yes,' I answered slowly, 'I'm pretty well sure by now that it's not the same thing at all; that these two experiences are different. If your sleep and mine are a pair, then we are moving about in places we know and we can recognise this place or that. Only more real. Only in splendour. Great houses and courts and terraces climbing the sky from squares and steps and streets. A perfectness.

'When we're awake, as we are now, sitting together, it is much more like ordinary living, extended in time.'

He interrupted: 'That's it. Trailers for half the films that have made Paris, or a hundred and one ways of Queer Street.'

I agreed. I have a weakness for Queer Street, and people who have that are soon past being astonished at anything. So I did not ask him the questions I might have asked, but took it as I found it that a boy from the other side of the world should have walked straight up one of my own particular streets. A long way further up than I had ever gone.

I followed his eyes again, pitched high on the roofs on the other side of the street beyond the trams.

'It's there it all begins,' he said. 'Every corner you turn will be the next and the last. How'd you describe that?'

I tried again: 'An extraordinary, a unique sense of all sorts of mixed pasts, a sense of the ancient city and all the fury of life that went to make it. Especially for me, in Villon's time and in the seventeenth century. That and' – he gave me a quick look – 'that and something else. Like something out of which they *all* came. A matrix, which is Paris and the secret of Paris.'

'The pot-boiling,' he said, 'and the bubbles coming off the stew.'

'You can go home,' I said, 'when you've prowled enough, and pick it over and make plans and patterns. Even maps. But I think we're right to be careful, to keep this whole separate from what we see in sleep. For there is nothing glorified about it.' The look in his eyes troubled me, the look of the hunter of his race at a terrible quarry approaching from a long way off, a quarry that made him the hunted as much as the hunter.

'"Glorified" is the word,' he said. 'Alone there in a light of a finer quality than day. Funny I didn't meet you. D'you know the white cliffs with the poplars and the fountains, east of the city near the old fortifications?' (I did, it was one of my 'places', and I knew the Orphic tablet too.)

'No one to speak to – just a few lovely quiet people about on their own blessed business. All Edens man's been working on. But what are the great birds?'

'Of course you're right. It *is* two different things. But what luck on my first trip to have walked back straight into the lot.

History by day and Plato's patterns by night – *Garçon!*' He ordered two long, golden, starry drinks.

Like two travellers we compared notes. Yes, any time of day did, but a misty dusk was propitious in the broken hill-country at the back of the Sorbonne. Yes, and we both knew the ancient church at the foot of the wicked slum, called after Port Royal; and I had broken new country in the three great parallels along the river, of which the lowest was the Rue de l'Université and the highest the Rue de Grenelle. To us both had come the moment when walls slid in and out, to reveal others; both understood *crains dans le mur aveugle un regard qui t'épie.* Pure past or pasts, with their mystery and their passion; and as it were *through* them, the over-powering sense of one energy roaring through each, the crucible, the power-house in which each was formed.

After such wandering you could go home, turn over in your mind what you had walked through. That was why I had spoken of maps. For by now I had in my mind a chart of the place, of a Paris upon which the city of our time was no more than superimposed. One aspect of a central fire, or the womb of Isis, eternally fertile, eternally bringing forth. An activity of which we were the latest *eidola.* Admitted perhaps to this knowledge because we had not been content with her carnal gifts, had never boasted that we had seen her face.

Not even in our dreams, though there was no intellectual work, remembering or researching. There we strayed. Into the courts of her perfected work, the threshold of the completion of her labours; within and beyond the *simulacra* which were all we, in our bodies, could share.

It is one of the curious things about such experiences, whatever their reality, their ultimate significance or insignificance, that no one can discuss them for long. (It has been years before I could bring myself to write this.) After that morning we saw a good deal of one another, Currer and

I; and though we knew perfectly what each was doing, what each was thinking about, we never spoke of it again.

Yet I thought of him as well, this young man, strayed round the side of a planet, carried across an ocean to stray again, awake or asleep, in two wholly new forms of experience. The dreams, so I concluded after some meditation, were safe. So long as you work up in time. Nor could you prevent them, nor had I ever come to harm in that country. Rather I loved them, as a promise and an exquisite reassurance; knowing too that like the 'sensible fervours' of prayer, they were not to be sought or asked for or even longed after, but, like the grace of God, only to be enjoyed.

So much for the Goddess's more legitimate work. No, it was the other business, this waking awareness of what one could only describe as 'goings-on', the furies of dark energy, for which our Paris, with its brilliance, its exquisite sobrieties, was the mere shell – it was there that I felt less happy about him.

He did not know (for one instance) that along the line of my three glorious streets was once the waste place where the witches met – *quartier des Sorciers*; that when it was known what had happened in the little church by the river, the judge ordered a cloth to be hung over the crucifix, in sign that man if he could would spare God the knowledge of what had been done there.

He did not know, and I shied at my own guess, why Tour St Jaques stands alone as it does, or who the Child is who visited there.

He did not know the things Strindberg did not tell – even less than the things Joris Karl Huysmans told – in part.

He did not know that it is a curious fact that Madame de Montespan could not even get buried properly.

He did not know that the work of Isis implies the opposite of its own activity, that the Courts of the Morning stand on ground won from the Waste Land. He did not know that there was a were-wolf in Paris as late as the Franco-Prussian War.

He did not know what Hugo meant when he wrote about the Wicked Poor.

Any more than what the Surréalistes were up to.

He did not even know the Song of Paris, how every century she had taken civilisation and made it dance to her tune. Built it and sung it and dressed it, prepared it for the table, for the assembly, for the bed. For prayer, for wit, for treachery, for rhetoric, for devotion; for its life and for its death.

Nor understand what goes with this and what must go; until the αναкαταστασις, the renewal of all things, which Paris will be the last place to notice.

Puis ça, puis là, comme le vent varie – that most dreadful line of a terrible poet, the most dreadful line in French literature of the dead men rotting on Montfaucon, might have been written about a girl's scarf, fluttering in the Tuileries in a spring gale. Might be said of the Goddess, flirting with her admirers.

I went across the river, to the Paris of the Empire and the Third Republic, but only depressed myself by the sight of women buying lovely things I should never be able to afford.

Across the Seine, still high, still racing last winter's rains, ancient Paris sat watching the light splendours that had risen across her stream. So that it seemed that a giant, straddling the river, would have one foot in time and one foot out of it; and little doubt, for all the contrast and the easy splendours, on which side the Bird-Priestess who under Isis is the city's *daimon* has her nest and lays her eggs.

Anyhow all mine were in that basket, and I walked home across one of the bridges that have a spring to them like a bent bow.

II

The next time we met was in the Rue de l'Happe – this was in the days before the playground of the Wicked Poor had become one of those spots for vice without tears in which Isis specialises the first time you meet.

I had not thought to find him there, 'on the zinc', and the centime-in-the-slot-jazz, among the youth in their coloured linen and skimpy suits.

It appeared that he was expecting someone. A friend just over and calling loudly for adventure? He did not want to tell me about it and he did. It was an exquisite night. I suggested a cooling walk along the quays, away from, not towards, the Tour St Jaques.

We strolled west under the moon. The Paris moon, of all the moons the most nostalgic. For what? For everything. Love-in-a-mist at eighteen; for a night spot spent with a vampire in a vault; for a court ball; for an adventure at sea. For staying in Paris forever; for running away from it at once. For delicate vice, for sanctity, for a great laugh – the moon who creates out of all these longings the final mood of divine high spirits, for which again only Paris has the receipt. The laughter no other city can evoke – except Vienna before we murdered her – the joy and daring she distils out of one like a dance, a running up and down between the alcove and the stars.

Shadows on the moon-candied stones, cat-black and sharp. It was late. Spring night or no spring night, the city was indoors at its play. My companion in his tuxedo was black and white too, the stones not paler than his young cheeks nor the night brighter than his eyes. Nor any hunter moved on a lighter step – I thought of great woods, and of his forbears' watching in the woods for the feathered, silent warriors of the Five Nations, stepping, score by score, on the war-trail in the night. Then noticed him (we were silent) glancing right and left, checking his step as if to listen. For his friend?

With my mind on secular things, 'Who *are* you looking for?' I said.

As though already I was not there, and his question to the wide world (as our questions often are), to *anyone* who would answer:

'Have they never spoken to you in sleep?'

As I have said, you cannot dwell for long on these things. My active mind was on the Boeuf sur le Toit and to friends I had left. 'No,' I said, was suddenly glad now I came to think of it, that they had not. Even if they were the souls of just men made perfect (as one hoped).

'No, they never speak – why?'

'Well,' he said, with again that flash across his shoulder – 'believe it or not, when it happens in the other way, there are some about who do.'

'They're *not* the same thing –' I began, pedantically. Then suddenly felt as if I were pulled up short. By an intense cold. As though the little perfumed breeze that rose across the river were iced. Blown off some glacier – a breath, but a more than polar chill. And if you are to believe Dante, there is ice in hell. Then from behind a shadow I could not account for all but caught me up. Came up and dropped back into an angle in the walls. A little dark that had been following us, catching up and falling back, all the way, a thing that I had noticed and I had not noticed. A shadow thrown from one tree to another, traveling with them as they bent in the night airs on the embankment over our heads? I did not think so. Somehow I was wanted away. Instantly I wanted myself away also.

An interesting adventure, a perception to play with from time to time, wet one's toes in that sea. This man by my side had plunged straight in, with more intuition and even less knowledge, was already past hailing distance from the shore.

Argument and near-panic raced up me together.

'Don't,' I managed to cry, 'come away. It's not safe. Come tomorrow, and I will tell you everything I know about it' – I caught his arm and it felt as if it was something a long way – an infinite distance – off, and cold, and made of something else; and between us something that was no space, and cold from where cold comes from, was separating us. I heard myself saying:

'Ariadne it's like. You can't go without your thread.' Hearing his answer:

'He's got it. He's past the Minotaur he said. Round the next corner he'll wait.'

We had been standing facing one another. Now we began to walk again, and into my mind flashed images of men who had been too far. The young publisher who vanished to Olympus; the man in Buchan's story who discovered the corridors and that space, like murder, 'is full of holes'. We hurried as though driven. Already our feet were on the incline that leads up to street level again; as with the tail of my eye I saw the shadow dart out of its hiding place.

Just at that moment a taxi drew up to the curb at the top.

He did not follow even so far as to put me in; nor the taxi wait so long as for me to see what happened to the American left alone on the white moon road below the street, beside the stream.

It was an hour later, at the Boeuf, that I had remembered to wonder who had paid that taxi, and how he had known that he was to bring me there.

I was with friends. But not to one of them could I say: 'I've been out with a man who was followed by a ghost, and I left them making friends; and because I was upsetting its vibrations, it drove me away.'

Next day this dumbness Montagu James describes as 'common form' still held me; and it was three days before a mixture of conscience, curiosity and Paris high spirits sent me out to try if I could find him again.

I learned nothing at all; or rather that he had been seen, and that he had not been seen; alone and not alone (or possibly with a friend beside him, or with a bad character at his heels) by the concierge of his hotel, the *dame du bureau*, a waiter at the Deux Magots and one or two of his acquaintances.

Pensive, I left them, and walked east towards Notre-Dame along the Quai Voltaire.

Oh but the place was sweet! On the Quai des Fleurs I bought some country flowers, larkspurs and *giroflées*, and the orange marigolds the French call *soucis*. Looking up at the towers of Our Lady of Paris, thinking of Our Lady at Chartres, who could believe – in the demon who from her roofs looks down upon the city of Paris? That ubiquitous demon they can make into a door-knocker and the simple tourist's souvenir who may even be a fake, a restorer's idea for a devil. Who, set in the crown of Our Lady of Paris, is yet the best known portrait of the Evil One that exists.

On my way back I passed again by the very dirty deserted house, beside which an alley runs back into the web of old streets at the wrong end of the Boulevard St Germain. A house that saw the Musketeers and the Revolution out, high-pitched, crazy, the kind of house etchers love, rat-worn, with something abominable about it. On my secret map a black spot and a question-mark – *crains dans le mur aveugle* – and the alley beside it is filthy. It you could not see the far end nothing would make you walk up it. You never meet anyone in it, and from the river end I was half way up when I saw him cross the mouth of it; and could not be sure if the figure at his heels was accompanying him or not.

I hurried up, to find myself in a street market, in a crowd walking round in circles, and on the Boulevard a knot of trams, all starting at once.

It was clearly, perfectly Currer Mileson, seen with something of the small perfection of a figure seen down the wrong end of a glass.

Reassured, I walked back to the Café des Deux Magots.

It began to get about that he was gone, to get about and be contradicted. I said nothing, and as I have told, he was new to Paris and he had no close friends. No one to start the inquiries which set the machinery of society in action. It was some time after that a man from the *Sûreté* came to see me; and I suggested, which did not please him, that Paris was a city in which one might easily be lost.

'Have a look round here,' I said at last, 'and see if I'm hiding him.' It was the quietest of still days. The turquoise and gold dust of early summer – *maquillage d'Isis* – lay upon the city. Yet a picture, a map of old Paris, suddenly clattered on the wall, the *agent* turned his head, and a curious silence fell between us, like a shutter between his incredulity and my reserve.

You can only really give to people the kind of truth that is serviceable to them. I dined early, and when dusk came shut myself in to consider very carefully what I knew that I could be sure I knew, in the policeman's sense, in any sense, and possibly in another.

I ought to be able to believe that Currer Mileson was doing no more than wander about, neglectful of his meals, of the people he knew or his bed. That overwhelmed by his discoveries, by the release of certain imaginative and intuitive he was working off a crisis in himself. That in time he would either snap out of it or be picked up by the police. 'Partial loss of memory' was the phrase that rose – until I considered the sense of it and began to laugh rather shakily.

Yet it was the obvious way to approach it. It was what I should ordinarily have believed, even in the face of far stranger-seeming evidence. Only this time I did not believe it, I could not believe it, a single image recurring in my mind continually – of a young man to whom an order had been given: 'step out of your body'. An order he would obey (the means given, the means would certainly be given) as lightly as he would change his shoes.

Swept up, hurried off into an extension of that knowledge we both shared. Only an extension I had the sense to keep out of or the inability to pursue. *'Something far more deeply interfused.'* That was it. So far that he would never return.

It was after this that people came to see me. Americans mostly. People I had met and people I had not met. Few, or very few, with the idea that I had harmed him or even had some private knowledge, but (as I did not at first understand) as if some of them, at least, had a question to ask me they could not ask themselves. They came for help, and I had no help to give that would have helped them. Yet they seemed to feel that I felt something, and would one day produce it on a plate. One of them got so far as to hint about 'vibrations' – but they none of them knew Paris.

Now and then I would try them out. 'In the Rue Férou – did they remember who had lodged there?' Or did they know Jean Goujon's fountain, in a panel of which the inner genius of water is shown in stone? Or who had died on the Pont Henri-Quatre, calling upon a Pope and a King to meet him within a year before the Court of God? (A point which taken only provoked a reaction about the Templars and homosexuality.)

Or at Versailles even – had they noticed the silver birch that stands alone in the rough field beside the choked tank between Petit Trianon and Hameau?

Or that in the Bibliothèque de l'Arsenal there is a manuscript with the squares, and the receipts for letting out what, as Montagu James says, most certainly ought to be kept in? Or the emptiness of the Boulevard Arago where, for all its broad leafiness the horses shy because of the work that the guillotine does there? Or? Or?

It was during this time, too, more than once, as I had seen it that night on the quays, a shadow would follow me home. A slip of dark I could not account for; and like Punch hiding behind the curtains so it used my windows. Hanging half in, half out when my back was turned, as though keeping an eye on me to see if I knew enough either to be drawn in or to interfere. One evening it leaned out, shamelessly, stretched up over my shoulder, as though to follow the page on which I had been writing down my helplessness. An eye it had on me, but I did not know and I could do nothing; and that was what it wanted, what it had come to find out. And all the time I was aware of this also; that there was a step I could take, simple and obvious, that I was a person with a key in one hand, a box in the other, without the wits to make them fit. Like Punch it sniggered at me, like Punch it was somehow annoyed.

Until one night it gave it up; and this time I was so certain of it that I hurried to the window, to see what appeared like a thin blackness swarming down the face of the house, dart across the moon bar in the narrow street, to be swallowed up in the dark of the opposite wall. 'Goddess,' said I, 'keep an eye on your servants.'

But it seemed, too, that she was laughing at my ignorance; and as the summer drew to its height began to be bored with me, having given me, and in more ways than this, of her best and of her worst.

✖

The *agent* came once more. This time he was more amiable. It seemed that Authority was still asking questions. Strange as it seemed, even the most insignificant of Americans were not allowed to vanish utterly. As one European to another, he implied that I would see the point. As if one of them, supposing they came from the place they said, supposing there was such a place for them to come from, mattered more or less.

Especially, as I pointed out, the object of his inquiries did not seem to have made a good job of it. There always seemed – just to be a little ghost of evidence that he was still occasionally seen. Then, for the sake of trying to say something, I added:

'Last time, Monsieur, you would not admit that your city was a bad place to be lost in. Yet would you admit that it is a place where you might make a bad friend?'

His answer surprised me:

'I entreat you, Madame, to tell me what you mean.'

'I have told you all I can tell you, and you know that.' Again there was silence, again our eyes met, and this time it was his eyes led mine to the map on the wall.

Then he surprised me even more. He crossed himself:

'I am not of Paris – I am from Corsica, I: and I do not mean its brothels or its criminals, but I say there are parts of this city that were better burned to the ground.'

I nodded: 'That is why I do not think you will ever see him again. Can you not get a corpse, any corpse, and satisfy them as to its identity?'

'That,' he said simply, 'will no doubt be done.' Then surprisingly: 'It is not you, Madame, who could bring him back?'

'No,' said I, 'then there would be only be two of us. Besides, I assure you that if I could I would have done so long ago.'

He stood there, no longer the Paris policeman but a tall man from the pure mountains in the South. And he believed me.

'He met then?'

'A shadow. Who has drawn him into the shadows. But remember, he was good. He may come to no harm there.'

'How is that possible?'

'I mean that on the other side of the shadows there is another country, the Courts of the Morning that lie only just outside the gates of Paradise. When you are off duty, pray for him.'

The map on the wall was still.

10 'Ghosties and Ghoulies'.
Uses of the Supernatural in English Fiction

BY MARY BUTTS

FIRST PUBLISHED IN FOUR PARTS IN THE BOOKMAN,
JANUARY TO APRIL 1933

Today one form of popular writing – the detective story – has been developed on the lines proper to a new form of art. It has shape, rhythm and its own kind of epiphany. It has also become an elaborate craft; and for the reader an intricate, intelligent and enthralling game, allied to chess, insight into the spirit *in extremis*, a battle; crime-at-home in an armchair, with no after regrets, complications or visits from the police. (So far from being an incentive to bad conduct, as the cinemas are often called, one wonders if the perfection to which stories about sudden death are being brought, may not act as some sort of equivalent for adventurous wrongdoing to the blameless citizen, deep in the story of Death in the Train, the Tram, the Hotel, the Home, the Bath, the Bed.) A book, for example, like *The Murder of Roger Ackroyd*, with its pace and balance, the surprises and resolution of its theme, has qualities which are precisely those of a work of art; with its living characters, the well-locked joints of its events, like some old cabinet, opening and shutting smoothly and filled with secret drawers.

The subject of this essay is not the detective story, used only as an illustration that it is possible for the artist to handle any theme for the purposes of art, once he understands its limitations and its conditions. There is another form of letters, less popular, of longer descent, whose public is more anonymous and, so far as the writer knows, without its 'fans' – the stories commonly called 'psychic' or 'on the supernatural'. These, compared with the detective story, form a very small literature to-day; yet they continue to be written and by many of our best writers. This in an age when the accepted view is that anything may be true; that anything may happen; while that none of the explanations – especially the religious explanations – we were once taught, *can* be the right one. A point of view which is a legacy from the dogmatic materialism of the last century and still unconsciously powerful; whose influence to-day leads us to describe the beliefs and faiths of our ancestors as science misunderstood; or the visions of saint or artist, profound or fruitful, curious or bizarre, as nothing *more* than a way of externalising the unconscious. Yet in spite of this – in itself a half-conscious process and the common man's partial submission to it – people still write and turn out tolerable or even excellent work on the subjects they are not supposed to believe in at all – the old *motif* of ghost and spirit; and of our occasional sense of awareness of other forms of life other than those shown us by our senses.

It is curious, along with the sheikh story and other folk-themes, this class of work exists, without erotic or detective attractions. At the end of a ghost-story there is no one to be married and no one to be hung. Neither beds nor blood occur much in them. Their problems are not for ingenuity to solve. Their scope is wide, and for the worst demands some imagination. They range from sheer silliness to real literature. Even the greatest of poets has touched on witchcraft and the elemental powers, evil or exquisite.

It would even seem that writers are more and more making use of the 'supernatural' *conte*. Anthologies are devoted to it, and omnibus volumes. From conviction that there is 'something in it'? From pleasure at the material? But if the matter pleases, it should contain a minimum of truth. What sort of truth? Would a story – to take Professor Bury's suggestion of a hypothesis which can hardly be proved false – of a race of donkeys, alive on Sirius, who speak English and spend their time discussing eugenics – make a story of any interest or value? Only if the donkeys were really there, and another state of existence shown. Or if they were used symbolically, as a criticism on the life of man. Ghost-stories cannot fall into the last class. Their common business is 'to make our flesh creep'. And by that we mean, not simple horror or terror at a new and generally evil world, usually invisible but interlocked with ours; we mean also a stirring, a touching of nerves not usually sensitive, an awakening to more than fear – but to something like awareness and conviction or even memory. A touching of nerves inherited from our savage ancestors? Well, that is one explanation, drawn from the lately discovered fact that, like savages to-day, our forefathers thought 'animistically', endowed everything that lives with life, like or unlike his own. (All artists still do.) The kind of life depending on what piece of nature they were looking at, alive or dead; and on the *quality* each individual brought to his contemplation.

There is a tree, a scarred pine, in the park at Azay les Rideaux, which might inspire another *Golden Bough*. Any 'savage ancestor' of mine would have sworn that it pounced. when I stared at it (though it instantly frightened me), and talked about Van Gogh, instead of placating and adoring; and that the ring that slipped out of my ear and rolled through the only crack in the plank bridge, was the offering it had taken, since I had not made one; and that the sickness that came on me an hour or so later was the tree asserting its power ...

Like taxi-windows, stories of the supernatural fall into two classes. Their borders are sometimes indistinct, but the first order, implicitly or explicitly, assume theories of life existing beyond, or generally beyond our perception; theories which, in different makes-up – some hideous, some lovely, some awful, some idiotic – are immeasurably old; and not *all* accounted for by our increased scientific knowledge of the world. Theories which suppose laws, a range of beings from gods and bogies to daimones and God, an atlas of unknown worlds, physically existing regions beyond the senses of man. This is the first class. The second class are tales, well or ill told, about things happening which do not happen, all theory ignored. Their success depends on their getting the reader into a state, varying from desire to get into bed quickly and, most irrationally, not to sleep face to the wall and give horror a chance to creep up behind, to a sudden quickening of the mind to a sense that it is the bed, the book, the body that are shadows; or at least that there is a 'real' outside them, tangible as 'an army with banners'. While both classes unite in trying to persuade us that *'millions of spiritual creatures walk the earth unseen'.*

There is a third class that we can leave out altogether – the vulgar stuff, the sniggerers in the cheap magazines at stories of the appearance of the dead. Afraid of the dead and of what they call 'science'; doubly false, either by a cheap finale where Science is called in and patted on the back because it has declared such phenomena impossible. Or derided because it has shown man the way to such knowledge and his infinite capacity for error – above all, in a field where his five senses are not all that he needs to arrive at truth. Such work need not be considered, except for the light it throws on modern imbecility and superstition *à rebours.* Though now and again there is valuable material to be found in popular books which propose to tell of historical visions and hauntings; valuable either as story-material or as evidence; one notably in a volume in wide circulation, a rehash of appearances 'alleged to have been seen' in an Irish castle today.

A singular intelligence and a writer of degraded English assembled that book. Quotations from eighteenth-century anonymities are admitted as evidence; along with letters fifty years old from a Mrs X in India who dreamed that her daughter was dead. And dead she was. A girl forgets the name of a flower; dreams that she meets a woman called by its name. This is tabulated under 'occult' in 1923, by an author who drags in a quotation from Zeno that 'not until we study our dreams shall we reach truth'.

Yet the story, or rather the series of stories of things seen in that castle, culminating in one unspeakable apparition, is of sober and awful intereSt The story is a well-known one, apart from this version. A number of people – of whom several died soon after – wrote out their account of it. This evidence apart, there is some quality in the description that rings true, masters the commonplace eyes that saw it, the trashy English in which it is written up. If the whole business is a fabrication, it is one that moved an abominable writer to the use of simple and convincing words. It is the story of an animal-thing, seen, heard and smelt, but impervious to touch and infecting like a poison. If true at all it comes under the class of creatures called 'Elementals' – a very ancient belief and a name old enough to be decent. Ariel was one and Caliban another, in the antique supposed order of such natures, outside the skins, furs, shells and feathers of our earth.

But to leave this lowest class of our age's half shamefaced interest in supernatural beliefs, there is a considerable and variously entertaining literature worth examination. We have divided it into two classes: authors with a psychic axe to grind, who wish to persuade us that current materialism and credulity are alike insufficient; or those who seek only to produce horror and wonder; or at best, and without explanation, the consciousness of a universe enlarged. Starting with the last, the stories of Professor Montagu

James are in a class alone. He has no psychic axe to grind, no theory of which he wishes to persuade us. Cheerfully he says in each preface that he hopes these idle little tales will entertain, before proceeding to frighten us out of our wits. A master of plain style like plain-chant, a humanist, a scholar and an observer of men, half the force of his stories lies in the simplicity of their setting. The wailing, luminous nun in the ruined abbey may or may not wail and shine? Who cares? We rarely pass the night there. But no one can be quite sure that what happens in Professor James's tales may not happen to him. His 'terrain' is Trollope's, and as familiar. The garden, the library, the cathedral, the country hotel. The terror, in essence, that concerns his agreeable humanist gentlemen is the fear of a life, believed to be dead and buried, returning and rising to the contemporary surface like a bubble from some foul bottom, breaking on some clear pool where men usually whip for fish. The stories are without theory, pure evocations of man's still latent fear that there is an animal life outside the animals he knows, less than human life and more, and infinitely malignant. Such is the theory of the evil elemental spirits, implicit in Professor James, making him the principal master in our second classification; where the object is not theory or persuasion, but telling the tale and, with luck, evocation.

His second theme is the pleasant fancy of a body that is not properly dead. Not decently haunting in a luminous transparency, but hideously changed, and charged with a vitality due to its evil life on earth; in one form or another, beast, pest and ghost.

On these he rings hideous and awful changes, culminating in that masterpiece, 'The Mezzotint', sober little Cambridge episode, persuading us by the sheer perfection of its invention; forcing one to say: 'If this sort of thing can happen, it happens like this.'

While, for all his kind, sceptical disclaimers of any intention but to amuse, there are implications in Professor James. It would not surprise me if once – and he will never own to it – he has met something uncommonly like the presence or the work of an evil spirit. Or that there has been but one episode in his life which gave him a psychic 'turn', left an impress on his imagination. Even that someone underground once came up, and made him aware of it in no easy shape; and that this one encounter gave him the material for five books. Some experience, apart from his immense scholarship, he must have had. Or it is also possible that the belief and the experience in some old book came through and stamped itself on him and persuaded him.

As to the possible existence of such creatures, it is curious to note that men's gods have come and gone, but that the belief in 'them' (and in the evil far more than in the good) has not changed much. The last is inevitable and human enough. Isis and Osiris have passed from our devotions or, if evoked, not by name; but the kêrês of sickness and destruction seem as long-lived as the amoeba. Demons in short. And all nonsense and misunderstanding of natural phenomena apart, when imaginative writing reaches a certain degree of precision, produces such an effect of reality, it is difficult to see how this is done if the observation implied in the writing is without *some* foundation in experience. A love-song may not be about one particular love-affair but, if it is a good one, it is about love. A writer must, if only half consciously, believe in what he is writing about. Details he can invent, and setting; terror and wonder he must have known and may have reflected on; at least putting the question if their origin was only in himself. There is a Dutch Primitive of the mockers of Christ; faces, one hopes, that never have been seen on earth – their quality of bestial cruelty is not of this world. Where did the painter find them?

There are moments when one remembers Lecky. In his *History of Rationalism*, writing on the kindred subject of witchcraft, he says: 'In our day ... it would be altogether impossible for such an amount of evidence to accumulate round a conception which had no substantial basis in fact.' And that, 'When we consider the multitudes of strange statements that were sworn and registered in legal documents', the way to a wholly rationalistic explanation is hard. (Lecky went on to explain it by saying that fashions have changed; the persecution for witchcraft ceased, more because the belief in it went out of fashion, than for any failure of evidence.)

Still, granting every ghost-story ever written a lie, and that each phenomena examined by the Society for Psychical Research to mean, not what it is supposed to mean but, as Mr Aldous Huxley suggests, something else – a question remains, more easy to feel than to ask. Professor James can say as often as he likes that he only does it for fun, but through his masterpieces like 'The Mezzotint' and 'Casting the Runes', through all his books, the same theme repeats. Something called his attention to them; turned the mind of the archæologist and ex-Provost of Eton to 'ghosties and ghoulies and long-leggity beasties and things that go bump in the night'; from which the Scots Litany prayed that the Lord would deliver us.

Leaving Professor James to his fun, there is Mr E F Benson, who can write gaily and wittily about people of fashion; soberly and well about things which are supposed never to happen at all. He can go to the length of a novel about it, and it is not a subject which usually lends itself to full-dress. Lytton's *Zanoni* is written round a full-fledged theory, and would today I think be found unreadable, though the idea of it is interesting – and very ancient. Lytton was a serious student. Mr Benson's *Image in the Sand* is also a bad novel, tiresome and padded. Apart from the earlier chapters, in which he said all he had to say, the reader finds himself insisting: 'If any part of this business happened, and I feel rather that the beginning did, it did not develop and, above all, *end* like this.' But his collection of short stories, *The Room in the Tower*, has in it as good work as has ever been done. Brick kilns remain the brick kiln which could be seen from that house. A kiln with a man going in and out, with nothing particular about him but his hands, one of which carried a knife; and his wrists, round which played a small light, dirty and impure.

It is Mr Benson's attitude to his subject, today almost improper, as though one of the arts had had an illegitimate baby, which gives his work a great part of its charm. His sharp contempt for spiritualist humbugs and illusions; his pleasure in the more comforting kind of story (he is one of the few who deal with good spirits); his reasonable wish to convince us that our world, whether we like it or not, has more in it and more comfort for our spirits than it is fashionable to-day to admit; the belief that certain incredulities impoverish us, and are no more truly scientific than past superstitions; that change is the true name of death.

As in the story of the Long Gallery, where the tortured baby ghosts, who innocently bring death, lose their power to destroy when the girl masters her fear enough to sit beside them on the floor and bless them. It would be hard to find fault with Mr Benson's attitude, his impatience with the sentimentality and shameless credulity and wish-fulfilments of most popular spiritualism; whose follies hinder research by disgusting people capable of weighing the evidence; and aware how far a desire for personal immortality is responsible for the 'revelations' given under most conditions of trance. His 'Spinach' is a gay story of two young professional mediums, who by chance strike the real thing – contact with a boy struck by lightning, with something on his mind he is forced to tell;

this, and his slow fading-out into their usual subconscious fabrications about white robes and further shores. He knows the worst of fraudulent and silly psychism, the handle it gives to the materialist, the instrument he would have been called, in any age but our own, of despair. Immortality apart, a word none of us can realise, if there is no continuance after death for those who die when they should live, at ten years or ten months, or young of disease or accident, or young in battle, nothing can make this earth rational for the only rational animal known to it.

Mr Benson knows too the narrowness that confines the question to that of survival after death. With James, his stories pass in settings we know, are often obvious *contes*, arrangements of what might happen, whether it did actually or not. But now and then his story turns on what he obviously and passionately believes to have happened – our possession by the powers of good and evil, our logical blessedness or punishment after death. It is here chiefly that he wished to persuade or even to teach. (It is curious. Up to our age a writer, even the most detached artist, was allowed to teach. Having special love or knowledge of something, he was supposed to hand it on. The present world, its majority suddenly become literate, unless the subject is technical, faints at the thought. Until it is noticed that, having read any imaginative work from Aristophanes to Ronald Firbank, and taken pleasure in it, something of its quality has entered in and become part of oneself. Has made one more aware and *sensible*, using the writer's eyes. So that one finds out that, after all, one has learned.) But the present theory seems to be that one can learn about engineering or beetles from a book; not fortitude and faith from Marcus Aurelius. Even Wilde, founder, abroad at least, of so much of modern æstheticism, set out, in *De Profundis* and 'The Soul of Man', to persuade at leaSt

To return to the subject: it is also curious that, over all this field of letters, the opposite idea to that implied by 'possession' should be so little used. If man can be in contact with more than human intelligences, as Plotinus thought he was, and Socrates and Saint Joan of Arc, why are there so few stories about the man delivered by death after a life well spent, or of earthly contact with some spirit of life and grace? Ariel instead of Caliban. If the business of such writing is to awaken consciousness, why should horror be the form preferred? Is it that, without a shudder, interest is lost? But why should it be? Apart from Mr Benson, there is only one writer of distinction who has seen beyond this. Her place is later. In the past Hogg found an answer; but he comes at the end of a series, begun in the Middle Ages – the Scottish and Border magic poems, almost the only poems *on* magic which *are* magic. That no one can write now, unless one must count Mr de la Mare.

Thomas the Rhymer, whose prophecy quoted in the sixteenth century seems to have come rather accurately true in the beginning of the nineteenth, met on Huntley Bank a woman he took for the Virgin Mary. She told him that she was not, but queen of those people the Irish call the Sdì. He followed her, and they went off together on the Border Hills. There the transition took place, which has been observed before and after, when a place becomes another place; and you know what you have suspected before – that all the time it has been two places at once.

> It was mirk, mirk night, there was nae starlight.
> They waded through red blood to the knee;
> For all the blood that's shed on airth
> Runs through the springs of that country.
>
> It was mirk, mirk night, there was nae starlight.
> They waded through rivers abune the knee;
> And they saw neither sun nor moon,
> But they heard the roaring oi the sea.

That is one description of a state of consciousness enlarged. Thomas came out of it all right in the end, with his future as prophet and as poet made. His adventure has a certain relation with Plutarch's young man, and what happened to him in the cave of Triphonios. Variations on an initiation rite, public and sacerdotal, or accidental. And few people would dare to say that these experiences and these rites did not sometimes initiate. Remember E M Forster's definition of blasphemy, to the Northern mind a question of bad taste; to the Latin or Mediterranean, 'the incorrect performance of certain acts, especially sacramental acts'. Why? Because such acts were in their essence automatic receipts for taking a man out of his body and putting him, and even it, into another state of existence. The rules of the game, the natural laws set in motion, or even their existence, were and are imperfectly stated and never understood. While Heaven alone knew the consequences of tampering with them. Hence the danger of amateur meddling.

After the ballads, 'Lulli, Lulli', the 'Lyke Wake Dirge', even 'Tam Lyn' and the 'Wife of Usher's Well', who saw her sons' ghosts in hats of bark that:

> Neither grew not in syke nor ditch,
> Nor yet in any sheugh;
> But at the gates of Paradise
> That bark grew fair eneugh.

After these, there is little good writing about such things; though Shakespeare believed in his witches; he had seen in Warwickshire similar country hags. And Caliban, so it seems inevitable, is more convincing than Ariel. For the seventeenth century, one can say that Milton's preoccupation is chiefly with the supernatural. But what a supernatural! An educated and intelligent man – take the classic Chinaman – but entirely ignorant of our civilisation, what would he make of our religion and our theology from the study of *Paradise Lost*? How fantastic, how insanely improbable it would appear to him, wanting our saturation in its assumptions. While from what one reads of Chinese folk and mystery tales, 'Tam Lyn', to Professor James and even Mr Benson, would be familiar country to him, old hauntings newly set.

The Scots ballads died, came to life once, and have stayed dead ever since Hogg published 'Kilmeny'. His best poem, variations on the theme that is the theme of 'True Thomas', which haunts in infinite varieties the imagination of man:

> Late in the gloamin' Kilmeny came home.
> For Kilmeny had been she knew not where.
> And Kilmeny had seen what she could not declare.

Here he manages to persuade us, but from point of treatment, most of the poem is as objective and unsuggestive as a novel by Mrs Radcliffe; the girl's vision and adventures being no more than a translation of a translation of something half forgotten. Except for one verse, on which the whole poem depends:

> In yon green there is a wake,
> And in that wake there is a wene.
> And by that wene there is a make
> That neither has flesh nor blood nor bane:
> And down yon green wood he walks his lane.

Kilmeny's lover came from that place, where the bark was cut that shone round the heads of the sons of the wife of Usher's Well.

Scotland after that stayed mute, except for George Macdonald, who picked up the trail to that land by way of *The Back of the North Wind*. Strange company for Apollo on his winter journey there. After him, Fiona Macleod, probably unreadable to us today. Then, in full light of soldiering and Parliament, the easy writing of the finest adventure stories, Colonel John Buchan, in the books which have earned him least praise, writes with reserve and reverence, but with conviction, on his race's traditional material.

It is noticeable that men with a *flair* for life as it is lived – war and adventure and social relations – have often their mystical preoccupations as well. The more thoroughgoing the worldly activities, the deeper the preoccupation would seem. (The other way round, Desmond MacCarthy has something to say about the hard-headedness of the mystic.) Colonel Buchan can be called Rider Haggard's successor. Mr Benson knows his pre-War world. Colonel Buchan sets his stories up north, but not always in Scotland. There is one about the agony of the Emperor Justinian, transmitted through a bust of him, to a country house and setting loose forces of destruction there. Another of a stream called Fawn, and a haunting that went with it from classic times. A scholar, antique civilisation haunts his work also; as in a recent novel, *The Dancing Floor*. Colonel Buchan is a man with many of Kipling's prejudices about strong men and his distrust of the arts. This with real scholarship and love of life; the natural beauty of his land assimilated until his descriptions have a classic beauty. His *Dancing Floor* is one of the first novels to owe its origin to *The Golden Bough*. There, in an obscure Greek island, owned by a girl the peasants hate on account of her father's sham obscene sorceries, the ritual of the Kouros and Koré is evoked by them against her. Colonel Buchan knows the first law – for whatever it may mean, the law is there – of the interaction of other worlds with ours; that it can somehow by described by a parallel with the knight's move in chess. The other moves are comparable with ordinary activities. Only the knights move two square and a diagonal, on and sideways and can jump.

The young man in the book, has had all his life a recurrent dream to show that an adventure of profound significance is on its way. Mistranslates its nature, and yet is there in time to play Kouros to her Koré and save her. And dress she wore when they passed through the fire, which had shocked him in a London night club, was the one the maiden would have worn twenty-five centuries back. But it is in the young man's dream that the kernel of significance lies.

The *conception* of 'Brushwood Boy' is exquisite. Variation on the significant theme of *The Dancing Floor*, the realisation of a dream-sequence, shared by a 'gentle girl and boy'; Freud ignored, but not without parallel in one's experience, as in many folk-tales also. There is a tradition, old as humanity, that sometimes in sleep, instead of hanging about the body and play-acting its desires, we leave it, and go off on an adventure where no body can go; visit a country whose relation to this world is like that of our world to the stage set, with its painted trees and sky.

'What does it mean?' the girl asks the boy, another Koré with another Kouros, as they draw up their horses after the ride, which was not unlike the Thirty-Mile Ride they had taken together in sleep. 'If it means anything, it means this,' he answered. 'This' being marriage, India, children, a country house. They had done better in sleep, and had the sense to take this world as they found it. In this story there runs through what Paracelsus, I think, and Swedenborg called the 'signatures'. The law of signatures or correspondences is familiar to everyone in experience, but usually hustled out of consideration under the name of coincidence. What the mediæval mystic, and perhaps the Cambridge Platonist, meant by it was this: that every significant event or happening which quickens the individual life is, as it were, announced by trivial physical accidents, fortuitous, unconnected, a kind of pun on the event in progress or to be.

You see in a shop and buy a ship in a glass snowstorm, or fill a glass wine-jar from the Midi with water, and call it the 'sea-at-home'. Then comes the event itself – a friend returns, a sailor, after years, and a friendship is very deeply renewed. You turn up the Encyclopædia for the name of a Siennese primitive, and in a parallel column see the name of the man who has come back – but this time he has only some oblique connection with the sea. After that, the sea gets loose all about the house. A jug of salt water is served in mistake for sweet; a small child, who has not heard about the sailor, will talk about nothing but boats. A friend arrives who can eat nothing but fish. These go on until they die out. But they can reach a point past coincidence, the important incident signing itself a dozen ways in different varieties of matter. Observed by early man, they account for divination becoming official, part of the state. While today the pursuit of their significance is a thing to be wary of, if one would escape Strindberg's walks through Paris, driven by imaginary enemies to crazy terror – fear which came out again in illuminated prose – as he trod on the crossed sticks in the Rue Cardinal le Moine.

If the test of these stories is evocation, no trick of technique is more useful than the use of 'signatures'. In the 'Finest Story', the finest moment is when Charlie, the bank clerk, once a Viking with Thorfin Karlsefne, once a galley-slave, crosses London Bridge and heard a cow bellowing, with a book-bill chained to him.

It is not in Mr Kipling to indulge in theory; his gift is a unique eye for what things look like. All his 'uncanny' stories – including an extraordinary one in his last book, being closely allied to the strictest scientific experiment – carry, if not in the *dénouement*, but by some beauty of detail, as in the 'Bisara of Pooree', profound knowledge, and the necessary kind of physical awareness in Mr Kipling's own nature. This sensitiveness is unique in kind, and absolutely necessary for this sort of work. Its absence makes D G Rossetti and his attempts to handle magical material outside the scope of this essay. The success of works, such as 'Rose-Mary' and the 'Ballad of the King's Tragedy', is the success proper to poetry; as evocation of the supernatural they are no use.

There are stories by Mr Kipling which have had children by Lord Dunsany and Mr Metcalf. The last published, not long ago, *The Smoking Leg*. Well-written tales, if rather too sensational, at least for one whose taste is all for the lovely sobriety of Professor James, for the rational hope of Mr Benson. Still, the story 'Nightmare Jack' is ghastly – too ghastly for sober telling. And it is perhaps not impossible that the stories, so outrageously ill-gotten, saturated in the rites of an East Indian god of priest-pæderasty, charged with the ritual, the cult, the desire, may have had peculiar effects on men who did not know what they were handling, whose hands were bloody, and who were mortally afraid.

What a man can conceive, he can become 'like'. Meditate on Apollo and on Artemis – in the right way – and concepts of radiance and swiftness will possess even the body; until, with luck, a young man or woman may become not entirely unlike the Twins 'whom Fair-haired Leto bare'. This is the truth about the gods. Give yourself up to your conception of them, and you will become in some sense a repetition, an image of them. Many a testy, fussy, vengeful, rather righteous old gentleman is the direct responsibility of the Protestant Jehovah. From where do they come, these objects of contemplation, changing and developing down the centuries, of whom our conception, Christian or pagan, seems, at certain moments of intensity, to be outside normal experience? We know their geography, their ritual, hardly their vitality's source. What is it in the universe which gave to the tribal gods of the Achæans something like immortal life? Developed the tribal mascot of the primitive Jews? Vitality which seems to shift and draw new power, out of each and to each of the generations of men. Artemis and Apollo show signs of lasting longer than Jehovah. He began as a small godling, as humble as they. The Second Isaiah exalted him: Greek speculation or taste arranged him in a group of three. Join him with Ammon, Zeus and later Odin, and you get God the Father. The Brother and Sister crystallised earlier, never claimed universality and remain 'Gods to whom the doubtful Philosopher can pray ... as to so many radiant and heart-searching hypotheses'. It is infinitely subtle, this making-over of vision by generations of minds. Visions that harden and slowly lose their quality; become dull, stucco and plaster: stages of the Cheshire Cat: that flash out again and repossess men's minds by means of some brilliant restatement: 'Queen and Huntress, chaste and fair ...'

Mr Metcalf's 'Smoking Leg' is one of our last 'occult' additions and an original one. But it is the story that the reviewers passed by which has the most value, the soundest originality – a quiet little tale, without properties, but curiously persuasive; variation on the antique motion that a place can be two places at once.

In the past certain holy spots, caves and 'temenoi' were, at one and the same time, a place on this earth; a place where once a supernatural event had happened; and a place where, by luck or devotion or the *quality* of the initiate, it might happen again. The cave on Mount Ida was a cave and the birthplace of Zeus. Also, if one is not mistaken, a place where a supernatural event could happen again, and man 'become God'. At Eleusis, at certain times and in different ways – during a play, 'mime' of a 'sacred marriage', or in the dark, by an 'ear of corn, reaped in silence', upheld in a beam of light, an even physical change came over man; he was translated, 'converted', initiated, 'saved'. So far as these were ceremonies and the rites symbolical, any Church may be counted in the same order. By such circumstances men profited; drew out in proportion to what they put in. The crux of the business carries us a step farther when, as in the case of Triphonius in the cave, things happened to you whether you liked it or not. No doubt mechanism was used – 'Sometimes, I do not say always, very simple and innocent contrivances whereby the priest fortifies the faith of his flock.' But outside what may be called the regular places where men went for initiation, to have their souls strengthened by contact with reality outside the observation of their senses, man has kept a belief and a tradition that certain places exist, of themselves and quite unofficially, charged with Mana and taboo. Not always places you would expect. Explanation or theory apart, a good many sensitive persons have a list of their own. For instance there is a neolithic earthwork in the south of England. It is better not to say where. The fewer people who pollute that holy and delectable ground the better. No shepherd, no farm-hand will go there after dark. In medieval romance, a place identified with it was a 'temenos' of Morgan le Fay. (The country people have forgotten her.) But there are other earthworks nearby, including Stonehenge, where they will camp out all night at lambing time. Not that one. It is, or was until lately, mana of high potency and, at the same time, strictly taboo. The writer of this essay discovered it when young; and it is no exaggeration to say that a great part of her imaginative life was elicited by it and rests there. Archæology had begun to interest me, but I knew none of its stories then. It entered into me, 'accepted' me. That was all at first; but through the years, what was begun there has continued; where one grew decades of imaginative life in an hour. Returning from there once, I fell into an abnormal sleep, caused probably by the may in full bloom with which my room was filled. I found myself there again, but in mid-winter. It is difficult to find words to describe what I saw. I can only speak of part of it as a seeing of what was really there, the true nature of the place. Hanging above the grove that crowns the earthworks was a face. Fifteen years later I met the owner of the face; or rather the translation of its unthinkable loveliness into flesh and blood. We stared and immediately recognised each other. And with that began another sequence.

This story is as true as I can make it, but a personal digression, and so not very satisfactory. (Though it is hard to say why in this respect alone personal experience should be suspect.) It is an attempt to explain what is meant by the experience, so often used by writers on the supernatural, that a place can be more than its assembly of wood and leaf and stone visible to us; more than the atomic structure common to all things. Ossandovsky writes of a barrow in Asiatic Russia, one of the tumuli which mark the road of Genghis Khan, which the peasants do not like. He saw it, once a round grass mound, and once a whirling grey miSt Apparently his camera saw it also. Sometimes he could photograph it, sometimes he could not. His evidence is called suspect, but a big-game hunter and mining engineer is not usually over-fanciful. To quote again one's own experience: there is a part of Lincoln's Inn which does not always 'stay put'. Also Great Russell Street. But that, whatever it is, is something projected *out* of the British Museum. Mr Metcalf's story, 'The Bad Lands', makes the most of this. A man, a confessed neurotic, takes a walk each day in a countryside most perfectly described. Each day the walk gets worse; until one day he goes to the house that is not there, to burn it; because of the downstairs room he has looked in at, bare but for the table and the infernal spinning wheel. He is arrested for arson and the attempted destruction of the barn. The spoke of the wheel, he had put into his pocket for evidence, is the handle of the patent separator, marked with the angry farmer's name.

So far we have divided the literature of the occult into two classes – those which are written round a theory of the nature of matter, space or time, and those which ask us to believe in no theory. We have observed a few of the second, and that their success depends on evocation, a state (to which 'bogy' fear is only the accompaniment) of wonder in its rarest sense, of *clarté*, of a universe enlarged. The first class is more elaborate – exposition of a theory which has to appeal by its interest, by its reasonableness; and we have to be persuaded or half persuaded that our three-dimension space and time arrangements are no more than an arrangement of our senses, a setting for our play; a conception to which science itself, as even the newspapers are beginning to remind us, gives more and more its authority.

Here we are a long way from Professor James and his sheer skill; the divine trick by which the artist draws tales out of anything, raw fish on a plate, a piece of common sentiment; from a god men have long since ceased to pray to; or from things which are not supposed to happen at all. (Or if they ever do happen, make doubly sure of the existence in nature of hideous evil and fear.)

We have glanced at his work. and at the earliest, purest, least theoretic origins of all such work, in the ballads and in the practices of antiquity. While writers such as Hogg and Mr Wells, Kipling and Mr Metcalf – to take a few names at hazard – may sometimes assume theory, but they have no theory to back up. It is now time to consider the writers of distinction who have set out to prove a case.

In modern letters, Bulwer Lytton began it. His long short story, 'Haunters and Haunted', is a classic, and is reprinted to-day when boys and girls refuse to read *The Last Days of Pompeii* any more. His theory is explicit. The old London house is what might be called a 'mixed haunt'. Ghosts of the evil woman, the drowned man and the child. A host of light balls and elemental shapes. These are set in motion and in different patterns of horror because Cagliostro once lived there, and left behind some sort of focusing and materialising mechanism, closely described, in a space between the walls. A kind of compass, I think, in vibration, which by troubling the atmosphere made the phenomena visible. The word 'vibration' starts an old theory – the utility in the Middle Ages of the ringing of bells, whose ringing purified the air, released the holiness stored at the altar for the driving out of evil spirits. Such were the sistra of Isis, descended today to the bell-strokes before the Elevation; the drums and flutes of the Bacchantes degraded to the Salvation Army. And many people know what a sudden bell will do. So we arrive at the whole range of the effects of music, from Beethoven to jazz.

Zanoni is a full-dress novel. A young man, so far as I remember, wishes to acquire supernatural powers, and accepts the long initiation period supposed necessary for their safe use. Got bored – and no wonder, with the amount of fasting and prayer considered obligatory – for he was to be a respectable magician. Finally, mastered by his impatience – for a young woman, I think, who he hoped to get out of it – he tries a short cut and expires. For the theory go to *Dogme et Rituel de la Haute Magie*, by Eliphas Lévi; *magnum opus* of the cold Latin-Jewish mind; where the history of the descent of the Logos into matter is described as if Lévi was writing a treatise on cookery. William Butler Yeats said he was a man who would have said anything; though his huge book reads plausibly, not as though he wished to deceive other people, let alone himself. Did any of the experiments, so seriously vouched for, ever come off? Perhaps, but never in the way he expected. On the analogy of the knight's move, one can say that his work bore fruit, indirectly and successfully, in Huysmans' great novel, *Là-Bas*.

After Bulwer Lytton came a writer to whom Buchan is

again in some sort the successor, Rider Haggard, famous in one's childhood as Dumas, father in letters to them both. One wrote *King Solomon's Mines*, the other *Mr Standfast* and *The Thirty-Nine Steps*. But already in *King Solomon's Mines* there is a hint of the author's chief preoccupation, which was to be the theme for his other great success, our youth's best-seller and even now reprinted – *She* and its sequel, *Ayesha*. Even now in memory they seem to me to be very good books, great illuminators for adolescence; and they are written round theories, so precise and so strongly held as to be the essential structure of the tale and of the writer's conception of what is most important in life. Moreover one was left at the end sure that Mr Haggard knew very much more than he cared to write down; that some experience of no common order lay behind the country gentleman turned popular novelist; who laid that aside in turn to become an agricultural expert – like another man of the same order, the Irishman, 'Æ'.

This essay is not the place to examine the Celtic field. Ancient or modern, there is too much of it. Today it can be smug. Can assume, without so much as a polite gesture in the direction of evidence, that it is the mind of the debased Saxon, lost in materialism, which questions the stories of a supernaturally enlightened peasantry on the existence and nature of the Sidhe. Who exist in Ireland for the Irish; sole inspiration of the only art worth mentioning in Europe. I have heard a young woman nationalist say, on what philological grounds I know not, that the Tuatha da Danaan were Homer's Danaans, come there to repeat Hellenic civilisation ...

It is cult that is fatal. And the Irish today seem to make of their folk-mythology a national asset. This with admirable exceptions – Lady Gregory's sober classic *Vision and Belief in the West of Ireland*; Mr Yeats, Mr Stephens and 'Æ' at their beSt But in most literature that is specifically 'Celtic' there seems to be a shapelessness. Things happen as we know they do not happen, and as we do not want them to happen. The magic princesses – for this is just an explicit in their earliest epics – are too magic. Thirty invincible knights fight thirty invincible giants for thirty nights and days; without, as Professor Murray points out, any interval for meals. Not only do these things not happen; we do not care to pretend that they happen. Nor are they made symbolic for any of the invisible tides in human affairs. Very different are the true countrymen's stories, of a small, green, strange, gay, earthy, child-stealing folk. Moreover it will be found that an overdose of Celtic 'magic' can give a sense of something very like a special kind of evil, a spiritual quickening that soon turns to poison, as it might be from some drug.

Compare some of those stories with True Thomas's sober tale, stirring a hope in most hearts that in some way it might be possible to share that adventure, to go on that ride.

Compare them again with a supernatural story so good that I have seen it reprinted in a recent anthology, side by side with Bulwer Lytton and Mr Benson – 'Glam's Ghost'. Chapters xxii to xxv of the Grettir Saga. It is sober, awful and precise. There is 'something wrong' up at Thorkall's sheep pens, and with incomparable skill it is suggested that there is 'something wrong' also – though Thorkall does not know it – with the shepherd he has got in to deal with it. The shepherd is found hideously dead. Then *his* ghost begins to trouble Thorkall's dwelling and the whole settlement. The description reads like that of a 'poltergeist' turned dangerous. Then Grettir arrives to see what he can do. Meets Glam's ghost in the stables at night, fights with it and destroys it. But the fight has drawn him out under the cold Icelandic moon. It is the saga's turning-point to tragedy. For the evil spirit, about to be made to depart, speaks; tells Grettir that the encounter has been fatal for him; that he shall grow no stronger; that what he has done, his looking on the ghost's face, shall bring him early to defeat and death. And Grettir, when he has heard that and seen the creature's eyes, kills it. But ever after he fears the dark, and suffers pitifully on account of that fear. Until, not many years later, he is killed – and this time by plain witchcraft – on Drangey.

Observe the knight's move again. While it is impossible to give any idea of the sober precision of the telling. It might be a report written by an imaginative, simple and accurate person for the Society of Psychical Research. *If it happened at all, it happened like that.*

One of Dr Hyde's stories, in his classic collection of the best Irish fairy-tales, is on the same matter – an evil corpse, which makes a man carry him on his back, all night, running over stone walls. And there is pure evocation in another, on witches, who come visiting a woman nightly, until a voice out of a well tells her how to rid of them. 'And they departed to Slievennamon which is their chief abode.'

Rider Haggard has written more books than people are ever likely to remember again, and of priceless value for adolescence. Apart from some of the African series, they are forgotten. Who today reads *Stella Fregelius*, *Cleopatra* or *The World's Desire*? One hopes never to read them again. Many of us have an excellent version of them written in our heads, which we do not want disturbed by a tactless reference to the text. Perhaps the best thing that can be said about them is that they awoke imagination and curiosity in children; *Stella Fregelius* is about love, sacred and profane; *Cleopatra* about a great moment in history, where his evocation of the goddess Isis was a 'variety of religious experience' to children about to become sensitive to such things.

From these and other forgotten books one learned also the rules of mysticism, the sentences which crystallise the mystic's experience and belief. An exciting story illustrated them; and if Victorian morals and a certain historical ignorance made him condemn Cleopatra for not being married to Antony, his portrait of the queen is not vulgar. He had a sense of the mysterious links and repetitions of history – Cleopatra strung like her own pearl on a thread of beauty and disturbing power running through man's history, opening at its dawn with 'Heaven-born Helen, Sparta's queen'. Reborn, now here and now there, making one feel sure that such happenings and such repetitions are not fortuitous.

He made the ancient religions live; re-evoked Isis; led one into the heart of the Pyramid to the grave of Menkau-Ra. In *The World's Desire* he invented a small materialised form of the evil forces in nature; a *motif* used neatly in *The High Place* by Mr Branch Cabell. In Mr Haggard it is a kind of animal, not described – almost a foretaste of Professor James. Mr Cabell too can evoke when he likes – the only American writer outside Poe and Henry James who can. And some tastes find Poe, especially in his much-praised 'House of Usher', too lyrical by half. The stage set is over life-size – if one's preference is for small, neat wonders in a familiar world. Or if they must pass in a grandiose setting, let it be in a pyramid we all know to be there, or in a cathedral where we can hear evensong.

In *The World's Desire* the scene is bold enough, but not unfamiliar. Odysseus's second wanderings, Penelope dead, to find Troy's Helen, his first love. Then his death at the hands of Telegonus, Circe's son. Interesting to youth, just alive to Homer, and made acquainted on the way with Plato's theory of the division of souls. This is really Mr Haggard's theme. Even in his Zulu tales he wrote about little else but a piece of some absolute beauty, divided up, usually into three, bodies of men and women; trying again to unite, slipping through each others' fingers; and according to their quality, realising or destroying themselves.

Throughout the adventures and the big-game hunting, the

battles, the lost treasures, he made it understood that here we are no more than shadows, working out a play on our true existence, and aware of it as shadows might be of their body. His little preachings are those of a Victorian gentleman. His vision persists, if my memory does not fail me, of a singular breadth and exaltation. It is also civilised. His Zulu chiefs are men like ourselves. In one book, written round T'chaka, his 'nigger' tribesmen contain princely boys. One of them, who had suffered greatly, hunted with a pack of ghost-wolves.

There were once words, cut on an emerald, whose understanding would deliver mankind. The emerald is loSt Some of the words are remembered. He told them. There were other things like that. A distant cousin, though I never met him, there came from his mind to the mind of a child, wandering and reading in a Dorsetshire garden, the first idea of an earth 'one great city of gods and men'.

If it is difficult to end this study, it is harder to draw conclusions from it. So many names occur, and there is no space in which to deal with them. Ghost-anthologies have become popular, and contain such names as Conrad, Ethel Colburn Mayne and Violet Hunt. Œnone Somerville and Martin Ross slip in, between their hunting and shooting comedies, the story, here and there, of a ghoSt Not on the traditional Irish material, but what one may call 'plain ghost', the sober kind, fit for the ears of the Secretary of the Society for Psychical Research, and no less convincing for that. While Miss Somerville in her memoirs tells simply how once she heard a ghost-pack hunting on the Irish shore.

Marion Crawford, with his plain, deep love of the sea, wrote two classic sea-horrors – 'The Upper Berth', story of a cabin on a liner which each night smelt of stale sea-water; and there was a port-hole no one could keep shut, and a berth which had in it the body of a man long-drowned. With that there is 'The Screaming Skull', a tale worked up from that object, supposed still to be seen in a south-country farm-house, high and dry on the rafters, and better left there, because it squeaked if you displaced it and invariably found its way back. With him, though in very different keys, is Mr Tomlinson and Conrad. In another style and content altogether, Mr Barry Pain. In the Victorian past there was Mrs Oliphant, who wrote one masterpiece of sober loveliness, 'The Library Window'. Dickens and Wilkie Collins, neither very successful; and Le Fanu, sole example of an author who rarely wrote about anything else. It is curious; the rest of his work for us today is practically unreadable, but his short stories, like 'Mr Justice Harbottle', are fresh and enduring. There are many of them; it is becoming the fashion to include them in anthologies; and they were written from his heart. Dreadful tales, chiefly about the evil and unresting dead.

At this moment new authors are appearing – Mr Harvey, Mr L White, Miss Lawrence and Miss Naomi Royde-Smith. Certain of these have a peculiar quality, which will be noticed later; but if they have one thing in common, it is an absence of the facetiousness or stressed scepticism, which the Victorians thought essential, and which has lasted in the least distinguished of this work till today. A class which I have left out of account, to be dismissed now in a paragraph – the books which say that they are not fiction, which profess to describe hauntings and disturbances, traditional in certain houses, known of from generation to generation. It is a pity. I do not know of a single even tolerably good writer who has devoted himself to this. These accounts seem to written by persons whose style has not developed beyond the commonest journalese; whose ability to judge between fiction and possible fact, hardly exists at all. The evidence for such stories is suspect enough, yet it is of the greatest importance that it should be tested. For if it is all rubbish, the sooner that it is known to be rubbish the better. While if there is any truth in these traditions, the sooner that it is determined *what* truth, the better. At least the business is one that should not be left to third-rate journalists.

Outside 'Kilmeny' and the Ballads, we have not spoken of poetry – poetry one of whose qualities is the evocation of the invisible. It would agreeable to compose a 'magic' anthology – it would not be a large one – of English 'supernatural' verse.

There is still another attitude of mind before this subject, best left to the end, so that there may not be time to say all the rude things that occur to one – the class of story whose writers set out, not to evoke or examine, or to frighten us into a fit, but to prove a case; who have a theory of the unseen and set out to insist on it. One knows no surer source for a pettish scepticism than some books I read once, issuing from some theosophical association in America, in which the most preposterous things happened – to the dismay of unbelievers in reincarnation, auras and the ecclesiastical possibilities of Tibet. But better writers than the authors of those books have fallen into the same trap, and out of pure good-will. There is Mr Algernon Blackwood, who may be quite right about his nature potencies. But he – except on occasions – so wishes to persuade us, so multiplies his presences, that it becomes difficult to be sure what he is writing about. In actual experience, the exasperating point is that, to us, there is often no discernible point. While Mr Blackwood, in trying to tie down the elusive reason, seems only to succeed in obscuring it further. His contact with nature is deep, his reactions and his reverence stimulating, but it is often all reiteration, all multiplication of effect. So long-drawn-out that one thinks of Miss May Sinclair's God of Pantheism – 'as though He had sat down on the piano, on all the notes at once'.

There seems to be a new school in these stories, the newest school of all – at least the most recently printed. In them is developed what may be called a novel horror, descended perhaps from Professor James in its detachment and absence of theory, but without either his faultless style or lucidity of mind. But Mr Metcalf in 'The Smoking Leg', Mr Harvey in 'The Beast with Five Fingers', and Mr E L White in 'Lukundo' have given a turn to horror which is hardly tolerable. Perhaps Poe is their master, but to some minds he is too literary to be convincing. With infinitely less accomplishment, what they have to 'put over' may actually carry more persuasion. The beastliness of those stories, handed out, without so much as a comma to indicate a possible explanation, may have affinities with something that is appearing in our society, a wantonness, a want of standard, an acceptance of unreason, which may not be without parallel, but has a quite peculiar flavour about it. Until lately, it would hardly have occurred to anyone to invent such things for their own sake, and without much literary excuse. No one would have thought them up; or if they had, the point, in part at least, would have lain in their explanation.

There is one writer of great reputation who in these matters has gone further than most others in our time – Miss May Sinclair who, round variations of pure theory, has written one very remarkable book. With assurance enough to be banal, she called it 'Uncanny Tales'. It came out some years ago and has been reissued lately in a cheap edition. I do not know if Miss Sinclair has written many other stories like these, nor what prompted the book. Only that she is a metaphysician and, I believe, the usual open-minded, sceptical member of the Society for Psychical Research. Some of these stories have a most persuasive enchantment. They are chiefly on the reappearance of the dead or the conditions of life after death. Miss Sinclair is one of the few who can make the return of blessed spirits to their loved ones as interesting as the horrible thing Mr Landon thought of – the dried body of a tortured nun at the foot of a bed, whose rags and bones, tangible and finally broken up, seemed to have collected themselves together and gone back to wherever such things go. At least the people, whose agony of terror is as convincing as one's own would be, hear steps outside the room where they have taken refuge, and, on going out, there were no rags and no bones. Miss Sinclair has none of these terrors. On her theory, they would depend on the will of the dead. And her dead are young wives and tender mothers and wise old men; who even though his chauffeur murders him and cuts him up, comes back to forgive him and advise him in a shape of radiant old age; with only a hint as to the form he might have taken had he wished for revenge. That story, 'The Victim', is well known. It deserves to be. There is a perfect charity about it, understanding and reasonable hope. No one who has read it could find anything to say but – 'If there is a life after death, and it is not a leap into a logic unknown to us, this is what it should be.'

Even better done, and more valuable because there Miss Sinclair explains her metaphysics, is 'The Finding of the Absolute', the realisation by several spirits, to whom death has been a deliverance, of their lands of the heart's desire. A high-spirited tale. One 'got in' to the reality he had desired by love of beauty, one by the service of love, two by the love of truth; each by more than the love of pleasantness, or being well-thought-of or by virtues instead of virtue.

Perhaps in the story 'Where Their Fire is Not Quenched', Miss Sinclair is too hard on her poor ghosts, giving way to a prejudice Mr Strachey has quoted from Newman on 'the high, severe ideal of the intrinsic excellence of virginity'. One of them had never pretended to love other than coarsely; the other had been mistaken in thinking that she had. It is not 'pitched' quite right for a sermon on pretension in love. Which should open hell, if hell there be – the hell that is implicit in the nature of things.

After Miss Sinclair there remains Mr E M Forster, whose special sensibility, curiosity and faith make him indifferent to any ultimate distinction between pagan and Christian supernatural values. Capable of observing 'one form under many names', for him it is 'all Hermes, all Aphrodite'. This is explicit in some of his short stories, and implicit in his *Passage to India*, perhaps the chief novel of our generation, where many varieties of 'magic' are shown or suggested or described – with scepticism, with faith. While the whole book is shot through with a light – that radiance so incalculable, so recurrent, so variously described, whose power of suggestion is greater than any other; light of the stuff that grows

> Not in holt or heath.
> Nor yet in any sheugh ...

but always in that country man has never been able to mark on any map, yet is the ambiguous place of origin for his most durable works.

Mr Forster knows the knight's move, its oblique turns in human adventure. He is also the historian on Alexandria, and in 'Pharos and Pharillon' he describes the adventures of its founder in the oasis of Ammon. That story and Mr Forster's query on it will serve to end, illustrate and sum up the subject of this essay. We all know what happened, the little event on which so much depended, and which has so impressed itself on the imagination of the world.

In the temple at the oasis the priest, who was not supposed to know who he was, saluted Mr Forster's 'young tourist' as 'Son of God'. As he points out, there are two or three explanations to this. One is that the priest spoke bad Greek, and said: 'O Paidios' ('Son of God') for 'O Paidion', which means 'my child'. Or that the supernatural salutation, however correct it afterwards proved to be, was a put-up job on the part of the Egyptian authorities, anxious for the young man's favour. Or, finally, that the priest meant what he said. For at least, so far as humanity can judge, he was right. There is no such thing as a divine man, or, more exactly, a divine in man, if Alexander was not such a man, had not something of a divine nature in him. Or if there is no such thing as a divine nature anywhere, what is Alexander? (Alexander or Buddha; Plato or St John of the Cross; Akbar or Asoka. Or ... or ...?) Today the balance of powerful thought is inclining, not to a change of definition for the Divine, with the supernatural that accompanies it – we are used to that – but to a denial of Divinity as a whole, or else of its effective existence in terms conceivable to man. (Not unlike Epicurus who, if one has understood him properly, admitted the gods of antiquity, but on the understanding that they could not affect, in any way, any person or any circumstance or any thing.) This last seems about as far as anyone outside the religious professions is willing to go to-day. While the men in power who still profess belief are easy to drive into a corner, and somehow do not put up a very satisfactory fight with their backs to the wall.

To the common man of intelligence, neither party in this most fundamental of all controversies manages to convince. He feels that both sides profess either too little or too much, and his chief hope to lie in the study of religious origins; and there less where faiths have differed than where they have agreed. Meanwhile he continues to read and to write, according to his vision, taste or imagination, about any sort of supernatural that may conceivably be true. There was never more curiosity than there is today about 'the uncanny' or 'strange things' – 'things' that even in our fathers' day it was improper to believe in at all. Things of which the smallest proof would prove very much more than the actual event. 'Things', from the appalling horrors of Professor James to the exquisite and delivered spirits of Miss May Sinclair; to the bright and dark thread running through the world scene of Mr Forster. *'Brightness falls from the air ...'* Very tentative, very inventive, wisely theoretical or mercifully untheoretical happenings, that so many writers are trying to invent, to display, to evoke for us.

After them all, there is no better book than the late Miss Harrison's *Prolegomena to the Study of Greek Religion*, or Miss Weston's *From Ritual to Romance*, the work to which T S Eliot owes so much. There is set out the *natural* history of many of our beliefs, in bogy, ghost, daimon, demon, angel or god. Some were absorbed direct into Christianity; all have affected our culture; not one of which has not been, in its time, material for the finer orders of men to see more deeply into the structure of reality, and to make others see also.

So perhaps we shall find ourselves back again where our 'savage ancestors' began – back again to initiation rites that really initiated, so long as you brought something to them; good health; faith; knowledge and good-will – to whose men peace was promised. That conception may come round again – a great wheel turned and ground gained – to initiations which will really initiate; not by haphazard; not by fraud or hypnosis or superstition, but inevitably. Because we shall know to what further fields of veridical experience they take us.

Even now old formulæ haunt and stir:

> LOVE: I have fallen upon the breast of Despoina, Queen of the Underworld.

> DEATH: You shall find on the left of the House of Hades a well-spring. Beside it is a white cypress. Say: 'I am a child of earth and the starry heavens. But my race is of the stars.'

Formulæ that are very old. The time may be coming when, their ritual origins traced, their risings and settings chased through our subconscious, we shall know what powers we have evoked exterior to us. How far also it depends on man which he chooses; who, at his word, from among the seraphim, the angels, the demons, the daimones will come.

If we do not find out, we had better look out for ourselves. We have been careless lately what spiritual company we have kept; in our choice of ghostly guests. The results are observable.

Paris–Sennen, 1928–1932

Notes on the text

BY KATE MACDONALD

1 Man-Size in Marble (1893)

Liberty's: the fashionable new department store off Oxford Circus where William Morris fabrics and art nouveau decorations could be bought.

do for us: to come in daily to clean and cook as needed.

little magazine stories: Edith Nesbit earned her living writing stories for the magazines.

Monthly Marplot: an invented magazine name.

rise in her screw: she wants a pay rise.

reticulated windows: tall windows divided into vertical bars, topped with a network of circles; a style of structural decoration typical of the early fourteenth century in English churches.

blackleading: the standard method of cleaning a cast-iron kitchen range, by polishing or painting it with a paste of black lead and white spirit, and then buffing it up when dried. It is notoriously messy and hard work.

Rubinstein: probably the prolific Russian pianist and composer Anton Rubinstein (1829–1894) of whom it was remarked that he composed enough for three.

cavendish: a treated tobacco with a sweet taste and a strong smell.

Arcadian: from Arcady, a mythological place of harmony, joy and peace.

vesta: an early form of match.

2 No-Man's Land (1900)

shieling: a settlement, often only of one family or person, in lonely parts of Lowland and Highland Scotland.

Farawa, Allermuir: all these placenames were invented by Buchan, sometimes as pseudonyms for real places and sometimes they were complete fabrications, which he developed into a personal fictional Lowland landscape in which he set much of his Scottish fiction.

fly-books: where he keeps his fishing flies pinned into a 'book'.

forwandered: lost

Schools: the final exams at Oxford.

Lochaber: the western Highlands of Scotland above Glasgow and south of Skye, a Gaelic-speaking area.

Erse: Irish Gaelic.

Eddic: from the Eddas, the collections of medieval Icelandic legends.

the Isles: the Inner and Outer Hebrides off the west coast of Scotland.

benty: grassy.

mosses: bogs, covered with various species of water-absorbing moss.

mica: a flaky rock which catches and reflects light, commonly found in granite.

temenos: Greek, a sacred space or sanctuary.

links: flat grassy stretches.

corpus vile: Latin for (literally) 'worthless body', meaning here the unpromising material from which to draw conclusions.

dreeing his weird: Scots phrase meaning 'to accept his fate', taken from the poem *The City of Dreadful Night* by James Thomson (1874).

backwoods: not in Oxford, or in London, but somewhere remote from the centres of civilisation, as the speaker would know it.

toddy: hot toddy is a hot evening drink made with whisky, water, sugar or honey, and sometimes spices.

tinklers: travelling people, gypsies.

brose: oatmeal mixed with hot water and left to stand, sometimes eaten with butter or cream; a very basic diet.

Bedlamite: after Bedlam, a notorious London hospital for the mentally deranged.

carrier: a deliverer of miscellaneous packages and orders in remote rural areas.

banal quotation: it is from *Hamlet*, and is very commonly used.

tableland, watershed: the watershed is the point at which streams flow downwards in different directions, according to the topography. It will usually be a ridge, but can be a high-level plateau.

burns: streams.

'They ca' the place Carrickfey,' he said. 'Naebody has daured to bide there this twenty year sin': It's called Carrickfey. No-one has dared to live there for twenty years.

'Five pair o' twins yestreen, twae this morn': Five pairs of twin lambs yesterday evening, two this morning.

yowes: ewes.

sicht: sight.

smoke: from Psalm 144: 'touch the mountains, and they shall smoke'.

exegesis: interpretation of Scripture.

box-beds: beds built within wooden frameworks like a large cupboard along the walls, with doors or curtains.

grocers' almanacs: similar to illustrated trade calendars of today, an advertisement with extra information, decoration and illustration.

drake-wing: a fishing fly.

trolling: trawling, pulling the minnow through the water to imitate its natural swimming pattern.

thole: endure, survive.

away: stolen.

gang mysel': go myself.

kenna: ken not, don't know.

the morn: in the morning, tomorrow.

Revue Celtique: a scholarly journal founded in 1870 for Celtic studies, now called *Études Celtiques*.

bides: lives.

cleuch: a steep hollow or valley.

Gaelic: It's not thought that Buchan knew more than a few words of Gaelic. The literal translation of 'The place of the little people' would be 'Àite nan Daoine Beaga'. But the Gaelic word 'Sìthean' also means a fairy hill or place of the little people, and is a common element in Gaelic place-names, so it's likely that this is what Buchan may have had in mind.

toun: town, civilised places.

Eumenides: the Greek Furies, or instruments of vengeance.

Good Folk: traditional Scots name for fairies, elves, and other supernatural creatures living among humans.

had not stood the wear: flint tools do not weather by exposure, but by use. This is a classic technique of Buchan's storytelling, asserting a thing that he wants the reader to believe for the purposes of verisimilitude, yet with research the reader will find that the assertion is deliberately false.

'a muckle flat stane aside the buchts': a huge flat stone beside the sheepfolds, the enclosures where the sheep are kept during lambing.

'I mind o' lookin' out o' the windy': I remember looking out of the window.

bit errow: little arrow.

'wunnered a wee': wondered a little.

faulds: sheepfolds.

hoggs: unshorn yearling sheep.

aince: once.

speir: ask.

wizands: throats, gizzards.

ill: difficult, hard.

ae place: one place.

whae wark wi' stane errows: who work with stone arrows.

Muckle Deil: Great Devil.

I trow no: I think not.

ony ither: any other.

twalmonth: twelvemonth, a year.

sing safter: sing softer, not be so sure of yourself.

whilk: which.

aucht: anything.

een: eyes.

corries: Scots name for the high-level shallow hollows on the sides of mountains, formed by erosion and abrasion, that are usually the last places to lose their snow, and are treacherous to walk across or below due to their unstable surface layers.

tarn: Northern term for a stream.

rig: ridge.

abune: above.

sair: sore, or difficult.

straucht: straight.

scart: a scrape or scratch.

sair guidit: badly led.

articulate-speaking men: from Book 11 of *The Iliad*, meaning mankind.

Jabberwock: from Lewis Carroll's *Through The Looking-Glass, And What Alice Found There* (1871), an invented chimerical creature made from different animal elements.

brae-face: hillside.

calico: nineteenth-century maps were printed on glazed fabric for durability.

rudely: with primitive skill, roughly.

moraine: flat areas of rock-covered terrain made of the debris carried along by glaciers.

spout: a vertical or near-vertical channel, usually a waterfall but not in this case.

spit: a natural promontory formed by wave and wind action, driving stones together at the edge of the land from two directions.

strait: hard, difficult.

hags: where peat accumulates it forms natural miniature gullies and ramparts, which are usually boggy at their base. The hags are the mounds of uncut peat which are worked by peat-cutters.

jaws o' the Pit: the mouth of Hell.

fand: found.

bide and keep the house: stay and look after the house.

the day: today.

steeks on the windies: locks on the windows.

trap: a basic horse-drawn carriage.

linns: deep pools.

shouther: shoulder.

bagman: a travelling salesman.

Lorne: a district in Argyll in the west of Scotland.

battledore: an older name for badminton.

smurr: a type of rain that moves in a damp obscuring cloud.

herds: shepherds.

ava: an intensifier, used as 'at all', but with a more negative inference.

ostler: a groom from the stables.

fortnicht syne: a fortnight ago.

blind-fou: blind drunk.

siccan: such.

muirs: moors.

bogle: a supernatural creature, less terrifying than a demon but more malevolent than a fairy.

wise: sane, in his right mind.

stoot: hearty, strong.

a saved soul: the shepherd is a Presbyterian who believes that his soul will go to Heaven on his death, no matter what he does in his life.

threepit: begged and argued.

the bodies just lauch'd: the people just laughed.

grip: take.

conning: learning, memorising.

In tuas manus, Domine: Latin, in Your hands, Lord.

At first he bore the treatment bravely: the text from this sentence to 'Whether he had been soured' had been edited out of later reprints of this story, whether for space or as a revision by Buchan is unknown.

quack: deliberately false, purporting to be other than what it is for profit.

Though a fellow-historian: this line and the text that follows to the end of the story were replaced by the following single sentence **in later versions:** 'That which alone could bring proof is buried beneath a thousand tons of rock in the midst of an untrodden desert.'

3 The Willows (1907)

Pressburg: now called Bratislava, in south-western Slovakia, due east from Vienna.

sunken chain: chain ferries operate in areas of strong current, where the ferry is pulled along the chain on a fixed route.

bioscope: a type of early film camera.

Brer Fox: a popular trickster character in American folk tales from the Deep South.

Undine: a female water spirit.

antediluvian: animals from before the Flood, that is, dinosaurs.

Vienna-Pesth steamers: steamers sailing from Vienna downstream to Budapest and back.

4 Caterpillars (1912)

ilex: *Quercus ilex*, a holm oak, with a thick head of evergreen leaves.

en suite: linked to each other with doors and without a corridor.

Sirocco: a Mediterranean summer wind originating from the Sahara, that produces dry and dusty conditions over the landmasses that it covers.

5 The Bad Lands (1920)

fly: a small one-horse carriage used as a taxi.

frore: archaic term for exceedingly cold, verging on frozen.

Salterton: both this name and Todd are invented, and are more likely to be found as parts of place-names in the west of England rather than in the east.

sere: archaic term for dried-up and withered.

impropriety: in this period it was incorrect for men to introduce themselves to young women, and should rather wait to be introduced by a person who (in ideal circumstances) could guarantee their respectability and prevent her being annoyed by people with whom she did not wish to socialise.

terre-mauvaise: French, literally bad lands, land afflicted with a curse or some other kind of polluting influence.

6 Randall's Round (1929)

easy: an easy time.

Michaelmas term: the winter term, ending at Christmas, when students are supposed to be getting seriously down to work.

Guy Fawkes' Day: 5th November, with a traditional rhyme, 'Remember, remember, the fifth of November'.

figure: a set of steps to make a movement in the dance.

ordnance: the now familiar maps of Britain produced by the Ordnance Survey (OS) were originally made for military purposes. Calling the map an ordnance (military supplies), map shows that the military use was still predominant in the popular mind.

'Tumulus': Latin for a man-made mound, the term used on all OS maps for a barrow or burial mound, whether prehistoric or otherwise.

worthy: holder of a local office.

groining: architectural term for where the splayed edges of ceiling vaulting meet.

'diuers Persouns of ys Towne': divers persons of this town, some local people.

'a yong and comely Lad of 20ann': a young and attractive boy of 20 years.

'wherefore ye sd. Jno. Beale didd openlie declare and state yt ye sd. Son Frauncis hadd been led away by Warlockes in ye Daunce (for yt his Ringe, ye wh. he hadd long worne, was found in ye Fielde wh. ye wot of) and hadd by ym beene done to Deathe in yr Abhominable Practicinges': wherefore the said John Beale did openly declare and state that the said son Francis had been led away by warlocks in the Dance (for his Ring, which had worn for a long time, was found the field you know) and had been done to Death in their Abominable Practices.

'ye ill repute of the place, the wh. was unknowen to Himm when he didd entre into his Bargayn': the bad reputation of the place, which was unknown to him when he entered into the bargain.

'ye Lewd Games and Dauncyng, ye wh. are Seruice to Sathanas and a moste strong Abhominatioun to ye Lorde': the Lewd Games and Dancing, which are Service to Satan and a most strong Abomination to the Lord.

Conuicti et combusti: Latin for 'convicted and burned'.

hedged: avoided the subject.

7 Lost Keep (1934)

mean: poor, shabby.

Tilbury: an area near the London docks.

bearer bonds: an anonymous and unregistered certificate of debt security, meaning that Peter could have cashed them in as funds.

multum in parvo: Latin, a lot in a small space.

8 N (1934)

N: N is the old post code for north London.

Victoria: Arnold thinks the table is about thirty years younger than Perrott claims.

Walpole and Gray: Horace Walpole wrote the first Gothic novel *The Castle of Otranto* (1764). The scholar and poet Thomas Gray wrote *Elegy Written In A Country Churchyard* (1741), which Walpole helped to popularise before publication, and which anticipates the Romantic movement in poetry, moving away from the earlier Gothic.

gliding signs: the stars.

***Bolton Abbey in the Olden Time*:** an 1834 painting by the Victorian landscape artist Edwin Landseer, which depicts a stout monk considering which farm produce, alive and dead, to buy.

Mafeking year: 1900, the year that the town of Mafeking was relieved from its siege by Boer forces during the Second Boer War. The news of the lifting of the siege caused widespread rejoicing in Britain.

***Sherry, Sir*:** an 1851 painting of a housemaid carrying a tray with sherry and a glass, by William Powell Frith. The friends are clearly connoisseurs of Victorian domestic art that celebrates Victorian values.

wax fruit: another Victorian art form, in which wax fruit is displayed for the perfect beauty of the models, that will never decay.

bars were up: after 1890 many of the private areas in Bloomsbury had their gates and bars removed to allow traffic to use the public streets.

Bell: the Old Bell Hotel, also known by many other names over the years, including the Bell Inn, at 123 Holborn.

Dryden's house: Fetter Lane in London did contain surviving seventeenth-century houses until the 1880s, from which date they began to be pulled down. John Dryden (1631–1700), the Poet Laureate, appears to have lived in Gerrard Street in Soho, further to the west near Leicester Square, but the 1851 etching 'The House of John Dryden' by John Wykeham Archer in his series *Vestiges of Old London*, connected Dryden with the Fetter Lane survivals.

Cliffords Inn: a London Inn of Chancery, where barristers are trained, founded in 1344 and largely demolished in 1934, the date of this story.

David Copperfield: Charles Dickens' celebrated novel (1849–50) is largely set in London.

turnovers: newspaper articles that carried on to the next page.

Nutt's bookshop: David Nutt's bookshop moved to the Strand in 1848.

Lyceum pit: the cheapest seats in the Lyceum Theatre.

'Oh, plump head waiter at the Cock': lines by Alfred Lord Tennyson memorialising the Cock Tavern on Fleet Street.

Misce, fiat mistura: Latin, mix to make a mixture.

Clare Market: a former street market from the seventeenth century, demolished in the early 1900s to make the Aldwych and Kingsway, between Fleet Street and the Strand.

Canon's Park: there is a Canon's Park in Edgeware, west London, but not one in Stoke Newington in north London. Machen would know that some of his readers would know this perfectly well, and that others might not be quite sure.

St James's Market: Haymarket exists, as a street running between Piccadilly and Pall Mall, but St James's Market is an invention.

the war: the First World War.

Traherne: The poet Thomas Traherne (1636–74) nearly disappeared from knowledge because most of his manuscripts were held unpublished by his family for nearly 200 years. They were discovered on a bookseller's barrow in 1898, and *Centuries of Meditation*, and other poems, were recognised for what they were and finally published from 1903.

Hampole: Machen had invented this author and *A London Walk: Meditations in the Streets of the Metropolis* for his earlier novel *The Green Round* (1933).

supernal: celestial, from the divine, or from the sky.

***veritas contra mundum*:** Latin, truth against the world.

SN: Stoke Newington.

soothing cup: tea.

***homo protoplastus*:** Greek, the first-formed man.

fiat: authoritative permission.

cot: archaic term for cottage.

Mrs Todgers and Mr Pecksniff: characters in Dickens' novel *Martin Chuzzlewit* (1842–44). She ran a boarding-house and he was a self-taught teacher of architecture.

H G Wells: the most influential British science fiction author of the early twentieth century.

Indian rope trick: a famous illusion involving a rope apparently ascending under its own power from a basket on the ground, first described in the nineteenth century as performed by Indian fakirs, but may actually have been invented by a Chicago journalist.

Kubla Khan: reference to Coleridge's poem *Kubla Khan, Or, A Vision In A Dream* (1797/1816), which begins: 'In Xanadu did Kubla Khan a stately pleasure dome decree'.

Old Man of the Mountain: Marco Polo's book of travels, very popular in the thirteenth century, tells the story of the Old Man of the Mountain who would drug followers with hashish, promising them a glimpse of paradise.

S P R: Society for Psychical Research, founded in 1882.

made no doubt: did not doubt.

beat the coverts: a fox-hunting term, to search in all the usual places where the quarry is to be found.

warm men: rich men.

pineapples: an indicator of the wealth needed to build and maintain the special warmed frames for growing the fruit in the English climate.

crabapple, Cox's pippin: two kinds of apple species; one hard and sour, the other sweet.

9 Mappa Mundi (1937)

noli me tangere: Latin for 'stop holding on to me', 'stop touching me'.

Isis: Egyptian fertility goddess, also considered to be another aspect of Aphrodite.

Apuleius: Latin author from the 2nd century AD, most well known for his *The Golden Ass*.

Hecate: Greek goddess of death, and latterly of witchcraft.

St Geneviève: 5th-century patron saint of Paris.

Tamar Karsavina: Tamara Karsavina (1885–1978) was a ballerina in the Imperial Russian Ballet and danced regularly with Diaghilev's Ballets Russes in Paris. She was a founder of the Royal Academy of Dance in London. She wrote largely about theatrical technique and ballet.

Café des Deux Magots: Les Deux Magots was a centre for intellectual and literary life in twentieth century Paris.

Boul' Miche: the Boulevard St-Michel, one of the principal thoroughfares in central Paris.

Sorbonne: the building housed one of the earliest universities in the world in the thirteenth century, and now forms part of Paris's networks of higher education.

Strindberg: August Strindberg (1849–1912), a Swedish playwright and author, investigated alchemy and the occult, recorded in his autobiographical novel *Inferno* (1896–97), and referred to in Mary Butts' diary on 11 October 1931.

Julian's baths: the Thermes de Cluny, Gallo-Roman baths built in the 3rd century AD, located now between the Sorbonne and Notre-Dame on the Left Bank.

Cluny Museum: now the Musée National du Moyen Age.

Villon: François Villon (1431–63), the most well-known medieval French poet, particularly popular in modern times for his criminal activities and dissolute life.

Orphic tablet: a carved stone associated with the religious devotion to Orpheus and his descent into and return from the Underworld.

***crains dans le mur aveugle un regard qui t'épie*:** 'fear the gaze in the blind wall which spies on you', from 'Vers dorés' by the French romantic poet Gerard de Nerval (1808–55).

eidola: Greek, spirit-images of humans dead or alive.

***simulacra*:** Greek, likenesses or representations of a thing.

***quartier des Sorciers*:** the wizards' quarter ('sorcières' is French for witches, this may have been an error with the original French).

Tour St Jaques: the surviving tower of Saint-Jacques-de-la-Boucherie, a sixteenth-century church marking the beginning of one of the pilgrimage routes to Santiago de Compostella. The rest of the church was destroyed during the French Revolution.

The Child: possibly Butts' invention of a Christ-Child worshipped in the church.

Joris Karl Huysmans: French novelist and critic (1848–1907) whose work charts the evolution of his personal philosophy from Naturalism to Decadence to Catholicism.

Madame de Montespan: this implies that she was believed to be a witch or some other unholy creature who could not buried in sanctified ground, but seems to be a fantasy.

The Courts of the Morning: the title of a 1929 novel by John Buchan which describes a private coup in a South American dictatorship.

The Waste Land: T S Eliot's poem from 1922. Butts may be making an anti-intellectual joke here, by saying that Buchan's work was made possible by Eliot.

Franco-Prussian War: 1870–1871.

Hugo: a reference to Victor Hugo's novel *Les Miserables* (1862), a novel about the poor of Paris, with the plot ending in the 1832 June Rebellion.

Surréalistes: artists and activists in all media active in Europe from the 1920s, creating new ways of looking at and representing the world.

Puis ça, puis là, comme le vent varie: 'Then this, then there, as the wind changes', from the *Ballade des Pendus* (ballad of the hanged) by Villon, published in 1489, widely believed to have been written while he was awaiting execution.

Bird-Priestess: this seems to be part of Butts' personal belief system, connected with white witchcraft.

Rue de l'Happe: possibly Rue de Lappe.

on the zinc: at the bar, zinc being a common material for bar counters.

Love-in-a-mist: *Nigella damascene*, a blue flowering plant with its stems supporting clouds of upright fronds, a romantic flower.

Five Nations: the Iroquois or Haudenosaunee people of North America.

Le Boeuf sur le Toit: a Paris cabaret bar.

Buchan's story: 'Space' (1911), by John Buchan, in which a man discovers a fourth dimension and its inhabitants.

Montagu James: Montagu Rhodes James (1862–1936), medievalist, formerly Provost of Eton College and Vice-Chancellor of the University of Cambridge, best remembered now for his exceptional ghost stories, labelled 'antiquarian' for their conspicuous use of his own scholarship and literary interests, though told in an unsettling realistic style.

***giroflées*:** wallflowers.

***Sûreté*:** the French police.

Jean Goujon's fountain: the Fountain of the Innocents (1547–50).

Boulevard Arago: was built by Haussman in the nineteenth century to open up Paris.

Punch: Mr Punch is a puppet who appears from behind the curtains in a Punch and Judy puppet-show to perform. He is comic, angry and terrifying.

11 Ghosties and Ghoulies (1933)

***The Bookman*:** the leading English monthly magazine about books, authors and bookselling, at its most influential in the first half of the twentieth century.

The Murder of Roger Ackroyd: celebrated detective novel from 1926 by Agatha Christie which revolutionised the form.

conte: French for a tale, in the traditional sense of an adventure or a romance.

Professor Bury: John Bagnall Bury (1861–1927), Irish historian and classicist. The donkeys are in his *A History of Freedom of Thought* (1913).

Azay les Rideaux: one of the most celebrated of the Loire chateaux.

Golden Bough: *The Golden Bough* by Sir James Frazer, subtitled *A Study in Comparative Religion*, later changed to *A Study in Magic and Religion*, published in various editions from 1890 onwards.

bogy: an imaginary spirit that annoys, persecutes and harasses.

daimones: plural of the Ancient Greek 'daimon', a spirit or lesser deity concerned with destiny or fate.

à rebours: against nature, unnatural. Also the title of an 1884 work on extreme aestheticism by Joris-Karl Huysmans whose themes are in line with what Butts discusses in this essay.

Zeno: possibly Zeno of Elea (c. 495–430 BC), a Greek philosopher whose teaching was celebrated for his paradoxes.

Ariel and Caliban: characters in Shakespeare's play *The Tempest*.

Trollope: Anthony Trollope (1815–1882), English novelist, most famous for his invention of Barsetshire, an English county much concerned with clerical society and marriages.

Isis and Osiris: the Egyptian god Osiris enacted the resurrection with his wife and sister Isis, the great fertility goddess.

kêrês: the plural of the ancient Greek conception of fate, the ker, who brings an end to human life.

Dutch Primitive: this could be any number of paintings, but 'Christ Mocked (Crowning with Thorns)' by Hieronymous Bosch (1510) seems a likely candidate, also 'The Mocking of Christ) by Matthias Grünewald (1505–07).

Lecky: William Edward Hartpole Lecky (1838–1903) was an Irish historian and political theorist, one of whose first books was *A History of the Rise and Influence of Rationalism in Europe* (1865).

Society for Psychical Research: see p284.

Aldous Huxley: English novelist (1894–1963), at this date mainly known for his society satires, for editing the letters of D H Lawrence, and for *Brave New World* (1932).

Scots Litany: not so much from the official Litany, but rather a traditional rhyme claimed to be a prayer.

E F Benson: prolific English novelist and memoirist (1867–1940), and author of very high-quality supernatural short stories.

Zanoni: 1842 novel about the occult by the English writer and Conservative MP Edward Bulwer-Lytton.

The Image in the Sand: 1905 novel by E F Benson, set in Egypt.

The Room In The Tower: 1912 collection by E F Benson, which includes 'Caterpillars', republished in this volume.

Long Gallery: 'How Fear Departed from the Long Gallery', also collected in *The Room In The Tower*.

'Spinach': short story collected in Benson's *Spook Stories* (1928).

Ronald Firbank: avant garde English novelist (1886–1926) whose novels largely consisted of complex, allusive dialogue and innuendo.

Plotinus: third-century Greek philosopher and metaphysician.

Hogg: James Hogg (1770–1935), Scottish poet, essayist and novelist, most famous now for his novel on demonic possession, *The Private Memoirs and Confessions of a Justified Sinner* (1824).

Mr de la Mare: Walter de la Mare (1873–1956), English poet, novelist and acclaimed author of horror stories.

mirk, mirk night: from the seventeenth-century ballad 'Thomas the Rhymer'.

Triphonios: Trophonius was a Greek mythic figure with associations with Apollo and the Delphic Oracle. The Latinised version of his cult involved a cave from which one would emerge having been terrified, as described in Plutarch's *De Genio Socratis*.

Kilmeny: poem by James Hogg, about a girl who is taken away by the fairies.

George Macdonald: George MacDonald (1924–1905). Scottish author and poet and a Congregational minister. His works include *Phantastes* (1858), *At the Back of the North Wind* (1871) and *The Princess And The Goblin* (1872).

Fiona Macleod: pen-name of the Scottish author and editor William Sharp (1855–1905), also the creator of the faux-Gaelic poet Ossian.

John Buchan: novelist, biographer, journalist, publisher, and Director of Information during the First World War. His military rank, which he had stopped using in the early 1920s, came from his service in 1916 writing General Haig's military communiques. He was Scottish, hence 'his race'.

Desmond MacCarthy: well-connected literary critic and editor (1877–1952).

Rider Haggard: Henry Rider Haggard (1856–1925), prolific author and agricultural reformer, most famous for his novels *King Solomon's Mines* (1885) and *She* (1886).

Emperor Justinian: 'The Watcher By The Threshold', first published in the collection of the same name (1900).

Fawn: 'The Green Glen', first published in *The Moon Endureth* (1912).

The Dancing Floor: Buchan's novel about Greek religion and possession by the old gods (1926), influenced by both Frazer's *The Golden Bough* and the work of the Cambridge classicist Jane Ellen Harrison.

the Kouros and Koré: ritual figures of the Youth and the Maiden.

'The Brushwood Boy': Rudyard Kipling's story about a dream dreamt by two children destined to meet again as adults (1895), published in *The Day's Work* in 1898.

Paracelsus: fifteenth-century Swiss theologian and philosopher.

Swedenborg: Emanuel Swedenborg (1688–1772) was a Swedish theologian, philosopher and mystic.

Siennese primitive: a medieval painter from Siena.

Strindberg: see above.

'Finest Story': Rudyard Kipling's story 'The Finest Story In The World' (1891), in which a bank clerk lives a parallel life as a Viking galley slave. It was republished in *Many Inventions* (1893).

'Bisara of Pooree': 'The Bisara of Pooree' (1887, published in *Plain Tales From The Hills* in 1888) is a slightly facetious story about an Indian curse embodied in an eyeless wooden fish.

D G Rossetti: Dante Gabriel Rossetti (1828–1882), English-Italian poet, translator and artist

Lord Dunsany: Edward Plunkett, Baron Dunsany (1878–1957) was an Anglo-Irish author and playwright, notable for his fantasy fiction.

Mr Metcalf: (William) John Metcalfe (1891–1965), an English teacher and novelist whose supernatural short stories, including 'The Bad Lands' published in *The Smoking Leg, And Other Stories* (1925, also in this volume) displayed his talent for generating unease.

Leto: Leto gave birth to the gods Artemis and Apollo after having caught the eye of Zeus.

Achæans: the peoples who lived on the Peloponnesian peninsula before modern Greece had evolved from city-states and small fighting nations.

'Gods to whom the doubtful Philosopher can pray': from Gilbert Murray's *Four Stages of Greek Religion* (1912).

Cheshire Cat: a character in Lewis Carroll's *Alice in Wonderland*, who slowly appears and disappears, with the smile the last to go.

'Queen and Huntress, chaste and fair': the first line of Ben Jonson's poem 'Cynthia's Revels'.

Eleusis: the Greek site of the Eleusian Mysteries, devotional rites to Demeter and Koré that celebrated the possibility of life after death.

Morgan le Fay: from the Arthurian cycle of stories, a witch and the half-sister of Arthur.

may: hawthorn, which has a powerfully-scented and profuse white blossom, usually flowering in May after the leaves have come out.

Ossandovsky: Ferdynand Antoni Ossendowski (1976–1945), Polish explorer, scientist and writer.

Lincoln's Inn, Great Russell Street: areas of London near and adjacent to the British Museum.

The Last Days of Pompeii: a very popular 1834 novel by Edward Bulwer-Lytton, much adapted for theatre and film.

Cagliostro: Count Alessandro di Cagliostro was a stage name of the adventurer and occultist Giuseppe or Joseph Balsamo (1743–1795), who performed magic for the eighteenth-century crowned heads of Europe.

sistra: plural of 'sistrum', an ancient percussive musical instrument used in votive ceremonies.

Dogme et Rituel de la Haute Magie: an influential work on rituals in magic, first published in 1854–56.

Là-Bas: 1891 novel about occult magic by Joris-Karl Huysmans, one English translation of the title being *The Damned*.

'Æ': also 'AE', the pen-name of George William Russell (1867–1935), the Irish author and mystic.

the Grettir Saga: Grettis Saga or Grettir's Saga, an Icelandic saga first written down in the thirteenth century.

Dr Hyde: probably Douglas Hyde (1860–1949), Irish language scholar, founder of the Gaelic League and the first President of Ireland.

Branch Cabell: James Branch Cabell (1879–1958), American author of fantasy fiction. *The High Place. A Comedy of Disenchantment* was published in 1923.

'House of Usher': 'The Fall of the House of Usher', a short story published in 1839 by Edgar Allen Poe (1809–49), master of American gothic and horror fiction.

Conrad: the Modernist author Joseph Conrad (1857–1924) wrote some short stories with supernatural elements, but he objected to them being reviewed as ghost stories.

Ethel Colburn Mayne: an Irish novelist and short story writer (1865–1941), and a close friend of Butts.

Violet Hunt: British author, feminist and literary hostess (1862–1942), who published two collections of supernatural stories, in 1911 and 1925.

Œnone Somerville and Martin Ross: Edith Œnone Somerville (1858–1949) and her cousin Violet Martin (1862–1915) wrote stories of rural Irish life and hunting together as 'Somerville and Ross'.

Marion Crawford: Francis Marion Crawford (1854–1909) was an American novelist and short story writer, with a strong line in high quality horror short stories.

Mr Tomlinson: Henry Tomlinson (1873–1958), biographer of the avant garde writer Norman Douglas and author of novels and short stories, particularly of life at sea.

Barry Pain: English journalist, poet and short story writer (1864–1928), specialising in gentle comedy, and, in two volumes, horror stories.

Mrs Oliphant: Margaret Oliphant (1828–1897), Scottish novelist and historical writer, blending domestic realism with the supernatural.

Le Fanu: Sheridan Le Fanu (1814–1973), Irish writer of the supernatural and the leading Victorian ghost story writer.

Mr Harvey: William Fryer Harvey (1885–1937), English writer specialising in the macabre.

Miss Lawrence: Margery Lawrence (1889–1969), the pen name of Mrs Arthur E Towle, was a prolific author of fantasy, horror and romantic fiction.

Naomi Royde-Smith: English writer and literary hostess (1875–1964), the first woman editor of the Westminster Gazette and a patron and close friend of many British literary figures from the 1910s.

Algernon Blackwood: Algernon Henry Blackwood (1869–1951) was a broadcaster and a journalist and one of the great British literary figures of his day, a prolific writer of stories of the supernatural.

Miss May Sinclair: the pen name of Mary Amelia St Clair (1863–1946), prominent and influential literary critic and novelist credited with inventing the term 'stream of consciousness'.

Prolegomena: Jane Ellen Harrison (1850–1928) was a leading British Classical scholar and theorist. Her *Prolegomena* developed a new approach to interpreting Ancient Greek visual art and religious ritual.

From Ritual to Romance: by the medievalist and folklore scholar Jessie L Weston (1850–1928), a 1920 work connecting Arthurian legend with early Christianity.